STONES

By

Jason Denaro

Avid Readers Publishing Group
Lakewood, California

Stones

Avid Readers Publishing Group

http://www.avidreaderspg.com

ISBN-13: 978-0-9801438-6-7

Printed in the United States

PROLOGUE

AS THE AUDI RIPPED through the countryside, the Russian turned, grinned at the semi-conscious man and passed the near empty vodka flask to his comrade sitting in the rear alongside their victim. Travis Craven now subdued, squinted as he tried to focus. He saw the muzzle of the .45 Magnum inches from his nose.

"What happened, who the fuck are you people?" No reply.

The driver eyed his comrade in the rear view mirror and widened the grin. The larger Russian's hand jolted Craven's head as he delivered a heavy blow with the barrel of the .45. As Craven slumped, the man slipped the revolver into a shoulder-holster, took out a cut-throat and quickly placed the razor at Craven's throat. Craven could not remember feeling like this. He was unable to draw breath without pain. The feeling of being totally helpless.

The driver's accent was heavy Russian, he said, "Let us find a quiet place where we can have a little chat." The Audi veered off the road, pulled into a heavily wooded area. It was hidden from the road and obscured from aerial observation by large heavily foliaged trees. An old barn came into view, the driver made his way toward it. The barn appeared abandoned, a large rusted tractor serving as a tombstone sentinel beside double barn doors, perhaps a reflection of better days. Its wheels embedded into the ground, rust corroding the wheel arches.

The door hinges were well rusted, and the large Russian strained as he manhandled one side of the large wooden entrance. Years of weed growth had made the door one with the earth. Vines had further consummated the arrangement. The driver cautiously moved the Audi into the barn. The door groaned back to its closed position and two large rats scurried across the damp ground, taking refuge in a damp rotting haystack. It bordered on compost.

The smaller of the two men stepped from behind the wheel, dragged Craven from the car, placed a fist firmly into Craven's rib cage. There was a cracking sound followed by a muffled groan, and Craven slumped to the ground. Pain shot threw his body. Revenge would keep him alive. A length of rope and a roll of duct tape dropped beside him. The small man said, "These were in the trunk. They should do the job."

The two men raised Craven to his feet. Struggling to draw breath, he clearly knew the blow from the big man had broken at least one of his ribs.

"Drag him to that post and tie his wrists," the smaller man said grinning. "Here, throw one end of the rope over that beam and raise him up."

Craven now fully stretched, balanced on the tips of his shoes. The smaller Russian began to remove Craven's belt, unfastening his trousers. Craven lowered his eyes and watched in horror as the man fondled his genitals, removed his penis and stretched it out painfully from his arching body.

Craven began screaming as the pain swelled. The larger man drew back his fist readying himself to deliver another blow to the rib cage.

"No, it will kill him; we need him alive, for a little longer anyway. I need some time with him. I have waited for this." He placed the razor at the top of Craven's pubic hair and began shaving downward. Craven held his breath, *won't give this sadist the satisfaction*, he thought as he raised his eyes to the timber beams above him. He held his breath. Wanted God's help. God was predisposed.

CHAPTER 1

HER EYES WERE THE color of the moon in the daylight sky.

The pinot noire glimmered ruby red as it snaked its way along the spaces between the terra-cotta tiles. It slithered toward the lower level of the floor, eventually merging into the hot, dark blood, the spilled wine now pooling alongside the charred body that lay crumpled on the floor. A body which only minutes earlier beamed life. She had been a stunning girl, a lady men admired, lusted for her. Lusted for her youthful aura, the very aura that had led her into the circle of responsible for her demise. She'd spent the previous night with two of these men. They'd arrived at eight o'clock.

"Michelle you're more radiant than ever," the first man said as he entered. He handed her some white lilies, her favorite flower. His friend followed two paces behind.

His friend said, "Ramone she's more stunning than you described. Her eyes are so - so very beautiful."

Ramone flashed a near perfect grin, a row of white teeth, too good for a Frenchman. A hint of mint freshener escaped through the smile. He chuckled. The chuckle was tinged with a certain French delivery.

"Philippe please, she'll want more for her time than what we've brought along with us."

"You two," she giggled girlishly. "It's been a long time hasn't it Ramone?" She continued to giggle as she closed the door behind them.

She moved toward a cabinet, opened the heavy carved oak doors and placed a hand on a cut crystal decanter. She said, "I have Pinot Noir. As I recall Ramone, that is your favorite, correct?"

The Frenchman blushed. He thought, *Philippe will think I live here* but he said, "Thank you Michelle. Just a little, you wouldn't be trying to get me tired early now would you?"

The two men removed their coats, followed the girl to the

nearby bedroom. She feigned coyness. "Are you boys up for a night of fun?"

Ramone, the taller of the two men, nodded excitedly. He resembled a caricature of a human Goofy, very lanky, very awkward. For him, finding willing women was a task, paying for services a necessity. Philippe wiped the saliva from his lower lip, and looked about the room. His eyes protruded sufficiently to add a Jackie Gleeson touch to Goofy. He'd been short changed by the good-looks God. He was at the end of the queue when chiseled features were handed out. He tried to appear cool and it worked . . . just a little. In a suave voice he said, "You have a lovely home Michelle."

"Thank you. It's comfortable. Just myself and the cat . . . and of course . . ." She smiled, tilted her head at Ramone, and added, "My occasional guest."

She flicked a thumb toward the bed. "Don't be shy. Make yourselves at home. I am taking a quick shower and will slip into . . ." She hesitated, blushed just a little, threw in a well timed giggle and added, "Something a little easier to slip out of."

This will be a memorable evening, Ramone thought. He'd spent many evenings with Michelle. Each had gone well. Her ecstatic cries, the groaning, staged as they may have been, had worked their magic. Her cries to God remained indelible in his mind. Her cries kept him returning. The multiple orgasms, staged as they certainly were, made him feel manly. Feel needed. Feel appreciated.

He'd told his friends how spectacular the girl had always been. He'd returned with a third party, would he still be as appreciated or would Michelle's affection be noticeably diluted now that she'd be spreading it between two men?

It was different for Michelle, the switching of partners. She gave each man time to recuperate. With the arrival of dawn, the time between each man's sexual fantasies became extended until all three lay exhausted, the odor of sex permeated throughout the small room. The three slept until the sound of the phone disturbed their repose. Michelle raised herself from the bed, Philippe's arm dropping from her waist as she reached to answer. As she spoke to the caller, the two men stirred and began to wake.

"Certainly, I'll look forward to it. I'll call you back in an hour or so Susanna." Michelle placed the phone back on its base and turned toward her now awakening guests. She wore nothing but a radiant smile, a smile so enchanting it nearly kept the men's eyes from surveying the beauty of her nakedness. Ramone slowly moved from the bed toward the bathroom.

"Morning Michelle," his voice called from the bathroom.

"Hello Ramone. Sorry for the early call, it was my sister. She is an early riser." She placed the phone back on the receiver and moved to the kitchen to begin brewing fresh coffee. Her golden hair hung just below her shoulders, her naked figure like that of a goddess. When time for the two men to leave arrived, Ramone reached into his pocket.

"You're a true gem Michelle. I told you we would reward you handsomely for treating us well."

Ramone stretched his closed fist toward the girl, smiling in anticipation of her reaction. "Here - for you." He opened his hand. Michelle's eyes opened wide and her smile beamed, her perfect white teeth created for a tooth paste commercial.

"Mon dieu Ramone! For me? You're far too generous."

In his hand sat an exquisite diamond of at least three karats. It was probably worth more than Michelle could earn in a year. Far more than her services for one night could ever demand.

"This is far too generous of you," she said using her best coy schoolgirl voice.

"It is in appreciation of your warmth. Your beauty. You more than surpassed our expectations. It was a night we will never forget. I can only hope we're welcome back to spend time with you once again. Of course when we've regained sufficient energy," Ramone said, lowering his eyes as he blushed.

The three laughed and exchanged hugs.

"Perhaps we can add further to your jewelry collection."

Ramone and Philippe hugged her again, neither passing up the opportunity to press themselves against her firm breasts. Then the two men turned, wearily made their way out of the apartment. It was the last time they'd see Michelle. The magnitude of their involvement would far outweigh the pleasures of that night. The girl didn't die alone. Beside her lay the Persian cat she'd lavished with so many hours of grooming. The burned cat looked like a rabbit straight off the spit. The girl too, burned to a crisp. The stench resembled barbequed pork. It hung in the air. Her phone rang, 'till eventually the answering machine picked up. Michelle's warm voice was all that remained of the soft stunningly beautiful girl with the sky blue eyes.

"Hello, you've reached Michelle. Please leave a message. I will call you back shortly."

CHAPTER 2

WHEN THE BODY WAS discovered, the French cops were mystified. There was no evidence of injury aside from the burning. No entry wounds. The apartment showed no signs of fire. It was immaculate, very much the model home. Just Michelle and her cat looking like shish-kebabs. Investigators were unable to determine the cause of death. Spontaneous combustion was one suggested possibility. But the bodies were burned from the outside, ruling out that possibility.

Inspector Claude Chevalier was placed in charge of the investigation. Chevalier was unique, as a highly praised and collectible landscape artist, he was able to live a lifestyle far beyond that affordable by other police personnel. His most recent canvas fetched in excess of sixty thousand pounds at Sotheby's Auction. Chevalier arrived at the scene with a more reluctant demeanor than his usual official entrance bravado. He'd been briefed on the gruesome scene, knew where he was headed, knew who lived in the apartment. He held a handkerchief to his mouth as he entered, lowered his head as though moving beneath a chopper's rotary, his eyes darting from side to side. Not the body language his men were accustomed to, his edginess being clearly evident. His assistant Penoir followed close behind. He slowly moved to the inspector's side. They stood looking down on the remains. Penoir said, "It's her isn't it Claude?"

"Yes, her mother was . . ." Chevalier choked, began to gag and said nothing further. He raised a hand to his eye, tried to derail a tear about to trickle down his cheek.

"That's okay Claude. I'm sorry, it's okay," Penoir said quietly, placing a sheet over the girl's remains.

It was back in Chevalier's early days as a cop. He'd been assigned the duty of enforcing the law on some ladies of the night. Catherine du Blanc, a ravishing brunette with an hour glass figure and black eyes that would turn back the Trojan fleet, was his first incursion into the world of the red light madams. Chevalier had a brief but tempestuous relationship with Michelle du Blanc's mother. Chevalier and the woman were close for months. The romance resulted in an unwanted pregnancy. Chevalier wanted nothing more than to marry Catherine, to raise the child. It wasn't to be – Catherine fled and Chevalier never saw her again. He never heard about the child. Years later, he investigated a robbery in this very place, this apartment Michelle was laying beneath the sheet. Her small body burned to a cinder.

The pictures on the mantle were of his Catherine. By her side stood a pretty young girl about three years of age. It was Michelle together with a smaller girl no older than two years of age. A young man about six years older than Michelle stood by her side. A good looking boy with soft aqua eyes. The four were in swim suits, enjoying a hot French summer vacation. Chevalier studied the photograph, studied the birthmark. The young man's birthmark was identical to his own. A dolphin shaped patch on the lower left rib cage. If Chevalier had given nothing else to his only son and heir, he'd given him that birthmark. It was an indelible family heirloom. He'd asked Michelle about the young man at the time, but she just shook her head. Said the boy was her brother who'd disappeared years earlier. She'd been too young to remember much about him. Said his name was Trudeau. Apparently he'd had some kind of illness, which came to light after the family cat had been found writhing in pain in the rear yard. Its skin had been totally stripped from its body. The police report said the boy was found hiding in a nearby park, his hands still blood soaked. He was sent to an institution. That was the last the family had seen of Trudeau. Chevalier had a copy of the picture. He'd spent many hours sitting quietly in his office, cigarette in hand, coffee by his side. Stared at the young man and wondered. He wondered if it really could be. If in fact this boy was his son.

He'd had made an effort although apprehensive; to trace the boy's whereabouts. He'd run into one dead end after another. Subconsciously, running into dead ends was welcomed by Chevalier. If he found the boy it would introduce a new element into his life. A life already too set in its ways with police investigations and his artwork. The investigations, the galleries – he had no time to become a parent. His commitment to search for the boy was well - it was out of guilt. He hoped he would never find the boy but made occasional attempts to seek him out. Deep inside Chevalier believed that should the boy Trudeau ever enter his life it could change things forever. He asked himself can I live with a kid in my life. The answer was always the same, no. Such a change was not in Chevalier's destiny.

The death by fire of Michelle du Blanc necessitated the formation of a special task force. The case was running into nothing but dead ends. No doubt the personal interest of the inspector placed extra emphasis on the investigation.

CHAPTER 3

THE 747 QUIETLY GLIDED through the air en route to Paris. Karen sighed heavily and took a final official glance at the French landscape below as she made her final flight as a flight attendant. She'd flown for fifteen years and it was now time to take off the wings and become more grounded. Can't wait to see Amy again, she thought. It's been three months since we last saw each other in San Francisco. Amy Van Doran was an attractive blonde. Her life consisted of flying around the globe meeting new people. She lived the good life. She often wondered how she would maintain her lifestyle once her flying days came to an end. Until the day she met Raoul Ramirez. It was following her final flight; she'd dropped her bags at the usual Paris hotel and was still wearing her flight uniform. She carried an attaché case containing some paperwork she planned to go through, maybe at her favorite roadside café, relaxing over a coffee.

It was a balmy spring day on the outdoor patio of the trendy Parisian garden restaurant. She sat quietly over a not-too-frothy cappuccino, a little on the flat side. This isn't quite Starbuck's, but this is French coffee. *Hmm, should I complain? Ah, not much the use,* she thought.

She smiled at the passing parade; let the past years filter through her mind like an old eight millimeter home movie. They were good years, she'd traveled to all four corners, seen it all, some good, some not so good. At first she wasn't aware of the stranger. The rather handsome man in the linen suit drew a chair at the adjoining table. She began to turn; perhaps it was someone she knew.

"Amy Van Doran?" He spoke quietly with an educated, polished accent. His eyes were shifty. They darted from side to side, never moving to meet hers. She turned toward him.

"Please don't look. I've a proposition you'll be interested in."

She abruptly turned away, but remained peripherally aware of the man as he spoke. She leaned in his direction, strained to hear. As he began to speak a shrill sound came from the street nearby. The scream of the Pirelli tires shattered the calm of the restaurant. The 911 squealed as it tore through the tables, scattering them about the restaurant's exterior garden. A body launched by the impact sent tables sprawling as it smashed across the plaza. Those people, who moments earlier were relaxing over croissants and coffee, were now screaming amidst the carnage. Raoul Ramirez experienced his last glimpse of life. Ramirez had left the planet. Amy, thrown to the ground by the impact, crawled between the tables, dazed, instinctively clutching at her attaché case. She fumbled her way out of the destruction. Her nails breaking as her fingers clawed their way through the carnage. In her shocked state not realizing she had inadvertently grabbed hold of the case bearing the initials R.R. The similarity to hers made miss-identity an easy error. It was a long, painful walk to the hotel. She stared at the case, didn't realize her mistake. The sound of the horrible French sirens whaling, as well as her pain, drove her onward toward the Hotel.

She stumbled on, still unaware that she had the wrong case. Her pain medication - the Oxycodone - was in her case, not much good now. So too were her passport, diaphragm and a selection of female junk stuff. She didn't need most of the stuff, but couldn't afford to be without the passport. The Oxycodone she could replace, but the diaphragm, well the diaphragm, hmm . . . she could refrain, for a while anyhow. Discomfort and fear far outweighed other emotions. Dazed and still in shock, she by-passed the desk clerk, struggled with the stairs and limped to the third floor. She reached into her pocket, searching, fumbling, found the key, found the key-hole, and slid the key into the lock. Once in the room she let loose her grip on the case and stumbled to the bathroom, found clippers, removed the torn remains of three finger-nails.

She stared down at the torn nails, needed to cut way down, the pain throbbed through her head, she gazed up into the mirror hanging crookedly over the wash-basin, saw the trickle of blood along the edge of her ear, stared at the wound.

"Must have hit my head, Jesus the cut looks deep," she mumbled. "Oh shit, fuckin' Christ." She wasn't shy to audibly express her emotions. No one heard. She looked at the initials on the attaché case.

"R.R . . . What the fuck?"

She dropped the case onto the chenille bed cover. She said aloud, "Oh shit!"

She sat besides the case staring, *looks like mine* she thought. She lowered her head into her hands and tried to suppress the throbbing.

She whimpered, "Who the fuck is R.R.? Oh shit my head, my fuckin' head."

She gingerly massaged her temple and cringed as she rolled her head from side to side. She tried to rotate her head and heard her neck clicking. The clicking made her cringe even more. Her rough nails snagged on her blouse. She slowly lowered her body into a fully reclined position, dragged her bloodied fingers through her hair. She let out a long, half-muffled groan as she pondered the situation. Exhausted, sore and tired, she stretched out on the bed. An hour passed as Amy drifted in and out of sleep, when she was reasonably aware of her surroundings she realized the blow to her head had probably caused a minor concussion. She squinted at her watch. The glass on her Omega was cracked. It didn't upset her, better the watch than my face, she thought. She rubbed the balls of her palms into her eyes, tried to use her fingers but the pain in her fingertips made it impossible. She shifted her focus to the case. For ten long seconds it held her gaze. She painfully tried to raise her body from the bed, pushing down with her closed fists on the mattress, trying to balance as she half stood. She repeatedly stamped her foot on the carpet and let out a shriek, she screamed at the ceiling, "Jesus fuckin' Christ. What the hell happened?" But Jesus didn't answer.

Amy stumbled around the edge of the bed, limped to the kitchen. She came back in with a large table knife. The attaché case resisted her efforts to forcibly open it. She wasn't surprised. Her fingers were far too sore to force the locks, to push on the knife. Annoyed; she flung herself back onto the bed, burst into uncontrollable sobbing. She drifted back into a half-sleep. Searing pain prevented comfort in any position. She tried lying on her right side, couldn't do that. She moved to her left – even worse. She jabbed at a pillow, forced it under her knees, flat on her back. This position gave some relief. Amy accepted the best her body would offer and drifted in and out semi-sleep. She drifted, thinking about her friend Karen. Thought about how as children Karen had teased her with an ice cream cone. How Karen ate the whole thing herself. Amy wanted that ice cream so badly. Now she experienced a similar craving - needed to open this case. The case wasn't going to stop her. It owed her. She tried again, forced the knife under the lock. The lock held. She asked herself questions. Was the stranger singled out by the Porsche driver? Had the car targeted in on his table? Was he a target or was the incident an accident? No one else at the restaurant was hurt, just the stranger in the linen suit. What was it R.R. wanted to talk over with her? What was his proposition? *Has to be something to do with this case*, she thought.

She recalled how the stranger held it, so securely. *This's driving me crazy; I gotta open it.* As she thought about the Porsche careening into the tables she was suddenly snapped back to full awareness by the ringing of the bed-side phone.

"This is the desk clerk madam. There is a person in the lobby. He has a case which he retrieved at the scene of an accident an hour ago. It appears the bag contains your personal effects, your passport, and your hotel paperwork. He would like to return the bag to you in person. It appears you have taken his attaché case in error. He says it has bares initials R.R."

Amy hesitated. She remained silent, moved the hand piece from her ear and stared in silence at it. Could hear the desk clerk's voice, "Madam, madam - are you there?"

She placed the phone back to her ear, said in a soft voice, "Leave it at the desk. The valet can come to my room and collect his brief case. Thank him for returning mine."

The desk clerk said, "He wants to exchange the case in person."

A long pause, "I'm not dressed. I was in the shower." Her mind was spinning. *Christ, I'm being paranoid*, she thought, *probably just someone bringing my case*. She could hear distant sirens, she thought *probably going to the restaurant*. It had been about an hour since the accident and the local network had already aired the story. She reached for the remote, turned the television, she was still playing for time with the desk clerk.

"Tell him I'll come down. I'll meet him in the lobby."

As she was leaving her room, the newscaster said, "an incident today that took the life of a tourist. His name is believed to be . . . " She was almost out the door when the television announcer's words caught her ear. He went on to say, "Police have identified the victim of the hit-and-run accident as Raoul Ramirez. The man is believed to be a tourist. No other information has been released at this time. Witnesses say the victim was seen speaking with a woman. It is believed the woman was seen leaving the scene with a brief-case belonging to the victim. Police are anxious to hear from anyone who might have information that could assist them in their investigation of the incident."

Amy stopped. *Okay, okay*, she thought. *Shit, what'll I do? This guy's downstairs has my case but wants to see me. Police want to question me. My passport's downstairs. Just go down, give this guy his case, get my stuff and we're done. That fuckin' case! I've a gut feeling this case has something to do with the entire incident; I have to open the case.* She reeled back into the room. Took a bottle opener off of the mini-bar, tried forcing the lock one more time. The case had seen better days. The skid across the paved terrace area of the restaurant had left it cut up, the leather along one side scarred. She pushed down, used her body-weight. The lock gave. She froze, almost unsure about what might be in the case. *Seen too many movies*, she thought. Nonetheless, she stood back, arm's length from the case, pushed her head as far back as she could, turned it away, slowly lifted the lid. She wasn't prepared for the contents of the attaché. Four clear acrylic boxes, each the size of a cigarette pack, each glistening, even in the bad light of the hotel room.

On two of the boxes were the words "Coordinates TC

24," and on the other two boxes - "Coordinates TC 25." She tried to open one of the boxes. It had no visible seams along its sides, no lid. It was a solid container with no way to empty its contents. Inside each container were several stones, beautiful diamonds calling her name. None appeared smaller than three karats. A fortune conveniently reduced to the contents of four clear acrylic cigarette-pack-sized boxes. *Oh yeah*, she thought – *a retirement nest egg! That guy saw that I was a flight attendant. Wanted me to smuggle the stones, what else could it be? No harm in that. They're not drugs . . . just diamonds.*

The telephone rang, jolting her back to the moment. She answered shakily.

"This is the desk clerk. The man with your case is still waiting, He is insisting on coming to your room. He is anxious to retrieve his brief case?"

"No, no. I'll be down shortly. Ask him to wait." She thought *I need to be in some place where there are people around. Don't want to be alone. This guy can be any nut case. I can meet him at the bar.* She replied "Tell him I'll come to the bar."

She fumbled about the room. *Have to hide them*, she thought. She lifted the lid from the toilet cistern, placed the four boxes into the water and replaced the lid. She quickly hid the brief-case in the closet beneath her luggage. She left the room and made her way to the lobby bar.

The stranger eyed her suspiciously.

"Miss Van Doran, you look far better than your passport. But then, don't we all?"

"You have my case Mr. . ."

"Heinzman, but you can call me Eduard."

"Well then Eduard or Eddy . . ."

"No – it's Eduard," he replied affirmably with a slight German accent.

His demeanor changed. He smiled a forced, indignant, thin lipped smile. She analyzed the smile. *You smile like a used car salesman*, she thought, *an Eddy – not an Eduard.*

"Okay then Eduard. Excuse me; I've had one hell of a day. I'm sorry. You've got my attaché case. Thanks for returning it. Are you after a reward or something?"

"I'm glad you asked. Please take a seat, allow me to buy you a drink."

Her reluctance showed, she didn't feel like socializing. Head still throbbing. They sat on high bar-stools, she groaned as her body lifted itself onto the stool. She forced a smile His hungry eyes made he feel like she was on the menu. He held her gaze. His body language was suggestive. He placed one hand on her knee. The sweat began to bead on his forehead. His lips parted slightly. Amy waited in anticipation of some obscene proposal.

His hand began to move along her leg. She slapped his hand from her knee.

"Hey," she barked. "The 'or something' was not a literal offer okay? Don't even think about it."

The man was briefly taken back. Trying to regain some composure he said, "I believe you've something that belongs to me, an attaché case, it's one very similar to yours. It has my friend's initials – R.R. I thought you would have brought it down with you.

Heavy weather was moving in. The crack of lightning signaled the storm was now overhead. The man's hand again reached for her leg. She froze. His fingers around her calf. He mulled her over like a starving animal set to devour its kill. He leaned forward, placed his lips to her ear. His breath caused tension to swell through her body. She moved back, as far back as the bar-stool allowed. The muzzle of the Beretta nudged her rib cage. Curiosity had always been a weakness with Amy, and this occasion would be on exception. She needed to know why the guy wanted the attaché case so badly. She could just as easily hand it over but that wasn't Amy's style. She didn't like this guy, but more importantly she didn't like being the pawn. She wanted control of the situation.

"Steady my dear, no heroic moves. You're quite dispensable, although that would be such a waste." His German accent now more pronounced. His sick eyes scanned her body, lingered on the cleavage between her breasts.

He slid his eyes down to the gun. "This gun is silent. I can leave you slumped at this bar. Take a look around you. No one will hear. No one will come."

She held his stare, slid her eyes to the left, then to the right, glanced nervously about the room. He sensed the nervousness; it gave him the upper hand. His stocks were rising.

"These people around us,: he said gesturing with his free hand. "They'd ignore you. Think you'd had a few too many drinks, think you're sleeping it off. They won't even know you're done. Now slowly, very slowly - let's stand up, look like a happy couple. Walk slowly to your room."

The Beretta dug deeper into her rib cage. She slid from the bar-stool, sensing the pain from her fall, she thought about collapsing, *I can do it right here, in the middle of the hotel bar area. How'll he react?* She threw a brief pleading look at the bar-man; he smiled and nodded back at her. *Shit, didn't work. Collapsing, will I just fake a faint?*

The Beretta again nudged her lower back. "Move along, don't look at anyone," the man whispered. They made their way up the stairs to the room. She fumbled the key, dropped it, she thought about kicking the man's balls. Considered she might be too sore to move that fast, to get her foot to hit its target. She turned the key, the door swung open. Satisfied the room was vacant he nudged her forward.

"Now, the attaché case, give me the case."

"I left it with a friend before I got back to the hotel. I was in too much pain to carry it. My friend said he'd carry the case after the accident. He's got it."

It was a pathetic attempt at lying and it showed. He placed the muzzle against her forehead.

"For your sake that had better be a fuckin' lie, if the case is not here you are a dead woman."

He laughed an insane cackle. And as he laughed he said, "The blouse." He motioned at it with a dip of his head. "Take it off."

She unbuttoned. *Not the time to argue*, she thought.

"Now, the brassiere. Take it off."

Amy flinched. He grabbed her hair, pulled her head back

and pressed the gun into to her throat.

"Fuckin' better do it or so help me God I am the last thing your eyes are going to see."

He moved across the room, switched the television onto a music channel and turned up the volume. The storm was rumbling above the hotel, raindrops beating against the window panes.

"Let us have a little background noise. I do not wish to startle the neighbors." He slowly reached for the remote, pressed the power button.

The network was running a replay of a '70s concert. Donna Summers was wooing the audience with a languishing rendition of "Love to Love You Baby."

"The bra, get it off - NOW," he shouted. "Get the fuckin' thing off; do not make me tell you again."

Amy sat frozen. Her knees began to knock. She stared at them, tried to control the trembling but couldn't. Her bladder weakened as the nearness of death became a reality. He raised his voice even louder, the excitement clearly showing on his face. He grunted, "Take the fuckin' brassiere off." He shouted, "NOW!"

She could see the beads of sweat beginning to run down his forehead. Amy quickly reached round back, unhooked the bra. He snuck the end of the Beretta beneath the cups of the bra and flicked the brassier across the room. The music continued its mesmerizing beat.

"It has been a long, long time. I am going to enjoy your company. When I am done with you . . . ." He ran a pointed tongue over his lower lip. "When I have enjoyed you every way imaginable, and some ways that are not imaginable - then I will find the case."

He enjoyed the fear in her eyes. Saw the trembling knees, enjoyed the power he now held.

"Of course if you cooperate willingly it will be far less harrowing. So why not just give me the case, and perhaps all that I will enjoy from you is a good touch."

He placed the end of the silencer onto her breast, gently rotated the end of the silencer on her nipple engulfing it within the cylindrical tip of the weapon. Donna continued groaning the background tune.

"Lady, you can be alive or dead, I will still amuse myself. It is up to you. I can finish you right now. I will eventually find the case - in my own good time. Some sex would make it easier for you; maybe I will be kinder if you if you cooperate." He sniggered, made lunging movements with his crotch. The bulge in his trousers, the excitement, it pushed on his zipper as he starred at the firm forty inch breasts.

"Do you have the case, yes or no? No? Then we will have sex anyway."

Amy pulled away as best she could. Heinzman lunged at her, delivered a blow to her shoulder, knocked her to the floor. He pounced on her, reached below her skirt savagely ripping at her underwear. He unbuckled his belt, struggled with her as he pushed his trousers down and dropped his boxers. He pushed her skirt up around her waist, parted her legs, and kneeled between them.

Amy began to cry. "Please, please, stop . . . I'll give you the case. Don't hurt me, don't hurt me."

"It is too late. You should not have made me wait. Now I need it, now I will take you."

He ran the muzzle of the Beretta along her inner thigh. She froze, drew a deep breath. The gun moved higher, higher. He held his erect penis in one hand. The beat went on as Donna sang, "I - love to love you babee. I - love to love you babee."

Heinzman panted, short of breath, struggled to speak, "You see, if I use this toy the way that I have planned, there will be no visible entry wound. To most, you will just look like a heavy period, a hemorrhage." Again, the snaking tongue ran across the lip, this time he flicked it to the tip of his nose. "Yes, a period, an extremely bad one of course."

He lowered himself and struggled to enter her. As he began to penetrate, she lay deadly still, gave him false confidence, then collecting every ounce of strength she bucked. The sudden move threw him off of her. He tried to regroup, moved the gun toward her crotch. Amy thought quickly; *best to try to pacify this maniac, no point giving him the satisfaction of a struggle*. He pressed his left arm across her throat, awkwardly began inserting the silencer into her body. He moved it slowly. She heard the click as he pulled back on the trigger. She stared at his insane grin, the look of a maniac, a man who enjoyed inflicting pain, his stone cold eyes. Amy forced a smile. It caught him off guard. He stopped grinning, the silencer abruptly ceasing its warm journey.

"Please, please. This is crazy. Let's get back to something you can enjoy." Slowly, cautiously she moved a hand to his gun hand, slowly moved it back, moved the silencer from her body. Amy said, "I'll let you do it, just don't hurt me."

This change of heart threw his plan into pause mode, the gun now removed from its intrusive position. As he paused, Amy brought both legs back. He stared at the inviting position, began to smile. She blocked the pain from her mind and in a sudden release of all the power she could muster kicked out at his chest. Heinzman stumbled backward. Amy rolled off the bed, struggled to her feet and stumbled to the kitchen. The bread knife was right there. She moved toward it. Heinzman tried to reach her, tripped as his trousers restricted his movement, still around his ankles. He lurched forward, grabbed hold of her hair, his other hand ripped at her skirt. It came away in his hand. Now naked she fought for her life. *The knife, if I can just reach. One more lurch.* Then she had it. She spun around, stabbing out. The music in its deepest groaning stage, Donna Summers at her best. Amy lunged at Heinzman, plunged the knife deep into his thigh. His eyes stared into hers, only inches away. His breath smelled strongly of the cognac, his drinks at the bar. The flow of blood from the wound seeped through his trouser leg. He pushed her back, raised the Beretta and took aim. She dived across the room, her naked body bouncing across the mattress and fell clumsily to the floor. Realized her next move could be her last, she reached for the phone and ripped it from the wall.

Heinzman wavered, tripped again as his trousers slipped to his ankles, he stared at his leg, saw the blood pumping from the wound, pulled the trousers back around his waist and quickly tightened his belt, his right trouser leg now red from thigh to cuff. His eyes closed as Heinzman dropped to his knees, now unable to aim the Beretta in her direction. She thought quickly, *I've just one shot at this.* She flung the phone toward him. He let out a deep groan, dropped the Beretta and raised both hands to his head.

The phone had opened a deep gash. The new wound was now pumping more blood than the injury to his leg. Amy scrambled to reach the Beretta. Heinzman fell toward her, grabbed at her ankle.

"YOU FUCKER!" she screamed.

Heinzman grabbed at the knife and missed it. His eyes were glazed. Focus blurred. His blood-soaked hand kept its vice-like grip on her ankle. The blood was slippery. His hand slid from her ankle and she kicked him away. He fell back, his head cracking as it made contact with the door-jam. He let out an enraged scream. Mustering the last of his energy he clawed his way toward her. She rolled away, rolled behind the bed. Heinzman crawled along the blood soaked door; found the knife. He clutched it in one hand as he dragged himself up, standing half erect, prodded against the door-jam. He opened his mouth and slid the bloody blade delicately across his tongue. He grinned, gave Amy a sick smile. Tasting the blood on the blade, his smile widened.

"The gun has a safety. You cannot shoot it." He began to laugh, the now familiar sick perverted chuckle. Amy's despair dissipated as she thanked her father for the many lessons he'd given her on the use of hand guns. She felt for the safety. It was there.

"Eddy you're one unlucky mother-fucker."

Heinzman glared in disbelief. His eyes squinted, he tried to follow her finger, saw what he hoped was not happening. She released the safety catch. His expression became solemn, like a man who suddenly knew he had missed an inside straight, a gambler whose horse had fallen one yard from the finish post. Like a man about to die.

Amy raised the Beretta . . . reeled off three shots, each into his chest. Heinzman gasped, his hands ripped at his shirt as he again fell to his knees. He stared down at the gaping holes, a look of disbelief, of despair.

She stepped forward, placed the silencer against his forehead and squeezed off one more shot. She watched as brain matter added a splash of color to the wall behind him. His body flung backward then recoiled toward her. The music groaned down to its climax. She sat on the edge of the bed. The room had taken on a strange new décor, redder than good taste would deem acceptable.

"What a mess," she said to herself. "What a fuckin' mess."

She made her way to the bathroom, placed a hand on either side of the sink, stared at herself in the crooked mirror, reached over, straightened the mirror, and let it all out. When she was done throwing up into the hand basin, she ran the cold water. Splashed it onto her face a few times, and tried to regain composure.

She thought, *can't look at him, I have to cover his body. If I cover him, some of the horror might go away.*

She took the blue chenille cover from the bed, laid it over Heinzman. She grunted as she pushed against him with her feet. She rolled his body over, wrapping him inside the cover. Before covering his face she took a last look at the crazed eyes of the late Eduard Heinzman. They were rolled back, only the whites were showing. His forehead was vented with a gaping hole from the Beretta. The back of his skull was dispersed across the wall and the television screen, amorphous tissue and bone slithers slowly making their way down the glass on the television. It took her back to when she was a kid and had flung her breakfast, a bowl of grits, at the television. Same effect she thought, well almost.

She showered, rubbed Neosporin into her scratches, and threw down an Oxycodone and four Ibuprofen. She dressed and left the Hotel. It was now two hours and forty minutes since the accident. She wanted out of this room. She limped down the hall, took the elevator, gave a slight wave to the desk clerk, and left the building.

CHAPTER 4

$\mathbf{T}$HE RED PORSCHE SHADOWED her as she slowly, painfully made her way to the crossing. Standing on the curb . . . red light, then "WALK." Each step was heavy, every muscle ached. The Porsche began to roar, just as the old Fiat cut across its path. Travis Craven hit the brakes.

Amy could still feel the weight of Eduard Heinzman crashing onto her less than an hour ago. I have to get today out of my mind, she thought.

Travis sat coolly behind the leather bound wheel and eyed his prey as she crossed. He was just a few cars from her. Strangely, the Porsche showed no sign of front damage caused by striking the tables at the restaurant. *Yeah that's her, I'd recognize her anywhere,* Travis thought. *She's definitely the one who left the plaza with the brief-case. Yeah, park and follow on foot.* Craven slowly drove the Porsche into a nearby side street, parked and continued tracking her on foot. He enjoyed stalking, relished observing his prey.

The cell phone in Amy's bag rang loudly.

"It's Karen, I haven't heard from you since San Francisco. What's happening?"

Amy was relieved to hear a friendly voice, she said, "Thank God. We need to talk, but not now. I'll call you back in a bit, keep your cell near."

The two women flew together many times and had shopped every corner of the globe, searching out bargains as only flight crew knew how. Amy slipped the cell phone into her pocket, sensing someone was following. Something caught her eye. The stranger following was not as inconspicuous as he would have liked. *I'm probably being paranoid*, she thought. *I'll slip into the coffee shop and sit a while, then see if he goes on his way.*

She put the cell phone to her ear, acted as if speaking to someone, carefully following his reflection in the shop window. He sat, reached for a newspaper, made out he was reading. He noticed the welts, some bluish swelling on her arm, on her face.

He looked beyond the marks, admired her over the top of the sports section, intrigued by her expressions . . . the way she moved her lips as she spoke, the way her eyes slowly blinked as though her lashes were too heavy, as though she needed to close them and drift into sleep. He fantasized about how he would like to join her. How he would look good alongside her. Then he thought more about it. *Why not? Why not just walk up to the table and join her.*

Travis Craven was a tall, ruggedly handsome man in his early forties with short cropped hair, chiseled features, emerald green lady-killer eyes, and lips that every woman envied. His body wasn't quite gym standard, but he still cut a neat figure in a swimsuit on the Lido in Venice.

Craven was the consummate professional. A perfect machine, finely tuned to take an assignment through to its successful conclusion. He went about locating and targeting his victim with sonar like precision. To his peers, Travis Craven was simply known as the Dolphin. The name Dolphin was assumed by many to indicate Craven's ability to home in on his victim with sonar like precision, but in reality, it originated from a female acquaintance in Marseilles who, while sharing intimate moments with Craven, had commented on his dolphin shaped birthmark, and subsequently affectionately tagged him '*The Dolphin.*'

For Craven this assignment had gone wrong, terribly wrong. The unexpected incident at the restaurant in the Plaza had not been part of the plan. The Porsche skidding on the slippery cobblestone around the fountain was inexcusable. One of those incidents a professional of the Craven's caliber was expected to have anticipated. To be prepared for. Craven had shadowed Ramirez for days. He suspected Ramirez would attempt to either run again or maybe – just maybe . . . switch the attaché case. Stash it someplace. He was most certainly planning to rendezvous with his contact and pass the attaché case on.

But now this stunning woman had the case. This was not what Travis Craven had been expecting. He locked his fingers, stretched them, placed himself into charm mode and made his way to where Amy was sitting.

"It's a good day to be alive, wouldn't you say?"

She glanced up at him. His smile was warm, as though he was an old friend who just happened to bump into her in some secluded corner of the world.

"Yes, any day above dirt's a good day. Do I know you?" Of course she didn't, but that was how the words came out.

"I believe so. I think it was a year back . . . was it Paris last spring?" Craven said bluffing.

Such an obvious line she thought. "No perhaps Moscow in winter," she replied.

He smiled, again replying, "*Touché*. So we didn't really know each other a minute back, but we almost do now. My name's Craven, Travis Craven. Do you mind if I sit with you for a while? We need to talk."

She reluctantly bowed her head, acquiescing to his request.

He continued. "You left the scene of an accident with an attaché case. Correct?"

Amy paused, took a slow sip from her cup and replied, "And if I did?"

"I need the case. You still have it?" His tone had become aggressive, *somewhat unbelievable*, Amy thought.

"Sure, do you know what's in the case?"

"I do. But I'm willing to let you keep what you found in the case. Some very important connections have a serious interest in the case, not the contents."

"Let me get this straight. There were diamonds in the case. I get to keep them?"

Craven stared directly into her eyes and answered without hesitation. He knew the only way he'd be led to the case was if this woman believed she could keep the stones.

"You keep the stones, I get the case. Deal? Now where is it? Oh, and by the way, you haven't opened any of the containers that were in the case have you?"

Amy glanced away from the intimidating stranger, hesitating a few seconds. She thought, *can I trust him?*

"I understand your reluctance to take me to the location of the case. Let's meet back at a place agreeable to both of us. You can hand it over to me there," Craven said with an assuring nod of his head as he spoke.

Amy slowly bowed her head in agreement. She said, "It's been a long day, one I'd like to put behind me, I'm sore, confused, tired and very pissed of. I'll bring the case, and we agree it'll be empty. Let's make it at ten o'clock tonight. No arguments."

Craven admired her bravado and reluctantly agreed.

"But you haven't answered my question, have you opened the boxes yet?"

"No. They really aren't consumer friendly, but I'll crack one open soon enough. Is that a problem?"

"A problem?" Craven quipped. "No problem. Not for me anyway." He smiled, and leaned back in the chair, balancing on its rear legs.

Amy sensed something ominous in his voice. Why was it 'no problem' for him, she wondered. Her stare was inquisitive, Craven was silent, and the question remained unanswered. The meeting place was set, and Amy walked away from the coffee shop. *What could he want with the case? Why no apparent interest in the diamonds? It's a bluff,* she thought. *He wants the stones as well as the case. That's got to be it.*

Amy started back to the hotel. She strolled about the shops, stopping to admire paintings hanging in a newly opened exhibition, all the time checking behind for familiar faces. She saw none. She headed up an escalator, across a store display of dresses, down a flight of stairs. She'd lost Craven, who was still negotiating a weaving trail between mannequins in the dress department. Craven, disappointed, sneered in disgust. He made his way to the parked Porsche. Took his cell from the car and hit a button.

"You'll be glad to know that she's agreed to return the case. She's got the stones. Once I've gotten the case, the stones will follow. I'm meeting her at ten o'clock. No problem, I'll take care of her and get the stones too."

Amy's phone vibrated. Karen Jones could be trusted.

She'd always been there for Amy in times of need, a big sister substitute. Amy spoke quickly, "Karen we need to talk. Where are you?"

A short time later, the two women met at a Panda Express restaurant. Karen carried a tray of food to the table. Amy was bruised, not looking the best for wear. Amy took twenty minutes to go through the course of events. She explained, as best she could, the Porsche, the body in her hotel room, the meeting with Craven, the diamonds in the unopened boxes – the whole day's unbelievable mess.

"Oh my God Amy, I can't let you out of my sight. What a mess! Okay, first things first."

As Amy picked through the now cold lemon chicken, Karen sat shaking her head at the story she'd just heard. Karen was a world traveler. Her brother Rick was a retired Navy SEAL. Rick also had some serious clout among the casino crowd in Monte Carlo. He'd survived as a professional gambler for three years since retiring from the SEAls. Rick Jones had earned the respect and favors of several gentlemen in 'high places.'

Karen accompanied Amy back to her hotel and they took the stairs to her room. Amy placed one hand on Karen's shoulder. She said, "It's pretty bad in there. I haven't cleaned the mess, you ready for this?"

The door opened and they stepped into the nightmare. Karen's hand rose quickly to her mouth. The blood had seeped through the quilt and was now an expanding pool on the outside of the chenille cover. Amy spotted the bloody footprints around the room. They weren't hers. She spoke through the gaps of her fingers, her eyes staring as one hand pointed at the shoe prints. She said, "Someone's been here. My God, someone knows."

Clothes were strewn about the room as though a frenzied search had taken place. The closet containing her luggage, as well as the attaché case, remained untouched. She thought that perhaps the intruder was disturbed before completing the search. Then she remembered the cistern. She gasped, "My God, the bathroom."

She took six large paces and pushed the bathroom door.

She raised the porcelain lid from the toilet cistern and found the four boxes where she'd left them. Karen stood staring down at the body, speechless and not believing the mess, not wanting to accept the reality, the horror. "Amy we gotta clean this mess, we gotta get the body out of here. Need some serious help."

Karen sat on the old chesterfield lounge, flicked open the cell phone and began her call.

"Hello Ricardo?"

The man on the other end of the phone knew it was a serious call. His sister didn't call him Ricardo unless she had a problem. It'd been a good week in Monaco. Rick was enjoying his favorite haunt, the Monte Carlo Casino. The casino was built in 1863 in the principality of Monaco. This architectural masterpiece had been the setting for Monte Carlo's finest hours. It was there that Rick felt at home. The casino accepted all currencies, and he preferred to be paid in U.S. dollars, making this the perfect venue for him. The Monte Carlo revolved primarily around table games. Roulette and blackjack were Rick's demons.

After he spoke with Karen, Rick took a cab to the heliport. Six hours remained until the meeting with Travis Craven, enough time for Rick to join the two ladies.

CHAPTER 5

RICK HARDLY UTTERED A word. His drive from the airport involved listening. His mind moved into clean-up mode. The plan was already morphing, was in motion. He walked into the hotel room, looked about, said: "Sweet Jesus. How could two people make such a fuckin' mess?"

"Wasn't easy," Amy said quietly, looking away from the bundle at one side of the room. Rick shook his head at the mess as Amy came from the bathroom. She laid the four boxes containing the stones on the table. All four were tightly sealed.

"Well look at this. These were in the case he wanted so badly, huh?"

"You think they're real?" Amy asked.

"I'd say so. Let's find out."

Rick tried to open a box. There was no lid, no joins. He placed one box on the tiled table top, retrieved a heavy handled bottle opener from the utensil drawer. With a sudden move, he brought it crashing down on the box. The two girls pulled away with a knee-jerk reaction. The crack was loud, the box split along one edge. A hissing sound, and then a strange green mist seeped from the crack in the box. In a few seconds the air cleared. He opened a Swiss Army knife and forced the blade into the crack. He tipped one stone from the container and studied it carefully, then walked to the bathroom mirror.

"Always wanted to do this," he said dragging the stone across the glass.

"What do you think the green shit is?" Amy asked.

"Dunno, maybe it's some kind of conservation chemical. Don't much matter. No harm done that I can see."

The scratch in the mirror confirmed Rick's suspicion.

"It's the real thing, not a cubic."

He put the stone back into the container and opened the attaché case. He carefully examined the lining. Wondered why the case was so important.

He ran his fingers across the velvet lining and felt something under the cloth. Again using his pocket knife, he separated the lining from the lid of the case. A computer disc, gold and shiny, slid out and dropped into the empty case.

"Well, well, well . . . what have we here?"

"I'd say what we have here," Amy replied, "is an attaché case worth absolutely nothing."

CHAPTER 6

WHEN CRAVEN ARRIVED AT the busy entrance to the cathedral, the popular late Mass had its usual roll-up. Parishioners entered the church in a steady stream. The full moon slid behind threatening clouds. A glow from antique Gothic lights of the church added a medieval mood to the surrounding landscape. Church goers made their way through large carved doors. Craven moved discreetly. He edged his way toward the front pews, nodding politely to the priest who smiled at everyone. People took up places along the rows. As Craven moved into a spot in the front row he slid his hand inside his jacket and gave the Glock a reassuring tap.

Surely this will be a safe rendezvous place, he thought. *What the hell are these people doing coming to church at this ungodly hour?*

A few minutes passed. Amy, Karen, and Rick arrived with the case. Rick said quietly, "I'm goin' round the side to see if there's another way out." He leaned to Karen's ear. "Once you reach the front row, make your way toward Craven. Tell him to look over at Amy. She'll be by that side exit over there." He nodded to an arched door to the far left of the altar.

"When he looks your way, be sure to hold the case so he can see it." Rick moved out of the church, walked its perimeter, checking for other exits.

Craven sat looking directly ahead as Karen made her way along the row. She positioned herself beside him and whispered, "I'm here with Amy. She's got the case." He flashed a quick look sideways at the whisper. She tilted her head. "Over there, by the exit."

He was surprised. This was a new player in the game. He gave Karen a full glance then turned toward the exit. Amy stood in the doorway conspicuously holding the case. She threw an antagonistic grin at Craven and motioned at the case with her head. Then she motioned to the doorway, luring him to follow.

Travis Craven, the consummate professional didn't feel comfortable not controlling a situation. He had no choice this time. They stood and began walking crab like, shuffling past the parishioners seated along the front row. As they got nearer to Amy, she moved out to the courtyard. Rick stayed hidden from sight behind a large hanging of bougainvillea. He looked about, felt he was there in anticipation of . . . whatever. Craven stood back from Amy trying to read her body language. But there was nothing to read. He lowered his eyes to the attaché case.

"The case, give it to me." He reached for it. Amy passed it toward him as he reached into his jacket, placing one hand on the Glock. He hesitated, thought better of it and pulled his hand back. He squinted, tried to stare into the darkness around the church. He always felt uncomfortable in unfamiliar surroundings. The stars had taken refuge behind heavy clouds, the night air was cold and a hint of fog hung suspended over their heads. A gentle mist swirled like translucent tissue paper around the gothic lanterns that were sparsely spread about the parking area.

"Tell me why the case is so important," Amy said drawing Craven's attention back to her.

"No concern of yours. Don't ask questions."

The silence of the churchyard was broken by the sound of a speeding motor-bike. It came from nowhere. No headlight. It headed directly for Craven, who leaped to one side, the same direction the rider swerved in an effort to grab the case from Craven's grip. Craven was unable to jump from its path. The bike hit hard into his side, throwing Craven heavily into a parked Renault. The Yamaha tried to turn away, the rider swerved, almost careening into Karen. The bike fell to its side, cart-wheeled about on the ground. The rider made a dash to the attaché case that lay on the ground between Amy and Craven. He scooped up the case. Accelerated through the parking area. Dodged between cars, bumped along a perimeter fence. Dropped the case. Rick sprinted toward him; the rider limped back to the bike. It lay on its side, the rear wheel spinning. He scrambled to set the bike upright as Rick made a full dive through the air. The two men fell to the ground. As he fell, Rick struck his head against the edge of the sidewalk. He lay there momentarily dazed. The rider limped to the bike, righted it, revved the motor, swung it about and accelerated through the gates. It was over before Rick had a chance to fully recover. The attaché case still lay nearby, very much the worse for wear.

"My God Rick, what was that all about?" She looked about, looked into the mist. "Craven is over there. We think he's dead. Are you hurt?"

"Think I'm okay sis, fuckin' lunatic on that bike."

He limped back toward Craven. A crowd now gathered around the unconscious man. Karen turned to Rick. "Did you see who that was on the bike?"

Rick passed the case to Karen, She picked at the imbedded gravel in its leather lid.

"This case has seen better days. That guy on the bike was fast," Karen said looking in the direction of the entry gates. "Seemed you were handling it okay, didn't need me over there. You're getting slow old man."

"Yeah, feelin' fuckin' old too," Rick groaned rubbing his lower back. "My back's killin' me. I can hear sirens, time to get the hell out of here."

They moved through the parking lot, across the grassy area of the courtyard, and out past the school bus. It was an old Leyland used for transporting children to church services. Rick quickly surveyed their options. He looked at the road leading away from the church, could hear the approaching sirens: "Can't go this way. Quickly, get in the bus."

They moved to the rear of the bus and lay on the floor in the darkness. Sirens made their way into the churchyard, the flashing squad car light-bars now adding a kaleidoscope of color around the inside of the bus. Within minutes cops mulled around Craven who was still laying face down by the Renault. An irate Frenchman argued with one of the cops about the damage to his rear fender. The result of the Yamaha's rebound as it made its rush for the exit.

An ambulance weaved its way through the parking lot, siren whaling. Separating the spectators. The arrival of so many cops together with the commotion caused by the accident ended Mass early that night. It had been a short sermon.

Cops cordoned off the area. The church had now emptied. Crowds gathered in the courtyard. A woman cop waved a flashlight about as she directed people toward the bus. Within minutes the seats were filled. The three at the rear of the bus slowly raised themselves and sat in the seats. No one noticed, they'd become part of the church crowd whose night Mass had been disrupted by an incident.

A young cop directed cars from the courtyard. The bus slowly exited and made its way along the poorly lit street leading away from the church. Its first stop was at a popular shopping area. A handful of late night and early morning tourists were hovering around a coffee shop. Other late diners were slowly leaving restaurants and curio shops. As the passengers filed out of the bus, Amy, Rick and Karen became part of the crowd.

Rick reached for his cell, placed a call, spoke for several minutes and then gave Amy and Karen an encouraging nod. He placed his hand over the phone and said, "Things are gonna be fine."

He flipped the cell closed and said, "Just spoke with an old friend. He owes me big time, got his sister out of the clutches of a bunch of bad mother-fuckers back in Miami. She was shootin' it up like there was no tomorrow. Lucky for her, she made it out okay."

Rick saw the look of *where's this going,* on the faces of each girl as each anticipated Rick's expanding on the story. He said, "We're meetin' some buddies back at the hotel, a sort of clean up crew. Let's get movin'. We've a few blocks to go. They're expectin' to meet us there round midnight."

CHAPTER 7

THE VAN WAS PARKED in the alley at the rear of the hotel, a neatly dressed man stood propped against its hood. He was smoking what distinctly smelled like a Gauloise - the national aroma of Paris. He smiled as Rick approached. "Good morning Ricardo." He glanced at his wrist watch and flipped open a Zippo lighter, held it to the watch and squinted at the dial. "Yes it is morning, twenty after one to be precise. It has been a long time Rick. Good to see you. Your call was most welcome."

Rick smiled widely, he said, "Thanks for gettin' this all together so quick. When ya move, ya really move fast. Meet my sister Karen and a good friend Amy. Have you brought the props?"

The Frenchman ignored the question, smiled at the two ladies, he said, "My pleasure to meet such lovely ladies."

He walked closer to Rick, lowered his voice. Spoke in a muffled tone. "Everything it is arranged. The van she is clean. From a Monastery in Nice, she will not be missed for some time. Her license plates, they have been taken from her. We found the van a few days back for another job we have planned. But of course she is yours for tonight." Rick smiled at the French touch, the gendering of the van. The Frenchman continued, "Most fortunate, otherwise it would have been most difficult to pull this together on so little notice." He shrugged and gestured at the van with both hands as though it was a favorite child.

Rick placed an arm around his shoulder and said, "You're truly the best. Really appreciate you getting' this together so quick. The props, you got 'em too?"

"But of course," he pointed to the rear. "They are in the van."

The van door slid open, a dim light reflected off the painted faces of the three occupants. They each smiled as they stepped from the vehicle. One was fully dressed as a clown. The other two were in various stages of clown attire. As though they were preparing to enter a three ring circus act. Two had faces painted with smiling red lips while the third sported a smile sloped downward, making him the sadder of the three clowns.

Yves said "You remember Philippe, Ramone, and Gustave?"

Rick laughed as they each shook his hand. He said, "Clean-up crew, huh? Good ta see you guys again. Y'all been briefed on the procedure?"

"But of course," replied Yves as he maneuvered the butt between his index finger and thumb the sucked down one final drag of the cigarette. He said, "We are ready to perform, just as we did in Rio."

"Now that was a heist. Glad to see y'all still in business Yves." Karen gave Rick an inquisitive look. He said, "Long story, tell ya 'bout it some other time; let's just say these guys are good. They got their shit together. You're gonna see professionals at work."

Amy and Karen were bewildered. They watched as all four men made their way into the hotel lobby. Rick smiled at the morning shift desk clerk and gestured with a whimsical wave toward the curious troop standing behind him.

Rick said, "These are my friends. We've just finished our circus act for the night and they're stoppin' by to collect some props for their next show. I realize it's late. I hope this ain't a problem. We'll be very quiet."

The clerk passed a quizzical glance at the strange gathering. "Not at all. Please go ahead."

Rick turned back to the troupe He looked around the lobby as though something was missing.

"Yves where's the trunk? We need to bring in the old stuff. Figure out what stays here and what we need to take to the show."

The desk clerk took it all in. His grin showed that he was enjoying being entertained by the colorful troupe.

Yves played along. He said, "But of course. Ramone, Philippe. Bring the trunk from the van. *Amener le tronc.*"

The two returned within minutes. They struggled as they

brought in the heavy trunk. As they took the trunk through the lobby area they strained under its imaginary weight. They let it fall to the ground by the elevator. Pushing down hard on it as it landed, making certain the landing made a distinct and noticeably heavy thud.

Ramone painfully regained his upright composure. Philippe massaged his back, stopped, wiped his brow with a red polka dotted handkerchief. Ramone and Philippe turned toward the grinning desk clerk and gave him their best Laurel and Hardy impersonation. Gustave clapped silently.

The door of the elevator slowly opened. The three men exaggerated their struggle with the trunk as two pushed and one pulled. The trunk inched into the small enclosure.

The message to the desk clerk was clear. This was one heavy trunk. All was going to plan. This scenario always had. This was the clean-up crew at its best.

Rick, Yves and the two women took the stairs. They arrived ahead of the elevator. It had seen better days. The wrought iron cage rattled and groaned as it strained toward the third floor. Once inside the room, the entourage stood in silence as though mesmerized by the blood bath. Blood was splattered about the walls and the furniture. Yves waved his hand across the room. He said, "We have much to do. *Aller, va. Commencer le nettoyage de ce désordre.*"

The two men opened the trunk. It was empty, except for an assortment of cleaning utensils and old towels.

Amy asked, "You made it look so heavy, why?"

Yves grinned and placed another Gauloise between his lips. Rick reached forward, lit the smoke. Yves took a long drag and said, "It will be heavy on its way out, very heavy."

Three hours after entering the room, the clean-up crew began a second scrub down. Going over all areas where blood had splashed. They sprayed chlorinated disinfectant on all the surfaces, then they methodically repeated the scrubbing procedure. The body was uncomfortably folded into the plastic-lined trunk together with the chenille cover. Ramone and Gustave worked at spraying cleaner, wiping all horizontal surfaces. Philippe began to make his way along a narrow ledge around the outside of the building.

Yves said, "Be sure to take the used soap from the shower, it could have prints." He repeated his words in French, as though the English was for the benefit of the Americans. He moved toward the bathroom, he repeated, *"Etre sûr de prendre le savon utilisé de la douche, il pourrait avoir des caractères."*

Rick grinned, "I'm impressed Yves, very good."

Philippe slowly inched his way along the narrow ledge toward the adjoining room's external window. The lights were not on. He took a quick glance inside. Made certain the room was empty. The window was conveniently unlocked. A few seconds passed and he was inside. He walked quickly, made his way to the bedroom, and was pleased to see the chenille bed cover. It was the same color as the original cover, which was in the trunk. In the bathroom he found a bar of un-used soap, slipped it into his pocket.

"I have the cover," he proudly proclaimed as he re-entered the room.

Yves smiled and nodded his satisfaction. "Place it on the bed Philippe. Our work here is almost done. *Nous sommes finis.*"

Philippe passed the soap to Gustave who held up the used bar.

"Good, take it with you. *Essuyer par-dessus les bouteilles.* The shampoo bottles, wipe them as well."

"Don't worry Yves, *la salle de bains est propre.*" He turned to Rick and said, "The bathroom is as clean as new," Gustave said proudly.

Their brightly colored jackets were neatly folded on the sofa. The three clowns retouched their painted faces, retrieved their jackets turning them inside out to reveal more brightly garish colors. They slipped into their new outfits and started to carry the now genuinely heavy trunk from the room. The elevator door groaned open. Rick was now at the desk, engaged in an animated conversation with the clerk. The desk phone rang. It distracted the clerk. The voice on the other end made an fake inquiry into room availability for some future date. It created enough confusion for the clerk from being too close an observer. When sufficient time passed Yves thanked the clerk and flipped his cell phone shut. The three men now grunting and puffing exited the lobby, struggling desperately with the trunk as they went.

This was to be last ride of Eduard Heinzman. Mr. Heinzman was leaving the building. He'd make an inglorious exit from Paris in the rear of a transit van, through the back streets of the city. Of little consolation was his departure in style. After all, he *was* jammed into a leather YSL travel trunk.

They closed the rear door of the van, Rick grinned at Yves acknowledging another job well done. Rick extended a hand to Yves, who brushed the hand aside and gave his friend the customary hug and French air kiss. Rick reached into his jacket, feeling for the box of stones. He carefully squeezed it open, forced the crack, and removed six stones.

"Thanks Yves," Rick said appreciably. "Here, take these for a job well done."

In Rick's palm were six diamonds, all large and each stone around three karats. Yves looked down at Rick's palm, stunned by the stones.

Yves said, "*Mon Dieu.* For removing that stone dead man, why not . . . stones. *Ils sont magnifiques.* They are beautiful. Thank you Rick. Until next time, I bid you *adieu*, my friend."

Yves, Ramone, Gustave and Philippe slowly drove off. Yves rewarded each of his assistants with a single stone. They were more than grateful. Ramone returned Yves to his home, and as Yves stepped from the van he tapped on the trunk, he said, "Sleep well my friend, sleep well."

He called to Ramone, "Drive to the west end Ramone. Gustave be sure you go where the water is deepest. Be sure there is no one by the lake. Do not want any witnesses. The windows . . . leave them down so that she sinks quickly."

The three men nodded to Yves as they drove away. Ramone turned to Philippe and smiled. "Philippe, with one of these stones we can make a fantasy come true, you and I are spending some time with the infamous Michelle."

Gustave, who had a wife at home, laughed, "Yes, yes, the

life of a single man. Ah well, at least I get regular meals, and the same warm bed each night."

The three men laughed and the van rattled onward toward the lake. It was ten to four when Rick returned to the room. A typical Paris morning was looming and the two girls had fresh coffee brewing.

"I know it's a ridiculous time to have coffee," Amy said, "but I had to make it, if for no other reason than to kill the smell of this disinfectant and those horrid cigarettes." She waved at the air, trying to rid the room of the array of odors.

"Fresh coffee, thanks. Just what the doc ordered," Rick said, relaxing for the first time since arriving at the hotel.

Karen asked, "So we're clear then?"

Rick stretched out on the sofa, pushed off one shoe. He stretched his toes and said. "Yeah, yeah. Those boys'll get rid of the trunk. It won't be found. It's all over. How long will the coffee be?"

As Amy and Karen prepared cups and a few crackers, Rick stretched across to the table where he'd slid the contents of the attaché case. He removed the bundle from its hiding place and un-wrapped the velvet cloth. Amy and Karen re-entered with an early breakfast. The gold disc had the immediate attention of all three.

"Is this what men have been dyin' for?" Rick asked. "Is this what the threats and risks have all been about?"

"What do you think Karen?" Amy asked.

"It's a disc, maybe a coded master disc," Rick said. "Whatever's on this thing, it must be valuable to someone. In a few hours we'll find out precisely what those guys want so badly. Until then, let's try to grab forty winks . . . I got dibs on the sofa."

The bedside clock was the only light. It let off a digital glow. It was sufficient enough to do away with the need for a night light.

Rick had hated the dark when he was a kid. Saturday matinees would do more than their share of scaring the living daylights out of him. He'd lie in bed at night, hearing the creatures under his bed. Someone or something definitely lived in the closet. No one could convince him otherwise. Shadows hung over the windows. Monsters wanted to devour him. The sound of car horns below the hotel window woke Rick and Amy.

"I had the worst nightmare," Amy said.

"Nah, no nightmare," Rick mumbled. "It really happened."

"Shit, you're right," she replied rubbing her eyes with softly closed fists. "It did happen, oh my God."

"So then, eight o'clock, let's get down to business." Rick said. He turned toward Karen and called aloud, "WAKE UP SIS."

The coffee pot was rejuvenated and all three washed up and sat at the small table, in silence, than when a few minutes passed, Rick interlocked his fingers, stretched his arms away from himself and cracked his knuckles.

The percolator beeped; another round of fresh coffee was his again his savior. Three sugars, coffee creamer, a dash of whipped cream, and voilà . . . a perfect start to another day in Paris.

CHAPTER 8

SAN DIEGO DEFINITELY HAS much to offer, its proximity to beaches, attractions, and international travel. As Saffrey Bell savored the final drops of his creamed brew, his attention was diverted from the television to the low buzzing of the phone.

"Yeah," he snapped, not 'good morning'. Friends knew better than to expect a 'good morning' from Saffrey if they called before his coffee, before nine o'clock.

"Hey man, how's it hangin' stateside?"

Bell said, "Rick? Rick, is that you, man?"

He hadn't heard from Rick in years. The two men had shared some exciting times in the SEALs. On leaving the force they had gone separate ways. Rick enjoyed the casino scene and the last Saffrey had heard, Rick was doing very well.

"Hey Saff it's good to touch base with ya after so long."

"Jesus Christ Rick, what's the time man? I'm sleeping here for Christ's sake. What's up?"

"Too much to fill ya in on by phone . . . can ya travel? Like now?"

"Is this employment or fun?"

"Definitely employment and the payoff is huge."

"When and where old buddy?"

"Right now, in Paris, I'll have a ticket ready for ya at the American Airlines counter at Lindbergh Field. Say around ten o'clock departure tomorrow mornin'?"

The 767 touched down at the Charles de Gaulle International Airport on its scheduled arrival time. Saffrey Bell cleared customs with the usual barrage of questions: "Any beef jerky? What is the purpose of your visit? How long are you staying in France?

Same old questions, same old answers .Blah, blah, blah. He gave the same old answers. "No jerky, for pleasure, and God willing I'm not here for long."

A skeptical glare from the uniformed Frenchman, and a quick and curt, "Move on, move on."

Saffrey collected his one piece of luggage, flicked his cell open, and called Rick. The two hooked up twenty minutes later at the Admiral's Club.

Rick gave the usual gentleman's greeting,

"Lookin' good man, lookin' good. Ten years hasn't left its mark."

"Yeah you too. Okay enough of the ass kissing, what the hell's this all about Rick?"

Rick filled him in on the chain of events. Saffrey followed as best he could, although there were a few loose ends. Loose ends have a way of tying into something along the way. Big knots can often be worse than the loose ends from where they originated.

"Okay so where the hell is this disc?" Saffrey asked.

"In a safe-deposit box with the three sealed boxes. Can't take any chances. These people are deadly serious about getting' this stuff. They don't give a rat's ass who gets killed along the way!"

The two men had the cab stop a block from the bank. They took a stroll through a few shops. Made sure no one was tailing them.

The bank was old, musty, and mortuary cold. The type of building one would find in an old World War Two movie. A swastika flag hanging in a depressing Nazi headquarters. They retrieved the disc from the bank. The three sealed boxes remained in the bank's vault. Feeling like criminals, the two men made their way to the Champs Elysées, up a narrow cobble stoned street to a small, inconspicuous hotel.

"We're located here until Yves and the boys are done cleanin'. Can't risk . . . I just can't risk . . . sorry buddy, sometimes I feel a bit paranoid with all this shit goin' down, but my sister and Amy . . . her and her friend, they can't take much more of this."

It was only the second time Saffrey could recall seeing Rick uptight about anything. The other time was on an assignment in Cambodia. They weren't there . . . officially. They'd just come across an old deserted Vietcong stronghold. They poked about looking for evidence. Evidence of MIAs. There walked into a shack, the walls made of old bamboo sheeting; it covered the entry walls and into an adjoining room. Time had caused the bamboo to move, exposing the once concealed opening.

Rick entered ahead of Saffrey and reeled about, spewing as he turned. Saffrey was caught in the spray of Rick's breakfast.

Rick screamed, "Jesus Christ, those sons of bitches," as he continued ejecting what little food remained in his gut.

The count was seventy, no dog tags, no bodies, just heads, each with one common feature, a bullet hole in the forehead.

Rick squatted over a group of the skulls, one hand touching a bullet-hole. He asked, "Are these our guys or are they local villagers?"

Turning away, Saffrey's reply was subdued: "Look at the dental work, that's American dentistry. They're ours all right."

Rick left the shack, fell to his knees, and sobbed. He stayed that way for ten minutes. Saffrey couldn't get much out of Rick for several hours. The first words he spoke were no more than a whisper.

"Saff, what do ya suppose they did with the bodies?"

"Let it go man. For Christ's sake, let it go."

Comforting a hardened soldier wasn't something Saffrey Bell needed to do. This was an exception. He placed his arm around Rick's shoulder. Rick broke down again. Saffrey said, "Time to call it quits, buddy. This is the end of the line for both of us." Rick's eyes were bloodshot. His hands trembled. Burn out had arrived. They left Cambodia three days later. Neither man spoke of the incident again. It was as though it had been a nightmare, one they each pretended never happened. The glances each gave the other during those three days were burned into their memories. That body language had said it all. They'd seen children with missing limbs, women raped by soldiers wearing the same uniforms as their guys, and those U.S. officers, each turning a blind eye to it all. The worst thing was they'd learned how to separate most of it from what they considered "reality." Didn't want this part of their lives coexisting with *reality*. At least, not reality as they preferred reality to be. They wanted to build a fantasy shroud, one that would take away the past. One far removed from the very world they now preferred to exist in.

On his return to the States, Rick underwent psychiatric care for eight months. The powers that be determined Saffrey Bell was not in need of the same. This of course didn't make his dreams any less disturbing. Strange thing how adversity when shared, can bring two individuals closer together. Rick had been like the brother Saff Bell never had. The brother who had left a part of his soul in Cambodia. As for Rick's dreams, the monsters remained ever constant, taking the place of Saturday matinees.

Amy and Karen greeted the two men on their arrival at the hotel. Saffrey had met Karen on only one other occasion while he was in the SEALs. She was as beautiful as he'd remembered. A little more mature, and even more arousing.

Saffrey chewed on a toothpick, he said, "Amy, you're in one hell of a pickle."

She smiled at Saffrey, the look of a child pleading for guidance, searching for a way out. The phone rang. Rick spoke quietly for several minutes: "Sure and you have the equipment? Okay then, we'll be there around five o'clock." He turned to the others, "That's our computer guy. He's ready to run the disc. Let's get goin'. You girls are welcome to come along but . . ."

Karen cut him short. She said, "In your dreams. No way are we staying away from this."

CHAPTER 9

AT A QUARTER TO five they arrived at a small computer repair store. Rick pressed the door bell and stood back looking at the open window above. "Henri? Hey Henri . . . Rick."

A voice from above replied, "Come in, come in."

The lock opened, and the four entered the small dark store. As they entered, a woman appeared from a room at the rear. She was nursing a fat gray cat. The cat was resting its head comfortably on the woman's matronly bust.

Her English was broken. "Welcome. Henri is expecting you, please come this way."

They brushed past a collection of monitors and peripherals, boxes jammed with VHS tapes, floppies and discs. A small security camera tucked away in a corner of the ceiling flashed a red light every few seconds. Hardware and software were in abundance, sufficient it seemed, to recreate the command deck of the Starship Enterprise. A very French gentleman wearing bifocals entered the room and sat at a table. He had Einstein hair, an empty pipe wedged between his teeth, and a warm friendly smile. He extended a hand to Rick, he said, "Welcome my friend. Good to see you again Ricardo."

After introductions were made, Rick took the disc from his jacket pocket and gave it to Henri. The Frenchman glanced at it. He slowly raised his eyes, removed the pipe from his mouth. He pulled a pouch from his shirt pocket and began to refill the pipe with an aromatic blend of tobacco. The gray cat purred contentedly, casually dropped from the busty woman. It wobbled over to its master and began to rub against Henri's leg.

Henri struck a match, tilted his head and took several strong draws on the pipe. Three matches later, clouds of white smoke billowed like incense around the old man's head. He squinted as the smoke stung his eyes, waved furiously to clear visibility. He said to Rick, "Are you not forgetting something?"

"Yeah, yeah, sorry Henri," Rick reached into his pocket and took out a small box. He placed it on the coffee stained tablecloth. Henri smiled, chewed hard on the pipe with his yellowed teeth.

"Ah but of course, the fruits of one's labor," he said smiling. "For such an enticement Henri will gladly unravel the mystery that technology has placed on this mysterious golden disc."

"One thing Henri," Rick snapped firmly. "Whatever ya see here, it stays here. No one can hear 'bout the disc. Understand . . . no one."

Henri sucked in, chewed even harder on the pipe. "Mon dieu, but of course," he said still staring at the small box. "Henri's lips are sealed."

"And the woman?" Her lips good too?" Rick motioned toward the woman standing by the door, nodding his head in her direction as he spoke.

Henri slid the smoking inferno from his mouth, tapped it against an old Cinzano ashtray. He looked at the woman and said, "*Marie, prendre le chat et aller*. If you please Marie, leave us now." He stared at the ashtray as he spoke, continued tapping. As the woman began to move from the room, Henri slowly raised his eyes to meet Rick's, he nodded toward the woman and said, "My wife, she is not a problem."

His wife smiled, picked up the gray cat which was comfortably curled up by the monitor, and together they left the room. Henri inserted the disc. After more than an hour had passed, Henri's attempts at several access codes had failed. The disc was unique. He couldn't access the information it stored. Rick was now beyond his limit of endurance when it came to computers. He said "Come on Henri, I was told you're the best at this shit. How much longer before you . . ."

Rick didn't complete the question. The monitor sprung to life. The words began to appear. A deep mechanical voice, reminiscent of Darth Vader said, "Teleportation, Doorways, and Neutron Technology: A Compendium of Recent Findings. Theory has it that a dark hole can act as a doorway when a unit hits the speed of light and withstands the force of the pull of the dark hole's gravity. This suggests a doorway can act as a teleport through which a unit can travel from point A to point B without going the actual distance between. This therefore is a way for travelers to pass from one galaxy to another."

Saffrey Bell stared mouth opened at the monitor, he nudged Rick: "Rick, do you realize what this is all about?"

"Oh yeah Saff, sure I do. I grew up on this shit." Rick gave Saffrey a look of *"yeah, really,"* and scratched his chin in bewilderment.

The voice continued: "The doorway is stabilized to allow safe passage through. Using highly exotic matter is key. In order to stabilize the doorway the throat of the singularity would have to be threaded with this matter, which would be spherical in nature. The property this matter has is negative mass. It is therefore capable of exerting a positive surface pressure."

Amy leaned toward Rick. "Is this about time travel?" she asked. "Are you getting any of it?"

"I think that's the gist of it. Yeah, time travel. That's where it's headin'. Interestin' shit."

The Vader voice went on. "It must have these two properties for very specific reasons. The negative mass ensures that the opening of the doorway lies outside the protected region. The positive surface pressure is the property that prevents the opening of the doorway from collapsing. We have determined this is the type of space-time geometry most likely needed to produce a stable doorway. The energy-momentum content of matter exists in an area to produce the needed geometry. From as general a standpoint as this can be, these are the properties needed to stabilize a doorway. The energy allows a unit to jump from one location to another. It is a jump, not an actual journey involving distance traversed."

"Yeah, you're right," Saffrey said. "Time travel, going from one galaxy to another I'd say."

"Gonna drive me nuts with this stuff," Rick said in a quizzical voice. "Are you buyin' it?"

The monitor scrambled. The voice faded behind the sounds on poltergeist. Within seconds the commentary resumed. "We therefore conclude that the doorways, which are now considered safe and stable, will be chronologically preserved for all those who follow. We must, however, take all precaution to see that the information herein is preserved for present and future posterity. Past times and galaxies are not ready for or aware of the consequences of attempting tele transportation of this intensity."

"Okay, okay, let's move on," Saffrey said. "This stuff's too heavy for me." He had little patience for anything resembling what he perceived as computer jargon.

"Just take us to 'computer for idiots' Rick mumbled wiping sweat from his forehead. Saff grinned, nodding in agreement. The camera settled on an image, a ship of World War Two vintage. On its sides were the markings DE 173.

"Looks like a destroyer." Saffrey said with a feeling of déjà vu. *I've seen this ship somewhere before*, he thought. "I know this ship; it's from the Philadelphia incident. I remember the movie,"

Rick turned and then, moving closer to the monitor, nodded his head in agreement, "Christ, your right. Isn't it the Eldridge? It is. It's the USS Eldridge, the invisible ship. Remember how it disappeared for a few minutes and re-appeared in Virginia at some Navy dock, then next thing it was back in Philly, crew, everything. It went away, and then it came back. The Navy denied it ever took place. After the incident several of the crew was hidden away in mental institutions, the Navy will tell you otherwise."

"Yeah, poor devils, more than half of them were insane because of the effects of pulsating energy fields. I recall hearing how they were kept in Bethesda Naval Hospital for around a year, not permitted to communicate with anyone, Saffrey said. "Rumor has it the Navy was attempting to make its fleet invisible. What happened was more than invisibility, it was teleportation. You remember that Rick?"

"Took brass fuckin' balls to be on that ship, kinda like *'beam me up, Scotty'* huh," Rick answered.

"In a nutshell," Saffrey said.

As they continued watching the monitor, pictures of the USS Eldridge were continually shown. One showed a crewman partly embedded into the steel deck, another with just his arms, shoulder, and head protruding from the steel siding of the hull.

The voice on the disc explained briefly how Einstein's 'Unified Field Theory' was the basis of the experiment. The invisibility experiment was a complete success, but to the men aboard, the severe mental and physical after effects made it a total disaster. Letters written by sailors and officers affirming the secret U.S. experiment have turned up. The Navy denies it ever happened.

"Just like Area 51," Rick said. "What d'ya make of this so far?"

Saffrey glanced at him. "Scary shit man, scary shit. Frightens the hell out of me just wondering what else is on this disc. I know this, if the CIA gets their hands on it, it'll never see the light of day."

Henri sat transfixed, mumbling, "*Mon dieu, mon dieu.*"

"Guess we're gonna find out soon enough," Rick said.

Saffrey ran his fingers across his cheeks, said to Rick, "Guess we will. Soon enough."

CHAPTER 10

THE IMAGE OF THE destroyer again appeared on the screen. A strange green mist swirled around it. A huge magnetic generator was shown below the ship. Notes appeared on the monitor coinciding with the images.

Saffrey read the words aloud hoping it might make more sense hearing them rather than just reading them. "The generator is pulsed at resonant frequencies so as to create a magnetic field on, as well as around, a floating vessel. Jesus Christ, sure sounds impressive Saff, don't you think?"

"Sounds like a fuckin' nightmare in the makin', a science fiction nightmare."

All four watched the monitor for what seemed like hours. Magnetic fields, electric fields, characteristics of mass, it went on and on. Amy came to life. Stood, began tapping on the monitor. Excitedly she said, "Stop, stop. It's Craven standing by the red Porsche."

Rick said, "Travis fuckin' Craven. Last saw him at the cathedral, with a severe concussion at best."

Saffrey said, "Henri, can you zoom into this guy and print it out?"

"Yes, just one moment."

They continued to studying the screen. Craven turned around, waved to the camera. He paced out an area of about ten meters and placed a small box at each end of a line. He got into the driver's seat and began to drive toward a group of cones either sides of a spot on the roadway ahead.

A green mist hovered around the cones. As the Porsche approached the markers, it began to vibrate as though leaving our focus. Craven spun the Porsche about, gunned it toward the space between the two small boxes. And then he was gone. The mist dissipated. Only the orange plastic cones and the two small boxes remained. They were marking the spot where the speeding Porsche had vanished.

Rick's eyes widened as he said, "Holy shit. You see that? Tell me this is trick photography."

Henri played the scene again. After viewing it several times the four sat in silence. Not a word. Three minutes, four . . . Rick spoke first: "Okay, okay. It's some charlatan parlor trick, some kind of digital trickery." He said, "Hit the play button Henri."

The camera focused on the orange cones. Then as suddenly as it vanished the car roared back through the fine green mist. It stopped just short of the camera. The monitor showed more footage of the Porsche driving into and out of the green mist. They continued watching the monitor, and as they watched, once in a while one of them would break into words of disbelief. The camera continued panning, finally focusing on a gathering of white robed men, a group of scientists perhaps. They were standing around a bank of monitors. With them was a Hispanic man. He smiled, waved to the camera. The whole group then turned, waved in unison in the direction of the camera.

Henri played around with the volume control. The Hispanic man turned and acknowledged the person running toward him. She was an attractive woman, and as she called out loudly, Henri finally got the volume up. Their voices were now clearly audible.

The blonde said, "Andreas, it's good to see you again. We made it."

She limped toward him, and the two gently embraced. The monitor then lost the picture. The screen was white.

"Interesting," Saffrey said.

Amy asked, "Who were those people?"

Henri stood, made his way past each of them, careful not to turn his back.

"Wait Henri please," Rick called. "This is for helping, and for forgettin' the shit you saw here."

He reached for the box on the table, twisted it open, handed a single stone to Henri. Pressed the box closed. The old man stared at Rick, then down at the stone. Shook his head, nodded his appreciation. He said, "I will never speak of what I have seen tonight, never." He left the room, looked toward the ceiling, and blessed himself.

They sat and stared at the monitor, then slowly the image re appeared. The blonde and the Hispanic man were gone. The monitor was focused on yet another green mist. They waited for the red Porsche to roar onto the scene. This time it didn't happen. The disc continued. A group of laboratory workers were inspecting what appeared to be diamonds. The men were dressed in contaminant-control outfits. They stood around a cylindrical contraption that looked like a heavy duty coffee percolator outfitted with a bolt-on porthole. A preternatural greenish glow shined from the window.

The camera switched to one of the white robed men, possibly a laboratory assistant. He began to discuss the procedure.

"This procedure involves placing pure carbon under enough heat and pressure . . . 2200 degrees Fahrenheit and fifty thousand atmospheres to be precise, and allowing it to crystallize into the hardest material known. Those were the conditions that first forged diamonds deep in the earth's mantle 3.3 billion years ago.

"The production of 'cultured diamonds' will open the doorway to the development of diamond-based semiconductors."

Rick nudged Saffrey and quizzically asked, "Am I followin' this, are they makin' diamonds?"

The man moved toward a large machine and placed one hand on it.

"This unit is eight thousand pounds. The machine uses electricity and hydraulics to apply large amounts of pressure and ever increasing temperature onto the core of a sphere. This recreates the temperature one hundred miles below the earth's crust, the depth where diamonds are created. A sliver of diamond is positioned in the core, we inject some carbon, and then the sliver becomes host to the formation of a larger diamond which grows around it. You are able to pass tremendous heat through a diamond without causing any damage, because a diamond has the highest known level of thermal conductivity known.

"By comparison, regular microprocessors run far too

hot, at temperatures exceeding two hundred degrees Fahrenheit. When called upon to increase their load, they fail. On the other hand, diamond microchips can sustain far higher temperatures. Regular silicon chips liquefy at these high temperatures. Diamonds in fact attain far higher speeds, and do not liquefy; this makes diamonds the most desirable solution as the perfect semiconductor.

"A project known as Code 6174 was conducted by the U.S. Navy, the Navy's diamond research arm, based in a highly secured area outside of Washington, DC. A civilian scientist named Butler, researched CVD diamonds and semiconductors for the military for some time. There've been three setbacks in the development of diamond semiconductors.

"First, diamond is seen as being extremely expensive, due to the scarcity De Beers creates with its control of the market. Synthesized diamonds created outside of the cartel will greatly reduce that problem. Second, there has never been a steady and dependable supply of large, pure diamonds. You can't depend on mined diamonds, as there is no way to ensure each stone will have the same electrical properties as the next. CVD diamonds have now solved that.

"The third big challenge has been the most daunting for materials scientists: To form microchip circuits, positive and negative conductors are needed. Diamond is an inherent insulator, because diamonds don't conduct electricity. But injecting boron into the lattice creates a positive charge. Until now, though, no one had been able to manufacture a negatively charged, or n-type, diamond with sufficient conductivity.

"The discovery of a novel way of inverting boron's natural conductivity to form a boron-doped n-type diamond provided a positive negative-junction, a diamond semiconductor that really works. This means there is definitely a diamond computer chip on the horizon. Diamonds represent a seismic change in semiconductors. Traditional processors are going to get hotter and hotter. Eventually silicon is just going to turn into a puddle. Diamond is the solution to that problem."

The four were bewildered by this barrage of technical

information, yet it seemed logical, and surprisingly, it did make sense.

The man went on professing the numerous advantages of the diamond chip. It seemed beyond doubt the silicon chip was doomed.

Then the diamond discussion began to take on a new track. They watched a stone on a table in a lab room. Suddenly there was a brilliant flash of light and the stone vanished, a green mist appeared then dissipated from where the stone once sat. The man continued to discuss the phenomena.

"We have perfected the neutron chip, coded the X11 stone. This eleventh generation stone will enable us to . . ."

The voice tapered off and the screen again turned white, the monitor let out a hissing sound and the disc in the computer drive ejected. Rick and Saffrey stumbled backwards, scrambling to regain their balance.

"Jesus Christ Saff, what the fuck was that?"

"Could be a malfunction or some kind of inbuilt security system, the disc was probably programmed shut down if played on a non compatible unit. Lucky we saw what we did."

Saffrey took the disc, wrapped it back in the lining. "Gotta hang on to this thing, God knows we'll be needin' it down the track."

"Yeah, good idea," Rick said. "Maybe there's some way ta . . . ya know . . . make the fuckin' thing work again."

They made their way back to the hotel. Amy and Karen chatted briefly, intermittently. Not much was said between the two men. They entered the room zombie like. It was eight o'clock. None of the four were up to discussing what they'd seen that evening.

CHAPTER 11

THE NEXT DAY THEY woke early if in fact they'd slept at all. The phone rang and jolted them back to reality.

"Get that will ya Saff? I'm fuckin' beat."

The voice on the phone sounded vaguely familiar but Saffrey couldn't quite put a face with it.

"You've something that's mine. By now you know of what's on the disc. Aren't you the least bit curious about where it's from, what it all means?"

Saffrey held his breath and thought very quickly. He knew the voice, just couldn't place it.

He replied, "Curious? Yeah sure we're curious. Is it safe to be curious, who the fuck is this?"

"Never mind who it is. You and your friends will be fine if you follow my instructions. We need to meet."

Saff hesitated momentarily. "Call me back in one hour. I need time to think this over."

The voice said, "Agreed. One hour."

Rick asked, "Who *was* that?"

"Dunno. Darth Vader I think," Saffrey said.

Exactly sixty minutes later the buzzing phone broke the silence. Saff picked up the receiver, placed it to his ear, didn't need to speak. The voice said, "Do we have a decision?"

"Yeah okay, we'll meet with you but it's gotta be in a safe place, plenty of people around."

"Agreed. You choose the meeting place."

"McDonald's on the Champs Elysées at eleven. Okay?"

"Patriotic of you. McDonald's it is. In an hour then, and only the four of you."

"What did he say?" Rick asked. "Did you pick the voice?"

"He said okay to McDonald's. Strange though, he knows there are four of us."

McDonald's was like any other Mickey Dee's. Big Macs, French fries, shakes. All at a bunch more euros than the dollar equivalent. But this, after all - this is Paris. Just like being back in San Diego but four times the price.

Good meeting place, Saffrey Bell thought, *safe, secure, and busy. Good old McDonald's.*

The four found a booth and sat nervously. They eyed each person entering, like singles anticipating the arrival of a blind date. Two men entered and looked about the restaurant. They were heavy, rough looking, not what Saffrey and Rick were hoping to see. They spotted the lavatory and made their way toward it. *Close call, glad they came in for a leak and not for us*, Rick thought. *Okay, can only get better.*

A few minutes passed and like a ghost, he floated into the restaurant. Craven smiled, and walked toward the table, he grinned at Rick and said, "Would have been so much easier if you'd handed the case over back at the church."

He took in the looks of disbelief on their faces.

Rick said, "You're alive? We left you for dead at the church, who the fuck was that bike rider?"

Craven chuckled as he sat in the booth alongside Amy, he said, "He's a dead man, a former partner of a disgruntled associate. Of the man who died in the plaza, Raoul Ramirez. He had an accomplice. When I went to your hotel room to retrieve the case the bike rider was already there. I almost had him but slipped on Eduard's blood, it gave the man time to escape."

Craven looked about the restaurant, checking to see if there were any suspicious observers. He turned to Amy, looked into her eyes. He said, "Speaking of Eduard that was a good number you did on him. He always fancied himself as a ladies man. Ah well, live by the sword. But to cut a long story short, our bike rider has left the building and joined his accomplice Ramirez. Neither was much of an asset to your time or mine. Good riddance to them both. I don't expect you to understand. We need to move forward. All of this, the information on the disc, will be explained. If you are cooperative, no harm will come to any of you. You have the disc?"

Rick looked at Saffrey, then he winked and turned back to face Craven. He said, "Nature calls. Give me a minute."

They waited as Rick made his way to the bathroom. Once inside, Rick searched desperately for a secure hiding place for the remaining stones. He stood on the toilet seat, lifted one of the insulation bats in the suspended ceiling, slid the box into the ceiling, carefully replaced the bat and returned to the others. Saff removed the disc from his jacket pocket, passed it to Craven.

They left McDonald's and accompanied Craven along the Champs Elysées. Craven led them to a large Lincoln limousine. They settled back, not taking their eyes off Craven. Rick leaned forward and attempted to make conversation. "So then you're some kind of time traveler. What do you eat in your, hmm . . . your world?"

"Food is food, ours is a little different to yours, it's a better quality. Parallel dimensions are exactly that, parallel. It's not drastically different, food is food. The technology is the greatest difference as you will see."

The limo traveled for what seemed around twenty minutes. They saw no scenery. The journey seemed as though it passed while each was in some kind of hypnotic state, as though they were in a zone during the journey.

"Where do you think we're going?" Amy whispered to Karen.

"Where are you taking us Craven?" Karen quickly asked.

"It'll all be explained shortly. Until then, just relax, okay?"

Relax? Easy for him to say, Rick thought. Amy looked at her watch. It was showing twenty-two minutes after eleven. *How can that be? We left McDonald's at around twenty after. It's been more than just a few minutes. We seemed to have traveled for so long.* A light appeared in the distance. The limo driver headed toward it. When they passed through the light, they emerged in a huge hangar, the type of hangar you'd find a Good Year blimp anchored in. *A Hindenberg sized garage*, Rick thought as he looked about. The green mist was there to greet them. *How very comforting*, Saffrey sarcastically thought as the Lincoln cruised to a stop. Craven opened the door and said, "Follow me; you'll need to be familiarized."

They headed toward a white building. It was built mostly of clear glass blocks. From outside they could see the shapes of people inside, people wearing white, busily going about their chores. Craven stopped at the door, placed his palm on a screen, and after a few quick beeps they were inside.

"This is it, make yourselves at home. Someone will be along shortly to brief you."

The air was heavy. Saffrey glanced around the sterile surroundings, a stark white work area. White outfits. White floors. A group of about thirty were going about their tasks. Computers were prevalent and filing cabinets were large and of course, white.

They whispered among themselves, motioning this way and that with their heads as they spoke. Craven returned, entering from a side door. He spoke with one of the workers.

"Hey Craven," Rick called. "How far did we travel in the limo?"

"I know you've a number of questions and they'll all be answered in time," Craven replied. "Come this way."

They followed and made their way along a long white corridor. It led them into a large round room. Craven gestured toward a table. Three white robed men and one woman, similarly dressed entered the room seconds behind them. They sat opposite the four. Karen bit down on her lower lip. She was far from feeling at ease. The lights dimmed and soft music began to play. Rick leaned to Saffrey and said, "Fuckin' elevator music, even got it here."

The girls nervously looked around the room. There were no speakers to be seen. In fact the only furniture in the room was the table and a large monitor fitted to a far wall. The woman in white said, "Please watch the screen."

One of the white robed men motioned toward the monitor. The face of Ramirez filled the screen. Amy turned to Saffrey, and pointed at the monitor. She said, "That's the diamond guy, the guy who came to me back at the restaurant, the one with the attaché case, the bike rider's partner."

"Yes," interrupted the robed man. "He was one of ours."

"Ours?" Saffrey queried. "What's *ours*?"

"We sent Ramirez back to retrieve the disc. Our diamonds were the payment to Ramirez for the safe return of the disc. Ramirez together with one other defector Velasquez, was able to secure the disc from the defector Eduard Heinzman who had stolen it.

Somewhere along the way Ramirez decided to stay in your time. He conspired with Velasquez to keep the stones as well as the disc. We believe they planned to contact a world-power as a possible buyer for the disc. We could not allow this to happen. We could not allow technology from our time to affect the balance of power, and inevitably change the course of world history."

Rick turned to Saffrey, whispering. "Clear as fuckin' crystal hey Saff?"

The white robed man continued. "We sent Craven to retrieve the disc and eliminate Ramirez and Velasquez."

Amy interrupted. "Why did Ramirez attempt to give me the attaché case at the restaurant?"

"Ramirez knew he was poled." The white robed man replied.

Rick asked, "Poled, what's that mean - poled?"

"We are able to trace our people through polarization. Once one is poled we are able to send a tracker such as Craven to terminate that person who is poled. It is similar to your medieval microchip technology."

Amy asked, "But why did Ramirez want me to take the attaché case?"

"We assume Ramirez believed the polarization had honed in onto the case and not onto him, that the disc or the content, were attracting the poling beam. If you had taken the case from Ramirez, Craven would have redirected his tracking to you instead of Ramirez. After Ramirez was terminated by Craven at the plaza, his accomplice Velasquez followed you to your hotel." He nodded toward Amy as he spoke. "He was disturbed during his search by Craven. He escaped Craven with the use of a motor cycle. His reprieve was temporary. Craven has since terminated Velasquez."

The four white robed people stood as one and motioned for the visitors to follow. They followed like school children nervously filing into a classroom, like day one at kindergarten. The elevator music followed along the way. The white gowned entourage led them down a winding passageway that to two opaque glass doors. They entered an enormous room big enough to host a Super Bowl final. As they walked along they passed by dozens of large canisters standing side by side along one wall. They appeared were constructed of a clear material. Each canister was filled with a green mist.

Craven said, "You see our time is millennia ahead of your primitive technology. Your military attempted invisibility and tele transportation, back in your year 1943. It was a disaster."

"Stop, let's go back a few bars here," Saffrey said in frustration, taking a long deep breath. "What the hell is going on here? Where are we? Who are you people?"

"Where are you? As difficult as you'll find this to believe, you're in a parallel universe. We've mastered tele transportation and subsequently, we travel between universes. Human consciousness in a quantum theory has long been resolved."

Craven looked at Saffrey and Rick. He grinned and said, "Give it time, you'll eventually get it. Our technology has mastered molecular transfer, more commonly known as time travel. We've also mastered invisibility. We can fragmentize atoms and teleport them to any place in time. We've created routing map for the doorways."

Saffrey shook his head, annoyed and confused. "This shit really intrigues me. Doesn't it intrigue you Rick? Do you feel enlightened? 'Jesus Christ . . . doorways? What the fuck are doorways?"

CHAPTER 12

CRAVEN SHOOK HIS HEAD as though disappointed in Rick's remark, but nothing fazed the white gowned men, no barrage of insults, no degree of obscenities; calmness was definitely an integral part of their demeanor.

The woman in white placed a hand toward Saffrey. She gave a warm smile saying, "Doorways are the openings through which we travel. Your world refers to them as wormholes. Visitors from many universes visit your world by the use of doorways. If they did not have this access, they would need many years to travel. The doorways allow what you refer to as aliens, to visit your time as easily as you're own traveling through a doorway and into the next room."

Wormholes? Sounds familiar, Saffrey thought.

Craven added, "This is why the disc had to be returned. It contains information we cannot allow to fall into the hands of any military power in your time. The destiny of your world depends on zero interference from outsiders. The universe, as you know it, is doomed. It will inevitably die. It doesn't need our interceding to accelerate this process. It will die in ice. Reach absolute zero. This'll make intelligent life extinct. Humanity as it exists in your universe will migrate to newer systems, parallel systems, to parallel universes."

Karen asked Craven, "When do you see this ice age happening?"

"In a few billion years, and make no mistake, it does happen."

Rick said, "You mean it *could* happen?"

"No," Craven said. "It happens."

"The Big Bang, as you call it was not the beginning of time as we know it. Time, space, it all existed before the universe we exist in. Big Bangs happen on a relatively frequent basis. In the same way a collision started it, it can occur again. In an extra-dimensional cosmos anything is possible. There may very well be another universe heading directly toward yours . . . it may only be a matter of time before they collide. Universes are not stationary, collisions happen."

The elder of the white gowned men said, "There are an infinite number of parallel universes. You live in one of them. These universes contain space, time, and strange forms of exotic matter. You my friends may already exist in some of them but in a mildly different form."

Saffrey exhaled, then in a frustrated tone asked, "How far away are these universes? I mean . . . in time, how far off?"

The man in white smiled, it was a wise knowledgeable grin. "Because of the doorways, these parallel universes can exist less than a millimeter away."

"Too fuckin' much for me," Rick mumbled.

It was the kind of stuff Saffrey remembered seeing on television, Twilight Zone, Star Trek, the whole nine yards.

The man said, "This is more than sufficient for you to absorb at this time. Allow me to show you to your domicile, where you can help yourself to an array of exotic foods and rest a while."

Yeah Saffrey thought, *just what we need right now, a banquet and rest. But let's be good guests. The time for any type of action is not now.* Saffrey grinned at what he'd just thought. *Yeah, we've literally all the time in the world.*

The 'domicile' as the man had called it, was sumptuous. Saffrey gazed about the room, he said to the others, "Wherever the fuck we are, they know how to eat. Look at those shrimp."

The shrimp were huge, bigger than any they'd seen at Harrah's. The lobsters were big enough to make the top restaurants at Pier 39 blush, and the fruit was so perfect it resembled wax reproductions. The taste of all the food was exceptional. Amy and Karen moved curiously about the quarters. They came across a Roman style bathing area. There were separate cubicles for each of them, sumptuous in every detail. The showers were refreshing, and they each felt much better for enjoying their absolute splendor: white marble, white bottled perfumery and cosmetics, and white towels. Their white gowned hosts were perfect - of course. As they moved from the shower area, they were surprised to find their clothing had been replaced with white robes. The same robes everyone else in the complex wore. *Why not? No individuality here*, Saffrey thought.

Rick sat pensively looking at Saffrey. "What's on your mind?"

"I'm trying to remember what I've read about wormholes. Have you any clue what all that mumbo jumbo was about?"

One of their hosts entered the room. Rick swung about on his seat, he greeted the man saying, "Glad you're here, I gotta tell ya, the food was spectacular. And the showers are great too. We all thank ya."

"You are most welcome. Are there any other ways I may be of service?"

Amy asked, "Yeah I've a question that needs answering. How'd we actually get here? Can you run that by me again?"

"The elder has kindly explained the arrival process to you… the doorway," he said, smiling with a condescending bowing of his head to Amy as he spoke.

Karen nodded as though she actually understood. She said, "You mean the wormhole?"

"Oh of course I do beg pardon of you. your time does refer to it as a wormhole. We call it a doorway."

"Sure, sure," Rick said. "So can you tell us a bit about what the doorway is?"

"A doorway is a black hole that has an opening or a mouth at its other end. To visualize this concept, imagine space being a long sheet of plastic with a hole in it. This hole is the one end of the doorway. It is known in your time as a black hole. Let's say that your journey, your very long journey, through space meant you're traveling along the sheet of plastic. Consider if there were a doorway nearby, you could travel through this doorway and arrive at your destination instantaneously. An instant short cut. The doorway connects two points in space as if they were right next to each other. Using the sheet of plastic analogy, it would be as if the plastic was folded back on itself. We have successfully discovered how to keep walls between the doorways, keeping the door from closing by introducing antigravity to it. Antigravity is the equivalent of a wall."

Rick pondered this monotone barrage of information. He had questions, far too many of them. His head was spinning with questions.

Rick asked, "So if a person was to go through a door and return, would he look the same as when he left?"

"If someone were to travel through a doorway, they could leave your time and return. Since they are traveling in a black hole, they experience a different acceleration rate than your earth. Their twin, or self, left on earth could therefore be older than they are upon returning." This was too much, Rick gave a *what the fuck* look to Saffrey. The questions stopped there.

CHAPTER 13

THEY ALL SLEPT WELL that night, secure in their surroundings, as strange as they were, as unexplainable as it all appeared. At daybreak they were woken by a strange piercing siren. They heard voices, many voices, as though the movie had just ended and the crowd was pouring into the foyer. Rick rose from the bed, slipped on the white robe, and made his way to the main hall area. A mist hung through the air and light emanated from each of the canisters spread about the hall. The doors on each were ajar. Rick approached with hesitation. As he drew closer he could see movement about the room.

The canisters were all empty except one. That one still had closed doors. Rick moved toward it. It appeared the door had begun to open but after a few inches it jammed. Rick slid his fingers behind the edge, forcing it, pulling, and slowly opening it. The thing set him back. *What the fuck is this? What are these people doin' here, some kind of sick experiment?*

Suddenly a hand rested on his shoulder. Rick felt his heart move to his throat.

"Steady man," Saffrey grinned. "It's just me."

"What the fuck Saff. Next time make some noise before you reach me, okay?"

"What's happening, what's goin' on here?"

Rick gestured toward the empty canisters: "Take a look. They're all empty, except this one."

They stared at the contents of the one canister. Neither spoke for what seemed minutes. They stared at the thing standing in the canister. It resembled Quasimodo. Facial features were horridly misaligned; one eye was positioned in the middle of the cheek. The nose was on a strange tilted angle and the chin was pushed inwards. No two teeth were parallel. They peered into its eyes as though expecting something to improve, for the face to somehow get a little better. The eye on the cheek was closed.

"Jesus Christ Saff, what d'ya make of this?" Rick asked.

"Not sure, but we . . ."

Before Saffrey could finish speaking, the hand of Quasimodo shot through the small gap and grabbed at his throat. The strength of the grip was vice-like. Rick sprung forward, brought both fists down heavily onto the white, damp arm.

The thing squealed, released its hold on Saffrey. The two men shouldered the canister, slamming the door closed. The thing in the canister groped at the transparent door. Its contorted nose and cheek pressed firmly against it. Slime forced from its nose ran down the glass. Eventually the green mist enshrouded the grotesque captive.

Totally traumatized, Rick and Saffrey turned to rejoin the girls in the safety of their quarters. Neither of them spoke as they moved along the passageway. Voices were getting closer. Rick and Saffrey sidestepped into a doorway, entered a small room, waited in semi-darkness until the voices faded into the distance.

The air in the room was damp, cold, and had a smell of something rank, something rotting. They tried to identify shapes, but needed to move further into the semi-darkness, to move closer . . . but closer to what?

Rick edged ahead of Saffrey who said, "Slowly Rick, feel your way man, I can't see a thing . . . too dark, fuckin' slippery." Then Rick grunted, "Jesus,"

Saffrey felt Rick's weight pull on his arm. The weight of Rick's grab caught Saffrey off balance. They began a long fast slide, down, down. They felt the air smacking against their skin, damp against their faces. The downward spiral continued for minutes. The speed of their descent began to slow. They huddled together at the end of the slide, dazed and disorientated. In the distance a strange glow seeped from a huge shiny metal dome. The sphere had windows placed about twenty feet part. Looked like a typical UFO. The dome was a fixture, not going anywhere. It laid the UFO theory to rest. They edged toward the silver shape. Saffrey reminded Rick that continual stepping on his heels would only impede their progress. Rick backed off a few paces.

Saffrey heard a chattering noise. He whispered, "Rick . . . is that you doin' that?"

"Ah shit. It ain't me. Please tell me it's you."

It hovered twenty feet above them. Then it moved down at lightning speed. Saffrey's body turned limp. The limpness he recalled feeling as a kid, an anesthetic taking effect for a tonsillectomy. His world entered a slow spin, then faster, faster and soon it turned black. His last thought, *is this death?*

CHAPTER 14

IT WAS AN UNUSUALLY cool Paris spring day. The birds were chirping and the stench of Gittanes and Gauloises hung like an early morning mist.

French cops were out in force. The small street buzzed with gendarmes. Police lines were set up, curious passersby strained their necks, their ears, for information on what had happened. The coroner's van meant bad news for someone. No ambulance was called for. The sign above the door said Java Heaven. Smokers were permanent residents in the small coffee shop. Exhaled cigarette smoke added a strong stench to the air. Cops hung around the computer repair store, for them it added a new twist to the start of their otherwise mundane French day. An older cop was accompanied by a younger understudy. They made their way past the uniforms and entered the computer store. Three of the uniforms stumbled to regain their balance as the understudy dashed to the curb. He started heaving up breakfast.

The people standing outside of the coffee shop groaned. Cups began banging down hard onto tables. Heads turned away from the spewing cop kneeling in the gutter. Two uniforms helped him to his feet. He didn't want to re-enter the stench filled store.

Two men cowered over a crumpled lump in a corner of the room. The body of what might have been a woman was propped against a wall. The skin resembled a pig on a spit. The hair was gone; what might have once been eyes bulged from their sockets. The young cop put his hand over his mouth, headed for the gutter again, but nothing came out.

"Inspector Chevalier is on his way. He wants nothing disturbed," one of the uniforms grumbled.

Not what Claude Chevalier needed right now. He still had his hands full with the unsolved death of Michelle du Blanc. This scene was identical.

Michelle du Blanc's death days earlier, was somehow

connected with the deaths of Henri and Marie du Maurier. Chevalier arrived in his Ferrari. It was a reward to him for many years of extracurricular activity. What had once began out as a hobby, as therapy, had become a lucrative sideline. Chevalier had become one of France's most sought after contemporary artists. His grandfather was a cop, his father was a cop, his brother was a cop, and so the tradition continued. The artist in Chevalier was quite happy to create two canvases each year. He had buyers ready to snap up originals for amazingly high prices. The subsequent licensing of rights brought in regular royalty checks. Chevalier pulled the Ferrari into the spot coned off by his subordinates.

"Inspector, it is terrible in there. Have you been told of the details?"

"Yes. I have brought along the file on Michelle du Blanc. The similarity is beyond question."

Chevalier entered the computer store; stripped of his leather driving gloves, handed them to the cop accompanying him.

The driver of this Ferrari would always be expected to be appropriately attired, and as the air was somewhat brisk for this time of year, Chevalier took advantage of any opportunity to dress appropriately, on this day he had started for his office at first light and still wore cool weather clothing. He removed his hat, his cashmere knee-length double breasted driving coat. Passed them to a uniform. The uniform followed his every move.

"The bodies are burned to a crisp inspector," the older cop said, hand over mouth. "The rest of the place is untouched. What do you make of it?"

The inspector went down on one knee, removed the sheet from the woman propped in the corner.

"Was this the man?"

"No that's the man over there by the computer. The cat is here, by the woman."

"The cat, there is a cat?"

The man that answered wore a suit "Yes, is that imp p p portant?" stuttered Antoine Penoir, his longest serving assistant.

"There was a c c cat at the apartment of Michelle du B B Blanc," Penoir stuttered, his affliction prominent in times of stress.

"Fingerprint the place from front to back Penoir. Contact me when the prints are ready. Work on it all night if you must. Run computer matches for the past month."

Chevalier left the store, slid into his Ferrari, and sat for a while, thinking over the two cases.

Was there a common denominator?

Was the cat a clue or merely a coincidence?

He suspected a connection might exist.

He slipped a CD into the player. Sinatra began singing Strangers in the Night.

"Strangers in the night, if it were just that easy," he mumbled to himself.

It was eleven o'clock when the phone rang.

Chevalier lowered the volume, another Sinatra melody crooning away in the background. He hummed a few bars of 'The Summer Wind.' Slid across the sofa and stretched for the phone.

"Hello, Chevalier speaking."

"Inspector this is Penoir, I have some very interesting news on the prints. I think you should see this."

The drive time from the apartment to the police station was twenty minutes.

Chevalier could do it in seven.

He set a new record - six minutes - his siren screaming for the entire drive, Sinatra delivering another three favorites; they conveniently lasted the duration of the six minute dash. It wasn't until he turned the motor off that he realized just how hard Frank had been straining to be heard above the shrill wail of the siren.

He took three steps at a time as he sprinted up the stairs leading into the station.

"Penoir, what do you have for me?"

Antoine Penoir stood by the percolator.

"Coffee inspector?"

"For God's sake Antoine, it is almost midnight. I set a new land speed record getting here. My Ferrari is panting at the curb.

Its Italian tongue is lying on the roadway. You say you have some interesting news?"

"The prints that we gathered from the du Maurier's computer store. They match."

"They match what, the du Blanc apartment?"

Penoir grinned, and then thought better than to play games with Chevalier at this late hour.

"Inspector they match the prints found in a van dumped thirty kilometers into the country the day before the Michelle du Blanc death. The van was found at the bottom of a lake by a weekend fisherman. When it was inspected closer, a body was discovered in a travel trunk inside the van."

"Did forensics go through the van or find anything on the body?"

"It's an unidentified male, stab wound and bullet wounds."

"The prints were in the van?"

"On the travel trunk. Four sets of prints, and two prints matched those we found in the apartment of Miss du Blanc."

"The van, any trace on the owner?"

"No good, the van turned out to stolen from a convent in Nice a few days earlier. No connection."

"I want the bodies taken to the morgue, same section as the other burn case. Take the cat, too."

Philippe stepped into the door of the small pawn shop. A bell suspended above the door jingled as he entered. He instinctively gazed up, slowly closed the door and proceeded to a second door, made of wire meshing, forming a cage around the main counter area.

"Hello Philippe, what brings you here my friend?"

Philippe reached into his pocket and placed the diamond onto the counter.

"Well, well . . . very pretty."

The paunchy man behind the counter placed a jeweler's loupe to his eye and lowered his head to the stone.

"This is so beautiful. Where did you come by such a diamond? It looks . . . almost flawless." He studied the stone closer. "However I do see a very small strange inclusion."

His saliva accumulated until it dribbled from the side of his mouth, one arm slowly wiping it away with his shirt cuff.

"How much can you give for the stone?"

"Not so quick my friend. This stone requires more expertise for a true value to be established. Can you leave it with me overnight? I will have an answer for you tomorrow."

As Philippe left the store he wondered if he should have mentioned the existence of the third stone that Gustave still possessed. It was nearing sunset. Gustave sat at the lake, fishing rod in hand. He had several small fish, mostly undersize. They would make one good meal, all on the one plate. His old truck, which had seen better days, was parked beneath a tree twenty meters from where he sat. The breeze began to pick up. Gustave reeled in his line, threw the leftover bait into the water, and wearily got to his feet, making his way to the truck. He sat for a while, rolled a cigarette, lit it, took a deep pensive breath, and exhaled slowly, blowing a perfect smoke ring into the cabin of the truck.

The smoke ring floated toward the windshield and then slowly blended into the glass. He stared across the lake, flicked his ash from the car. He reached into the glove compartment and took out a small pouch. Undoing the drawstring he let the diamond slide onto the seat beside him. He sat admiring its beauty as though he were looking down into the eyes of a beautiful woman. He pondered his future, where he might be if he were to cash in his stone. He knew Philippe had taken his own stone to the pawn shop that same afternoon. He would call Philippe and ask for the good news. This he would do, as soon as he arrived home. So he sat, sat and dreamed of a large fishing boat, a villa in Marseilles, maybe both.

The drive from the lake to his home was not a long one. Gustave drove along at a comfortable sixty kilometers per hour. The suspension in the old truck was not as good as it once was. The road had more than its share of bumps, and the recent storms had made the potholes deeper than usual. The front wheel groaned as it jerked savagely to the right. Gustave who was driving in a semi-sleep state, he veered the truck back to the left, the stone on the seat by his side flew off the seat onto the floor.

A bright orange light engulfed the cabin of the truck as it veered out of control into a hedge along the roadside. It plowed through the hedge, traveling some fifty meters before coming to a stop, its doors jolted open by the rough ride and sudden stop.

The roosters crowed as the sun began to rise on the horizon. It was a typical spring morning. The truck was out of view, behind thick hedges, where the farmer could not see it from the fields. He began to work the tractor. It was noisy, the clatter of its diesel motor breaking the silence. His two retrievers frolicked in the pasture, running well ahead of their master. The dogs were trained to fetch when the pheasant season was in full swing. The farmer would rent them out to hunters. The two dogs supported themselves admirably. Two hours passed, the farmer had lost sight of the dogs for some time. He headed back to the house, switched off the diesel, and called the dogs.

He heard them in the distance, beyond the hedges. Hearing their master, both retrievers headed home. They bound into the small house and each placed a large bone onto the mat that lay by the table. The farmer and his wife ignored the dog's find for a few minutes as they went about preparing breakfast. As the farmer moved to the table, he kicked the bone from his path. His wife let out a hideous scream as the skull and vertebrae of what once was a human rolled across the kitchen floor. The other retriever picked up its bone, not wanting to see it kicked away. It was a forearm and hand, or the remnants of them.

It was another busy day for Inspector Chevalier. The drive to the farmhouse was pleasant enough, but the gruesome sight that awaited him was one he was becoming regrettably accustomed to seeing. He arrived at the farmhouse. The wife was hysterical and the farmer was comforting her as best he could. She was on her third glass of cognac and wailing like a banshee. Chevalier arrived ten minutes after Penoir. Penoir was also attempting to pacify the farmer's wife.

"P p please madam," he stammered. "Have a little more c c c cognac. It will help you s s settle down."

She was making headway into the fourth glass when Claude Chevalier sat alongside her. The human remains were covered with two sheets. Chevalier glanced beneath the sheets, looked at Penoir and gave him a confirming nod.

"Good man. Stay here with the woman Antoine. I will have the husband take me to the site."

The truck had not suffered a great deal of damage. It had come to rest against hedges. The door was ajar and what resembled the remnants of a human body had been dragged from the truck and scattered around the ground a few feet from the open door. The dogs had apparently discovered the human barbeque and considered it quite a delicacy. Chevalier poked around the truck, did the usual crime scene inspection and was soon joined by the forensic squad and a van from the coroner's department.

"Carefully remove the remains; there are more in the kitchen of the farmhouse."

Penoir had finally managed to settle the sobbing woman. "There, there madam, the cognac has helped, no?"

The woman slowly looked up at him, her eyes red and swollen. She managed a very strained smile as she nodded her head at Penoir, who by this time was feeling very proud of himself for settling the poor woman down. Then with a chuckle in his voice he proclaimed, "Good madam, let us hope that your d d d dogs have not acquired a taste for barbeque."

The woman again broke into hysteria. Antoine Penoir slowly backed out of the room, his head hung in dejected disappointment. As expected the truck showed no signs of damage, no burned interior except for the seat. The cop completed their combing of the scene. There was nothing remaining to be done.

"Have the truck towed back to the impound yard. Let me know when the prints are available."

Penoir called the tow truck and the usual clean up began. Chevalier was almost back at headquarters when his cell phone rang.

"Inspector this is Dupre from the Central Directorate of the Judicial Police."

The Central Directorate of the Judicial Police included

the territorial and central administration of the National Police for the prevention and the repression of the organized criminal and specialized delinquency. They had a territorial competence either regional or national in scope, and implemented approaches and techniques of investigation adapted to countering complex and serious criminal phenomena.

"We're investigating a strange incident that occurred thirty minutes ago in a large jewelry store downtown."

"Dupre, I've my hands full with my own headaches. What could you possibly want with me?"

"I was told you're investigating a series of burned bodies that have turned up over the past few days. The jewelry store has eight people, all deceased and well fried. Does this sound familiar?"

"No signs of damage to the store, right Dupre?"

"None inspector, however we've found a high radiation count throughout the shop. Can you meet me here now?"

He passed on the address for the store. Chevalier recognized the location.

"Twenty minutes Dupre, twenty minutes."

He gunned the Ferrari and arrived at the Jewelry shop in fourteen minutes. The site was taped off, and pedestrians were directed to walk on the opposite side of the street.

"I don't know what's going on, but it smells very good," said a curious spectator. The aroma of cooked pork wafted from the shop door, not the usual scent that permeates the air in this very trendy street of highly fashionable upper class boutiques and perfumeries.

Dupre briefed Chevalier. "We are still tracing the identities of the victims. So far we have turned up the ID of two as being from the American embassy. We have called their office and there is an official on his way here now."

"Good work Dupre. And the others, what of their identities, any leads?"

"Well inspector, I suspect two are from another embassy, a man and a woman. We're waiting for a call from my man who took prints this morning. We found several clean sets on the glass showcase, enough to run computer scans."

"So why do we have embassy personnel meeting in a jewelry store at . . . what time do you believe this occurred Dupre?"

"Probably between nine thirty and ten thirty this morning, we've witnesses who saw them arrive in embassy cars, two people in each of two cars. The other four bodies in the store were probably the staff, the jewelers."

Philippe was sleeping late; he figured a phone call with the valuation on his stone would be his waking call. But it was a knock on his door, followed by three harder knocks that woke him.

"All right, all right, I'm coming."

He reached the door and peered through the spy hole. Ramone stood on the other side, a drawn look on his already French drawn face.

"What are you doing here this early, what's wrong?"

"Philippe, I had a call from David at Gustave's factory. Gustave didn't turn up for work today."

"So he took the day off. Maybe he's going to sell his stone and live off the fat of the land for a few years."

"I think something's happened to him. He went fishing and didn't return to his cottage. The police were there today asking questions. Do you think this has something to do with the van and the body?"

"Not possible. I'll call Yves and ask if he's any knowledge of Gustave's whereabouts."

The phone in Yves's apartment rang several times. He tried the call again. No answer.

"Yves isn't at home. I'll stop by and see him later today. Meanwhile see what you can find out about Gustave."

Later that day the phone on Chevalier's desk rang. He picked up the phone and answered gruffly, "Chevalier."

"Inspector I've news on the prints from the jewelry store. We've two Russian agents and two American diplomats. As suspected the jewelers were the remaining four victims. We had a call from a pawn dealer. He said he'd dropped a diamond by the jeweler's for a valuation. Said it appeared extremely valuable and left it with the jeweler for an appraisal. We had an independent jeweler inspect the inventory at the scene. There was no stone found."

Chevalier could see a light at the end of the tunnel. "We must speak with this pawn dealer as soon as possible."

It took forty-five minutes to reach the pawn shop. The dealer sat in his cage and opened the security doors for the two cops.

"How can I help you gentlemen?"

Dupre stepped forward. "We're here to talk about the stone you left with the jewelers. What can you tell us about the stone? Where'd you get it?"

"It was brought to me by a regular customer. He wanted me to buy the stone but it was far too difficult for me to estimate its worth, so I took it to a specialist for an appraisal."

"So you took it to the jeweler for the appraisal."

"Yes."

"Who's this person that brought the stone to you?"

"I only know him as Philippe."

"Where'd he meet with you?"

"Right here where you're standing."

"Did you clean over this glass counter this morning?"

"No why?"

"Did he place the stone on the counter?"

"Yes."

"About here?" Dupre pointed to an area where a hand would touch the glass while a person stood at the counter.

"Yes he stood right there."

Dupre got right on the phone. The fingerprint team was there in thirty minutes.

"Inspector we've many good prints, and we'll go through the matches. We'll call you as soon as we have a result."

CHAPTER 15

THE AMERICAN CONSULATE GENERAL in Marseilles is located at the Place Varian Fry, in the city's central sixth arrondissement. Chevalier flew on a small commuter plane to Marseilles, five hundred and thirty-six miles south of Paris. It was found that the U.S. Diplomats were from the Marseilles office. He parked his rental outside the Préfecture de Région building, the American flag flying proudly across the street from the prefecture's main entrance. Chevalier met with the senior official.

"Good afternoon inspector. I believe you are here regarding the two men who met with some kind of regrettable accident in Paris."

"Yes, can you tell me why they were in Paris?"

"Pleasure I believe. They were there on their own time. Not official business."

Chevalier didn't believe him. He had his old gut feeling, the lack of direct eye contact. Something wasn't right.

"Your two men were in the company of two Russian agents. Were you aware of this?"

"No. This is news to me inspector. Look I really must excuse myself. I've a staff meeting in ten minutes, thank you inspector, and good-day to you sir." He walked toward the door, opened it, and nodded to Chevalier.

Chevalier slowly left the room as the door closed none-too-friendly behind him. The return flight to Paris gave him the necessary time to think, to let the pieces fall into place. He slipped off his shoes, stretched out and tried to relax.

Chevalier picked through a few magazines, feeling that somehow the involvement of the diplomats as well as the condition of the crime scenes were not only connected, but somehow radioactive neutron technology was involved. A more in-depth report awaited Chevalier on his return to Paris; the report indicated that all burn victims showed unbelievably high, off the chart levels of radiation. The truck found near the farm had readings higher than any ever recorded. The two dogs that carried parts of the body into the cottage were both showing severe signs of radiation poisoning. One was not expected to recover. The veterinarian believed the animal had consumed highly contaminated matter. Dupre met Chevalier at the station.

"Have you been told of the radiation find?"

"Yes all sites are being decontaminated before any further forensic work is allowed."

"I want to return to the du Mauriers' store. Arrange whatever protection is required for safe entry."

Penoir was at the computer store ahead of Chevalier. He had a knack for being prompt. He was not recognizable in his white protective suit and full head cover.

"Inspector it is me Penoir. Your suit, it is in the van."

Chevalier stepped into a white unmarked van. Three suits hung on hooks along one side, and a system of cupboards along the opposite wall contained a periphery of first aid and rescue equipment.

"Inspector what do you hope to find? We've been through the shop very thoroughly."

Chevalier didn't answer. He proceeded to enter the store; the smell of burned meat was still prevalent. The chalk outlines of the bodies were clearly visible.

"Tell me Penoir, which way do you think the two victims were facing at the time they were first exposed to the heat?"

"Possibly sitting at the table inspector."

"I remembered a security camera mounted in that corner."

Chevalier pointed to a far corner of the store. The camera was still there. "Yes Penoir, the camera is still there."

The two men slid the table across the room.

Penoir stood a chair onto the table and stepped onto it.

"Can you get it down Penoir?"

"No good. It is just the camera, no tape."

Chevalier said, "It must be a relay to a mother unit."

They followed a thin cable. It passed through the wall

into an adjoining storage room.

"Ah yes, here it is."

The unit contained a large tape which appeared to be on a loop system.

`"Perhaps this has something of interest on it, so we'll take it back to the station and run it there. Let's get out of this place it gives me a most uncomfortable feeling."

Once back at the station they placed the tape into a processor and began watching the film. The first thing to appear on the screen showed a short man carrying a monitor into the store. Henri du Maurier inspected the monitor and wrote a receipt for its owner. The man left. A few more customers came and went. Chevalier was beginning to lose hope. Marie du Maurier entered and sat at the table. She reached into her pocket and placed what seemed like a gemstone onto the table. Henri began to drink from a wine glass and with his glasses low on his nose, peruse the daily newspaper. Marie placed her index finger on the stone and moved it about, watching the sparkle change under the light that hung above the table. Chevalier could see the lights refracting off the stone.

"This stone is very impressive," Chevalier said. "Where do you think people of the du Mauriers' income level could come by a stone like this?"

Penoir was about to answer when a brilliant flash caused both men to instinctively raise their arms to their faces. The screen turned to white. When it cleared, a green mist filled the computer shop. As the mist subsided the blackened figures of the du Mauriers were on the floor, their cat lying nearby.

"The jewelry store Penoir. It also has a security camera."

They arrived at the jewelry store, donned more protective suits and proceeded to locate the master tape in the rear of the store. Back at the station both men sat and watched as the gathering of eight stood around a velvet pillow beneath a large, glittering diamond. The four suited men were arguing. A great deal of hand gestures came from the two larger men. Suddenly one of the larger men reached into his jacket, stepped back and aimed a weapon at the other two suited men. His accomplice moved back with him, also drawing his weapon. The jeweler waved his arms furiously; frustrated at the breakdown in negotiations or in the discussion. The diamond remained on the velvet pillow.

"What's going on inspector, what do you make of this?"

"I think the larger two are the Russians and ..."

Before he could finish speaking there was a white flash followed by the familiar green mist. When the monitor cleared, the burned remains of all eight lay on the shop floor. Each one in a neat singed pile.

The two men stared in silence. Penoir turned from the screen, and unable to reach a basin, threw up a few feet from Chevalier. Chevalier ignored him, he said, "Antoine I suspect that in some way the culprit is the stones. The stones could be the common denominator. What if each of the victims had a stone in their possession? The stones could actually be the killers. What we need to determine is where they came from, how they're activated or whatever, and how many more are out there."

CHAPTER 16

SEVERAL HOURS HAD PASSED since Amy and Karen had last seen the two men and they were beginning to worry. There was a soft knocking on the door. The white robed man smiled as he entered. Both girls forcibly returned the smile.

"Your friends have strayed from your quarters and it may be a while before they return."

"Where are they?" Karen said showing concern.

"They are quite safe. You need not be concerned."

He motioned to the girls to follow him out of the room. "Please, the Consort wishes to meet with you."

The Consort was a tall, thin man. Deep set blue eyes and white hair protruding from beneath a white hood. The girls sat in another large room, the chairs were plush, very deep. They each sank into their seats and waited a few minutes. A door opened and three other people in similar white robes entered and took up positions around the room.

"You are the one who received the stones?"

The Consort peered at Amy. He waited on her answer. *They seem to know the truth*, she thought, *no point lying.*

"Yes the stones were kind of given to me in Paris. Do you know the man who gave them to me?"

"Yes," replied the Consort.

"He was one of our operatives, Raoul Ramirez."

"Why did he give me the case? Why was he killed?

"Ramirez was a renegade operative. He knew he was being poled by Craven. That is why he panicked and attempted to pass the case on. Ramirez was sent to retrieve the case from the operative who stole them, his name is Eduard Heinzman."

"Mr. Heinzman, really!" Amy replied with a look of disgust. "Why did Craven want the case and not the stones?"

"We believed the stones to be harmless as long as they remained in their sealed containers. They are Generation Four prototypes. They are defective when exposed to the atmosphere, far more defective than first thought. They contain highly volatile neutron chips. We had hoped to eventually recover the stones. It seems you have changed those plans."

Amy and Karen looked at each other; they passed an inquisitive gaze from one to the other.

"The stones looked beautiful," Amy said." So why do you say they're defective?"

The Consort dropped his eyes from theirs; he slowly turned toward the other occupants in the room, let out a deep sigh, and regained his composure. Just as he looked as though he was about to explain the defective stone question, one of the other four abruptly stood.

"No Consort!" he snapped. "You should not disclose the stones issue to these travelers."

The Consort raised one hand, pointed his index finger at the interjecting man. The man squealed in agony, quickly raised both hands to his throat and dropped to his knees as a blood bubble inflated on his lips.

"Do any others among you here wish to intercede?"

The other three remained seated. The Consort walked around the table. Paused. Stood directly over the fallen man. He reached out with both arms outstretched. A strong light emanated from each hand as they hovered above the stricken man. The other three sat, not looking at the scene before them. All three sat smiling at Karen and Amy. The two girls stared in awe as the white cloaked unconscious body began to glow. Then, in an instant, it vanished.

"Oh my God, oh my God. Where'd he go?"

"Jesus, Amy, did you see that?" said Karen.

"You killed him, why?"

"I am the Consort. My decisions are not open to discussion. I will not be interrupted by inferiors. He has been teleported to the Dead Zone. He is of no further use in the living world."

He looked at the remaining men, then at the two girls, "The stones were defective. They were manufactured in our Quantum Zone. When we realized the neutron chips were not programmable, they were set aside for destruct phase. Before they could be terminated, an associate of Ramirez, Eduard Heinzman, gained access to the Quantum Zone. This runner terminated two security units. He stole the stones as well as a programming disc from the master files and found his way to the doorway."

"The doorway?" Amy asked.

Karen looked sideways at Amy. "The wormholes, remember?"

"Hmm," Amy said quietly lowering her eyes.

The Consort continued on. "The runner went through the doorway and into your time with the stones and the disc. We sent Ramirez to retrieve the case and terminate the runner. He was joined by another dissident, Eduard Heinzman."

The picture began to become clearer. Craven it seemed, was sent to bring back the disc and terminate Ramirez and Heinzman, he'd succeeded with Ramirez in the Plaza, and Amy had taken care of Heinzman in her Hotel room, however as the disc had shut down at the computer store, Craven had not been able to totally complete his assignment.

"The stones must now be destroyed or returned. Do you know of their whereabouts?"

"What happens if they stay where they are, in our universe?" asked Amy.

The Consort touched a button beneath the table. A large monitor lowered from the ceiling. He motioned the girls toward the monitor.

"Watch the monitor," He instructed.

On the screen was a group of disheveled ruffians, they resembled homeless vagabonds. They were in an enclosure. No windows or doors were evident, and a strange blue glow gave the room an eerie science fiction mood. The men were arguing among themselves, and a fist fight broke out. The blue light became more intense and the group in the room stopped their squabbling and covered their ears, appearing to be in unbearable agony. The light returned to its original hue. The group settled back to a peaceful calm. Just then a table began to rise into the center of the blue lit room. It slowly rose as the men gathered around it. The box on the table contained what appeared to be loose diamonds. One of the men reached for the box. He slowly removed the sealed lid. The men all grabbed at the stones. There were enough of them to go around. Amy and Karen watched the scruffy group curiously.

"They *are* diamonds right?" Amy asked the Consort.

"They are Generation Eight," he replied. "They possess they same flaw as Generation Four, the stones that you now have back in your time."

The Consort directed the girls to watch the screen. He reached into his gown and took a small control from the pocket. "Observe," he said. He pushed a button on the control. There was a sudden flash in the blue room. The screen went to white followed by a green mist. Burned bodies were all that remained of the group. The two girls put their hands to their mouths, Karen turned away vomiting her breakfast onto the spotless white marble floor. Her reaction was contagious. Amy turned and retched forward, barely missing Karen. When the two girls had finished throwing up, the Consort rose from the table. "So now you see why the stones must be returned. More importantly they must remain in their sealed containers. They have a specific application, they are paramount for setting the coordinates for the doorways, the entry and exit points from our time to yours. Once the stones are placed they become the doorways, we are able to enter and egress through these coordinates, we have these locations specifically mapped on the tracking screens in our vehicles, somewhat similar to your satellite guidance screens, yet far, far more advanced."

He went on to explain, "The stones in your possession have a faulty timing crystal. They are meant to remain inert until a control triggers the heat release. This is when they destroy all life forms within a ten meter radius. If a stone is released from the sealed container, it will self-destruct anytime within a few weeks of its exposure to the air. I can only hope that your stones all remain within their sealed boxes. The boxes must not be opened."

The two girls were led back to their quarters by the three gowned men. The Consort called out to them as they departed, "You will tell me the whereabouts of the diamonds, or your two friends will be terminated. They are in my keeping. Make no mistake they will become victims of the stones, unless you cooperate."

Karen turned to Amy and whispered, "My God do you realize we've given the stones to the cleanup crew as well as the du Mauriers, we left the rest at McDonalds. If what the Consort said is accurate, the stones handed out have detonated by now. There are dead people back home."

The two men lay with their eyes open. They couldn't move.

"Rick, you okay?"

"Christ Saff, what the fuck was that?"

"Some kind of drone, a security unit I think."

"You mean we were zapped by some kind of robot?"

"Could be, can you move?"

"I can move my eyes and I can speak, but that's about it. How about you?"

"Jesus, me too."

They were both laying on their backs, paralyzed, each staring at the ceiling. A strange clicking sound could be heard coming from a room not too far away.

"Thank God that fucker's gone. My legs are feelin' more awake now, how about yours?"

They began to move their fingers, their arms, their legs. Minutes passed. Mobility slowly began to return.

Saffrey struggled to sit, propping himself against the cold wall. Rick followed. "Okay let's get out of here before that fucker returns."

Rick moved toward Saffrey, each helping the other to stand erect. "This is more than I can figure out Saff, what do you make of it?"

A high-pitched mechanical whirring could be heard coming from their right. A light at the far end of a long passageway caught their attention. The two men began to make their way slowly toward the source of the luminescence. As they drew closer, they could here the chatter of workers. Then a flash of brilliant light caused them both to squint. A few seconds of temporary blindness passed. Their eyes readjusted, vision again returning. The large silver dome lay right ahead of them. The windows were twelve feet above the floor. They looked about. There was no way they could see into the dome. There was a lowering of the lights, and the glow diminished.

A door opened as a white uniformed worker exited the dome. Rick and Saffrey stood back in the shadows. The worker removed his coveralls and hung them alongside others by the door. As he passed, Rick and Saffrey saw that he was carrying a clear plastic box. They couldn't see the contents of the box. Whatever it was, it had the worker's absolute attention. He walked like a man on a mission. Passed by them as they stood hidden from sight. Saffrey motioned to Rick to follow. They made their way to the door, removed two sets of coveralls and two head covers, and put them on. The clear plastic face plate showed their eyes, but not enough face to reveal their identity. Rick opened the door. They entered without attracting attention.

It looked very much like any laboratory, sterile and spacious, a dozen or so technicians working at benches. A large vault-like container at the far end stood humming, as though it were a generator of some sort. The workers were too immersed in their tasks to notice the two men's presence. They slowly edged their way into the work area. The workers were busily weighing and calibrating small stones. The stones were placed on trays. Saffrey took his best guess. It resembled the lab work they had observed on the disc back at Henri's computer shop.

"Hey Saff, these are the diamonds right?" Rick was a few steps ahead of Saffrey. He leaned toward the workers. One turned and passed a tray, and Rick instinctively reached for it. Obviously confused, Rick turned to Saffrey with a look of despair. Saffrey took the tray and proceeded to walk in the direction of the other trays but his grip slipped and the tray immediately fell to the hard floor, rattling and clattering as it spilled its contents. The white garbed men were obviously not aggressive. They stood staring at Rick and Saffrey. They then slowly moved toward the spilled stones. One quickly began picking up the stones. He then pressed a button on the work table. A deafening siren blared. The sound bounced off the walls. The lighting in the room became a hot red.

The doors slammed shut.

Accepting their resolve Saffrey and Rick waited for their next move. It didn't come. The workers stood in a trance like state, staring at the huge steel doors. The doors slowly opened. The Consort entered followed by an armed squad of uniformed guards. They moved around the room, pointing their weapons menacingly toward Rick and Saffrey. The Consort stepped toward the workers. He reprimanded the white garbed men. Dismissed, they repeatedly bowed, nervously exiting the room. It was clear that the Consort held some strange power over all of his subordinates.

"You are most inquisitive!" he snapped at the two intruders. "So you wish to see the power of the stones? Then so be it. But once you are privy to this knowledge your stay here will permanent."

"And if we choose not to have you disclose 'the power of the stones,' are we free to leave?" Saffrey asked.

"You are beyond the point of returning. Your doorway is closed. Your existence here and that of your female companions is now at my leisure."

He led the two men to the large 'incubator' in which stones were being grown. "These are slivers of diamonds; the hydraulics and electricity will supply the necessary amount of heat and pressure to recreate the same conditions that exist one hundred miles below the surface of the earth.

"We inject carbon onto the sliver, and carefully place a minuscule neutron module onto the center of the stone. The diamond is then formed around the neutron device. To the most discerning inspection, the module appears to be nothing more than an inclusion. To better disguise the module, stones cannot be smaller than three karats."

"But what are the stones used for?" This, Saffrey decided, was the question that really needed asking, regardless of their fate, as they were doomed in any case according to the Consort.

"These specific stones were created as gifts for world dignitaries." He replied. "We have operatives in influential locations such as embassies, government institutions, jewelry houses, and museums. The stones will be designed into jewelry as gifts for your world leaders and highly influential dignitaries. We have other stones which are only used for coordinates, similar to gateways in and out of this time zone. We are striving to develop absolute tele-transportation without the necessity of stone placement, without having to physically set the stones at the entry and exit points."

He slowly walked behind the two men as if gathering his thoughts prior to proceeding. "This is known as 'Operation Genesis.' It is a precursor to the total balance of power, insurance you might say. Yes, definitely insurance. And as an added bonus, a limited number of the Generation Eleven stones have been created with a special inclusion . . . listening devices, when we need to listen, and explosive when we need to detonate. We are able to eavesdrop on world leaders with these stones and have our operatives intervene, or terminate, whenever a situation warrants their intervention."

Saffrey thought he was following the Consort's effort to rationalize the insanity. Nevertheless he asked, "Insurance? Insurance for what?"

"We have intervened many times in the direction of events in your time. In drastic circumstances our intervention can be initiated by the mere transmission of a destruct code to any one stone. The stone will destroy all life within a few meters, without damaging any of the surroundings.

"We attempted to assist your Navy in its misguided invisibility attempt in your year of 1943. The magnetic field was badly configured. Molecular transfer was disastrous. Invisibility resulted. Men were regenerated impaled into the metal sheeting of their ship the Eldridge. This is typical of why you cannot take evidence of our technology back to your primitive time."

He gave deep thought to his next words before continuing. "We intervened in the Cuban Missile Crisis of your sixties era. We have terminated presidents whom we knew would lead the world into a major nuclear war. We could not allow the Kennedy regime to remain in power. We could not allow Richard Nixon to remain in power. His removal changed your history. We made certain that documents would fall into the right hands, perpetuating what you now know as Watergate. Your future president will clash heavily with Iran. That president will also be terminated."

"Jesus Christ. You can move into the future too?" Rick asked.

"Time travel is not unilateral. Yet still we have our own complications with tele-transportation. Molecular transfer has not always gone as it should. Deformity is sometimes a side effect of the return. The doorways have a price and that price has often been too high. We are not always pleased with the condition in which our travelers re-enter our universe, or yours. Bodily disfiguration can be commonplace. The pods cannot always regenerate natural features. Their entry containers need to be correctly coordinated; if they are disturbed during the re-entry process, the unit attempting reentry can suffer what is known as transcription errors, leaving the re-entry subject scrambled, partly fused within the body it was traveling."

"The pods?" Saffrey asked inquisitively.

"They are the dwellings for the units. Experimental at this point, a type of infirmary. The haze refines their properties. They are subsequently repaired; it is a way to minimize transcription errors."

Saffrey realized he was referring to the green mist in the canisters. The obvious deformity to the Quasimodo unit must have been directly attributed to reentry error. "What's the fate of those who aren't repaired by these pods?"

"If they survive they are sent to the Interior."

"The Interior, what's the Interior?" Rick asked.

"The Interior is a forbidden zone to all but those who have failed the pod reconstruction, those with irreparable transcription errors as well as the watchers."

"The watchers?" Saffrey asked making a face.

"They are the keepers of the Interior."

"Are these uh, damaged travelers eventually repaired in this Interior?" Rick asked.

His reply lacked emotion, it was clear and cold. "They are terminated in the Interior."

A darker side of this strange world was beginning to emerge. It left little doubt in each of their minds that they were slated for termination. The Consort gestured to the guards. They moved in, tightening their circle. He held a hand toward the guards, gesturing. He said, "Please accompany them to their quarters."

He stepped aside as the guards escorted the two men from the room. They were directed into an elevator, large and reflective, as though lined with chromium. It seemed to ascend for several minutes. When it stopped, the doors opened to bright light. They were back in the large glass building.

"My God," Karen said in relief. "Where've you been?" The girls half walked, half ran to greet them. "We've been worried sick, what happened Saff?"

All four sat as the two men filled the girls in on their talk with the Consort. Saffrey spoke slowly, deliberately, "The stones that were given out would have detonated by now. Thank Christ we didn't open all the containers. The remaining boxes are okay, so long as no one opens them to get to the stones. If they do, they better be darned sure they close the box up really tight. Like, seal it. God knows how many have died so far."

The door opened. A tall man wearing the usual white gown entered. His eyes were a cold pale blue, almost white. The tall man motioned for the group to follow him. He led them through a maze of passageways until they eventually came to an exit door. The door led them to a docking station where several guards were escorting a group of people onto a large transporter. They stepped aboard and took their seats.

The gray headed man sitting opposite them held his hand out as he stared at the four visitors, but did it as though he wasn't really seeing them. He raised his eyes to meet Rick's, tilting his head in a gesture of defeat, as though his grim resolve was preordained.

The transporter continued along a long winding road. The guards followed in a smaller vehicle. Three armed men sat in the front of the transporter. They traveled for what seemed an hour. The hills were green and wildflowers dotted the roadside.

Definitely springtime, Saffrey thought. The occasional farmhouse gave variety to the landscape; cows and horses added to the setting. A distant building appeared out of place with its rural neighbors. The transporter came to a split in the road, veering off toward the building. As they drew nearer they could see it was well guarded, at least two armed men at each entrance. Alongside each guard hovered a large white sphere. Each seemed suspended some six feet above the ground. The vehicle drew nearer. The spheres began to gravitate toward them. Each was the size of a large beach ball, a meter in radius. The old man sitting opposite them began to tremble. It was clear the presence of the sphere was causing him great discomfort. The gray haired man leaned forward, trembling. Amy placed her hand on his shoulder to steady him, asking, "What is it?"

"They are watchers. They are our keepers."

So these were the watchers, these strange floating spheres that looked in no way like any type of threat to them. Rick felt relieved. When the inevitable escape opportunity presented itself, these spheres or watchers would appear to be far easier to shake off than the armed guards. As Rick was soon to discover this was not one of his wiser first impressions.

"Saff, look at the guards. They aren't goin' into the quarters."

"Keep a low profile Rick. We need to blend in with these people."

"The floaters are entering the building with the girls. What do you s'pose they do in there?"

"I think they're just guards. Relax, we'll find out soon enough. We need to get a plan together."

They were ushered into a large room containing a sitting area and a rectangular stainless steel table. The watcher levitated about the room. Familiarized itself with its charges. As it drew closer Saff leaned toward it. He bumped into it. Bad idea. The surge of electricity sent Saffrey sprawling across the room. Rick ran to his side, "You okay?"

"What the fuck happened?"

"I gotta think we ain't able ta touch the spheres; they give off some kinda current, like puttin' your finger on a spark plug while the motor's runnin'."

Saffrey thought about this for the next thirty minutes. Came to the conclusion the electric shock was the only deterrent the watchers possessed. Strike two. Wrong again as they'd all find out soon enough.

The next morning Craven paid them a visit. He was alone. "Good morning. Have you adjusted to your new surroundings? I'm here to give you what you might call a familiarization tour, there's plenty to see."

He walked to a closet, pointed to white laboratory coveralls and handed them to the group, "Okay slip into these and follow me."

CHAPTER 17

THEY SLIPPED INTO THE outfits. Craven motioned for them to follow. They accompanied him to an adjoining room. There were two watchers, one levitating on either side of the door. Saffrey didn't brush against either one. A bank of computers busily displayed information unfamiliar to either man at first glance. They stood together, watching the monitors. A voice called to them from the doorway.

"Welcome travelers." It was a warm voice, an inviting friendly tone. The four turned as one. The white robed figure was female. She was ravishing.

"I am the Consortessa Angelica." She raised a hand in a waving gesture.

Rick said, "Saff this is fuckin' déjà vu, remember the scene on the disc?"

"Yeah the waving scene, that's exactly what this is."

"But how? I don't get it."

Saffrey replied quietly, "Don't even try."

Amy gripped Saffrey's hand, squeezed tightly. "I'm scared Saff," she whispered. "This is losing me fast."

The Consortessa moved toward them. Her perfume was alluring, her gaze hypnotic. She reached toward Saffrey, her hand beckoning his. Her eyes were alluring, her skin milky white, and her voice in a word, captivating. She directed her gaze at Saffrey Bell. He felt like a school boy meeting his first love. Was this some kind of mesmeric power these people possessed or was this feeling he was experiencing genuine attraction?

Craven bowed his head as she approached him. "Consortessa, this is a nice surprise. I'm pleased you could visit."

She returned his gesture with a minimal head nod, very slow, very deliberate. "Leave us now Travis, I would like to join the travelers. Stay by the door and let me know if anyone approaches."

Craven smiled, left the room. The tall beauty smiled again,

"You know about the power of the stones?" she asked gently. "It's unfortunate that a defective batch found its way through the doorway. They should never have left the laboratory. Heinzman has placed us in a bad situation."

She moved about them, carefully searching for her next words.

"What I'm about to say mustn't be repeated. Do you understand?"

They nodded in agreement.

"Recently our research into cultured diamonds went a little astray. Some stones were produced without the placement of the neutron chips. These specific Eleventh Generation stones were inclusion free. Once cut they were indistinguishable from natural stones. In effect they are flawless. These stones still exist. They are stored in a heavily guarded shelter in the Syntec Zone. They are known as the 'I11 Stones.'"

"Why are they called that?" Rick asked.

"The 'I' represents Illusion. These diamonds have ideal-cut proportions, with internally flawless clarity. The 'eleven' represents the eleventh generation, producing near flawless specimens. Their chemical makeup is very rare, constituting less than one percent of all white diamonds, rare because they contain virtually no nitrogen, the impurity that causes more common white diamonds to have varying shades of yellow tint."

"Why are you telling us this?" Saffrey asked.

She paused, not accustomed to having questions leveled at her.

"My father is the Consort. He won't allow your group to return to your time. You'll be terminated. Only I can guarantee your safe return. And that is on one condition."

Her eyes once again locked onto Saffrey. "If you refuse my offer, rest assured . . . you will be terminated at my discretion."

"And your proposal is?" Saffrey asked.

"I've had one longing for many years; my existence is preordained in this world. I wish to permanently enter your time and live my life as a mortal citizen. You are my opportunity to escape this . . . this prison in which I'm bound by birthright. I'd planned to travel with Ramirez into your time. He was dispatched to retrieve Eduard Heinzman. It appeared Ramirez had plans of his own. As it turned out these plans did not include me. When my father passes on, I'll become ruler of this world. I don't want to inherit that position. If I refuse to become ruler I'll be terminated. This is law; this is the way it'll be."

"Why can't you just leave with one of your own people? Leave on your own?" Rick asked.

"I attempted this twice, each time I failed. Once because of the watchers, I'm continually under surveillance . . . continually."

Saffrey asked, "You say you tried to leave twice, what happened the second time?"

Angelica looked uncomfortable. She turned her eyes to her right, then to her left. She raised her gown and showed a prosthetic left leg.

"Jesus what happened?" Saffrey asked.

"The watchers, they don't discriminate when it comes to stopping anyone trying to escape the Zone, even *I* have no advantages."

They listened in amazement. No one spoke for what seemed an eternity. She continued to explain. "The Syntec Zone is well guarded. It contains all that is precious to our technology. The watchers abound there. They see everything."

"So why is the Syntec Zone of any importance to your escaping?" Saffrey asked.

"I'm aware of the value of the stones once they enter your time. The inclusion-free stones will see to my safety and lifestyle in your time. You'll all share in my good fortune if you take me with you."

"Do you have a way for us to get back home?" asked Karen.

"I've got the keys to the doorways. Their locations are encrypted in my memory. This knowledge is only possessed by the Consorts and their appointed Mizzas."

"Mizzas? What are they?" Rick asked.

"Travis is a Mizza; he has the location of the doorways encrypted. He knows the passageways. He delivers the coordinate containers, he sets the doorways. Your journey to this time was through his guidance, through his coordinated placement of the containers."

"In the limousine?" Karen asked.

"Yes, and we'll return the same way, the guidance system will correctly align the transporting vessel so it passes between the coordinates."

Saffrey didn't have a problem with what he'd heard. Angelica wanted out bad enough. She needed their help to make the plan work. They needed her help to get the hell out of there.

"We'll meet again soon. Travis will keep you informed of my plans. He is my trusted Mizza, my protector. Until then, enjoy your stay and keep this discussion confidential."

She gave them all a comforting glance, the type of look a mom gives her kids when promising them dessert if they eat their vegetables. Whereas the dessert sounded tempting, they could only wonder what vegetables they'd be eating.

CHAPTER 18

CHEVALIER SAT WITH THE task force. Penoir and Dupre rifled through folders, each of the men in the squad held an identical folder. "Welcome gentlemen. It appears there is a common denominator in these crimes," said Chevalier. Two of the specialists in the group had flown in from the FBI. It seemed the death of the two U.S. Embassy staff members had raised a red flag back in Washington. Neither of the U.S. agents spoke French. An interpreter sat between them and helped with explaining the conversation. To accommodate them, Chevalier rarely used French when foreigners were present.

"We're trying to retrace the steps of all involved in the incidents. A neighbor of Michelle du Blanc saw two men leave her apartment the morning of her death. Their prints were also found in the van that was pulled from the lake. Prints matching one of the men were on the glass showcase of the pawn shop. The witness who saw the two men leaving Miss du Blanc's residence has identified one of the men. He turned out to be the one whose prints were in the pawn shop. His name is Philippe Bouvier."

Chevalier took a long slow sip of his coffee, placed a cigarette between his lips, lit up and took a deep breath.

"The pawn shop owner also recognized the man as Philippe Bouvier. We have an all points out on him. He has prior convictions of breaking and entering as well as car theft. I am certain that he will have answers to many of our questions. The prints found in the truck by the farmhouse also matched those found in the van that had been pulled from the lake. We can only assume that the driver of the truck, whose body the dogs had partially devoured, was the owner of the prints." The cell phone vibrated in Chevalier's pocket. He decided to take the call.

"Claude this is Paul Laroche at headquarters. We have a girl on the line. Her name's Susanna du Blanc, says she is the younger sister of Michele du Blanc. She wishes to speak with you about her sister's death."

Chevalier took the phone number and immediately called the girl. "Susanna du Blanc. This is inspector Chevalier. You wish to speak with me?"

"Inspector . . . my sister . . . her death, I've information that might help your investigation. I need to speak with you. Can we meet?"

An hour later they sat across from each other in a small apartment in the South Bank area in central Paris, just south of the Seine River. Artwork in various stages of progress stood on easels. Chevalier passed an admiring glance at the canvases.

"I see you're an artist, I dabble a little myself."

"Yes inspector, I've seen your paintings. I'm one of your biggest fans."

"So then Miss du Blanc, what can you tell me about your sister?"

She hung her head, paused, reached for tissues, and wiped the tears. Chevalier waited, heard her blowing her nose. He swallowed. *Not too subtle of me*, he thought.

"My deepest apologies, I didn't mean to be so heartless. Please forgive me."

"Yes of course. I haven't spoken about Michelle since her death. It's very difficult."

"Please take your time. Just tell me what you know of the incident."

"I received a call early on the morning of the day of her death. She was very excited. She was hmm . . ."

"I'm aware of her business," Chevalier interrupted. He quietly said, "She was a professional escort."

"Yes, an escort. She called to tell me about a diamond. She was with two men who had hmm . . . visited her for the night. They rewarded her for her time with a diamond. She said it was large and beautiful. She was going to meet with me for lunch, and bring the diamond."

"She didn't meet you, correct?"

"I waited for over an hour. She always keeps her lunch dates with me."

"What did she tell you on the phone?"

"Just what I've told you, the two men."

"I would like you to come to the station. You'll need to fill out a report on the conversation. Did your sister mention any names?"

"Yes one was Philippe; the other has slipped my memory. I think it could've been Raphael, Roland, something beginning with 'R'."

"Philippe . . . Philippe Bouvier."

"You know the man inspector?"

"Yes, we are searching for him. We'll locate him soon no doubt. But the other man remains a mystery at this time."

The phone conversation ended after a few more minutes. There was nothing further for Chevalier to shed light on. Michelle had been a girl struggling to get by.

Dupre laid out a large sheet of butcher's paper, pointed to diagrams, names and arrows. He said, "Inspector, this is the schematic chart I've put together on the case. We've several dead people and two baked cats," he managed a smirk as he pointed to each of the squares. "Each person had possession of a diamond. Yet there was no evidence of a diamond at any of the crime scenes. Security video from the shops shows diamonds as they explode in a fire-ball leaving a strange green mist and the victims. Among the dead we've Miss du Blanc, a computer technician and his wife, the du Mauriers and a truck driver Gustave Broulett, who's been identified from fingerprints in his truck. It's interesting that this man's prints were also found in a van containing a body; the body was neatly folded into a trunk. The van was fished from this lake." He tapped on the location of the lake. "Also in the van we found more prints, those of Philippe Bouvier, Yves St Clair, and Ramone Flourette. All four of whom we've records to show collaboration in numerous small crimes such as motor vehicle theft and burglary. We're expecting early apprehension of the three surviving felons. This'll shed light on the mystery of the stones."

Chevalier nodded approval. "It appears all's going as well as can be expected Dupre. You've done well. We'll reconvene our meeting later. Meanwhile I've a task I must tend to."

The pawn shop owner sat in his security cage. Chevalier entered accompanied by Penoir. The bell over the door jingled.

"Inspector, what brings you to my humble premises?"

Chevalier asked politely, "May I smoke?"

"But of course."

He tapped the Gauloise on the glass counter. Penoir hurrying to light it had the flame burning seconds before it reached Chevaliers lips.

"Merci Penoir," he said courteously. "Tell me Monsieur Charvon, if you were to place a, as they say in America, a *ball park* value on the stone Philippe Bouvier brought to this shop, what figure would you choose?"

"The stone had unbelievable brilliance. I don't often see stones like that in my business."

"Is the brilliance the sole factor that makes the stone desirable?"

"Brilliance is the most important feature of a beautiful diamond. At the simplest level, brilliance is reduced if light leaks out the back of a diamond. In a more complex analysis the direction that light enters and leaves the top of a diamond becomes very important inspector."

"Was this particular stone deep or as they say, shallow?"

"It had a deep pavilion. A very deep pavilion diamond returns light straight back at you, so in fact when you look face on to the table, your head blocks the light, and the diamond looks dull. Some diamonds that are too shallow suffer a similar problem. But this stone, well, this stone was both deep and brilliant."

"Did the stone possess any individual properties?"

"Yes there was a very small inclusion. That's why I felt a second opinion was needed."

"Did you call anyone and tell them about the stone?"

Charvon hesitated. He swallowed deeply. His brow began to shine beneath the jeweler's lights; noticeable beads of sweat formed.

"Monsieur you can answer me now, or at the station, it's your choice."

Chevalier was playing a strong bluff hand, typical of his detective training. He had a great deal of luck using this technique. He was suddenly feeling very lucky.

"Please inspector, they told me I'd be dealt with if I spoke to anyone."

"Charvon, I'll see to it that your store is boarded up. You'll never operate a business in France again. Now, who are they?"

"Please assure me you'll never disclose your source of information. They've many informants. I'm sure they've paid similar visits to most stone dealers in Paris."

Charvon was trembling. He took an old polishing cloth and wiped his face. "I need to lock the door. We cannot have any interruptions." He unlocked his cage, moved down into the entry area. Charvon locked the door, pulled the shade.

"Go ahead Charvon. I'm growing impatient."

"Do you remember the incident at the restaurant when a tourist was struck and killed by a driver?"

"Yes of course. The Restaurant De Fontain about a week back, yes I'm familiar with it."

"A man came to my store shortly after the death of the tourist. He told me he was a friend of the victim."

Charvon walked to a small basin, pulled a paper cup from a dispenser, drank some water slowly, it brought him some time. He continued with his story. "He told me an attaché case belonging to the dead man was stolen from the scene. He said it contained a quantity of diamonds."

"And he figured that the thief might approach you for a sale, right?"

"In a way, although he was most interested in the means by which the person brought the diamonds to my shop," Charvon took another drink, took more time. "He particularly mentioned the attaché case with initials R.R."

"Did he give his name or a number where he could be reached?"

"Inspector please, I was scared for my life."

"You've already contacted this man, yes?"

"He told me he had knowledge that a stone had found

its way to my store. He came just after I'd given the stone to the jewelers for a second opinion."

"Describe this man."

"One hundred and eighty three centimeters, average build, dark hair, strange eyes . . . ice blue. They were dead eyes, an unforgettable individual."

"Penoir call back to headquarters and get the witness's description of the Porsche driver."

"What's your reason insp p pector?" Penoir stammered.

"A hunch Penoir, but lately my hunches are having a run of luck."

Chevalier continued his interrogation of Charvon and after minutes had passed, Penoir stepped back into the room holding a computer print-out. "No one saw the license plate on the P Porsche, but three p p patrons of the restaurant caught a g g glimpse of the driver."

Chevalier glanced through the report and smiled. "Looks like our man. Thank you for your assistance, Monsieur Charvon. We'll be in touch. Meanwhile I need not remind you to call me if any further interest is shown in the stones, or the attaché case." He passed Charvon his business card. "My mobile number's on the card. Call me."

Chevalier sat in the Ferrari. Penoir waited for his summation.

"Very curious, why would this person be interested in the attaché case more than the diamonds?"

As Penoir began to answer, Chevalier waved him off. "Please don't interrupt my thoughts," he said abruptly, tapping another cigarette on the car-dash. "We've Ramirez departed, the driver of the Porsche calling on the pawn dealer, and we've our friendly little conglomerate of locals who've their fingerprints all over the place. Where's the connection, where?"

Penoir remained silent.

"Come Penoir," Chevalier snapped. "Don't you have an opinion?"

CHAPTER 19

CHEVALIER DROVE TO THE seafood restaurant *La Fonderie*, his favorite. "Come along Penoir and join me for a snack, perhaps you'll find an opinion."

The waitress sat the two men at a booth." Welcome, our special for tonight is *huîtres aux crépinettes.*

Chevalier raised an eyebrow. "Oysters with spiced sausages Antoine, a very good choice."

"I c c c cannot eat oysters inspector. They don't agree with me," Penoir replied apologetically as he browsed through the menu. "Aha, I'll have the b b brochette *d d d dijon flambe.*"

"Very good choice Penoir, very good indeed."

Twenty minutes later the food arrived. The plate in front of Penoir contained a chicken-flavored coating with a mustard herb mixture threaded on skewers, grilled and then flamed with *Drambuie*. Chevalier's dish featured flattened *crépinettes,* baked, basted and well-browned. The waitress spooned the melted lard over the *crépinettes*. Chilled oysters lay by the steaming hot crêpes. The food went down well. A few drinks later the two men slowly rose from the table.

"Antoine do you mind driving? I feel a little hot and shaky."

CHAPTER 20

TRAVIS CRAVEN RELAXED BEHIND the wheel. He waited for the all clear from the men in white. They stood silently as though waiting for the word. The word would come from an indoor controller. A hand was raised. The man with the raised hand nodded to Craven. The Porsche accelerated toward a row of orange cones. A green mist formed a cloud between the cones. The 911 flashed into the mist, then vanished. Craven had again entered the doorway. In a matter of seconds, he emerged at a point on a quiet road south of Paris. Cows bolted away as the roaring Porsche appeared from nowhere, interrupting their leisurely graze.

Craven decelerated to a respectable one hundred and twenty kilometers an hour. He shot the Porsche past a farmer's truck carrying straw, waving apologetically as he flew by. The farmer cursed as the draught from the Porsche dragged loose straw in its wake. His instructions were clear. Locate the disc and bring it back. His first stop would be another visit to the Charvon's pawn shop.

Craven waited in the coffee shop and waited for the sunset. The pawn shop was directly across from him and its door was closed. He sat watching passers by, waited 'till the street was empty, thought about a fast escape. Everything looked good, the last light was smothered and a heavy cloud bank blocked the moon. There was no one strolling about and Craven made his move. He'd parked the Porsche in a side alley. It was obscured from sight by a huge dumpster. He moved sideways, crab-like, stepping into the shadows of a small shop alongside the coffee shop. Recalled how the bell above the pawn shop door jingled. Looked at the upstairs window, it glowed softly. Charvon was not in the darkened shop below. Charvon was in the room with the light.

Craven sighed, slid his hands into his pockets, let his shoulders slump and moved toward the alley alongside the shop.

The mobile in his pocket began vibrating.

"Craven," he answered.

"What went wrong Craven? We lost two operatives. What the fuck happened?"

"Some of the stones were defective. We had no way of knowing which were bad and which weren't. The bad stones had inclusions, bad timing sensors." Travis Craven needed to talk fast. Perhaps his very survival depended on it.

"Our embassy's been dragged into this mess. Interpol and the FBI are all over it like flies on shit. This is one hell of a mess you've gotten us into. First the fuck up with the Eldridge, now this. Your people back then were supposed to have the technology figured out for that fuckin' mess. And now we got this fuck up Craven."

"That was before my time, not my problem, nothing to do with what's going on here."

Craven's frustration caused him to give an abrupt annoyed reply. "I'm on top of this." He swallowed, took a deep breath, thought *can't alienate these people*. "Just give me time to clean up. I'll fix the problem. More than make amends." Craven waited for the reply. It was a long silence.

"There's a French cop, an Inspector Chevalier handling the investigations for the Paris cops. He's getting too close. He needs to meet with an accident. You follow me Craven?"

"I'll take care of it. I'll call you later. Give you an update."

Craven waited, another long pause, then "One more thing Craven, we didn't appreciate the two Russian agents showing up at the meeting. Don't try to play both sides again. It'll turn around and bite your mother-fuckin' ass. Do I make myself clear?"

Craven was puzzled. He said, "Russian agents? What are you talking about? I contacted your two operatives like you told me, told them a stone had reached the jeweler. No Russians."

"If you didn't, who the fuck did?"

"Maybe the jeweler," Craven said. A quick attempt at self defense. "Let me work on it."

"This isn't a fuckin' auction Craven. We don't do bidding wars with other nations. Make sure of it. Have you been able to turn up any leads on the missing stones?"

"Not yet. Leave it with me; you'll have your answers."

The phone clicked. Craven shuddered, stared at the cell, angrily snapped it shut and re-focused on the window above the pawn shop.

On the sidewalk outside of the pawn shop, Craven gazed at the window. His mind drifted for a few seconds, thought about the French cop, Chevalier. *This French cop could be problem. Have to get him out of the picture*, he thought. *But first I'll take care of the only person who can identify me.*

He crossed the narrow street, had a quick look around, slipped the silencer from his jacket and fitted it to the Glock. He took a mini-roll of duct tape from the other pocket. Tore off a strip eight inches long and stuck it across the glass on the front door, next to the lock. A few more strips of tape and covered an area eight inches square. With the butt of the Glock he made one fast blow on the tape. The glass shattered. Made no noise. He reached through the hole, unlocked the door, opened it just enough to slide his hand along the inside edge. He found the bell, stuffed a piece of plastic tape inside the bell h. The bell was silenced. The door silently opened. He could smell coffee, it was coming from upstairs.

The stairs leading from the shop to the residence had no door. Charvon lived alone. He was almost sleeping, oblivious to his television. It was loud and blocked out any other sounds. The bell wouldn't have been heard. Craven started up the stairs, careful not to place his hand on the railing. *No fingerprints,* he thought.

Charvon turned the volume down. He raised himself from the sofa and made his way to the kitchen. Craven heard the movement, heard the television go quiet. He stopped. The refrigerator opened and Charvon took cheese and placed it on a wooden chopping block. He sliced off a large chunk of camembert. The coffee was slowly bubbling on the cook-plate. Charvon took a cup from the cupboard, poured coffee.

Craven glanced around, waited, just three steps from the sitting room, just three steps from the crime scene. He kept the gun below waist level, out of sight, held in one hand.

He took the coffee and cheese to the sofa, placed them on a small table, sank back into the chair. Filled his mouth with camembert and took a full swig of coffee. The comedy on the screen held his attention. He began chuckling and the coffee trickled from the corners of his mouth. He wiped his sleeve across his roughly whiskered chin and took another swig of coffee.

Craven stepped into the room and raised the gun.

"Hey!" Charvon cried as he spilled the coffee, spitting the cheese from his mouth.

He stared into the black hole at the end of the silencer. "No, no, no," he begged as Craven stepped toward him. "It was Chevalier, he knew everything. I told him nothing. He already knew about Philippe."

"Philippe?" Craven paused. "Who's Philippe?"

"Philippe Bouvier, the one who brought the stone to me."

"Why didn't you tell me this, when I first came to see you?"

"I didn't think it was important. I didn't know his name until Chevalier took the fingerprints. I only knew him as Philippe. There is more than one Philippe in Paris, what does it matter?"

Charvon was panicking. Craven pressed the silencer against the trembling man's temple.

"I mightn't kill you tonight. Might even let you live. But I've a favor to ask."

"Please, anything, anything. I'll do anything monsieur." Charvon looked down at his trousers. The crotch was soaked with pee.

Craven smelled it, became annoyed. "ON YOUR GODDAMN KNEES," he shouted. He recomposed himself and after a few seconds he said, "On your goddamn knees. I'm going to stay here with you tonight. In the morning you'll call this Chevalier. Tell him you've some new information about the stones. Get him to come here."

"Yes, yes, of course. I'll call him. I'll do just as you ask."

Craven smiled. "Good, then why don't you be the perfect

host. First thing, go take a shower and change your trousers. Then make some fresh coffee."

Travis Craven sat back in the sofa, lit up a cigarette. He kicked off his loafers and chuckled at the television.

CHAPTER 21

"**P**OLICE HEADQUARTERS," THE RECEP-
TIONIST answered.

"Good morning. This is Pierre Charvon. May I speak with Inspector Chevalier?"

"The inspector hasn't arrived at the station yet. Can I take a message?"

"It's urgent that I speak with him. Can you have him call me at my pawn shop when he arrives? He has my number."

"Certainly, I'll place a note on his desk."

"Please tell him I have information about the stones."

Charvon hung up the phone and turned to Craven.

"He is not . . ."

"Yeah I heard. We'll wait. What do you have here for breakfast?"

*****

Antoine Penoir arrived at the station in his usual prompt manner. He sat at his desk in the room alongside Chevalier's. Had his morning coffee in one hand and began reading his copy of *Le Monde*. He placed the cup on the desk and pulled a cigarette from a silver case, placed it in his mouth and reached for the lighter. It was missing. He looked about for matches, but found none. He made his way to Chevalier's office. Found matches on the inspector's desk. As he reached for the matches, he couldn't help but see the note on the inspector's desk. He read it twice and quickly dialed the main desk.

"Have you heard from the insp p p pector?"

The receptionist answered in a matter-of-factish way.

"Mrs. Chevalier just called. He won't be in today. He's been up all night. Seems he ate something that didn't agree with him. Oysters I believe she said."

"Aha the oysters, I knew it." Penoir smirked to himself.

Penoir strolled back to his office, finished enjoying the cigarette and coffee. He thought about the note on the inspector's desk.

"Time for an executive decision," he mumbled to himself.

As he passed by the reception counter he said,

"I'm g g going out for a while. Take messages but do not c c call me directly."

Penoir drove to the Charvon pawn shop. Traffic began to block his route. He flicked the siren on, slowly weaving his way through the congestion.

Craven heard the siren coming. He moved to the window that faced the street below.

The squad car was still a block away, siren wailing.

"Our boy's on his way. Go on down and put the open sign on the door, then come back up. Don't try anything stupid. I've got you in my sights. My gun is silent and I never miss."

Charvon quickly went down the stairs, Craven following a few steps behind.

"Charvon remember . . . I don't miss from this range, nothing stupid."

Penoir stopped the patrol car outside the store. He walked to the door, wondered why it was open for business at this early hour. Saw the shattered glass. He gently nudged the door a few inches, remembered the bell. It was silent. Slowly opening the door, Penoir glanced up at the bell. Saw the duct tape stuffed into it.

"CHARVON! CHARVON!!" he called aloud. "Are you there? What happened here, have you had a robbery?"

"Everything's fine, someone tried to break in last night, please inspector, upstairs. Please come up."

Penoir thought nothing of Charvon's mistaking him for Chevalier, his voice was similar to Chevalier's and after all, Charvon was expecting the inspector, not Penoir.

Craven raised the gun to Charvon's temple, he whispered, "Thank you Charvon." He leaned toward the stairs, heard the footsteps getting nearer. "Now if you want to live, think before you make a sound."

"Hello Charvon? I read the m m message that you called in this morning," Penoir said as he arrived at the top of the stairs.

Craven stepped forward from behind the door; in a heartbeat he placed his silencer at the base of Penoir's skull. Two shots dropped Penoir. Each of the bullets exited above his eyes, the front of his face burst open. Charvon choked, and at the top of his lungs began yelling, "NO, NO, NO."

Craven grinned at him and calmly said, "If you don't shut up . . ."

Charvon became even more hysterical. Craven swung the Glock around, landing hard on Charvon's head. Charvon went down. Craven grabbed the screaming man by the hair and twisted him around. "Shut up, shut up you dumb bastard, shut the fuck up!"

Craven's cool demeanor had gone. His eyes widened, the look of a crazed killer, he once again grabbed hold of Charvon's hair, pulling him toward Penoir. He dropped to his knees and reached across to the dead mans face, scooping a handful of blood from the forehead wound. Charvon continued screaming. Craven rubbed the bloody mess from Penoir into Charvon's eyes, into his mouth and through his hair.

Charvon cried hysterically. Craven dragged him to his feet, pushed him into the bathroom, and smashed his face against the mirror. The mirror smashed. Charvon fell to the floor, glass shattering about him. He grasped a dagger-shaped piece of the broken mirror and quickly turned in a last-ditch effort to defend himself. He lunged at Craven with the glass. Craven let out a scream as the glass sheath dug deep into his thigh-muscle.

Craven grabbed onto Charvon's blood-soaked hair, dragged him back into the living room. Craven stumbled across Penoir's body, regained his balance, and pointed the Glock at Charvon.

"I'm going to enjoy this, you fuck," he lowered the silencer and fired one shot into Charvon's crotch.

The scream was silent. Charvon's mouth opened, but there was no sound. He rolled across the living room floor, wreathing in agony. Craven followed him, laughing as he pointed the Glock at Charvon's stomach. Fired again.

"This is too much fun. Are you enjoying it, Charvon?"

He laughed his insane laugh, a psychotic killer, out of control, a pseudo-orgasm for Craven. The 'cool' that once was . . . was now gone from his demeanor.

"This gun holds thirteen bullets. My guess is we have nine left. You'll take all nine before you die."

Three quick shots to his stomach left Charvon writhing for breath. His eyes bulged, tears flowed, and blood ran from his mouth. Three more shots to his legs had no added effect on the pain threshold. The threshold had been reached.

Craven stepped onto Charvon's chest, pinned him under his right foot. Lowered the Glock, placed it a few inches from Charvon's temple, and reeled off the final three shots.

Penoir's failure to return to the station raised concern. His mobile was not being answered. The note still sat on Chevalier's desk. It stayed there until the next morning. The inspector arrived early, poured a coffee, and made his way to his office. He sat back at his desk and lit a cigarette, took his first sip of coffee for the day. He gazed across the desk at his window, blew out two smoke rings. The phone rang, breaking his day dream, pulling him back to the moment.

"Inspector good morning, this is Susan Penoir. Antoine didn't come home last night and I've not been able to reach him by phone. Is he at the station?"

"Hello Susan, no I haven't seen him. I was at home yesterday. I'll check around and call you right back."

The note didn't catch Chevalier's eye until he hung up the phone. Two squad cars accompanied the inspector as they made their way, sirens blaring, through the city toward the pawn shop.

The Ferrari arrived first. Chevalier pulled the front wheels onto the sidewalk, leaving his door open as he ran from the car. The shop door was not locked. He pushed it open. Felt the glass crush under his shoes. His eyes immediately went to the muffled bell. Four cops were right behind him. He motioned for them to stop. Pointed to the stairs and placed his index finger over his lips.

Guns drawn, they moved cautiously toward the stairs. Blood stains dotted the floor from the door to the staircase. There was a rank smell that Chevalier recognized. He had a bad feeling. He really wanted to be someplace else.

Reaching the top of the stairs, Chevalier abruptly stopped.

"Oh no, oh no." He bowed his head, placing it in his hands. Penoir's body sat propped against a wall. Placed there for effect, to greet whoever entered the room. The badly mutilated body of Charvon lay at the feet of Penoir. Both bodies were covered in blood. Chevalier turned his back on the scene and angrily beat the butt of his gun into the wall. He reeled about and kicked the small table by the sofa. It tumbled across the room. Tears swelled in his eyes. Two cops moved forward to comfort him. He brushed them aside.

"Touch nothing. I want every inch of this place gone over. Get the forensics team in here now. See if anyone heard or saw anything. I want the son of a bitch." He took a handkerchief from his pocket, wiped his eyes, blew his nose. "Call the medical examiner; tell him to get down here."

Chevalier moved toward his old friend and kneeled at his side.

"Antoine my friend, I'm sorry." He nodded his head as tears continued to run from his eyes. He continually wiped the wet from his cheeks. He draped a sheet of cloth from the sofa over the face of Penoir.

"I will dearly miss you my old, old friend."

Chevalier stood, made his way out of the shop. Cops had already established lines around the perimeter. Crowds formed and questions were being asked by cops mixing with the spectators.

"Inspector, this man says he saw a person leaving the store. He says he was limping."

"Which way did he go?"

"Toward the alley."

Chevalier started toward the alley at the side of the store.

Blood drops made a trail toward a large dumpster fifty meters from the street corner. He lowered himself one knee and touched the blood with his index finger, rubbing it between the finger and his thumb. He looked ahead. Walked further, came to the spot where the blood trail ended.

This must be where he got into a car, he thought. He noticed stones against a wall a few meters from where he stood. A chalk circle was near the stones. Initials were written on the roadway as though children had been playing a game and recording a score. Every door within three hundred meters was knocked on. A young woman answered the blue door down the alley from Charvon's store.

"Yes, I have two children. What's the problem monsieur?"

"We're investigating a crime that took place here yesterday. Can I please speak with the children?"

The two children spoke with Chevalier. They explained they regularly play the stone game in the alley but were away visiting their aunt the previous day. Chevalier showed them photographs of the chalked initials, the circle by the wall. They recognized the initials as belonging to three other local boys who regularly played the game in the alley. He accompanied the children as they took him to the cottage where the three boys lived.

"Yes we did see a man limping in the alley," said the taller boy.

"What time do you think it was?"

"We came to play about nine o'clock. It was about thirty minutes after that."

"What can you tell me about the man, was he alone?"

"Yes, I think he had blood on his leg. He got into his car. It was by the dumpster."

"What color was the car, what type of car?"

"It was my favorite, a red Porsche."

"Did you see a license plate or any marks on the car?"

"No sir, it was all very quick. We were playing our game and didn't pay much attention to it."

"Was the car a convertible or coupe?"

"It was the model I want when I save my money, a Targa."

"Would you recognize this man if you saw him again?"

"Yes," all three boys replied in unison.

Chevalier took notes, thanked the boys for their help, and made his way to Penoir's home.

Susan Penoir took the news as Chevalier expected. The day following Penoir's death Susan called Chevalier. "Can I see him Claude?"

"No, I prefer you don't. It's not necessary. I'll sign the paperwork."

"Claude I need closure. I need to see him for myself."

"I'll call you Susan, "Chevalier said. "When he's satisfactorily prepared, I'll let you know Susan."

It had been a very bad day. Chevalier wanted to lock himself in a dark room, to speak to no one. Susan Penoir sobbed for as Chevalier placed a call to headquarters.

"This is Chevalier; please send a police woman to Antoine Penoir's home. Have her stay with his wife a few days."

He hugged Susan and quietly said, "It's late. I'll call back by in the morning. Please call me if you wish to talk. I'm here for you Susan."

Chevalier had the traffic section run a trace on every Porsche on record. Nothing matched the red Targa. Leaving no card unturned, he had them run the same model in different colors. This also failed to find a match. An all points bulletin was put out throughout the city. No sightings were reported.

Chevalier sat in his sofa. His best friend was gone; the case involving the burned bodies had run into dead ends. Life was not good. He lay back, rested his feet on the armrest at one end of the sofa. As he was about to drift off, the phone jarred him to consciousness. He reached forward, answered slowly, "Chevalier."

"Inspector we received a call from a farmer who says he was nearly run off the road by a red car fitting the description of the suspect."

CHAPTER 22

THE NIGHT WAS BRIGHT. The full moon made it easy to see the road ahead. The Ferrari purred toward the city limits and within minutes was surrounded by the countryside. The trees glowed in the light of the moon, creating large monsters that leered over the roadway.

The inspector pulled the Ferrari into the dirt driveway, turned the volume down on Sinatra, sat looking over the scene, felt all was as it should be. He turned the ignition off, walked up the wooden steps leading to the porch and knocked on the door of the old farmhouse. "Monsieur this is Inspector Chevalier of the Paris police. Can you please open the door?"

"Coming, coming," the voice replied.

The door squeaked open. An elderly withered man smiled at Chevalier. His teeth were stained, his posture wilted.

"Please come in, you have identification?"

Chevalier showed his badge. The two men sat at a table.

"What can you tell me about this red car?"

"It came from nowhere, almost ran me off the road. My cows gave no milk that day."

"Did you see the driver?"

"Yes, he waved to me. It was a young man, dark hair."

"Dark hair, that's it?"

"He was traveling very fast. He waved to me."

"You said that already."

"He made the straw fly from my truck. His car was not there. And then it was. It came from nowhere."

This old man is clearly senile, Chevalier thought.

"So monsieur, this red car, it just appeared from nowhere, is that what you're saying?"

"I can see cars coming along the road, but this red car was just, well . . . it was just there."

Chevalier thought for a minute. He stood, thought a few more seconds, and walked about the room.

"If I was to drive from the direction in which the red car came, would I just appear from nowhere?"

"Of course not, I'd see you approaching me. Why do you speak to me like I'm a senile old fool? I am not a stupid man. I know what I saw. The red car just appeared on the road. It was on top of me."

"Did it drop from the sky - drop from a plane?"

"Of course not, there was no plane. It was just there."

Chevalier scratched his head and asked the old man, "Do you mind if I smoke?"

"Of course not, go ahead."

"Tell me monsieur, do you drink?"

"Not at that hour, are you saying I was drunk?"

"Do you take medication?"

"Yes, for a back pain, that's all."

"If I return in the morning, can you take me to the place you first saw the red car?"

"Yes of course."

"Then I'll see you tomorrow."

He drove away from the farm more confused than ever. *Surely this red car doesn't materialize from nowhere. But that's what the farmer is saying. Ah, well,* he thought. *Tomorrow's another day; we'll see what tomorrow brings.*

*****

The day began with a call from Paul Laroche at headquarters. "Claude this is Laroche, my condolences on the loss of Antoine. He was a very good man. He will be greatly missed by us all."

"Thank you Paul. He'll be avenged, I promise."

"Claude I have some good news. We have Philippe Bouvier in custody. He was apprehended last night in a stolen vehicle."

Chevalier answered in an elated tone. "I'll be there in thirty minutes, thank you Paul."

Philippe Bouvier sat forlornly in the small cell. Chevalier

arrived and headed directly to the holding cells. Paul Laroche was sitting with Philippe.

"Aha inspector, allow me to introduce Philippe Bouvier."

"Philippe you've been a hard man to track down."

"It was just a car. Why am I being treated as though I've robbed the Louvre?"

"I'm not interested in the car. I want to hear about the diamond you left with the pawn shop. Do you admit to taking a stone to Charvon's store for valuation?"

"Yes and why not? I left it with him. That's not a crime. Why's that of concern to the police?" Philippe was genuine in his delivery. He still had no knowledge of the plight of the victims in the jeweler's store." He'll call me when he has a valuation."

"Charvon won't be calling you. Charvon is dead."

"Dead? How can that be? He was fine, what happened to him? Was it a robbery? How can I get my stone back?"

"Where did you come by the stone Bouvier? Who gave it to you?"

"I was given it as payment. It was payment for a job that I completed."

"What job?"

"I cannot say, it is confidential."

"You'll tell me Bouvier, or so help me God you will not see daylight again. This I promise you."

"You cannot do this! I have rights."

"RIGHTS?" Chevalier shouted. "RIGHTS? YOU HAVE NO FUCKIN' RIGHTS!" He regained a little composure, said, "You are the scum of the earth Bouvier, and I will squash you underfoot like the cockroach you are if you don't cooperate."

Philippe began sobbing. Chevalier pretended not to notice.

"Paul, take this scum to the old cells below."

"But inspector, we haven't used the lower cells in twenty years, they're rat infested and . . ." Laroche didn't get to finish the sentence.

"Take the swine down there, now!" Chevalier demanded.

". . . and leave his hands cuffed behind his back." Philippe stood to leave the cell, Chevalier gave him a solid slap across the head as he passed by.

"You will tell us everything. Everything! I will return to speak with you after I have eaten, a lunch that you Bouvier, will not be having."

The stairs to the lower level were damp and slippery. A dull light failed in its struggle to illuminate the way. Paul Laroche prodded Philippe with a night stick. He stumbled down the walkway falling heavily, landing on his face. The skin began bleeding and Philippe let out a muffled groan. Slowly he raised himself to his feet.

The door slammed shut behind him, rattled violently as it did. The floor was putrid; the smell of human feces was prevalent.

Laroche pointed to the ceiling. "It is the stench of leaking sewers. You will get used to it, the longer you stay."

Philippe could hear the squeaking and rustling of rats as he huddled in a corner. He listened to Laroche's footsteps as they faded into the distance. He heard them reach the top of the stairs, heard the heavy steel grated door rattle as it slammed shut. He heard the rats, he was alone. Alone with the rats. He felt blood trickle down his face. He didn't dare drift into sleep. The rats could smell the blood. Something scampered across his leg, squealing as it passed. Philippe screamed, jumped to his feet, striking his head against a low beam. He saw brilliant flashes of light, felt the searing pain. Unable to stay erect any longer he dropped to his knees, slid to the damp pungent floor and drifted into unconscious.

It was two hours before Chevalier returned. He and Laroche made their way down the steps to the dungeon. Laroche flashed a beam about the cell.

"Inspector I can't see Bouvier."

"Shine the light into the corners."

The huddled form of a man lay on the floor. Several rats scurried from his head. Chevalier ran toward the body, kicking at the rats, almost slipping as he trod on one, fell to the side, and placed a hand out against the wall, watched as the rats scurried away.

"Help me Paul; get him to his feet."

Laroche called, "Bouvier! Bouvier! Answer me, are you all right?"

Philippe was silent. The two men carried him from the cell, laid him in the passageway outside of the rat infested enclosure.

"Get a stretcher down here quickly. I'll stay with him."

Laroche returned with two more uniformed men. Rolling Philippe onto the stretcher, they proceeded up the steps. When they were in decent light the full horrifying extent of the injuries nauseated them.

"My God Claude, look at his face. The rats have . . ."

"Get him cleaned up. Get a doctor, a very quiet doctor. I don't want this to get out," Chevalier said quietly. "This could cost us both our jobs. We'll be writing parking tickets in Marseilles.

A cop placed smelling salts under Philippe's nose, jolting his head backward, bringing him back to consciousness.

Chevalier leaned forward, placed his mouth to Philippe's ear. "Bouvier I promise you this, I'll put you back in that cell with your rodent friends if you don't tell me who gave you the stone?"

Philippe began to shake, tears swelled in his eyes. "Please, please. I am a good person. I have never harmed anyone, not even a dog. I am a very good person. I do not deserve to be treated this way."

Philippe began crying uncontrollably.

"I can't watch this. Take him back down there for the night," Chevalier snapped.

"No, no. I'll tell you all that I know."

"Very well, start at the beginning. Where'd you get the stone?"

Philippe explained all that took place during the cleanup operation at the hotel.

"I see. You say you arrived in a stolen van. Did you personally steal the van?"

"Yes I took the van; it came from the monastery near

Nice."

"How many others were with you?"

"There were four of us."

Chevalier slowly took a cigarette, waited with it between his lips. Penoir was not there to light it. *A bad habit*, he thought waiting for the light. Paul Laroche reached forward and lit the cigarette.

"Thank you Paul. Antoine's spoiled me."

He turned back to Philippe. "Give me their names, now."

Philippe answered, "Yves St. Clare, Ramone Flourette and Gustave Broulett."

"Who was in charge of this clean-up operation?"

"Yves contacted me and asked for a van and two more assistants. He asked that I bring a large trunk and for us to come along dressed as clowns."

"How did St. Clare know about the clown outfits?"

"He has been to the circus. He knows we sometimes do a little work as clowns."

"Who was it that called St. Clare about removing the body from the hotel?"

"I don't know, maybe the Americans that were in the hotel room."

"Did you see these Americans?"

"Yes." He paused, swallowed hard. "There was one man, his name was Rick, and there were two women, I cannot remember their names."

"Can you recognize them if you see photographs?"

"Yes probably."

"Do you know the identity of the victim in the trunk?"

"No, I heard the women saying he was an intruder. They didn't seem to know him."

"Who gave you the stone?"

Philippe paused, swallowed hard again. "The American, the one named Rick, he took a box of stones from his pocket, he gave six stones to Yves. Yves gave us each one stone."

"Are you aware your friend in crime Gustave Broulett was found dead in his truck?"

Philippe gasped, "Oh my God. No. No. How did it happen? Was it an accident?"

"No, it was a fire, he was burned to death."

"Burned? Did his truck crash?"

"You don't know do you? It is obvious you know nothing about the implication of the stones. Tell me Bouvier, do you know a woman named Michelle du Blanc?"

"Yes. She's a very beautiful young woman I visited."

Chevalier replied in a calm matter-of-factish way, "She's a professional prostitute."

He walked toward the ashtray, extinguished the cigarette, kept his back to Philippe as he asked, "Did you give a stone to Miss du Blanc?"

"Ramone gave her a stone as a gift. Is this a problem?" Philippe replied.

"The woman is dead. She was killed Bouvier. She was burned. You've obviously not heard."

Philippe began sobbing, his bloodied lips now bleeding freely as his sobbing stretched them wider across his raw face, he placed his hands over his eyes and shouted, "OH MY GOD . . . NO, NO, NO." It took a full two minutes for the sobbing to subside, he managed to say, "She was such a beautiful girl. Who would want to do such a thing to her?"

Philippe ran his hands through his hair, obviously distressed.

"She too was burned to a crisp. Bouvier you're heavily implicated in these deaths. You'll remain in custody until we're able to speak with other witnesses."

"Please inspector, ask Ramone and Yves. They'll tell you the same as I have, we do not have any other information."

CHAPTER 23

THE NEXT MORNING AT first light both Ramone Flourette and Yves St. Clare were arrested and brought to the station. It hadn't take much persuading to get their addresses from a broken Philippe Bouvier, far be it for him to spend another night with the furry occupants of the dungeon.

Yves and Ramone corroborated Philippe's story.

"St. Clare where are the stones you were given?"

"They were stolen," he replied.

"Stolen?" Chevalier snapped. "Did you report their theft?"

Yves took on a quizzical expression. "No inspector. I had them in my house. I locked the house and went out for a couple of hours, when I returned the stones had vanished."

"Had the door been forced?"

"No, the house was secured. The windows and doors were locked. Whoever it was tried to set my home on fire. The cupboard in which I'd placed the stones had been badly burned; I thought perhaps the thief was trying to destroy any possible fingerprints."

"Why didn't you report the incident, report the fire?"

"I was worried I'd be asked how I came by the stones."

"Perhaps you were fortunate you weren't at home when the stones vanished," Chevalier said while scratching the side of his head as though not sure why he was saying it.

"And you Ramone Flourette, you gave your stone to the girl Michelle."

"I gave it to her as a gift."

Chevalier folded his arms and let out a deep breath. "You'll all remain under arrest as accessories in the death of the unidentified victim in the trunk."

CHAPTER 24

CHEVALIER SET OFF TO for his meeting with the farmer. He arrived at the farmhouse, thought of better times, of times when Penoir had always been there for him. They'd grown close over the years. The reality of his death was affecting him more today.

"I will get him Antoine, I will get him," he said quietly. "Whatever it takes, outside of the law if necessary. He won't escape me. I promise you." A tear ran down his cheek. Wiping it away, he put on a hard face and stepped from the Ferrari and made his way to the door.

The farmer greeted him, motioning him toward his truck. The drive was a rough ten minutes. The suspension on the truck had died some thirty years earlier. It groaned to a shaky halt and the farmer pointed to the roadside. "You see over there. The straw's still scattered along the edge. This is where he passed me, where the straw was sucked off my truck."

Chevalier stepped out of the truck. "Where did you first see the red car?"

The farmer walked back along the road some one hundred meters. Stopped, looked back at the truck, turned and looked in the opposite direction. "This is close to the place where the car first caught my eye."

This is a straight stretch of road, no curves where a car could have first come into sight. This is the middle of a straight road. It's not possible for a car to come from nowhere at this point, Chevalier thought.

Then he found the dark tire tracks. "These tire marks, they could only happen if a vehicle was to brake suddenly, or if it was to hit the roadway and accelerate as it landed," Chevalier said talking softly to himself.

"I don't understand inspector."

"It's nothing. Nothing at all monsieur, I'm just thinking aloud."

A car approached. Chevalier turned to the farmer. *An opportunity to test the farmers eyesight,* he thought.

"Can you see the car in the distance?"

"Yes of course, it's a blue sedan."

It was a long, slow drive back to Paris. Chevalier remained deep in thought. *It's not possible for the car to just appear. The farmer must've been hallucinating. His vision appears to be normal, but the whole scenario is too crazy.*

He took the cell phone from his jacket, called headquarters. "This is Chevalier; let me speak with Paul Laroche."

He waited as a series of beeps transferred him to Laroche who said "Hello Claude, so how did it go with the farmer?"

"Nothing, it was a waste of time Paul. Have you got anything on the Porsche?"

"We have a witness who says he saw a car matching the vehicle. Says it was traveling fast toward Nice. Tried to catch up with the Porsche but says it just vanished on the road ahead of him."

"Catching a Porsche is difficult, very fast."

"No you don't understand, the car was in view, then poof, nothing - it was gone Claude. It vanished into thin air."

"Really?" Chevalier picked up on the chuckle in Laroche's voice. "Was the witness sober Paul?"

"He had a few drinks with his lunch but says that he was sober."

"Have him take you to the spot where he last saw the Porsche. I want every location of this car marked on a map. Meet me in my office when you're through."

Laroche and Chevalier sat speechless as the locations of the Porsche coincided on the map.

"This is crazy Claude. It came and went at the same coordinate. How can this be?" Laroche cleared his throat. "Really Claude, diamonds that disappear, a car that appears and then vanishes? I can't begin to guess at answers. This is driving me insane."

"It's more than you and I can comprehend Paul. There's no logical explanation. But we'll treat it as fact. I want a squad car placed at this location twenty four hours each day. I want a record of every Porsche that passes this spot. Position a second squad car two hundred yards along the road to apprehend any vehicle that fits the description of the Porsche."

"And if we do '*apprehend*' a suspect?" Laroche held his two index fingers in the air, drawing imaginary quotation marks as he said *apprehend.*

"If he resists I want him dead. Penoir will be avenged."

"But Claude, we need to interrogate this man. We must have him alive. Don't let your emotions cloud your judgment."

"My God you're right; this whole mystery is getting to me. Of course *alive*, what was I thinking?" Chevalier turned away from Laroche, didn't want him to see the lie on his face.

Chevalier invited Laroche to join him for a meal. They arrived at the restaurant, *Cercle Ledoyen "Rez de Chaussee,"* a classic restaurant in the true French fashion. They ate well. No oysters this night. The table was cleared of the empty plates and both men relaxed in silence over a bottle of Merlot. Paul Laroche began to doodle on the disposable table cover. Chevalier pulled back on a freshly lit cigarette.

"The Americans are our mystery solvers Claude."

"What do you suggest Paul?" Chevalier asked in a disinterested tone.

"It all comes back to the Americans at the hotel. They were the ones who gave the stones to those four. Surely they can give us the answers to the stones."

"How's this connected to the Porsche?"

Laroche continued to draw on the table top. "We know the Porsche killed the tourist Ramirez at the restaurant by the fountain. We know from witnesses that a woman left the scene clutching a case that some say belonged to the dead man."

Chevalier leaned forward, looked closer at the doodling on the table cover. His interest in Laroche's summation began to grow.

"The red car and the diamonds seem to be connected. The driver of the Porsche, the dark haired man - he was seen leaving

Charvon's pawn shop and he is clearly the suspect in Penoir's death. We know Penoir went to the pawn shop after reading the note on your desk. Perhaps the killer wasn't laying in wait for Antoine; he was waiting for you Claude. Penoir was unlucky, you were fortunate. Perhaps the same man is involved in the deaths of the du Mauriers at the computer store. The death of Gustave Broulett is still open to conjecture. He had a stone of his own, and it's gone. Each person who had a stone is either dead or, if alive, their stone has vanished."

Chevalier lit another cigarette, drew on it deeply and puffed the smoke skyward. "This is very deep Paul. I follow your logic but I still can't see where it's leading."

He leaned forward, placed a hand on Laroche's shoulder and said as if sharing a secret, "Without apprehending the driver of the Porsche or locating the Americans we've no further leads. We're as they say, up a creek without a motor."

It was a dry conversation as the Ferrari headed toward the apartment where Laroche lived with his wife and two daughters. Neither man spoke. As Chevalier pulled to a halt he turned toward Laroche and said, "Paul I'm getting too old for this work. I'll celebrate my sixtieth birthday in a week. Penoir was to celebrate his fiftieth just three days later."

Laroche passed a sad but comforting smile to Chevalier. "Penoir will always remain forty nine. He's in a far better place. Go home Claude. Get a full night's sleep. You'll feel better in the morning."

Chevalier smiled. "Good night Paul." He placed a hand on his friend's shoulder. "And thank you."

Laroche returned the smile. "Good night Claude."

CHAPTER 25

TRAVIS CRAVEN HAD SLIPPED into a deep sleep in the front seat of the Porsche. The loss of blood was excessive. It was sheer luck he'd driven the red car into a secluded side street away from pedestrians, away from prying eyes. The tapping on his window caused him to stir.

He forced open one eye and squinted as the sunlight momentarily blinded him. A few seconds passed. Adjusting his vision he saw a face staring back through the glass. The stunning young girl staring down at him was no older than twenty.

Craven opened his window and attempted a smile. It was difficult; the pain in his leg was all he could bare.

Seeing the blood soaked trousers she asked in a concerned way.

"Are you injured, can I help you?"

"Where am I?"

"You're in *Auvers-sur-Oise*, about twenty kilometers northwest of Paris."

"I . . . I . . . I don't remember driving here. I guess I passed out," Craven said. "I need to find a doctor. Do you know of one nearby?"

"There's a man about three kilometers along this road. He was a doctor. Perhaps he can look at your injury."

The girl raised a hand and, without removing her gaze from Craven, limply pointed in the direction of the doctor's home.

"Can you come along with me?" Craven asked.

"I think you can be trusted monsieur. Yes I'll take you to him."

She smiled and introduced herself. "My name's Bianca."

The girl sat in the car alongside Craven It took all of his energy to turn the wheel. The Porsche moved slowly as Craven steered it in the direction his passenger indicated. As he drove, the girl looked closer at his wound. She screwed up her nose.

"My God monsieur, you have a large piece of glass . . ."

"Yes, yes, I know. It was an accident, nothing to be alarmed over. I'll be fine."

They arrived at a small cottage. The girl sprang from the car and ran to the door. She rang a bell that hung alongside a sign that read '*La Bouterie.*'

Growing impatient she called aloud, "Please answer. Is anyone in there?"

"I'm coming; I'm coming, what's your rush Bianca. What are you doing here?"

The man was extremely stylish, a three piece suit, graying temples, and spectacles sitting on the tip of his nose. The pipe on which he was drawing gave off a rich aroma of caramel blend tobacco. He opened the screen door and stepped onto the verandah.

"Quickly, the man in the car has been injured. He's bleeding."

"Wait Bianca, you know this is my home, not a hospital. You should take him into the city and have him see a doctor there."

"You were a doctor in the village, and you cared for me when I was sick. Please can't you help him? He's lost a lot of blood."

The doctor hesitated, glanced across at the man in the Porsche and relented. "All right then. Come, help me get him into the house."

Craven was sluggish. It took all of their strength to move him into the cottage.

"Thank you for helping," Craven said to the tall man.

"It's not in me to turn a blind eye on an injured man, as hard as I try. Let's take a look at this wound."

He motioned to a sofa. "Let's get him over there," he said, as they both assisted Craven across the room.

Forty-five minutes passed. The wound was cleaned and six stitches had closed it. "You're very lucky monsieur, another few millimeters and you would be dead. The artery was close to the incision."

Craven didn't hear the words. He was drifting in another world, partly through a half bottle of cognac he'd consumed prior to the surgery, and partly from blood loss.

"He has a fever, we'll watch him closely. Until then, you can help me remove the rest of his clothing and clean up this mess."

Bianca sat by Craven into the night. She bathed his body, carefully dried him, and gently ran her fingers across the contours of his face. Even in pain, Craven was an extremely handsome man. She admired the muscle tone of his body, the curl of the hair on his chest; she drew her chair closer, resting her head gently on his shoulder.

The aroma of fresh coffee filled the small cottage. The tall man spoke softly. "Wake up Bianca."

She opened her eyes, looked at the sleeping man and asked the doctor, "Is he still feverish? He spoke in his sleep last night."

The tall man placed a finger on Craven's wrist, looked at his watch. "His pulse is normal."

Craven began to stir and Bianca wiped over his forehead once more. "Where am I?" Craven tried to lift himself from the sofa.

"You're fine my friend. You've lost quite a lot of blood, very fortunate that Bianca here found you when she did. I believe you wouldn't have lasted the night without her help."

Craven reached his hand toward Bianca. "Thank you, I can't repay you enough for helping," he smiled at the doctor and said, "Thank you both."

This was hardly the Travis Craven who danced about Charvon, pumping bullets into the dying man's body. This wasn't the Craven who in cold blood put two bullets into Penoir's head. This was a soft, appreciative Craven. His blue eyes caught Bianca's, and held them for a few precious moments. It was clear that she found this mysterious man very appealing.

Craven rose up onto one elbow. He asked, "Where's my car?"

"It's safe at the back of the cottage. I've been cleaning the blood off the seat before it dried completely."

"That's very good of you. I could do that myself but I appreciate your thoughtfulness."

"The car, it's different. I'm familiar with the 911 Porsche series, but you seem to have different instrumentation."

"Ah . . . yeah." Craven hesitated. "I had special features added, personalized - you know?"

Craven had forgotten the guidance system for the doorways had been left engaged, but it could surely be passed off as a satellite guidance system.

"It helps me from getting lost. I'm pretty bad with directions." He smiled and shrugged as if to dismiss his stupidity.

"I have an SGS in my car. It's quite different from yours. I find yours most interesting."

Craven thought quickly. "That's technology for you, huh doc, always changing?"

"Yes of course, German ingenuity at its finest," the doctor replied as he grinned back at Craven.

One point for Porsche, Craven thought as he returned the smile.

"Bianca, I'm going into the village, can you please look out for the repair man. He's coming to fix my television. It's not worked for several days."

"Of course, and please stop by my brother's house and tell him I'm here. He'll be worried sick, thank you doctor."

Craven drifted in and out of sleep. He knew the police search for him would be relentless, yet the doctor seemed to be oblivious to any news alert.

Of course, he thought. The television had been off the air, no news broadcasts had been coming into the cottage. But once the repairman arrived, his face or its likeness could be all over the television screen. The Porsche would certainly be mentioned. Time was not on his side.

"Bianca please, I need to get dressed."

"You can't get dressed. You have to rest, please don't get off the sofa." Craven was already standing, a blanket draped about his shoulders.

He slipped into his shirt and walked slowly toward the bedroom at the rear of the cottage. He found a closet with clothing; the doctor's trousers would have to suffice, a little tight, but passable.

"Help me into my shoes please Bianca."

Bianca could see that Craven had his mind set. There was no dissuading him.

"Please, why do you need to leave so soon? Are you in some kind of trouble?"

"Yes and I can't place you and the doctor in danger. I have to get away from this place. I'm feeling okay. Just help me to my car."

Craven sensed the uncertainty in her eyes, the look of concern, of caring.

"I'll come back to see you when things are safe again, but I must leave now."

She helped him to the car. The Porsche seemed lower than ever as he struggled to get the wounded leg into the car.

"Adieu Bianca, 'til we meet again. Thank the doctor for me. I'll reward you both on my return."

CHAPTER 26

THE PORSCHE ROARED OFF in the direction of Paris. Craven looked at the passing countryside trying to recognize any landmarks.

"This is it, these are the coordinates," he said aloud as though he needed self-assurance. "Turn around, face east, key in the reentry code, and drive into the doorway."

He sat in the Porsche for a minute, keyed in the code and began to gather speed as the doorway drew closer. Just as he was about to enter the final stretch, a flashing light emerged from behind a grove of trees by the roadside.

A solitary police car began to gather speed. Its siren blaring, it cut across the front of the Porsche. Craven struggled to keep the red car on the paved surface, but his weakened state made the steering far too heavy for him to maneuver. The Porsche slammed into the gravel alongside the roadway and careened across a vacant lot, sliding sideways into bushes.

The police car again tried to cut in front of Craven. He dropped the Porsche into second gear and spun the nose around in the direction of the roadway. The spinning wheels of the Porsche created a huge dust cloud. The police car, engulfed totally, lost precious seconds as Craven sped off into the night.

"Headquarters this is car thirty-six. We're in pursuit of a red Porsche. It matches the description of the wanted vehicle on our all points bulletin. The driver is attempting to escape. We request back up. He is headed in the direction of Auvers-sur-Oise. Please inform us of your location as you approach."

The voice answered immediately. "This is Laroche from headquarters. We'll be in your location within the hour. Keep this line open. Let me know your position every few minutes."

The phone on Chevalier's desk rang. His assistant answered using the speaker phone facility.

"Claude this is Paul. We've located the Porsche."

Chevalier almost choked on his coffee, He jumped from

his desk and snatched the phone from the operator.

"Paul I'm on my way. Where is he? Are you within sight of him?"

"There's a squad car in pursuit with another not far behind. He won't escape."

Craven thought quickly, he needed to get back to his coordinates. Turning the car around, he sped straight toward the pursuing car.

"HE'S DRIVING STRAIGHT AT US!" screamed the driver. "OVER, OVER!"

The squad car swerved off the road and crashed into a large tree. The two policemen fell from the car as the siren whined down to an off-key wail. The two cops remained sprawled across the road as steam hissed from the radiator of the Citroën. The second car swung in alongside them.

"Are you okay?"

"I'm okay, stay with the Porsche. Inform headquarters that we are unable to pursue the son-of-a-bitch. I think Pierre is injured. Have an ambulance sent."

The second squad car now accelerated in the direction of the distant tail lights. Chevalier sped in the direction of the pursuing squad car; the ambulance could be seen in his rearview mirror.

"Paul, this is Claude. Where are you?"

"We're about ten kilometers from the last reported location of the Porsche."

"Call back to base. I want a helicopter. No questions asked. Tell them to get going, now."

Craven pushed the 911 into fifth gear. The odometer was registering two hundred and twenty kilometers per hour. He checked his coordinates looking for the location of the nearest doorway, but nothing showed on his screen. Ahead he saw a large farmhouse, with some kind of wheel turning alongside, probably a generator of some kind, he thought. He veered the Porsche onto a long driveway, killing the car's headlights, and using the gears to slow down so as to avoid the brake light glowing. The car was still traveling too fast.

Craven pulled on the hand brake. It slowed down to a safe thirty kilometers. He steered the Porsche toward the entrance of a large barn, he saw it was clear and drove inside. No lights. No police. He'd managed to shake off the squad car.

He sat in silence, listened to his heart beat, listened to the distant sirens. Not getting any closer. He felt relieved. His leg ached. Working the heavy clutch had caused the wound to open. It began bleeding again. He pushed the car door open, tumbled onto the ground. He felt the straw under him. It felt good and he lay there trying to regain strength. Sitting up, he propped himself back against the open door, removed his belt, and pulled it tightly around his thigh. Hopefully this tourniquet would help quell the bleeding.

Thoughts of making peace with his God flashed through Craven's mind. He pondered his condition. Thought about Angelica, how he'd dreamed of her, how longed to join her. Would she ever know what had happened to him, if he never returned to her world? He thought, *I mustn't think this way. I'll find the doorway. I'll get back. Our plans won't be messed up a mistake on my part.*

Chevalier linked up with the squad car, his siren cutting through the night air. The procession seemed comical; all headed in the same direction, yet nothing ahead of them. Chevalier reached for his phone. "This is Chevalier. Where's that helicopter?"

"It's about to leave the base now inspector."

Something niggled at him, seemed not quite right. The red car should have been spotted by now. Chevalier eased off the accelerator and came to a halt.

He turned off his lights and lit a cigarette, stepping from the car he paced a few meters along the road, listening to the sound of the distant sirens, the birds in the trees, sounds of the night. He kicked a stone along the roadside as he drifted in thought. He began to talk to himself, a habit he had when problem solving.

"This man's far smarter than we give him credit for. Come on Chevalier, what would you do in his place?" He paced a few more minutes. "Of course, I'd pull off the road, Wait 'till the police search had ended. I'd not be on the damned road, Claude you idiot, he's hiding in his Porsche."

The inspector slid back into the Ferrari and began a slow drive back down the long dark road, his headlights switched off, moving slowly, silently. He passed a farmhouse, music coming from the main cottage. He cruised on by, looking to see if there was any sign of a car in the driveway. Saw the old tractor, a work truck, a motorcycle. No Porsche. Continued on further.

"What am I doing? I'm wasting time," he mumbled to himself as he cruised slowly by each cottage and farmhouse along the roadway.

Craven struck his last match. Carefully raising it to his cigarette, the light of the match startled the pigeons nesting above him. The sudden rush of flapping wings caused Craven to balk, and he dropped the match, his cigarette remaining unlit. Chevalier slowed as the pigeons flew directly across the front of the Ferrari. He stopped the car, very quietly using his handbrake rather than engaging the foot brake, avoiding brake light glare. He leaned across the passenger's seat and peered through the window toward the barn. It was just thirty feet from him.

Craven cussed as the match died. He stretched toward the lighter in the Porsche, but couldn't reach it.

"Fuckin' pigeons," he mumbled as the birds noisily flew from the old barn. Sitting back into the driver's seat, he pushed the lighter into the socket, waited a few seconds, then took it and slowly raised it to the cigarette. His hand shook as he touched the lighter to the end of the cigarette.

He took a long deep breath, relaxing as he exhaled. His legs were cramping. He stretched out both legs under the tight dash, inadvertently depressing the clutch . . . and the brake. The barn glowed red as the taillight came to life.

Chevalier felt his pulse gathering speed. He exhaled deeply, breathed in, and quietly announced to himself, "It's you, by God, I've got you!"

He jumped from the car, weapon drawn, calling out, "This is the police. You're surrounded. Step out of the vehicle with your hands raised above your head."

Craven was now in unfamiliar territory. He'd never been

at the wrong end of a gun. His first instinct was to start the Porsche and drive forward, crash right on through the wooden back wall of the barn. There might be a truck or tractor sitting on the other side. Not a good idea he thought. Could even be a pond or dam somewhere ahead in the darkness. *Okay, first instinct - not good, I'm definitely on hold.*

Chevalier for a second time, but now shouting, "STEP OUT OF THE VEHICLE."

CHAPTER 27

CRAVEN OPENED THE DOOR, stepped from the car. He raised both hands. Chevalier started the Ferrari and slowly turned it toward the barn. Had Craven in his high beam lights, trapped like a deer in a spot light. The light blinded Travis as he limped slowly from the barn. He raised one hand across his eyes, tried shielding the glare, and tried seeing the face behind the headlights.

"Drop to the ground, now," Chevalier demanded as he stepped from the car. "I've no patience, even on a good day, this is far from a fuckin' good day." Chevalier seldom cussed, it had a certain ring to it. The French accent seemed to make it, hmm, cleaner, more socially acceptable.

Craven gingerly lowered himself to his knees, cringed as the belt around his thigh pulled tightly on the wound. He placed each hand into the dirt in front of him and hung his head. He took on the look of a dejected, defeated prey. Craven was cunningly playing his last card; he dropped to his side and feigned collapse.

Chevalier moved closer, pointing the gun at the motionless figure. "Don't move. I'll shoot you and save the state the expense of a trial."

Chevalier moved past the figure lying on the ground. Circling, he looked carefully into the barn, walked backward toward the Porsche, placed one hand onto the rear spoiler, patted it and said, "I've got you my beauty, like a trapped animal."

Not taking his eyes off Craven, he moved back to where the wounded man lay. He kicked dirt into Craven's face, causing him to squint and turn away. "You're not fooling anyone; now get to your feet . . . very slowly."

He raised himself, taking two full hands of dirt as he did. Chevalier moved closer and took the cuffs from his rear pocket.

"Put your hands behind your back," he said cautiously.

Craven placed closed fists behind him and waited for

Chevalier to step closer with the cuffs. Chevalier lowered the weapon and moved to place the cuffs on his captive. Craven made his move, flinging the dirt into the inspector's eyes.

Both men fell heavily as Craven threw his weight onto Chevalier. The gun fell onto the side of the dirt track as they struggled. Chevalier reached out, got one hand on the Glock, dragged it from the dirt, spun it round toward Craven, squeezed off a single shot.

Both men stood frozen, Chevalier looking at Craven, and Craven looked at the gun barrel. Nothing happened. Chevalier squeezed the trigger again, nothing. The mechanism was jammed. It was the dirt. Craven grinned, turned away and hobbled toward the barn. Chevalier stumbled in the poor light, allowing Craven precious seconds. Once inside the barn, he reached for the handle of a large pitchfork protruding from a hay stack.

He swung around. Chevalier was on top of him. The handle of the fork struck the inspector as he crowded in on Craven, knocking Chevalier to the ground. Craven re gripped the pitchfork, raised it above Chevalier's chest, readied himself, and froze as a voice called out: "Drop the fork! You're surrounded, we'll shoot!"

A floodlight added to the glare from the Ferrari's beam. Paul Laroche began to walk quickly toward the barn. Craven lowered the fork, still holding it in one hand. Chevalier lay motionless on the straw, not believing his luck. Laroche stepped into the barn, looking at Chevalier still lying at Craven's feet.

"Claude, this is Paul, are you . . ."

Before he could complete the sentence, Craven swung the pitchfork about and thrust it at Laroche.

The three spiked tongs impaled Laroche, his eyes bulged in shock and his mouth opening silently, a blood bubble forming on his lip. Paul Laroche slumped to his knees, his hands helplessly holding the handle of the fork.

He stayed in a kneeling position; Craven grabbed a hold of the fork, placed one foot onto Laroche and jerked the fork from his chest. Laroche remained motionless, as though frozen; the blood ran from the three chest wounds. Craven turned his back on the kneeling man, then in an instant, reeled about delivering a savage blow to Laroche's head with the heavy wooden handle of the pitchfork.

Chevalier tried to get to his knees. He cried out aloud, "NO, NO!"

Craven picked up Laroche's Glock and reeled toward Chevalier, pistol whipping the inspector.

Travis Craven dropped to the ground, crouching behind the body of Laroche. He took careful aim at the floodlight shining into the barn, fired four shots, killed the light. Waited for return fire. But the night was silent. Laroche had come alone.

Craven moved carefully toward the barn door, holding the gun outstretched, pointed in the direction of the Ferrari.

Chevalier slowly crawled toward the large stack of hay, slipped beneath its cover. He lay deadly still. Craven was preoccupied outside the barn. He moved toward the Ferrari, reached through the driver's window. Switched the motor off. If there were any police on the road, they'd go right on by. Craven hobbled to Laroche's Citroën, started the car, drove it to the rear of the barn, and threw the keys into the darkness.

Moving back to the barn, Craven began to feel faint. He stumbled across Laroche's body, falling clumsily against the Porsche. D it was impossible to see it in dropped the gun in the fall. Lost it in the darkness of the barn. Groping about on the straw covered ground, he scrambled about, desperately searching for the gun. It was there, his fingers tightened around the butt. With his free hand he grabbed hold of Laroche's arm. He dragged the body to the side.

In a boyish almost gay tone he said, "Inspector, are you there?"

"Come out, come out wherever you are. It's open season on inspectors. Don't make me any madder; I know you're in here someplace."

Craven kicked at the straw, raised the gun, pointed it at the large haystack and hesitated. He aimed at the haystack and squeezed the trigger. The hammer clicked, but the chamber was empty. Craven laughed. It was a crazy laugh that echoed through the large barn. "It mustn't be your time. We'll meet again, and you'll be mine. We'll live to fight another day, so until then my friend."

Painfully easing himself into the Porsche, Craven reversed the car from the barn, kept the lights off. Slowly, quietly he idled the car to the roadway. Back on the roadway he gunned the Porsche in the direction of Paris.

Claude Chevalier heard the Porsche roar into the distance. Bleeding from the blow to the head, crawled from under the straw. Attempted to stand, stumbled and fell back down, his balance feeling the concussion. He lay still for another minute. He crawled in the darkness, feeling the ground ahead with his hands. His hands felt something, a face, cold, not moving. He ran his hands along the body until he felt the form of something solid in the coat pocket. He took it out, hoped his guess was correct. Chevalier clicked the lighter. Laroche's glazed eyes reflected the flickering flame; the hand holding the lighter began shaking uncontrollably.

Chevalier doused the flame. He sat for minutes unable to stand, his head spinning, the sick rising in his throat.

"PAUL, PAUL!" He shouted, and the shouts subsided into an incoherent barrage of shaky sobs.

"Paul . . . Paul . . . Paul."

CHAPTER 28

I**T WAS A COLD** morning. Amy woke feeling extremely uncomfortable. Rick, Saffrey and Karen still slept soundly. She made her way to an adjoining room. Walked to the white table where more fruit and drinks had been placed.

"I'd kill for waffles and maple syrup," she said softly, scratching her fingers through her disheveled hair.

"Make mine French toast," Rick called from across the room.

"Hey," Amy replied softly.

"Hey Amy. I couldn't sleep, been out here since four thirty."

"Me too, just laying there thinking about all of this.'"

Rick stretched again, walked slowly toward Amy. He said, "Ya know kitten, it could be a lot worse. We could be in Cincinnati, or worse still Kansas." He grinned knowing Amy grew up on a typical Kansas farm.

"Us Totos aren't too bad," she replied grinning.

"What?"

"Where is it you grew up? Chico was it, huh?" She laughed, saying quietly beneath her breath "Fuckin' redneck."

Rick coughed, and faked a spluttering sound, "Hey I heard that little lady," he said in his best John Wayne accent. "Pass me a banana honey."

"If I eat one more banana I'll start swinging from the chandeliers, my body is on potassium high."

Rick was in fine style this morning. "Say sweet pea, what did you do for kicks back on the farm, chase Toto along the Yellow Brick Road?" Amy shined it on, ignored the comment.

"Ouch. The strong silent type, a dying breed, private school upbringing. Must be the nuns huh?"

She grinned. "Actually yes, and they warned us about boys like you."

Rick laughed, placed his arm around her shoulder, and

gave an affectionate squeeze.

Angelica couldn't understand why Craven hadn't returned. She depended on him to assist in the final plan for entering the Syntec Zone, for retrieving the I11 stones. Three days had passed since Craven had entered the doorway. Maybe he's met with an accident. Perhaps he's gone the way of Heinzman and Ramirez, decided to stay. *Not possible,* she thought. *We've planned this for far too long for that to happen..*

Angelica scheduled another meeting with the travelers. She entered with two white robed protectors, sat, turned to the two men and said quietly, "Please leave us now." They each bowed graciously and backed out of the room.

She spoke in a subdued voice. "Travis hasn't returned. I'm worried something's happened."

It was now clear the relationship between Angelica and Craven was deeper than it first looked. She bowed her head and placed a hand over her eyes, the tears of emotion ran down her face. "Please, we have to move ahead with my plans for entering the Zone. Hopefully Travis will return and join us on the mission.

"Angelica exactly how dangerous is this 'mission'?" Rick asked with a feeling inside telling him he wasn't going to like the answer.

"It'll not be without risk. The watchers are in full strength at the Zone. The stones are heavily guarded, and the original technology for the culturing is safeguarded deep inside the Zone."

"There's gotta be somethin' I'm missin' out on here," Rick replied. "This place is guarded by these watchers floatin' all about the fuckin' place?"

The group's last brush with the white ball was still firmly implanted in their minds.

Rick asked, "What d'ya have arranged to help get us into this Zone?"

"We've a plan of action involving several units. Each unit contains eight specialist exterminators. They're trained in neutralizing the watchers. The watchers can be immobilized with the appropriate weapons. The units have this weaponry."

Rick raised a hand. "Permission to speak," he said calmly. Angelica passed a glance in his direction, and nodded to him.

"If we're expected to accompany you into this 'Zone,'" he said making quotation marks in the air with his index fingers, "What guarantee do we have that we'll be safe, you know, that we're not gonna be massacred by those things?"

"Your presence isn't mandatory, but appreciated. I expect our departure from the Zone to be a brisk one. How safe remains to be seen. I feel your safety is fairly assured."

"Brisk huh?" Rick replied. "My image of our rapid departure with a bunch of stolen stones leaves me very unconvinced that our safety is anything but fuckin' assured."

Saffrey entered into the discussion. "If your people . . . your units . . . are so good, maybe our involvement will be just a token presence, not physical?"

Angelica smiled and nodded, "Yes, you'll not be called upon to endanger yourselves. The units will neutralize the watchers."

"Who controls the watchers?" Saffrey asked.

"They're programmed by the Supreme Master."

"Supreme Master, is that the Consort?"

"The Supreme Master is above all. The Consort, my father, was appointed by the Master."

"The watchers are his guys then?" Rick asked.

"Yes you could say that."

Rick stood and walked to the fruit tray. "Tell me Angelica, what's a guy gotta do to get a steak around here?"

Saffrey waved him off apologetically. "He's okay," he said chuckling. "He's due for his distemper shot. Take no notice of him."

Rick growled, showing his teeth. "When do you plan to go to the Zone?"

"I've been waiting for Travis. We'll give him until this evening. If he's not back, we'll proceed at first light."

"Where will the Master and Consort be during the time of the raid?"

"Tomorrow's the celebration of the Divinity, all of the council members and their subordinates will be present. It'll be our best opportunity to infiltrate the Zone. A distraction will be arranged. This'll pull the watchers away from our planned entry point."

CHAPTER 29

CRAVEN GUNNED THE PORSCHE toward the preset coordinates on the old farm road. As he drew nearer, the night air became colder, the closeness of the trees cooling the temperature a few degrees. Lights of the small farmhouses flickered by. The old truck that had carried the straw was parked in a driveway ahead. Craven slowed, recognized the truck. He smiled to himself, checked the positional screen, seeing the doorway entry point less than a half kilometer ahead.

There were no headlights behind him. Craven dropped the 911 into third gear, watched the tachometer climb to four thousand, and headed directly into the doorway.

Angelica stepped from the large glass building, her eyes wandering toward the re-entry area. The cones had been replaced with two gleaming silver towers, standing about three meters high. Technicians working on the re-entry coordinates had replaced the orange cones with permanent towers.

She strolled to a large tree surrounded by a well planned landscape. The water trickled from a small waterfall, down a brook, and into a pond. The large colored Koi splashed about as they saw her image standing above them. She reached into her pocket, brought out a small container of feed. Sprinkling some onto the pond caused the Koi to splash about even more furiously. The floating food was soon gone. Angelica sat and watched as the fish calmly swam from one end to the other.

The moon broke through the clouds, sending razor like beams scattering through the tree tops, the shards illuminated the hills with spotlighted patches. She smiled, thinking of better times; times she'd shared with Travis Craven, under the same moon, feeding the same Koi. She began sobbing at the thought, the thought she might never see him again.

The silence was shattered by the roar of the motor. The Porsche flew from the doorway. He dropped through fourth, then third, then second gear. It cruised to where Angelica was standing, excitement in her eyes. Craven jumped from the car, limped toward her and the two were locked in an embrace for several minutes.

"Travis, Travis, I've been so scared. Are you injured?"

"Just a leg wound. It's okay, it's okay. Just hold me."

She cried a little more, held him tightly, reassuring herself that he'd really returned.

"This is the last time my love. We won't be separated again. Our next journey's together."

They sat and discussed the plan for the next day's incursion, how a distraction would pull the watchers away from the Zone, how the specialist units would immobilize the watchers. If all went to plan, '*if*' being the operative word, they'd make their way through the doorway within hours of the incursion. Craven returned to the Porsche, parked it by the limousine, by the glass building.

*****

All four sat at the large breakfast table.

"I've a bad feeling about today," Karen said as Amy began working on a huge peach."

"Me too, not good," Rick said making a face. "Last time I felt this way, a doctor raised me up by the feet and spanked my ass."

Saffrey chuckled and walking toward the doorway said, "Any of you hear a car last night?"

All three shook their heads sideways as they devoured the morning's offering.

"I'm sure I heard a car," Saffrey repeated.

As they completed their morning snack, a frightening scream came from the main room.

"What the fuck is that?" Rick said.

Amy quickly stood. "Jesus what was it?"

"It came from the canister room," Karen whispered.

A voice began shouting, "He's escaped. Get a watcher, stop him!"

The door burst open as Quasimodo ran crazily through

the room, falling over the small table as he tried to escape from whatever was chasing him. From nowhere, a large white ball floated through the door, making its way toward the fallen escapee.

"THIS THING'S A BIG MOTHER . . ." Rick shouted as the white ball took in the small group. Moving toward Rick it hesitated then discharged a thin red beam of light sending Rick flying across the room and the remainder of the fruit spilling onto the floor.

Saffrey picked up an apple and threw it at the watcher in an effort to draw its focus way from Rick. It moved quickly to one side, the apple missed. The watcher shot off another light beam, and Saffrey found himself suspended two meters above the floor, his arms and legs flailing away like a floating astronaut.

Amy and Karen backed away in fear, moving toward the far wall. Saffrey fell to the floor with a thud. Slowly getting to his knees he motioned to the two girls to stay where they were. He moved to where Rick lay as the watcher was joined by a second ball.

"Rick, are you okay?" Saffrey asked.

"Just dazed, what the hell was that?"

"Some type of force field. Best we don't mess with these things. Let the units worry about the bastards."

Quasimodo began to gravitate, rising two meters above the floor. Blood from a head wound began to float around its head, not spilling to the floor as one would expect. The watchers stayed a few meters behind the floating man, guiding him as if by some remote power, until he was out of the room.

Angelica entered, showing a high level of distress not before seen in her rather controlled demeanor.

"We've a problem. The disfigured unit was meant to be our distraction. Its escape was supposed to take place later this morning, so the watchers would take chase. Now that it's been apprehended we must create a new distraction."

Travis Craven slowly walked into the room.

"Welcome back Craven," Saffrey said.

"Took me longer than expected, it's good to be back. We still have a problem, the missing stones. When we travel back to your time, I'll need them returned."

Saffrey saw this as a bargaining point, perhaps the only one they had to insure their safe return.

`"When we're all home safely we'll take you to the stones, agreed Craven?"

"Sure, agreed." Craven answered.

The plan for access to the Zone was not fully outlined to the four travelers. Best they could assume was they tag along, being ready to exit the doorway when Angelica and Craven were set. But what of the specialist units that assist in entering the Zone? Were they to be left at the mercy of the Consort and his Supreme Master? Is this how they were to be rewarded for assisting the Angelica and Craven?

Something didn't feel right. Saffrey and Rick went back to their quarters with the two girls.

"Rick, what do you feel about the plan and our involvement in it?"

"I don't like it. There's no plan B. I always feel better when there's a plan B."

"What do you say we put a plan B of our own into place, as insurance against any fuck up?"

"Got my vote," Rick replied. "Wha d'ya have in mind?"

"Have you noticed how the entry point to the doorway has been set in one location? I propose we quietly move the marker posts. This could buy us some valuable time in the event everything isn't kosher when we make our getaway. Right now all I want is to get us all the hell out of this place and back to familiar ground. The diamonds are not a set part of the equation."

Amy interrupted. "That might be okay for you, but Karen and I've discussed this, and we both agree we want the stones. We've gone through a lot the past week, and if they're offering stones, why not accept?"

Karen moved to Amy's side. "We're in agreement on this so don't even go there. We want what we're entitled to. After all, we've agreed to hand over the bad stones we've got stashed away back home."

Rick intervened. "Listen sis." He only ever called her "sis" when running short on patience. "If push comes to shove, we have to have priorities. Those priorities are getting' us all out safely and, if possible, getting' a hold of their technology for culturing the diamonds. If we can't take stones with us, why not learn to make our own? The whole thing is nothin' more than a fuckin' robbery by Angelica and her boyfriend. They don't need us. What's to stop them from eliminatin' us?"

"They need the stones we've hidden back home, right?" Amy said.

"Why?" asked Rick.

Karen took a deep breath, let it out slowly, and set about answering the question. "They've all the stones they need right here. They can take flawless stones from this "Zone" place. What do they want with the stones back home, the ones which have faulty timing censors inside them? It doesn't make sense."

All four sat in silence, a pseudo think tank.

"Come on, any suggestions? Time's of the essence," Saffrey said in a quiet tone.

"Quiet, someone's comin'," Rick said, looking toward the door.

Craven entered the room with three assistants carrying clothing and what appeared to be an assortment of weapons. He passed new outfits to each of the travelers.

"Put these on now." It was an order. "You'll each carry a neutralizer, this weapon de-activates the watchers. The neutralizer is also a formidable weapon if we need to use it for self defense. The weapon's effective to a distance of ten meters, beyond that they're ineffective."

Saffrey thought, *ten meters, that's about the length of a telegraph pole. Really good, this'll be fun.*

Craven demonstrated the trigger mechanism. Not too much to it, remove the safety, aim, shoot. Just be inside of ten meters before you point the weapon at the watcher and thoroughly piss him off.

"Oh goody," Rick quipped with a look of *'what the fuck?'* on his face.

"How many of these balls are floatin' around this place anyway?" Rick asked.

Craven ignored the question and began to leave the room. Saffrey moved to block the exit. Craven held up a hand as the three assistants moved in on Saffrey. "Let him be," Craven said gesturing to the three men to stand off.

"Fuck this!" Rick said. "I'm about done with all this mystery bullshit. Tell us what we need to know or you can forget about our cooperation."

Craven spun about, striking Rick with a solid blow to the head. Rick bounced back, throwing his full body weight into Craven. The three men moved quickly to pull the two apart.

"You son-of-a-bitch, we're not done, another time Craven."

Rick wiped the blood from his face as he stumbled away from Craven. Travis Craven brushed off his jacket and grinned at Rick. "Your temper had best be put into neutral, together with your mouth. And yes, we'll have another time and when that time comes I won't be as merciful."

Craven turned to the three men. "Take them to the tunnel. We'll get underway within the hour."

The three men escorted the travelers along a winding corridor, leading to a moving footway. The incline became steeper and the sound of machinery could be heard growing louder. When the footway came to a halt, three groups of guards emerged from a barrack type structure. There were eight men in each group. They were all armed with an assortment of weaponry.

The guards stepped onto the footway as it resumed its journey.

"So this is it, only thirty of us. Just fuckin' great," Rick said.

As the moving footway began to slow, Craven emerged from a larger tunnel. He was driving the Porsche and had Angelica by his side. Craven stepped from the car and moved toward Saffrey. He said, "This tunnel leads into the Zone. We should get in without any trouble. The difficult part will be the main security area. Most eyes will be on the Divinity procession taking place at midday outside the embassy building."

"What's the Divinity procession?" Saffrey asked.

"It's a blessing by the Supreme Master of the selected ones, those trusted to produce the stones. Most of the workers will be taking place in the annual procession. This is the one day of the year when the culturing refractory is virtually unguarded, except for the watchers."

Craven turned back to the smaller tunnel and called to the guard, "Bring the unit now."

A familiar shouting began as the guard dragged the Quasimodo being from out of the shadows.

"We've kidnapped our 'distraction.' Let's see if we can keep him this time."

The deformed body of the pitiful Quasimodo clearly upset Amy and Karen. This helpless being really had no idea of what was happening. He was totally childlike.

"How'd he get this way?" Amy asked Craven.

"He was an early victim of molecular transportation malfunction. This unit traveled through the doorway several times, but the last re-entry resulted in feature misalignment, both aesthetic and internal. His brain no longer functions normally. His ability to rationalize is no more than that of a child, or perhaps, of an animal."

"Have you tried to help him, or ain't he considered worth the effort?" Rick asked angrily.

"We've had some level of success with the mist chambers, but this unit has far greater misalignment than any other. He's been returned to the chamber several times, but his days are about to come to an end."

Quasimodo dropped to his knees, reaching out to Amy, stretching one hand, palm up in a begging gesture. He began to howl like a puppy, tears running from his eyes. His mouth pouted as though he were trying to speak.

"P P Please, help me," he slurred, almost indiscernibly, his eyes pleading directly at Amy. Amy tilted her head to one side and reached a hand toward his. Their fingers touched ever so lightly. Craven lunged forward and stomped a foot into the rib cage of the pleading man, sending him howling across the floor.

"NO, NO, STOP! Amy shouted as she rushed to protect him. Karen also moved to his aid and was pushed aside by the guard.

"HE'S A DEAD MAN, LET HIM BE!" Craven shouted. "He made one too many journeys in the red car. He was my predecessor. My 'master,' you might say. We all take the same risks. He took one too many. But he's got one last task to perform. He'll be our bait. He'll draw the watchers away from the culturing refractory. He won't die in vain.

CHAPTER 30

CHEVALIER CALLED IN TO the chopper, giving it the approximate location of the escaping Porsche.

Ten minutes later, the chopper touched down on the roadway. The Ferrari stood parked with its lights on high beam, making the landing a little less risky for the incoming chopper.

Four squad cars arrived at the same time with sirens still blaring amidst clouds of dust, and plenty of action. An ambulance pulled in quickly behind the squad cars and its rear doors flung open.

Chevalier stood slumped, leaning across the roof of the Ferrari and the two medics scurried toward him.

"No, no, I am okay. Go to the barn. Paul is inside."

"Inspector, you're wounded." The chopper pilot called.

"No, just a head wound, nothing too bad." He then slumped to the roadway, where he lay for several minutes. A medic quickly ran to his side and began to clean the wound. Another ran to retrieve a stretcher from the ambulance.

Chevalier placed a hand on the medic's arm.

"Is Paul . . .?"

"I'm sorry inspector. He's dead," interjected the medic." There was nothing we could do for him."

"Did anyone see the Porsche?"

Silence. Chevalier mustered every ounce of his energy, shouting at the top of his voice, "DID ANYONE SEE THE FUCKIN' PORSCHE?"

One cop stepped forward. "Nothing inspector, we covered all roads. It was nowhere to be found. We're conducting a door-to-door search of all farms, barns; anywhere a car can be hidden. We've called for more officers. We'll continue the search throughout the night."

Claude Chevalier was not a man who endeared himself to sympathy. The stretcher was waved off as he made his way to a squad car.

"Have one of your men drive the Ferrari back to the precinct. I will collect it tomorrow."

The squad car drove Chevalier back to his home. He walked unassisted to his door, reached slowly for his key and entered the house. Without turning he closed the door and fell onto the large sofa. He stayed there until the ringing of the phone woke him at six twenty."

"Chevalier." He answered in a tired *I'd really rather sleep* voice.

"Inspector Chevalier, sorry to be calling you at home. We went to a great deal of trouble to get this number. This is Adam McDowell of the U.S. embassy. I believe we're working on locating the same missing persons."

"Missing persons?" Chevalier replied. "To whom are you referring?"

"It's a long story. Can we meet with you today to discuss the case?"

"Certainly. Say at ten, in my office?"

"That'll do just fine," the voice said, with a distinct Texas drawl. "We'll see you then, thank you inspector."

Chevalier arrived at his office earlier than usual. He made a call to the wife of Paul Laroche, extending his condolences. She'd already been given the news the night before, and was being cared for by two special officers, one of whom had just completed a stay with a grieving Susan Penoir.

The knock on his door came at precisely ten o'clock. Chevalier tapped the cigarette on his desk, lit it slowly, looked at his wrist watch, and reclined in his chair.

"Enter," he said calmly.

Two men entered, one with a sort hairstyle and wearing a seventies style suit, the wide lapels definitely dating the jacket, the second, a younger more handsome man was tall with dark wavy hair, piercing blue eyes and wearing a more tailored suit, possibly Italian cut.

"Inspector I'm Adam McDowell," said the seventies man, handing him a business card. "This is Drew Blake. We're here to discuss four missing Americans. I believe you're after the same people."

Adam McDowell had recently been retired by the CIA. Circumstances surrounding his untimely departure remained classified. There were rumors, but no one in the Agency substantiated rumors. The CIA was a breeding ground for rumors. McDowell met Sam years earlier and the two had forged an associate type of friendship, both were in the so called spy industry, each had a distant respect for the other. They had each worked in the business during the Nixon era, each man had KGB dealings, off the record of course. The formation of the American Interpol Division was timely for both men. Sam offered Adam a position. McDowell liked the work. Liked it . . . but didn't need it.

Blake stepped forward and handed his card to Chevalier. The inspector didn't trust Americans, in particular those working under a diplomatic umbrella. He gave the two cards a quick glance.

"Tell me Mr. McDowell, how can the French police help you?"

"The embassy had a call from a hotel downtown. It seems four of its guests didn't return to their rooms last week. The hotel manager became suspicious when the beds weren't disturbed for a few nights. He found passports and luggage in their rooms. The passports belong to four Americans. We're concerned they've run into trouble. We ran their prints, cross referenced them with Interpol. It seems your guys also have their prints from another hotel, one where a trunk was carried from a room by three men wearing clown outfits."

"Interesting, do you have photographs of the four in question?"

McDowell reached into his coat pocket and handed Chevalier an envelope. He shook copies of four passport photographs onto the desk.

"Hmm, I've not seen these people. I might have someone who can identify them. Take a seat."

Chevalier reached for the desk phone and called to the

main desk.

"Lobrech, bring the prisoners from cell nine to my office. Have two officers accompany them. Have Philippe Bouvier enter first. The other two can wait in the hallway."

Chevalier opened the drawer of a nearby filing cabinet, withdrew a bundle of photographs, spreading them on the desk. He then placed the four photographs amongst them. The knock on his door was followed by his loud reply. "Enter."

Philippe Bouvier walked gingerly into the office.

"Come in Bouvier. Take a seat here." He motioned to a chair alongside the desk.

Philippe glanced at the two strangers seated across from him. He nodded politely at them. The two Americans remained expressionless.

"Bouvier take a look at these photographs. Tell me if you recognize any of them."

Philippe leaned forward, scanned the thirty or so head shots spread neatly across the desk top.

"Go ahead Bouvier; pick out those you think you've seen before."

His hand slowly reached forward, all three men watched, realizing this was a pivotal moment in identifying four key players. The first photograph was a scruffy bearded man, almost a double for Saddam Hussein. The two Americans looked at each other, then at Chevalier. Claude held his stare at Philippe.

"Are you sure you know this man?" he asked.

"I . . . I think so. He looks familiar."

McDowell snapped in, "Sure, he looks like fuckin' Saddam."

"Of course," Philippe replied. "How stupid of me, that's why I recognize him. I've seen him on television so many times. Wait, this one I've met." He reached for a photograph and pushed it toward Chevalier. "This is the one they called Rick, he's the one who gave the diamonds to Yves."

"Very good Bouvier. And the others?"

"Yes, this woman, and the one at the end, by the man with

the patch on his eye."

Chevalier placed a finger on the far photograph and said, "You mean this one?"

"Yes, they're the two women. One is called Karen, and I think the other is Mary."

"Amy," Blake interrupted.

"Of course, Amy," Philippe replied smiling at Blake.

"Thank you Bouvier. Please wait outside." He nodded at the cop by the door. "Bring in Ramone Flourette."

Ramone sat and took only minutes to select the three Americans from the assortment of head shots. Yves entered the room and also separated the three Americans from the mix of head shots.

"Thank you gentlemen," Chevalier said to the three. "You'll return to your cell. I'll speak with you later today." He nodded to Lobrech, who escorted all three men back to the cell block.

Once the three had departed, the two Americans turned curiously to Chevalier. "Inspector what's this about diamonds?" Blake asked.

"It's a long story, one that I've not quite figured out myself. Do you have any leads at all on the whereabouts of the Americans?"

"Nothing, we believe they were last seen getting into a limousine near the hotel," Blake said. "Four of them; the fourth is a former Navy SEAL named Saffrey Bell. He served with Rick Jones in Cambodia, both Purple Heart recipients. We believe the woman Karen is Jones's sister, same name on the passport. We also believe Amy Van Doran is the witness sought following an accident two weeks back where a red Porsche killed a tourist named Raoul Ramirez. No doubt you know about that, right inspector?" Blake asked.

"Of course, I personally looked into the incident, but we were unable to locate this witness, this Amy whatever."

Chevalier scratched at his forehead, deep in thought. "Tell me Mr. Blake. What does your department know about the red Porsche involved in the accident?"

"We've followed the car twice, but . . ."

Before Blake could continue, Chevalier interrupted. "You lost him each time correct?"

"Could say that, actually he . . ."

Blake paused, looking sideways at McDowell and said, "He just plain disappeared."

Chevalier laughed aloud. "That's ridiculous. Disappeared . . . how? Like he went 'poof!' and voila, he's gone?"

The Americans seemed to swallow hard, blushing. "That's about the size of it inspector," Blake said.

Chevalier knew exactly what they were saying, but decided to hold a few cards back. After all, he really felt he'd first claims on the driver of the Porsche. He owed him for Penoir and Laroche, and there was no way he'd allow some outside agency to get their hands on the Porsche driver, possibly offering him some kind of immunity or extradition. In fact, Chevalier had personally set his goals on apprehending the killer and disposing of him, at his leisure. As a cop with thirty years of service, he knew how the legal system had often robbed him of satisfaction. The ways of 'justice' were tailored for the rich, the celebrities, the privileged few, but not this time. Chevalier vowed he'd be personal executioner for this one. The Porsche driver would never see the inside of a prison cell. He knew it, Penoir and Laroche, God rest their souls both knew it.

CHAPTER 31

DREW BLAKE SAT PENSIVELY, running the story over repeatedly in his mind. He wasn't one to leave difficult tasks to others. He wasn't about to leave this one to the French police. It was almost noon. He'd made up a set of duplicate photographs of the four Americans. Now it would come down to good old fashioned door-knocking detective work. He started by calling on all restaurants within a mile of the hotel. No luck. The day was getting hotter. The workers were setting off from their offices, and traffic was building up.

Blake needed a break. He'd walked miles. No one recognized the photographs. His knowledge of French menus being less than limited, Blake decided to stop at McDonald's. The Mickey Dee's menu was home grown, easy, and besides, he really was fancying a shake and fries. He placed his order, sat at a small booth, pulled the head shots from his pocket, and stared frustratingly at them.

"Hey man, you're from the States right?"

The bleached haired girl was about twenty years of age. "I heard you place your order. Are you visiting Paris or working here?"

Blake smiled at the attractive girl. She was a pleasant deviation from his otherwise uneventful day.

"Actually I'm working and visiting. Name's Blake."

"How's it goin' Blake? I'm Julia, nice to meetcha."

"Likewise Julia, what brings you to Mc Donald's?"

"This is the only place in town I can get good old American burgers and fries, what else?"

Blake smiled. Perfect white teeth flashed at her. He was a stunning looking man, never had a problem with women. They were attracted to him, his sky blue eyes, his rugged bone structure, his aura, his fine wardrobe. He was definitely a ladies' man.

"Me too," Blake replied. "When in France, French fries." They both laughed. "Would you like to join me Julia? Please take a seat."

"Don't mind if I do, but I gotta get a soda. I'll be right back."

She returned a few minutes later.

"Can you watch my stuff? I'm off to the bathroom," Blake said.

When he returned, Julia was holding one of the head shots.

"These friends of yours?" she asked.

"Not really. They're people I'm trying to locate. Not having much luck I'm afraid."

She picked up another photograph. "These are Americans. I saw them in here about two weeks back. They sat right there. I overheard their conversation, heard the accents. They were waiting for someone, and I remember the looks on their faces when these two thug-looking guys came in."

"Thug-looking guys?" Blake asked.

"Yeah, but they went off to use the bathroom. Then this other guy, American too I think, came and joined them."

"Can you describe him?"

"Sure, tall with dark wavy hair, mid thirties, handsome guy. They left with him."

"Were they carrying anything?"

"Nope, not that I can remember, one of them, this one," she said, pointing to Rick. "He went to the bathroom. The others waited outside for him."

"How long was he in the bathroom?" Blake asked.

Julia pondered the question. "Only a short time, maybe for about a minute, not long enough to pee, just time enough to wash his hands."

"Julia, if you were to see a photograph of the guy that met with them, would you recognize him?"

"Are you a cop?" she asked abruptly.

"Kind of . . . like the FBI. Does it matter?"

"Guess not. Sure I'd recognize him. He was real cute. I recall seeing him once or twice before, once at Montmartre, and another time on the Champs Elysées. He was arguing with a cop over a parking ticket. He thinks he's hot shit in that Porsche of his."

Blake choked on his shake, spluttering as he blurted out, "Porsche, what color?"

"Red of course, is there any other?"

Julia smiled a matter-of-fact smile at Blake, who was wiping the milk from the front of his jacket.

"Don't suppose he got that ticket, huh?"

"Nope, I watched him smooth talk his way out of that one, real cool character. He handled that cop like putty in the hands of a sculptor."

"Damn," Blake snapped. "Was that the last time you saw him?"

"Yeah, I don't go around stalking guys in Porsches." She grinned. "But I'll ask a friend of mine who hangs in Montmartre quite a bit. She knows the 'in' crowd that lives in the bars up there. Mostly Americans hang out there, you know."

She made quotation marks in the air with her fingers as she spoke. She took a long overdue drag on her straw, raising her eyes to meet Blake's and smiling as she rolled the straw between her lips.

"This is probably a dumb question, is there any chance you'd recognize the cop who almost gave him the ticket?"

She gave him a blonde look, head tilted to one side. He took it as a '*duh, no*' reply.

"Sure, this is his beat. He always does the ticketing along that stretch of the Champs Elysées. Usually tourists stopping to take shots of the Arc de Triomphe."

"Julia I love you, just love you," Blake snapped, beaming a wider smile than usual.

She grinned at him, replying with a girlish smile, "Hmm American men. I've missed their subtlety."

Drew Blake felt as though he'd won the lottery. *What a stroke of luck,* he thought as he drove back to his Hotel on the South Bank. *This girl just happened to be at McDonald's, the same one the missing four had eaten at. Jesus* Blake thought, *a million to one chance.*

He arranged to meet with Julia for drinks. They planned

to get together at a small restaurant in Montmartre, the *in place*, as she referred to it, for many expatriate Americans. Drew called a cab, knowing the parking in that part of town to be nonexistent. The cab swung up the cobblestone street. There were tourists jamming the roadway, small coffee shops brimming with life, and lots of cigarette smoke.

Edith Piaf impersonators seemed to be doing their best versions of La Vie en Rose in at least three of the cafés as the cab slowly rattled by, the suspension groaning as it struggled to survive the uneven stone roadway.

The taxi driver squinted into the rearview mirror, took one long last drag on his cigarette, expelling the smoke as a never ending stream of pollution.

"Here's the restaurant monsieur. That'll be twenty-two euros."

Blake reached into his jacket, a finely tailored Armani, and passed the notes to the driver. He handed him three ten dollar bills.

"These are dollars monsieur."

"Sure, there are thirty of them. Keep the change."

The Frenchman gave a shrug of the shoulders and a look of disgust. "Why can't you Americans be more French when you are in our country?"

He said *French* as though it was the divine nationality. Blake thought about his grandfather who as a young man had lost a leg fighting in France during the war.

"Ah excuse me," he replied in a defensive tone, yet with a smidgeon of sarcasm, a trait at which Drew Blake was a master. "Why can't you French be more polite when you're in any country? Oh and by the way, use the change to buy some deodorant, or maybe on second thought, put it toward an attitude transplant. Have a pleasant fuckin' evening, Francois."

Blake stepped from the cab, the driver accelerating off as the cab door was on its way to slamming shut. He watched as the driver weaved his way through the burgeoning street crowd, watching until the tail lights melted into streetlights and reflectors along the roadway.

He stewed for a few minutes, dusted off his jacket which now smelled of cigarette smoke. He strolled along the rue de la Bonne, making his way toward the rue du Chevalier. He passed the *Sacré Cœur*, wandering aimlessly until reaching the *Place du Tertre* in the heart of Montmartre. The artists were busily sketching smiling tourists. Oil paintings depicting French landmarks abounded, some reminiscent of French street scenes. They were all mass produced in Asia, exported to France, a French signature added, and *voila*! One French original work of art for the unsuspecting tourist.

Blake looked at his watch, ten minutes before eight, ten minutes before his meeting with Julia. He asked the painting vendor directions to the small cabaret.

"Ah yes monsieur, *Au Lapin Agile*."

Au Lapin Agile is a historic nightclub dating back to the nineteenth century and is frequented by intellects and artists, making it a prime meeting place for Americans. It was easy to spot, with a large painting of a humoristic rabbit adorning its outside wall. The air hung heavy with cigarette smoke, the ever present incense of Paris. Blake carved a passage through the fog, finally sitting at a small table at one side of the stage. The waiter approached him and asked in French, "Would you like a drink monsieur?"

Blake apologized and using his best French answered, "I'm sorry, I do not speak French."

The waiter mumbled to himself, strutting away from the table.

"Hey stranger," the voice called from the table a few meters from where he sat.

"Thank God Julia, can you handle the waiter? He doesn't speak any English."

"Of course he does." She laughed. "The French don't like admitting they can understand English. They want you to have to understand French. Try putting a few bills on the table and ask him if it's a tip left behind by the previous patron. His English will improve real fast."

"Point taken." Blake grinned. "Were you able to contact

your friend . . . what's her name again?"

"Sure her name's Camile. She should be here soon. I mentioned you were after the driver of the red Porsche. She told me he often visited Au Lapin. She once sat with him for drinks. I think she might even have dated him."

Blake was feeling extra lucky. It was a good night to be a special agent, he thought. He also considered letting Chevalier in on his progress, but maybe that would be politically incorrect, or would it be? Then he thought to himself, *Nah, fuckin' French, won't call him unless I really have to.*

CHAPTER 32

CAMILE ARRIVED, WAVED TO Julie, walked to her table. She was a happy girl on first impression. Her smile was warm, memorable. Her English was heavily accented, a hybrid French-Italian that caused her lips to pout as she struggled to pronounce his name. She smiled at Blake and said, "Drew Blake?"

He'd never heard his name spoken with such appeal, such savoir faire, such allure. He nodded, said "Camile, thanks for joining us." He slid her chair from the table, ever the gentleman.

"*Merci monsieur*. Oh I'm sorry; I will only use English, thank you."

Before sitting, she leaned to Julia, exchanged the customary French air-kiss. She sat alongside Julia and Blake wondered if there was an arbitrary period before he too qualified for that French greeting. They ordered croissants and coffee.

"It is too early for spirits," Camile said coyly. "Perhaps a little later."

Blake smiled. He thought, *hmm later*. He spread crème onto the croissant. The coffee was thick, black, and very strong and it complimented the pastry.

"You want to know about Travis?" she said as Blake took a large bite of the croissant. He almost choked, trying desperately to wash the overly full mouthful down with a too large swig of coffee, coffee far too hot to drink any time this side of midnight. He reeled as the coffee hit the walls of his mouth, tears swelled in his eyes. Remaining cool under fire was one of Blake's strongest attributes. He swallowed hard, reached for the pitcher of water on the adjoining table. He poured the water into an empty wine glass, showing great relief as the temperature inside his throat simmered.

The two girls chatted between themselves, allowing Blake time to recompose his demeanor. *How thoughtful of them*, he thought, *letting me suffer in silence, pretending not to notice.*

"Tell me about this guy Travis."

"He visits Paris often. He says he is in the import-export business."

"Where'd you first meet this guy?"

Camile took a slow sip of her coffee, raising her eyes to meet his. She grinned and said, "The coffee is very hot, no?"

"Yeah just a tad hot," he replied embarrassingly.

He said, "It goes well with the croissant." Then smiling she added, "And a pitcher of water."

He returned the smile and repeated the question, "Where'd you first meet Travis?"

"At the Hotel du Louvre in Paris. He was a guest there. He was attending a jewelers' convention about five months ago."

"Were you there on business Camile?"

"No, just admiring the jewelry, a girl's best friend you know."

"Did he give you a last name?"

"Just Travis, I am not sure but that may have been his last name. I am not certain."

"Can you describe him?"

"Of course, but I also have a photograph of us together."

Blake sat up quickly, eyes very alert. He said in a shocked tone, "A photograph, how the hell did you get a photograph?"

She passed a wise look at Blake, the kind of look a mother gives a child when she knows . . . when she just knows *everything*.

"My friend is a photographer. He visits all the restaurants taking photographs of the tourists, lovers, you know what I mean. He was in the cabaret one night when Travis was here sitting with me. He asked if we would like our photographs taken. Travis told him to let us be. My friend said he would take the photograph for free, just for me, you understand, but Travis insisted he go away. My friend got upset with him, so he took a picture from across the floor, with a new lens he was testing. He gave me the photograph the next day."

"Does Travis know you've got a photograph?"

"No. I thought he might be married. Perhaps that was the reason he did not want a photograph taken."

"Camile you're an angel. Where is the photo? Can I see the it?"

"I brought it along with me. Julia told me you were looking for him, so I brought it along."

"Brilliant. Clever girl, can I see it?"

Camile opened her wallet and passed the color photograph to Blake.

"Well, well, well, so this is the notorious disappearing Scarlet Pimpernel." Blake smiled at the girl. "You look great in the photo Camile."

CHAPTER 33

THE THREE SAT AND finished their coffee, Julia conveniently excusing herself to visit with a group of friends at a far table.

Blake asked, "Did you see the car he was driving?"

"Yes he drove me to my place one evening. It was very fast."

"What did he talk about?"

"I asked him about his business. He told me he imported diamonds. I must have shown disbelief when he said it. He had an attaché case with him in the trunk of the Porsche. He asked if I'd like to see a collection of diamonds. We went to my room and he brought the stones with him to show me."

"He took the diamonds up to your room? Didn't you think this was dangerous, inviting him to your room?"

"Please Drew, I am a big girl. I know when it is dangerous to go with a man to my room."

"Sorry Camile. So you went to your room, what happened then?"

"Travis opened the case, and inside there was a small box containing diamonds. They were all big and beautiful. He let me look through the stones."

"What did he tell you about the stones? Did he say where they came from?"

"I asked if they were from South Africa, just because that is where I thought most diamonds came from. He did not answer. He asked me what hobbies I had, if I collected artwork. I showed him some photographs of a painting I have recently completed."

Blake studied her expressions, her pouting lips, the way she pronounced words, words like - confused. *Her lips pout perfectly* he thought. *They'd fit nicely onto mine, very nicely.* The age difference of around fifteen years was hardly a dissuader.

"Hold it!" he snapped as though a light bulb went off in his brain "Did he handle the photographs of the painting?"

"He handled them as he studied them. Why?"

"His prints, they're still on the photos? You still have them at your place right? Please say you do."

"Of course, I placed them back into the box where I keep all my photographs." She looked at her watch and said, "It is getting late. I must be going." She began to stand and said, "Would you like to come back to my place to see the photographs, and maybe have one more coffee? It isn't too far from here."

Blake wasn't ready for this brazen request but, once again, ever the gentleman, he accepted her offer, *maybe it's more than just an offer for coffee* he thought, *or it might be just a friendly gesture*. Whichever way it went he was only too thrilled to spend as much time as possible with Camile.

Julia waved goodbye as the couple left the cabaret and she mouthed the words, "I'll call you tomorrow." Camile nodded, winking back at Julia as they weaved their way between the tables, heading to the exit. The outside air was clear and invigorating, a welcome escape from the smoky haze of Au Lapin.

The cab ride to Camile's was uneventful. A conversation between the driver and Camile served to remind Blake that his high school decision to study Latin rather than French was not one of his wiser choices.

CHAPTER 34

DREW BLAKE LEFT CAMILE'S at first light. She'd made fresh coffee, bacon and eggs. Blake was a happy man. All was well in his world. He was undecided on his next move regarding Travis. He had a photograph, a name and possible fingerprints. He headed directly back to the U.S. embassy. He needed to brief McDowell on his progress. Camile's photographs went to the lab where the prints were successfully lifted from the surface of the photographs. McDowell listened intently as Blake ran through the previous night's events.

McDowell tapped away at his desk with a long yellow pencil. He said, "There're a few things about this case I held back from you. I think it's time to give you the whole enchilada."

"Held back huh? Fuckin' lovely. Okay, so tell me."

"About two weeks back, the embassy had a call about some guy offering a highly advanced type of neutron device to the major powers, to the highest bidder in fact. Our Russian friends turned up at a meeting along with two of our operatives. The meeting was in a jewelry store."

"The same place where the eight charred bodies were found?"

"You got it; we've kept a lid on it, not really knowing where to take it next. We know there've been air drops off New Orleans. Some group calling themselves Boleros. We've had some of our guys shadowing the operation down there. You ever heard of anyone mention black boats?"

"Black boats huh. No, can't say that I have."

"These black boats make pickups out in the bay off of New Orleans, the DEA crews are on it, but word on the street is there could be more to it than straight out drugs."

"Do you think the Porsche boy, this Travis, and his diamonds can be tied in with the black boats?"

"Not sure, but his prints, the ones on the photos, well, they match with prints from the Charvon pawn shop downtown."

Blake, a non-smoker, reached across to a silver cigarette case. It had McDowell's initials engraved in Gothic lettering on the lid.

"Can I?"

"Be my guest. If they don't kill you, the transient smoke in this fuckin' city will."

Blake pulled a cigarette from the case. McDowell reached across the desk and lit the tip. He inhaled cautiously, held the smoke deep inside, then coughed profusely. When he'd regained composure he said, "A meeting at the jeweler's shop, black boats in New Orleans, what was it, a neutral device?" McDowell corrected him, said "Neutron, a neutron devise."

"Yeah whatever. And eight burned bodies, no other damage, hmm. If I recall my science studies, I believe neutron devices destroy living things but don't fuck up the surroundings. You heard that?"

"Yeah, in fact what tipped us off to a connection between Paris and New Orleans was when one of the black boats drifted crewless off the coast of New Orleans; there were three charred bodies on board. No damage, no evidence of drugs. That discovery threw a monkey wrench into the DEA boys' theory of drug smuggling. Set back the whole fuckin' operation, until these fires started in Paris, exactly the same scene, same type of deaths." McDowell slid an ashtray across to Blake. "Whatever took out the victims in the jewelry store and the black boat was far more specific and advanced than anything we have. Needless to say our people are creaming their jeans to get a hold on whatever the fuck this technology is."

Blake asked, "Have the French or New Orleans cops been briefed on this?"

"No, this French cop Chevalier, the guy we met downtown, he's come close to figuring out part of it, clever fuck for a frog."

Blake was surprised to hear McDowell display any anti-French emotion. He coughed out a mouthful of smoke.

"Sorry Drew, I get a little testy now and then. Seems the sharing of information between us and them is a one way fuckin' street. We don't see any reason to change that. What we know stays with us, fuck 'em."

"I'm thinking about the three guys the French cop has locked away. We need to show them this photo."

"Don't know what to tell you. We just don't want to involve the French any more than necessary."

"Way I see it, and believe me, I'd rather handle it interdepartmentally myself, but we need this Chevalier guy. He's been to each of the crime scene locations. He lost two of his top men this week trying to snag this fucker." He tapped on the photo as he spoke. "I believe he's got far more than an official interest in tracking this guy down. If it's more personal than *by the book*, he could work in our favor."

"You got a point. Let me think it over. I'll call you later today on your cell, okay?"

"By the way, who's been following the New Orleans side of all this?" Blake asked.

"We've got a pretty hot shot guy there. His name's Palmer, heard of him?"

"Palmer huh, yeah I think we met at a Christmas bash a few years back."

They discussed Palmer for a few minutes. When Blake left the embassy office he kept chewing over the evidence, the connections between Travis, the Porsche, the diamonds, the burned victims, the neutron theory, the missing Americans, the clowns carrying the body from the hotel, and now . . . the New Orleans incident.

Chevalier answered his phone on the second ring, holding his morning coffee in one hand.

"Inspector this is Drew Blake, we met . . ."

"Yes Mr. Blake, what can I do for you?"

"This might seem a bit out of order, but I'd like to meet with you, off the record, to discuss a mutual friend."

"A mutual friend, I wasn't aware we had a *mutual friend*."

"It's about the Porsche, the one we've been unable to throw a net over."

"So?" Chevalier paused, choosing his words as though each was costing him a user's fee. "So tell me, why is this, eh, as you said, *off the record?*"

"It's in both our interests to find the driver of the red car, don't you agree?"

"But of course," Chevalier replied, somewhat apprehensively.

"Can you meet me in an hour?" Blake asked.

Chevalier nodded, remaining silent.

"Inspector . . . you still there?"

Chevalier realized Blake had missed the nod.

"Yes, yes, yes, of course. I apologize, too much thinking. In one hour, that's fine. Where do you wish to meet?"

Blake said, "In the lobby of the *Castille Sofitel Demeure on rue Cambon.* Is this okay for you?"

"I will be there Mr. Blake."

"And please inspector, come alone."

"Of course," Chevalier replied.

Blake repeated the words to himself, *Castille Sofitel Demeure,* he imagined Camile saying the word 'Demeure', how her perfect lips would form a pout as the word rolled out, *'Demeure.'*

The Ferrari pulled into the hotel, Chevalier's curiosity was peaked as to why Blake was acting so secretive, so *off the record* as he'd said. The lobby was warm. Blake sat on a sofa across from the reception area. He flicked through a *Perfect Parenting* magazine, the only English magazine he could find in the rack.

"Mr. Blake." Chevalier extended his hand.

Blake stood. Both men shook hands, no cheek-to-cheek greetings for Blake. *Whew,* he thought, *what a fuckin' relief.* He'd wondered if the inspector would extend his hand instead of puckered lips. *Good start*, he thought.

"Inspector this meeting never took place, do you get my drift?"

"Get your drift?" Chevalier repeated inquisitively.

"Sorry. What I mean to say is well, we never had this meeting, you understand?"

"We've already established this fact. What is it you wish to discuss Mr. Blake?"

"I'm prepared to break with departmental protocol. How do you feel about us pooling our information, working together to nail this Porsche driver, without the book, none of the departmental bullshit?"

"Whatever it takes, I want him in my clutches," Chevalier replied. "He killed two of my closest friends. I want him."

Blake thought about the cards he was holding close to his chest. *Should I lay them all out for this guy to see?*

"I've a contact who's met the driver. In fact, she's given me a photograph. If we can get a positive ID from the three guys you're holding, we can pool our resources and nail this son-of-a-bitch. What do you say?"

"Can I see the photograph?"

He held the colored snapshot in both hands, for a fleeting moment he sensed he had some form of recognition, tilted his head, though about it . . . *nah, crazy*. For twenty long seconds he stared at it as though it were alive, made a comment that completely caught Blake off guard. "So you are the mother-fucker." The cussing had certain quaintness about it when delivered with a French accent, almost a tone of acceptability.

"Got that right, he's definitely *the mother-fucker* we're both after."

"Do you have a name for him?"

"Travis." Blake went a little further. "What do you know about diamonds, stones connected with the fire victims?"

Chevalier decided it was smoke time. He pulled a packet of Gauloise from his coat pocket, offering one to Blake.

"No thanks, those things'll kill you."

Chevalier smirked as he placed one into the corner of his mouth. "Ah my friend, there's nothing in this world as unique as a French cigarette."

"You got that fuckin' right," Blake quickly remarked with a smirk, "Their definitely unique."

The inspector continued. "There was a diamond at each

crime scene, but it vanished in a flash of light, and the persons near the flash were incinerated. What we cannot understand is why there is no damage to the surroundings."

"Do you know of any Frenchmen with New Orleans crime interests?"

"New Orleans? Not that I'm immediately aware of, why do you ask?"

"Not sure myself, just a hunch, we'll leave that one on the back burner. I'll let you know when I know more myself."

The inspector gave him a quizzical expression, clearly confused by the reference to any activity outside of his jurisdiction.

"You got any leads on the four missing Americans?" Blake asked.

"No, all we have is that they gave the stones to the clowns at the hotel, Yves and his three assistants. The clowns passed one stones on to Michelle du Blanc and one to the pawn shop owner. The American's gave one to the du Mauriers. Charvon's stone then found its way to the jeweler's shop."

"Inspector, the call to our embassy was from a man with an American accent. Weren't all of the staff at the jeweler's French?"

"This is true but that doesn't preclude another party from setting up the meeting."

"Travis could have set it up, don't you think?"

Chevalier raised his eyes slowly to meet Blake's. "Are you saying he actually did set it up, or he might have set it up?"

"I've got it from a good source that Travis was in Paris a few months back for a jewelry convention. He possibly uses a cover as a diamond trader."

"Your source of information, is it reliable?"

"She slept with him. Guess that makes her intimately reliable."

"Not necessarily, in Paris that'd still classify her as a passing observer."

Chevalier chuckled. Blake smiled. Thunder pounded overhead and the lights flickered. Both men instinctively bobbed their heads, as though the lightening were about to rip through the hotel roof and strike them.

Chevalier was first to return to a comfortable position. "Ah the Paris spring showers, simply delightful." He smiled and reached across the table to grind the cigarette butt into the glass ashtray.

There was another flash and more flickering light, followed by a clap of thunder, the rain beating on the hotel windows. Both men were clearly using the distraction as a means to gather their thoughts. It had become a dry conversation.

"Cognac, Mr. Blake?" Chevalier asked.

"Thank you yes," Blake replied. "Call me Drew."

"Call me Claude."

"Claude," Blake said raising the snifter, a toasting gesture.

Chevalier said, "Here is to us and success in our joint endeavor." The glasses clinked and the cognac swished about the inside of the snifters as both men relaxed in what appeared to be a newfound alliance.

Chevalier again picked up the photograph of Travis.

"Drew, tell me, the girl in the picture, is she the *intimately reliable source*?"

"Yeah, not too bad either huh?"

"Lucky man, but his luck's about to come to an end," Chevalier said passing the photograph back to Blake.

"Let's return to my office. It's time to confront our three clowns."

The two men rode together in the Ferrari. Blake was amply impressed by the Testa Rosa.

"Son-of-a-bitch, is this standard issue for French police inspectors?" Blake asked as the Ferrari shot along the roadway. Chevalier was well accustomed to snide remarks regarding his excesses.

"I'm also an established artist. I've been fortunate that my works appeal to collectors of inexhaustible means. Perhaps one day you'll allow me to show you some of my recent canvases?"

Blake was impressed. "I'd like that. I've always appreciated fine artwork. The French masters are among my favorites."

Chevalier looked sideways at Blake. The American had struck a cord, a good one.

CHAPTER 35

THE WATCHER FLOATED IN front of the large steel doors marking the entry to the Zone. Two of the special-forces guards approached the watcher, their weapons hidden. From around the corner of the building another watcher unexpectedly appeared. It moved rapidly toward the two men. The two men reached behind their backs, each placing his hand on his weapon. The watcher nearest the two men immediately blasted a red beam of light. It struck the nearest man, passed through him and struck the other man. Both fell to the ground, clutching at their chests.

"Saff, can't we help 'em?" Rick asked in a panic.

"Not without knowing what we're up against. Look at those dead guys, and they knew what to expect, didn't do them much fuckin' good."

Craven stood rigid. He spoke slowly and distinctly, his lips barely moving. "Angelica, do this very slowly: Place a neutralizer behind your back. Make your way over to me. No fast movements."

Angelica looked at Rick and Saffrey. Karen and Amy remained hidden away crouched behind the three.

"What are you going to do Saff?" Karen asked.

"Do? Not a thing. Not yet, let's wait and see which way the wind blows."

The special units were slowly moving around the watchers, contemplating their next move. Rick counted twenty-two men, more than sufficient to handle any situation, he thought, if they could just get within range.

Angelica walked to join Travis. She stood in front of him, her back close to his hands. Travis slowly removed the weapon from her belt. Just a few meters separated him and the two watchers. The watchers knew they'd allowed these two intruders to get inside of their safety zone, to be inside the strike range.

"When I tell you, I want you to drop to the ground, do it very quickly understand?" Angelica nodded slowly. "Here we go," he whispered. Then he said, "Drop."

Angelica was on the ground, and in a flash Craven fired the weapon at the nearest watcher and then at the other. Both watchers dissolved into a strange slimy liquid, both of them oozing to the ground, reminiscent of a Salvador Dalí painting.

The goo-like mess spread across the floor. Craven quickly stepped back.

"Don't step in this stuff. It'll eat through your shoes and spread through your body like acid."

"I guess that warning is for our benefit," Rick said.

"Don't want to ruin a good pair of Reeboks," Karen chipped in.

Craven reached for the door lock, placed a small plastic card inside of it and stepped back. After a muffled thud the door opened.

"Quickly, this way," he ordered. The twenty or so guards scurried inside the building, each jumping quickly over the remains of the two watchers. Angelica dusted off her white gown, then looked at Craven who was stripping down to reveal some type of uniform. After he'd removed the white gown, he brushed off the trousers.

"Christ Saff, that's a French cop's uniform. What the fuck's goin' on?"

Angelica had taken off her robes. Her body was trim, as though she'd worked out, Saffrey and Rick looked at each other. Karen glanced at her brother and rolled her eyes.

"You're lookin' fit Angelica," Rick quipped. "Work out do ya?"

Craven flashed a *keep your distance* look at Rick.

Saffrey interrupted the moment. "Rick's an admirer of the arts. I'm sure he meant that in a respectful way, right Rick?"

"Absolutely," Rick chuckled. "In the *most* respectful fuckin' way."

The uniformed men moved forward, crouching occasionally as if expecting more resistance to appear.

"How far into this place before you reach the mother lode?" Rick asked.

"Just keep up with us. I don't want to be coming back to rescue you four," Craven snapped back at Rick. The group moved onward, Quasimodo being prodded along between two guards. Karen and Amy lagged behind. Within minutes it seemed the spearhead had gotten at least fifty meters ahead of the two girls. From a side passage a watcher suddenly emerged. It didn't see the two women. They pushed themselves against the wall, hoping the watcher wouldn't turn around. Amy wanted to scream, to warn the others. Karen sensing this quickly placed her hand across Amy's mouth and placed a finger on her own lips.

"Stay quiet, we can't call out. It'll turn on us, and we've no protection."

"What can we do?" Amy whispered.

"We can go back to the entrance. The two guards the watchers killed, their guns are still back there."

The two girls quickly moved back down the long tunnel. When they reached the entrance, the weapons were where they'd been dropped right by the two dead guards.

"Thank God," Amy said as she passed one to Karen.

"Let's get back to the guys. They can use our help."

In her rush to re-enter the building, Karen tripped on the guard's body, she stretched one hand out to break the fall. It slipped along the ground as she landed, the hand slid into the slimy remains of the dead watcher. She pulled her hand back, flicked the slime from her fingers and began wiping furiously as she tried to get the mess off of her skin. The stinging became unbearable. She started sobbing the words "Oh my God, oh my God, oh my God!"

"Karen . . . Karen are you all right? Wipe it off quickly!" Amy pleaded as she too began wiping Karen's wrist.

"I don't want to die. I don't want to die here. Help me, please help me."

CHAPTER 36

KAREN SANK TO THE ground. The skin on her hand began to sizzle, to smoke. There was a smell of acid on flesh, and the decaying began to spread along her arm. Karen could do nothing but stare in pain at the spreading cancer-like mass engulfing her arm, now almost to the elbow.

Amy sprang to her feet, stood a meter from Karen, aimed the weapon at the arm and fired. The arm came off at the elbow. Karen passed out. Amy removed her belt and tightly wrapped a tourniquet around the stump. The bleeding seemed to be slowed by the heat of the blast. The beam had cauterized effect the wound.

"Karen - Karen wake up! It's over."

Not quite knowing what reaction to expect from Karen, Amy covered her arm with the discarded white robe left by Craven. Karen's voice was weak, shaky. She whispered, "Amy? Amy, are you there?"

"I'm here Karen, I'm here."

"My arm hurts, it really hurts. What happened? That stuff on my arm, has it gone?"

"It was spreading along your arm, I thought it was going to cover your whole body, I did the only thing I could think of to save you."

Karen raised her hand, went to place it on Amy's leg, but the hand wasn't there. The white gown hung over the remains of her arm. Karen stared, frozen. She opened her mouth, and Amy placed her one hand across it, muffling the scream that blasted from it. The tears flowed and Karen fainted into blackness.

Rick turned slowly, something was wrong. He hadn't heard the girls for a while. As he turned, the watcher closed in.

"LOOK OUT!" Rick shouted. Craven reeled about, quickly firing off two rounds. The watcher zigzagged, avoiding the red beams as they zapped past. Rick lay flat on the ground. He looked back, thinking, *where are the girls? They should've been right behind us.*

Craven and a group of his accomplices began rapid fire at the watcher. It ruptured, began to melt, oozing slime a meter from where Rick lay. Rick rolled to his left, calling aloud to Saffrey.

"The girls, they're gone. I'm goin' back to find them."

"Go ahead; I'll stay with the group. Be careful."

Rick back tracked; found the two girls huddled in a quiet passageway. The severed forearm lay on the ground beside them. He stared at the limb, couldn't just leave it there. Ripped a large section off of a white gown, wrapped it around the limb and scooped it up. He lifted Karen and prodded the semi stunned Amy, moving them into the passageway.

"Come on Amy faster," he said stumbling along, straining under the lifeless weight of Karen's limp body."

"Why'd you bring the arm?" Amy asked.

"Christ knows, at the time it seemed like the thing to do, couldn't just leave the fuckin' thing there. It's a part of her ya know."

The sound of humming came from another passageway off to one end of the room. Craven pointed in the direction of the sound. "That's the main refractory. That's where the stones are produced and stored. That's our objective." Saffrey glanced in the direction Craven had pointed. "It might be guarded, although most of the regular watchers will be at the Divinity celebration in the main square."

Craven gathered the group around him, gave instructions, he looked just like a quarterback calling a game play. Three of the men moved off to the right. The remainder split into two groups and headed toward the humming sound. Craven turned to Saffrey, motioning with one hand for him to follow. As he did, he realized the girls and Rick were missing.

"Where're your friends?"

"Don't know. The girls were separated from us. Rick went back to find 'em."

"Don't you realize we can't close the doorway unless all matter that entered through it is removed through that same doorway?"

This confused Saffrey. He took it in slowly, thought about it, and said to Angelica, "What he's saying is that without all of us, you can't leave this place. You can be poled and followed, same as Ramirez, you can be found. But if we all go out, Craven can seal off the doorway. Is that it?"

"Yes that's correct. We can't be traced as long as you're *all* returned. No one can stay behind. All molecular forms must exit exactly the same as they were teleported in. We can then seal off the only way we can be followed. Those coordinates will become inoperative. We'll be safe," Angelica replied.

"We must take all four of you with us, dead or alive, but either way, you'll leave in the same form as you entered. Travis can terminate the coordinates to that doorway. Others can be opened, but that'll take any follower's quite a deal of time. They can't follow along the same pathway. They might exit in another place, a great distance from where we exit the doorway."

It was becoming a little clearer. Craven and Angelica needed the four travelers. They needed them as tickets to freedom. Without them the Consort could send other units to pole the two runners. Send them as though they're on a railway track, along the exact same coordinates.

Craven continued to press forward with the main contingent. He turned to Saffrey and said, "You mustn't become involved with the fighting. You all have to stay safe. It's bad enough that the other three have fallen behind. They'd better turn up in time for our departure. It's crucial. You understand?"

"I think I'm starting to get the picture. But I'm worried about them; they might need help back there."

"Can't go off searching alone. Stay with us, we'll find them when our work's done here."

Craven signaled the leaders of the groups. They looked at the watchers as Quasimodo was released in the direction of the floating balls. The watchers were taken completely by surprise. They turned to confront the screaming Quasimodo who, now in frenzy, furiously waved his arms about and pleaded to the watchers not to shoot. His efforts were in vain. The watchers ignored his wailing; they could only see an intruder. All three moved toward the screaming man, who realizing the futility of his actions, stopped in his tracks and stared helplessly at them. The three fired simultaneously, their red light beams struck Quasimodo who slumped to the floor, finally set free of his torment.

In an instant Craven and four guards leaped behind the unsuspecting watchers as they hovered above the body of Quasimodo. The ensuing battle was over in minutes. Craven stood among the smoke and stench, the slime slithering about the floor. Eighteen of the elite guard lay dead. Only four had survived the onslaught.

The watchers were now no more than pools of bubbling green mass; their defenses had been rendered useless by the strength of the surprise attack.

"QUICKLY, OPEN THE REFRACTORY!" Craven shouted.

The doors were swung open. The sight was blinding, trays containing brilliant diamonds, large carry bags full to the rim with uncut stones. Black stones, white stones, yellow stones. All colors, all sizes. Craven dug his hands deep into the cut stones, laughing as he let them trickle between his fingers. He turned to Angelica. "Angelica my love, feast your eyes on these babies, all for us," and he began laughing uncontrollably.

Saffrey stared at the grotesque behavior. It reminded him of a Vincent Price horror movie, the mad scientist screaming, "IT'S ALIVE! IT'S ALIVE!"

Angelica threw her arms around Craven's neck, kissing him repeatedly.

"Save it my love. You four, get the stones into the carry bags quickly."

Craven emptied the uncut stones onto the floor and placed the five large bags onto the table. "Fill them all, only the cut stones from these trays." He said pointing at the stones he wanted, "Not the trays on the far side, they're colored, stay away from them."

Saffrey watched in silence, then after some seconds asked Craven, "What *are* those stones on the far side of the room? Why not take them as well?"

"They're inclusive. They contain neutron chips. We only want the flawless stones. These trays are flawless. They've been separated from the others because they didn't accept the inclusion.

Ironic isn't it, the rejects are priceless."

Craven lied well. His scheme was progressing nicely. All of the stones in the room were inclusive, Craven had planned way ahead, planned his perfect disappearing act, and the inclusive stones were in fact his ticket to freedom. The men began filling the bags. Their task was interrupted by a loud siren. The entry and exit doors slammed shut. Craven reeled about, a look of surprise wiping the ecstasy from his face. "WHAT THE HELL, ANGELICA? WHAT'S THIS?" he shouted.

"I don't know. Some kind of security system I have not been told of."

Craven shouted, "QUICKLY, PUT THE BAGS BACK ON THE SHELVES!" The men quickly shoved the bags back onto the shelves. The siren stopped. The doors re-opened. Craven said to no one in particular, "It's weight activated. When the stones are taken from the shelves, the weight shift activates the alarm, how primitive."

He turned to Saffrey and said, "Move to the far side of the room, now."

Saffrey backed up slowly; worried Craven had totally lost it.

"Don't you see we can't take stones from the room unless the equivalent weight replaces them on the fuckin' shelves? It's the only way to stop the security doors from closing, the only way to silence the sirens."

Saffrey wasn't ready for Craven's next move; reeling about he pointed the weapon at the four men who were loading the stones.

"Thanks for your loyalty and support. Well done." He opened fire on all four. One scrambled for his weapon at the end of the table. Craven cut off his dive, stomped his foot onto the man's throat, placed the muzzle of the neutralizer against his forehead, and smiling widely, blew a hole the size of a cantaloupe through his head removing his entire face.

"Oh yeah, haven't had a buzz like that since the Frenchman. Brains are brains. Seen one set, seen them all." Craven brushed part remnants of the man's brain from his shoe, wiping it with the cuff of the dead man's shirt.

"Messy bastard," he said grinning.

"YOU'RE CRAZY!" Saffrey shouted from across the room.

"No argument here. You stay safe. Remember I can just as easily take you out of here dead as I can alive, but I prefer you walk out under your own steam. My hands will be full with these bags."

Angelica sidled up to him." Please Travis, a little restraint."

"YOU'RE BOTH CRAZY, BOTH OF YOU!" Saffrey shouted standing with his back hard against the wall. Craven raised the weapon, aimed it at Saffrey.

"NO TRAVIS!" Angelica snapped. "He must stay alive. We need him to help carry the stones."

"You can carry your own goddamn fuckin' stones, you crazy son-of-a-bitch!" Saffrey snapped.

Craven walked toward Saffrey. He placed the weapon on the table. Saffrey stepped forward. "Come on you fucker, come on!" He moved to one side, readying himself.

His Navy SEAL background would be more than Craven could handle, Saffrey had no fear of an unarmed assailant. The two men got within an arm's length of each other. Saffrey made the first move. Craven side stepped, placed a finger to Saffrey's throat causing him to fall to the floor. He was unable to move, gasping for air, paralyzed yet still conscious.

"I don't need a weapon to fuck you." He reached down to Saffrey, held his head between his hands, snapped it quickly to the left causing a loud click. The paralysis began to slip from Saffrey's body and movement slowly returned.

"Put four bodies on the shelves. They'll counterweight for the five bags of stones. Problem solved."

Saffrey slowly stood. He shakily moved toward Craven, stumbled, growled, "You bastard, you killed these guys to use their bodies as fuckin' counterweights?"

"How perceptive of you, get them up there."

Saffrey struggled to lift each of the four guards onto the shelves. When he was done Craven pointed to the bags, he said, "Now gather up all the bags, quickly."

CHAPTER 37

THE DIVINITY PROCESSION HAD drawn huge crowds. Children danced around the many floats. The floating watchers lined both sides of the central plaza, hovering as though suspended from the fluffy clouds drifting overhead. The sun took occasional peeks through the clouds; the colors of the costumes came to life with each beam that broke through from above.

Each of the men was wearing a type of monk's robe as they filed along the street. Each white robed monk carried a gold tray, and each tray was almost filled to its rim with glittering diamonds. An open-top vehicle followed behind the monks. It slowly made its way between the cheering spectators. A man dressed in a red gown sat in rear of the car. He made slow waving gestures to those around him. As he passed the spectators they bowed their heads reverently perhaps out of respect, most definitely out of fear. This man was the Supreme Master. This was the man to whom the Consorts paid homage.

A squad of watchers followed closely behind the Master's vehicle. They numbered around fifty. It was a show of strength to quell the most enthusiastic adversary. Travis did well to time his intrusion to coincide with the procession. If these watchers had been at their usual posts, it would have been absolutely impossible to penetrate the refractory.

Craven carried two bags, Angelica struggled with the weight of one, and Saffrey carried the remaining two. They made their way to the Porsche.

"Put the bags into the car quickly," Craven said looking behind them to assure himself no one had followed.

The five bags filled the interior of the Porsche. Craven sat in the driver's seat, turned to Angelica and smiling said, "You know what to do from here. Bring the limousine to the tunnel entrance. Be sure to be there at sunset. Have all four of them on board. We'll transfer the stones from the Porsche to the limousine as planned and head off to the doorway."

Craven drove off as Angelica watched, looking somewhat apprehensive.

Saffrey tilted his head toward Angelica. "You mightn't see him again, or the diamonds."

"I am not worried; he'll be there, just as he said."

*****

Amy comforted Karen as best she could. The bleeding had almost stopped. The arm, severed off at the elbow, was wrapped in a large piece of a white gown, secured with strips of torn cloth. Some seepage of blood was finding its way through the end of the wrapping. Rick made a makeshift sling and placed it around Karen's shoulder, sliding the remaining top half of her arm into the cradle. Karen cringed, drifting between unconsciousness and reality.

The celebrating crowds were now within earshot of Rick and the two girls. They were out of sight of the passing parade, yet close enough to hear the revelers cheering and for the music to filter through. Rick observed Karen who was now in a fetal position, her head hanging. Tears swelled as Amy placed her arms around his shoulders.

Amy said, "She'll be fine. It was the only way I could think of to stop the spread. I thought it was eating away at her whole body."

Rick spoke quietly. "You did the right thing, the only thing." He turned his head, refusing to meet her eyes. As he faced away from her, he softly said, "That took guts Amy. Don't think I could've reacted as quickly bein' my sister and all. Glad you were there. Thanks."

Amy tightened her hug on his shoulders, consoled him a few moments longer, then asked, "Where's Saff?"

"Back in the building." He flipped a thumb over his shoulder. "Back with those two fuckers."

Angelica appeared from nowhere and placed a hand on Rick's shoulder." No, this fucker is right here," she said, digging the barrel of her weapon into Rick's rib cage. "Get to your feet, we are moving."

Rick motioned his head toward Karen then slowly moved his eyes to Angelica, playing for time. He said, "My sister ain't in any condition to move, look at her. The slime stuff's taken her fuckin' arm."

"She must move. Get her up," Angelica snapped as her eyes widened. She pointed the weapon at Karen, then looking about, saw the small wrapped bundle, blood stained at one end. "You have the severed arm, good. Get her up, she can either walk or you can carry her – but she must move," she waited a few seconds, then shouted, "NOW!"

Angelica took three steps toward a bucket that sat under a tap. She turned the tap handle, lowered her weapon. Rick noticed the muscles in her forearms. He didn't fancy having to fight her, not the way he was feeling. She partly filled the bucket, picked it up, and turned to throw the water on Karen. As she did, Rick scrambled for the weapon reaching it before Angelica realized what was happening. Rick brought the butt end down across the back of Angelica's head, stunned her momentarily. Karen groaned as Angelica fell to the ground beside her.

She raised herself on all fours and gave Rick a look. Rick returned the contemptuous stare. He pointed to Karen and said, "Help her up," Then he added through clenched teeth, "She can walk, or you can carry her."

*****

Craven steered the Porsche through the tunnel. The day's dwindling light told him he had only minutes in which to meet with Angelica. He fantasized about returning with the stones and his woman. She'd never traveled through the doorway, never seen the world in the parallel universe. Their lives together would be so different.

All that remained was to meet Angelica and the four travelers, after sunset, by the limousine. How brilliant she is to have devised such a plan. Attempting to access the stones at any other time of the year would have been suicidal. If only he had more success arranging the buyers from the embassy. They had been so close to closing the transaction. The faulty inclusions had been a costly error, and now he needed to begin the bargaining process from square one. These stones were controllable. These stones would behave as they should.

His first task, however, was to locate the remaining faulty stones. They must be accounted for and destroyed. Only Rick and the other three could get the stones. He slowly drove the Porsche to a stop inside just a few meters inside the tunnel. Craven stepped from the car, waited for nearly twenty minutes. Revelers were still celebrating as the sun made its exit, sinking into the horizon. The sky came alive as fireworks shot toward the clouds, exploding into showers of colorful sparks, adorning the surrounding panorama like sparkling jewels drifting to earth.

Craven couldn't allow himself to be seen in the Porsche. It would alert the watchers that something was amiss. His absence from the Divinity celebration was expected, he'd apologized earlier for his absence, said he wasn't feeling well, said he'd stay back. He wouldn't be able to explain if he was seen driving the red car with these five bags of luggage in the seats.

He looked along the roadway; the limousine was nowhere to be seen. Something didn't feel right. He wondered, *will I stay with the Porsche or make my way to the main building?* Could he risk driving the Porsche to find Angelica? *No. I have to leave the Porsche here in the tunnel.*

He stood at the entrance of the tunnel and looked across the parkland opposite. It was too late to step back into the shadows; he thought the men might have seen him. The two security guards casually strolled toward Craven. They were heading directly toward the Porsche. He was crouched low, his instincts had placed him in defense mode. He moved stealthily, moved sideways behind some artistically shaped bushes, slipped the long blade from the side of his boot. His thoughts of reaching the limo were now on hold. It had been a long time, not since the two Russians. This was food for the senses. As they drew nearer, Craven stood, staggered from behind the topiary. Laughing as though drunk he staggered toward the guards. The taller one, no older than twenty, approached Craven. The cop's uniform Craven was wearing gave the two guards a false sense of security.

"Hey are you okay. You been injured?" He reached a hand to Craven. The shorter guard stood back and turned to watch the procession as it moved along on the far side of the parkland. The plunge of the knife followed by a rapid upward movement destroyed the young man in an instant. The man had time to open his mouth to scream, but the shout was silent. The shorter guard turned still smiling, his expression reversed and he began screaming. Craven still had his back to the man. He didn't want the noise, didn't want the shouting. Then the man dived toward him, one hand pulling a weapon from its holster. Craven swiveled about, the long blade outstretched as it traveled across the second guard's throat, almost severing the head. The guard sank to his knees, his eyes wide open, he dropped beside the first man, blood gushing from his throat.

Craven reached out grabbing his hair in his left hand, stepped around, placed the blade to the man's neck and with a sudden thrust cut deeply through his throat. He regained composure and brushed off his cop's uniform, as though the incident hadn't happened, his demeanor cold, callous. He washed his hands in a nearby fountain, smiled as the water around his fists turned red, splashed water onto his right sleeve and tried to remove the last of the man's spray of blood. A car turned the corner and made its way toward the fountain. He stepped forward and waved the vehicle down, the two bodies obscured by the topiary.

The driver acknowledged the cop ahead, returning Craven's wave. "What is it, is the road ahead closed off?" the driver inquired.

"I was on my way to help with the procession, my bike had a mechanical problem, I tried to repair it, got grease all over my uniform, had to wash in that fountain" he stretched out his arm, showed the wet sleeve, pointed to the fountain.

"That's too bad officer, how can I help you? Always too pleased to help the police." the driver said smiling.

Craven laughed and answered, "Can you give me a ride? I'm running late."

The driver opened the door and motioned for Craven to step in. As he did he slid the blade from his right boot and swung his right hand with the shiny blade into the driver's chest. The man froze at the wheel. He sat for a second, for five seconds. His eyes glazed, he turned and faced Craven, a smile slipped onto his face as he slowly turned his head from side to side. His mind expanded, snapped, a quizzical look, again expanded, snapped. He forced out a single word, a drawn out gurgling sound - "Nooooo." He cooled, felt the chill. Gasping to draw his last breath as his mouth gushed blood.

Darkness.

Craven backed away momentarily as the blood spewed onto the seat. Bubbling. Warm. He smiled, absorbed the scene like a painter admiring a canvas, reached into the car; let his fingers feel the warmth.

The red beauty.

"Didn't your mother tell you not to give rides to strangers? Craven laughed.

He stepped from the car, opened the trunk, walked back to the car. Dragged the driver around back. Placed him in the trunk and began to sing aloud, "This little piggy went to market." He lifted the taller guard's headless body into the trunk, throwing the head in behind him.

"And this little piggy stayed home." He carried the second guard's body to the car. Dumped it into the crowded trunk.

"This little piggy had bread and butter." He slammed the trunk closed. Sitting in the car he readjusted the rearview mirror. Seeing his face reflecting, he tapped one finger on the mirror and completed his song.

"And this little piggy had none."

He started the car and drove toward the main plaza. As he approached, a barricade blocked his way. The procession route cut him off. Crowds of partygoers moved by the car. As each group passed by, he inched the car forward. People walked either side. He sat. Couldn't move any further.

The screams that came from the rear of the car stopped most people in their tracks. Craven turned, looked through the rear window. Women were screaming, pointing at the ground behind the car.

"It's blood! It's blood!" The words were screamed by a plethora of people at the rear of the car. Two men ran to the car door, opened it. Dragged Craven to the ground. He tried to regain his footing, swung at one of the men striking him on the temple, further infuriating the growing crowd. Another spectator unlocked the trunk. More screams. Two women fainted. Craven pushed his way through the screaming group, Hysteria spread, making his escape between the cramming spectators easier than expected. Those who were too far from the craziness allowed him to push through; after all, he was a policeman. The parade was just meters ahead. Craven pushed through the people lining the sides of the road, buffeting his way between the floats that made up the procession.

The crowd was at least ten deep around the parade. Trumpets blared. Clowns performed for the children. Police sirens screamed in the distance. *Police sirens*, Craven thought for several long seconds, *police sirens. What if they discover the Porsche in the tunnel? Maybe they've been to the refractory, seen what's happened.* He dashed down an alley, through a small park. Came across a series of tents. Costumed people were moving around the outside of the tents. Some wore full costumes, others just partially dressed. He darted into the nearest tent. Clown costumes and theater make-up were scattered about the change area. Didn't need to think twice. Picked up a baggy red and yellow outfit and an orange wig and quickly slipped into the outfit. Sat at a mirror and quickly opened a jar marked 'clown white.' The highly pigmented cream spread easily over his face. Splashed red onto his cheeks and applied a large red smile to his mouth. The red bulbous nose completed the disguise. He had become Travis Craven - clown. Liked it. Leaned toward the mirror, smiled widely at his reflection, the smile turned to crazed laughter. His escape was complete. He'd cheated capture. Again.

He looked into the mirror, whispered to himself, "You're good, you're very fuckin' good." His bellowing laughter reached to a new crescendo. Leaving the tent he continued on his way to the location of the limousine. He saw it. A hundred meters ahead. It was moving slowly toward the procession. He waved, tried to catch the driver's eye. Angelica spotted the clown running toward them. But it was just a clown.

"Think that clown wants you to stop," Rick said from the back seat. Amy sat beside him, trying her best to comfort Karen.

The clown was a few meters from the driver when he removed the orange wig and red bulbous nose, tore off the outfit. She saw the cop's uniform. Realized who it was.

"Travis?"

Craven opened the passenger's door and fell into the car.

Rick snapped, "Where's Saff?"

Craven looked around, realized he'd totally forgotten Saffrey. "He was in the tunnel last time I saw him. We'll collect him when we get back to the Porsche. He can't get far without us. We'll drive to the tunnel. Can't keep our treasure waiting."

CHAPTER 38

SAFFREY BELL STOOD BY the entrance to the tunnel. Gazed about, couldn't see the rest of his group. The crowds were thinning out. He wondered if he should try to blend in with the revelers or stay put until the streets were quieter. He carefully walked over to two large topiary bushes. Spotted the large pool of blood on the ground. The blood trail ended nearby. *Don't want to hang about this place much longer,* he thought. *Just a matter of time before others came across this fuckin' mess. Too many questions. Can't risk staying.*

The Porsche sat a short way off. Just inside the tunnel. He moved quickly to the red car. Opened the door, was surprised to see the key on the floor by the accelerator pedal. The leather bags took up most of the space. He opened one of the bags and stared at the treasure of shimmering stones. They held his attention for several seconds. Reached into the bag and let them run through his fingers. His mind pictured the things these stones could get him. Thought of how many lives he could change with just a few.

He reached into his pocket, feeling for the disc. It'd been worth the risk of staying in the refractory long enough to retrieve it from the large computer. *The secret to culturing the diamonds has to be on this disc.* He reached for the key, slid it into the ignition. The Porsche started on the first turn, the motor rumbling. It was the smooth growl of a beast awoken from a short nap. Angry at being disturbed. He slipped the car into first gear and nosed forward from the tunnel.

It took several minutes for the limousine to weave its way through the streets partly cordoned off for the parade.

"The tunnel's just around the next bend," Craven said excitedly as he neared his treasure. He turned the corner. Rick spotted the red car.

"The Porsche, I think that's Saff drivin'," Rick said excitedly.

Craven nodded, his head cocked to one side. He quickly turned the limo in the direction the Porsche was traveling. He blasted away on the horn to catch the attention of the driver. Saffrey lifted one hand to acknowledge the limo, now trailing in his rearview mirror. He motioned for the limousine to pass.

"Smart move," Craven said smiling. "He'd never find his way to safety without us leading."

The two cars snaked their way between costumed clowns. Between party revelers, staggering street people. Finally they reached a stretch of road where they were able to increase their speed.

"Yeah, we're clear," Craven said grinning into the rearview mirror. He increased speed to eighty kilometers. The Porsche stayed on his tail.

Craven began to drive faster. The Porsche hugged his rear. The brake lights on the limousine came on, slowing both cars to half speed. The roadblock ahead was manned by several police vehicles. A group of watchers hovered above the patrol cars. Craven stopped the limousine as Saffrey Bell drew alongside. Both cars sat facing the roadblock. Two dragsters waiting for the green light. Saffrey leaned from the window of the Porsche; he called to Craven, "What do we do now?"

"We can't outrun the watchers," Craven replied. "We'll need to get in closer, we need to take them out. We have to be within ten meters."

"Fuckin' great, and how do we do that?" Saffrey asked. "What do we do, throw rocks at 'em?"

Craven stepped from the limo, walked calmly to the trunk. He reached into the trunk, took out two neutralizers. He stepped toward Saffrey and handed him one of the weapons. "You've seen how this works. It seems we're on the same side; at least until we're out of here, agree?"

Saffrey took the weapon, pointed it at Craven's head. Hesitated. Craven grinned widely at him saying, "Go ahead, take your shot" He stood staring into the weapon. Saffrey moved the weapon closer, he said, "You so sure I won't shoot?"

"No time for fuckin' about. We need each other. We all

make it out of here or none of us make it out. What don't you understand about that? Now pass me the five bags."

Saffrey passed the leather bags to Craven. He put each into the trunk of the limousine, but held one back. "If you don't mind, I'll keep this one with me - insurance you might say."

"You just don't get it do you?" Craven snapped. "Go ahead, keep one bag. Your friends' lives are in my hands. That bag had better not leave yours, and by the way . . ." he leaned toward Saffrey, reached to the neutralizer and pressed a switch on its side. Winked and grinned. He said, "Safety switch."

Angelica called from the limo, "The watchers, they're moving this way. Quickly Travis!"

Craven shouted at Saffrey, "STAY WITH ME. This'll be a rough ride."

Craven quickly sat back in the limo, passed the weapon to Rick and gestured to the sunroof. He gunned the motor, driving straight toward the floating balls. Rick stood in the rear of the car, his upper body protruding through the sunroof, weapon in hand.

"NOT 'TILL WE'RE ON TOP OF THEM," Craven shouted at Rick.

Rick shouted back down into the limo, "GOT IT!"

Fifty meters, thirty meters, ten meters. The watchers were on both sides of the car. In range. The Porsche whipped around the limo and skidded to a halt behind the watchers. Saffrey fired upward at one of the hovering white balls, now just five meters above him. Direct hit. The ball began to sink toward the road. Its green contents oozing out as it dropped.

Three squad cars left the barricade. Moved toward the battle, sirens blaring. Craven swung to one side as a beam from the nearest watcher zapped by. Felt its heat as it flashed by his ear. It melted a clean hole through the glass of the limousine's rear window. Angelica and the two girls lay along the rear seat. Craven flung the driver's door open, threw himself onto the roadway, firing as he rolled. The watcher quickly shifted to one side. Avoided the blast from the neutralizer. Another beam zapped toward Saffrey in the direction of the Porsche. He whipped the car into gear, spun it around in time to confuse the watcher. It switched targets. Blasted away in the direction of Craven.

Craven rolled, avoided the blast. The ricochet deflected off the roadway and blasted into the Porsche tire. Craven paused. He was distracted by the blast of the tire. The distraction lasted just long enough for him to miss the cop taking aim from behind a patrol car. Angelica jumped from the limo and threw herself between the cop and Craven. The bullet lodged in her chest as she fell into Craven's arms.

Saffrey and Rick continued their fire-fight with the remaining watchers. Amy reached from the limo, picked up the neutralizer Craven had dropped. She fired two blasts into the air, bringing another watcher crashing to the ground. The final watcher fell after a quick round from Rick and Saffrey.

Saffrey darted across to Craven who was holding Angelica. He shouted at Craven, "GET HER INTO THE LIMO. IT'S OUR ONLY CHANCE."

Craven pointed to the Porsche. "Get the bag from the Porsche, I'll cover you."

As Saffrey retrieved the solitary bag from the red car, Rick and Craven sent a volley of blasts toward the two cops still firing from the patrol cars. Rick took careful aim, took out one tire on each of the two squad cars.

The drive that followed was at speeds not too often reached by any limousine. Another two patrol cars, sirens blaring, gave chase in the near distance. Craven drove off the main road, cut through a heavily treed parkland. Made a sharp turn and pulled to a stop in a bushy lot. Angelica lay on the floor in the rear of the car, Amy pressing one hand heavily against her wound, trying to stem the flow of blood. Rick had a firm hold on Karen. She drifted in and out of consciousness. Saffrey still holding the neutralizer, sat alongside Craven. Sat listening to the sirens. Getting closer and closer, passing, passing - fading into the distance.

Gone.

Craven turned, looked back at Angelica, asked Amy. "How's she doin'?"

"Not good. Needs medical attention bad. Got a doctor nearby?"

"There's a doctor back at the refractory. Going back is out of the question. Can't go back there, can only go forward. There's a doctor at a farmhouse through the doorway. He took care of my leg wound. He's her best chance. Once we get through, it'll be just minutes to reach him."

Saffrey thought for a few seconds. "How do you even know this doctor will be there? If he's not there, Angelica will die. Karen too"

"I'm feeling lucky okay? Don't have a choice," Craven answered. "It's safe to get going again. We're about ten minutes from the doorway. Buckle up."

"Sure," Rick replied with an air of sarcasm. "Buckle up. Let's not take any risks, right?"

Craven started the limo. The motor strained, spluttered, stopped. Turned the key again. The starter motor groaned, strained, eventually turned over. It chugged for around ten seconds, then died. Craven ran his eyes across the instrument panel. The temperature indicator was in the red zone. Saffrey jumped from the car, inspected the front grill area.

"Taken a hit through the radiator. Not good."

Craven walked to the front of the car. Both men stood as men often do when mesmerized by anything mechanical, hands on hips. Staring at the bullet hole.

"Any ideas Craven?"

"None come to mind. We've got at least ten minutes of hard driving. Then we're home safe."

"Need to plug this hole or we aren't going anywhere."

"Have to get another car, it's the only way," Craven said.

Craven and Saffrey set off walking. Five minutes passed, Craven knew they were running out of time. Angelica couldn't hold out much longer. He said to Saffrey, "I want you to lie on the roadside. When a car comes along, they'll stop. We'll take the car."

He heard a car in the distance. Saw the headlights getting nearer. He lay on the side of the road. The first car slowed but continued on by. *Smart driver*, Saffrey thought, one eye half open watching the rear of the car disappear. Craven remained hidden from sight behind roadside scrub. Another car approached. It slowed, drove past the body on the roadside. Stopped. Reversed to where Saffrey was laying.

CHAPTER 39

TWO MEN STEPPED FROM THE car and stood over the body. The pirate looking man man with the patch on one eye said, "Take his wallet, might be some cash in it." The other man was Jamaican. He too looked every bit a pirate, a thug. He rolled Saffrey onto his back and rifled through his coat pocket. The headlights from their car shining across the scene added an eerie touch.

Saffrey opened his eye, grabbed the dark man by the arm, and threw him to the ground. The other man stepped forward, put his boot into Saffrey's side. He let out a loud groan. The man with the patch reached into his jacket and pulled a gun from a shoulder holster. He aimed it at Saffrey who instinctively raised an arm, covering his eyes.

The blade ripped across the man's throat. Blood sprayed onto Saffrey. He felt the warmth as it sprayed across his cheeks, didn't see it coming, had his eyes covered. The eye-patch man fell to his knees. Took in his last taste of life. He dropped forward and landed across Saffrey's chest.

Saffrey lowered his arm from his eyes. Saw Craven rolling the Jamaican into a trench by the roadside. Craven leaned over the patch man, pulled him off Saffrey and rolled him into the trench beside the Jamaican. He wiped his blood soaked hands on the man's coat as he went.

"Jesus, you didn't have to kill them," Saffrey said in horror.

"Why not, they were going to kill you. Get into the car quickly."

The vehicle was a black Mercedes 500SL. Big, roomy. Not as comfortable as the limo, but good enough for the drive through the doorway. Saffrey held his side. Limped slowly around the car. Slowly got and into the passenger's seat.

"That son-of-a-bitch didn't have to put the boot into me."

"Lucky it was your side and not your head," Craven replied. He drove the 500SL back to where the limo was hidden. Amy stepped from behind some bushes, glad to see the two men had returned safely. She placed a hand on Angelica and slowly shook her head as she spoke to Craven, "Her bleeding's gotten worse. I can't stop it."

"Get the bags into the car," Craven said softly as he moved to Angelica's side. "Hang in there my love. I'll get you taken care of soon enough."

Saffrey opened the trunk, took a moment for the trunk light to come on, he jumped back. "HOLY CHRIST!" he shouted. "WHAT THE FUCK IS THAT!"

A body in the trunk, a security guard? The light bounced back off of his shield, a sliver and gold badge on the man's chest. He was bound and very dead. Alongside of him were three bags. First National Bank bags.

"Jesus Christ. Looks like those two guys made a large withdrawal. Didn't need my wallet. Greedy fucks. This car's hotter than the fuckin' limo," Saffrey said. He thought about waiting for another car. No time.

Craven said, "Look on the bright side. Now you don't have to feel so bad about me killing them."

Saffrey opened one of the bank bags, took out a bundle of notes. As he did, an explosion burst from the bag, coating him in fluorescent pink dye.

"WHAT THE FUCK!" he shouted jumping back. Craven burst into laughter, his hands holding his stomach as tears rolled down his white painted cheeks, causing the clown face paint to run.

"What a sight," he cried to Saffrey, his laughter echoing through the small treed area.

Saffrey said, "You're an ugly fuck Bozo . . . like, YOU look normal?"

"Yeah, but if I get caught . . . I mean, I can entertain them, but you . . ."

The pink man and the clown sarcastically complimented each other as they stepped into the Mercedes.

"Christ if we get stopped . . ." Saffrey said cringing, still favoring what felt like a broken rib.

"Yeah pinky, but at least mine'll wash off."

"You m m mean . . ." Saffrey stammered.

"You got it, the stuff's indelible," Craven said with his permanent clown's smile. "It lasts FOREVER."

The Mercedes headed back toward the city. Craven tried to relax. Knew the Mercedes was hot. They arrived back at the limousine. Expressions on the faces of those waiting were a good indication of how others would react to the two painted men.

Rick pointed at Saffrey, "Christ man, what the fuck is this?"

"Don't say a fuckin' word," Saffrey grumbled. He told Rick about their run in with the two Mercedes men, about the bank bags, the security guard, and the fluorescent bomb.

Craven leaned into the limousine and comforted Angelica. Asked how Karen was doing. A rare display of compassion.

He called to Rick, "Let's move the bags and guns into the car."

"Dontcha think it'd be a good idea if we switched cars one more time. Somethin' not hot," Rick said. "Whatcha think Mr. Pink?"

Saffrey smirked back, showing white teeth through his luminous face. "Fuck you!" He snarled.

Craven carefully moved Angelica into the Benz. Amy sat between the two wounded women with Rick on the offside rear window. Craven drove. Saffrey squeezed into the front seat. He carried two neutralizers.

After a few kilometers Rick said, "Don't look now, but we picked up a tail, it's flashin' a blue light," he focused on the fast approaching light. "It's a single light, a fuckin' bike cop."

Craven said, "Yeah, he's been with us a few minutes. I'm going to stop." He nodded at Rick. He said, "You stay low in the back. Get ready with the weapon." He turned to Saffrey. "Lay low, don't want him to see any of you."

Craven pulled the car off the road. The cop stopped some ten meters behind. He got off the bike, dropped to one knee.

Pointed his hand-gun at the car. Called out, "Out of the car. Hands where I can see them!"

Craven stepped slowly onto the road with both hands held high above his head. The headlight from the bike shined into Craven's eyes, the cop was a silhouette.

"Move away from the vehicle!"

"Absolutely."

Craven squinted, propped his head to one side, took three paces toward the cop.

"Lay on the ground, arms outstretched," then he shouted, "YOU, IN THE CAR . . . GET OUT."

"There's no one in the car. I'm alone."

"Alone? Where are the men, Martinets and Schumann?" the cop snapped as he got in closer to Craven. "Who the hell are you?"

Craven thought quickly, *the cop has to be an accomplice of those two. He knows their names.*

"We were pulled over back down the road. The other two were shot. I was a last minute addition as driver. The one good eye on Schumann was giving him trouble. They needed me to drive."

Craven had thought quickly, *Martinets must be the Jamaican; the patch had to belong to Schumann. Did I pick it right?*

"Schumann's dead?"

"They're both dead."

"Where's the money?"

"In the trunk."

"Open it."

The cop slipped his weapon into its holster, moved toward the Mercedes. He took a flashlight from a rear clip on his belt. Craven slowly raised himself to his feet, moving toward the rear of the car.

"Open it . . . NOW!"

Craven slowly opened the trunk. The pink dye glowed, covering the body of the security guard as well as the other two bank bags. The beam from the flashlight danced on the pink color. It took the cop by surprise.

He shouted, "WHAT THE FUCK HAPPENED HERE?"

"Thought we'd collect a pair of book-ends," Craven answered.

"What are you talking about?" the cop asked as he stared in confusion at the mess in the trunk, his hand moving back to his hand-gun. Craven quickly reached to his boot, slipped the blade from its sheath and pushed it deep into the cop's neck.

"Hey Rick, get out here and help me get his uniform off." He began unbuttoning the cop's shirt ahead of the blood flow. Shouted to Rick, who hadn't moved fast enough. "YOU'RE THE ONLY ONE OF US WHO CAN WEAR IT, PUT IT ON AND GET THE BIKE."

Rick didn't ask questions. He removed his clothing and dressed in the cop's uniform, wiping blood from the leather jacket. He left the cop's boots on the body. They were at least two sizes too small for him.

"GET THE BIKE!"

"I've never ridden a bike."

"Everyone knows how to ride a fuckin' bike."

Saffrey stepped from the car. "I do."

"Mr. Pink on a Harley, what a picture,"

Craven laughed. He turned back to Rick who was now every bit the cop. "Get the bike to the middle of the road, and flag down the first car that comes along. We need to dump this Mercedes. It's a magnet."

The lights were a minute away. Rick rolled the bike to the center of the road. Waved at the approaching car. The driver saw the blue lights flashing on the cop's bike. Saw the Mercedes pulled to the side. He though it could be an accident. The driver slowed. Rick stepped to the door of the car and pulled the driver from his seat.

"RUN LIKE HELL OR I'LL SHOOT!" he shouted at the driver.

The man was shocked. He stumbled as Rick fired a shot over his head. The man scampered into the nearby brush, making good his escape. He stayed still. Watched the two men argue. Listened.

"WHAT THE FUCK ARE YOU DOING?" Craven shouted. "HE'S GOTTEN AWAY."

"If I hadn't scared him off you would've killed him," Rick replied. "Didn't need to kill the guy, we got his car. Mission fuckin' accomplished."

Craven stared into Rick's eyes. He shouted, "YOU'RE LUCKY I DON'T KILL YOU. YOU'RE BECOMING QUITE AN AGGRAVATION. GIVE ME THE GUN."

"You'll have your chance," Rick said gritting his teeth and passing the cop's hand-gun over.

"We'll dance when the time is right." Craven brushed past him and moved to the car. "Everyone into the car, bring the bags."

Craven lifted the almost naked body of the motorcycle cop into the trunk of the Mercedes, slammed it shut. "He died a happy man, a nice Benz and a few thousand in cash. Even has a personal security guard," Craven said laughing. He threw the gun back into the trunk and fitted three bags around them. The other two bags of stones were pushed into the rear seat of the car, under the feet of the three women.

"It's a squeeze, but it won't be for too long," Craven said in an almost apologetic tone. They were safely in the white car. Craven turned to Angelica and speaking softly gently squeezed her hand. He said in a loving voice, "Hold on my love . . . we're on our way."

CHAPTER 40

DREW BLAKE ACCOMPANIED CHEVALIER back to the inspector's office. The ride to the station consisted primarily of *male bonding*. Claude described his artwork to a very impressed Blake, and Blake expressed a genuine interest in visiting his studio, look at his latest canvas. In the office Chevalier called to one of the cops in the adjoining room.

"Lobrech, bring the three men."

Twenty or so photographs were spread randomly across the desk. Craven's photo was placed among them. There was a knock on the door. Lobrech, a tall thin man with a black curled moustache poked his head into the room.

"I have the three men inspector."

"Show them in . . . one at a time."

Philippe Bouvier entered. He bowed his head in respect, he walked toward the desk.

"Come in Bouvier. How has cell nine been treating you?"

"Please inspector, we have harmed no one. Why must we stay imprisoned?"

"You are all accessories," Chevalier replied, his eyes staying on the spread of photographs. "You will remain as my guests at my pleasure. Now take a look at these photographs and pass me three you recognize."

Philippe looked slowly at the selection. He paused, reached for three.

"Thank you Bouvier. Wait outside." Chevalier called to Lobrech, "Send in Yves."

The next man entered the room and smiled at Chevalier. He passed a glance to Blake and pushed two photographs from the bunch, then reached toward the photo of Craven, hesitated and picked out a nearby shot.

"Thank you, wait outside."

Ramone Flourette entered and selected three photos. He

"

ignored the shot of Craven.

None of the three chose Craven. They'd each selected local criminals, all well known to Chevalier.

"That was a dead end," Blake said in a disappointed voice.

"Hmm, I am very confused. I really thought they would select our man."

They sat in a cloud of silence for several minutes.

"LOBRECH." Chevalier called aloud. "Return the prisoners to their cell."

There was a quick tap, tap on the door. Lobrech entered quietly.

"There is a Miss Camile here asking for Mr. Blake."

"Send her in Lobrech."

Camile entered the room. She spoke quietly as she apologized to Blake. "Please forgive me; I didn't want to be in trouble with the police, so I didn't tell anyone about it."

"About what?" Blake asked.

"The last night I was with Travis, well . . . I woke early, couldn't sleep. He had an attaché case, the one the diamonds were in, the diamonds he showed me earlier that night. I wanted to look at them one more time. I opened the case and took the stones from the box. As I did, the case slipped off the chair, spilling some of its contents. I quickly gathered the papers and replaced them, as well as all the stones. I was scared he would wake and find me rummaging through his personal effects. The next day when I was cleaning the room I found this disc under the sofa. It must have slipped out when the contents spilled from the case."

"You brought his disc? Good girl, do you have it with you?" Chevalier asked.

She reached into her hand-bag, took out a golden disc, handed it to the inspector.

"I played the disc on my computer. It scared me. I didn't know whom to tell."

Blake looked at Chevalier. They each had an inquisitive yet excited look of anticipation on their faces.

She said, "On the disc, there's his red car. The one I rode in with Travis. But . . . it . . . it just vanishes, drives along the road then disappears right before your eyes."

"Probably some kind of computer trick, some trick photography," Chevalier quickly interrupted. "You know how computers can do anything. I would not be too worried about it."

The three sat and talked for fifteen minutes. Once assured that they had all the information from Camile, Chevalier decided it was time to end the visit.

"Miss Camile, I will have one of my men drive you home. We will contact you if we need to see you again. Thank you."

Camile stood slowly, smiling at Blake.

"I'll see you later tonight okay? Call me on my cell," Blake said as Camile left the office.

Chevalier moved quickly to the computer desk. Both men sat as the disc began to play. Coordinates giving latitude and longitude appeared on the monitor. Very complicated data flashed onto the monitor. The road by the farmhouse where the Porsche seemed to vanish appeared on the monitor.

"Look Drew, this is exactly where we have lost him each time," Chevalier said tapping his index finger on the monitor.

The two men stared at the screen as the red Porsche zoomed into the picture.

"Jesus, look at this, it's him," Blake snapped.

The inspector sat forward, almost bumping heads with Blake. Both men were spellbound. The Porsche increased its speed as it gunned along the road, hugging the center line of the asphalt.

"Why is he riding the center line?" Blake asked. "He must be doing over 160."

Chevalier kept his eye on the screen. "Watch, he's going to go, very soon now . . . watch him."

As he spoke the very words, the Porsche vanished.

Blake blessed himself, he said "Sweet fuckin' Jesus, where did he go?"

"I do not know, but I am going after him."

The two viewed the remainder of the disc. It showed repeated scenes of the red car vanishing, each time from a different location.

"I recognize the farmhouse location, but the others would require more thorough investigation," Chevalier said studying the monitor." I only need the one location. If it works, I will find this Travis person."

Blake asked, "And when you do, what then?"

"It will be in the lap of the gods. Fate will play its hand my friend. Fate will decide what is to become of each of us. I will need more fire power than usual. It is worth the trouble to prepare well for this excursion. Who knows how I am to return from wherever the vanishing point takes me."

The following day the two men met up at the police retention depot. Chevalier strolled among dozens of confiscated vehicles. Blake accompanied him, curious as to why Claude would not take his Ferrari for the venture.

"I cannot take the Ferrari," Chevalier answered when Blake asked the question. "Because I will need to return with at least one prisoner, and who knows how many more. Besides, I need extra space for weapons."

The white Citroën had been confiscated in a drug bust. It was nearly new and perfect for what Chevalier had in mind.

"I hope you know what you're doing Claude. I really would like to come along," Blake said somewhat apprehensively.

"No, you have to remain behind. You are the only one who knows what is going on here, you know…with the vanishing car, the disc. We cannot both take the risk, it's too great. With you here - I at least have a cohort. Someone who can throw me a line, cover for me when questions are asked. Tell them I am off investigating a lead in Marseilles. I will brief Lobrech with such a story before I leave."

"When do you plan to get started?" Blake asked.

"At around one o'clock. You can come along with a camera. I think you should have this on disc, in case you need to explain why I've not returned . . . if worse comes to the worse, as they say."

"Good idea, I don't need a vacation at the funny farm. Don't need to explain how a car just vanished. Video huh, excellent idea Claude."

It was just past midday. The two men stood at the side of the road. The white Citroën was ready for its journey. Blake stood by the Ferrari.

"Take care of my baby," Chevalier said cautiously, nodding toward the Ferrari as he shook Blake's hand.

"Bon voyage Claude," Blake answered, as Chevalier stepped in closer, gave him the traditional kiss to each cheek.

"Oh man," Blake cringed, "that wasn't necessary." But Blake smiled, giving Chevalier another farewell hug.

"If I fail to return in three days, you are welcome to follow me, but please, not in my Ferrari," Chevalier gave a sad smile as he patted the fender of the Testa Rosa.

Claude stepped into the Citroën, started the motor. "Park the Ferrari by the vanishing point and video me as I drive toward you."

"Got it. Good luck. See you in a few days."

CHAPTER 41

THE CITROEN SPED TOWARD the point, faster, faster, the center line on the roadway dissecting the car between the passenger seat and the driver. It was just as they had seen on the monitor.

The car drew closer and closer to where Blake stood with the video camera. He kept an eye against the viewfinder. The Citroën was thirty meters from Blake's position. Twenty. Ten. *Getting too close,* he thought. As Blake was about to throw himself out of the speeding car's path, his mouth dropped open. The car was gone. No sound. Remnants of a dust cloud being the only evidence that any vehicle had been on the road.

The journey through the doorway was over in seconds, Chevalier emerging confused, yet in control of his emotions as well as the still speeding Citroën. As he pushed the Citroën to top speed, he could see the blue light flashing on the roadway ahead. He slowed the car down, could see a cop waving his flashlight at the Citroën.

"What is the trouble Officer?" he asked.

The cop approached Chevalier, opened the door and pulled the inspector from the car. He shouted, "RUN LIKE HELL OR I'll SHOOT!"

The inspector scurried off into nearby bushes as a shot whistled over his head. Crouching behind a large tree, he could see a group of people moving quickly to get into the Citroën.

"What the fuck are you doing?" one of the men shouted at the cop with the gun still in his hand. Chevalier watched as an argument between the two men developed. He listened closely and could make out some of their words.

The man shouted at the cop, "YOU'RE LUCKY I DON'T KILL YOU. YOU'RE BECOMING QUITE AN AGGRAVATION. GIVE ME THE GUN."

The shouting man appeared to have some kind of white paint on his face, the remnants of smeared red lips giving a hint of a clown's facial make up. Chevalier strained to see the face of the painted man. Something about him was familiar, but how could that be? The man with the painted face walked to a parked car at the side of the road. It was a large black Mercedes. He bent down and struggled to lift something into the trunk.

Chevalier moved forward for a better view, seeing the semi-naked body the man lowered into the black Mercedes. The man then stepped into the Citroën. Chevalier watched helplessly as the car sped off into the distance.

CHAPTER 42

BLAKE DROVE CHEVALIER'S FERRARI to Montmarlier. Earlier that afternoon he'd called Camile and arranged to meet with her for drinks. The atmosphere in the Lapin Agile had its familiar aroma. Blake took one final deep breath of fresh air before entering. Camile was waiting with Julia at a small table by the stage. A mime quietly went about his routine, white painted face and black clothing, pulling himself up an imaginary rope that was supposedly hanging from the ceiling. Blake made his way to the table. He was thrilled when both girls stood and greeted him with a kiss on each cheek.

Blake said, "Hi girls, great to see you both, wasn't expecting to see you here Julia."

"I hope you don't mind Drew. I was here with friends. Camile arrived. I'll leave you guys alone."

"Wouldn't hear of it, stay and have some drinks with us."

They chatted for over an hour. Blake became pensive, his mind wandered. *Where's Chevalier? What if he's in trouble, how can I help him?* The two girls rambled on oblivious to his absence; part of their dialogue was in English, part in French.

"Drew you are in another world." Camile laughed.

"Yeah, yeah, yeah - excuse me, I was thinking about a friend who's just gone off on a journey. I'm sorry." Blake turned to Julia. "Is there anything more you can tell me about this Travis guy?"

"Nah, not really, you know about as much as I do. If something else comes to mind I'll pass it on." She slid a sideways glance at Camile, saw she was eying Blake. "Okay guys, time to say *seeya,* gonna leave you guys to chat."

Julia stood, hugged them both, and made her way back to her friends' table. Camile leaned in closer and asked, "Tell me Drew, who is this friend that has taken the journey? Is it a person that I know?"

Blake thought for a few seconds, *should I tell her? After*

all, she did bring us the disc and gave me the information on Travis.

"Camile, can I totally trust you with some very important shit?"

"Important shit?" She grinned. "But off course, if you are in trouble I wish to help you. This shit, it is in confidence, yes?" She moved in closer to his side as though expecting him to whisper a secret in her ear. Two foreign looking men sat across from Blake. They'd followed him to the Au Lapin, or more to the point, they had followed Chevalier's Ferrari. One leaned toward the other. As he did he caught Blake's eye. He nodded his head toward Blake and Camile. A sideway nudge, just enough of a nod to let Blake know he was aware of being observed by Blake. Of being seen.

The nodding man said, "Our people tell me she has been to see the French inspector as recently as yesterday. Why have they not closed in on her before this?"

The other man took a handkerchief from his pocket. Blew into it. Blake slipped a tactless stare across at him, giving a look of disgust as the large nosed man again blew noisily into the cloth. The other man reached into his pocket, placed a packet of Sobranie on the table. Pulled one from the pack, placed it in his mouth and leaned toward the candle flickering on the table. Blake, still looking in the man's direction couldn't help notice the black cigarette.

He dropped his eyes, moved them back to Camile and said "Black Russians, haven't seen them in a while."

"Excuse me?"

"Hey? Aw, it's nothing. Just thinking aloud. Russian cigarettes, don't see 'em too often."

"Tell me Drew, what is this secret you wish to share with me? Who is your friend who has taken the journey?"

"Oh yeah, sorry Camile, it's been a long day. Actually, it's Claude. The inspector."

"The inspector?"

"Yeah, he . . . hmm . . . is after the guy with the red Porsche."

Camile gave Blake a quizzical look. "So why is his journey . . .?"

"It's a whole bunch of things. A very difficult story to explain. Just give me a few more minutes to mentally put it together."

Camile strolled to the bar, came back with two fresh drinks. The two men with the Russian cigarettes tracked her movement. Blake saw the tracking.

They were almost half way into the cognac when Blake said, "The whole mess goes back to a burned body, an escort girl named Michelle du Blanc." He went through the chain of events. Camile listened intently. She reached into her purse and lit up a cigarette. Finished the drink and signaled to the waiter. She ordered another cognac. Blake half nodded to the waiter.

"Me too."

He continued on. Camile was in awe of the story.

She placed her hand on his and gave a comforting squeeze as Blake relayed the deaths of Penoir and Laroche, how Travis was responsible. He reached the part where Chevalier drove off into nowhere, Camile's mouth opened, her eyes widened, a look of amazement.

"You mean what I saw on the disc was not trick photography?"

Blake expelled a large breath. "Nope, it's the real deal. Claude's driven into the doorway, or whatever the hell it is. He's gone."

"Well . . . when will he be back?" she asked shrugging her shoulders, making a French gesture with both hands.

"Soon I hope, maybe three days. He'll call me when he gets back."

"My God, this is so crazy; you lead such a dangerous life, you policemen."

He thought for a minute, and then snapped back, "What the fuck was I thinking? How could I just let him go off like that, let him do this on his own? Fuckin' delusional. I've gotta get out there and help him. Can't just stay here waiting."

"Can I come with you?"

"Are you nuts? This is so crazy; I don't even know where I'm going. It's just that Claude could very likely need help."

"Why don't you take someone along who can help? Another policeman perhaps."

Blake hadn't considered that possibility. Everything had been happening so quickly. Aside from the fact he really didn't want to involve another party, could he ask McDowell? No, far too departmental. *Have to go it alone*, he thought.

"Can't involve anyone else. It's bad enough that I've involved you Camile. Let's get out of here; I need some fresh air."

As they walked between the tables, Blake nodded at the two men with the Russian cigarettes. They returned the nod, and quickly tossed down what was left of their drinks.

Camile and Blake walked along the semi-lit street to where the Ferrari was parked. The two men from the café moved slowly behind, staying in the shadows of small shop doorways.

Blake turned, sensed something and looked along the street behind them.

"What is it?"

"Thought I saw something. Nothing I guess, getting paranoid. Let's get you home."

The Ferrari turned into a well lit street. Blake kept an eye on the rearview mirror, no one following. He eased off the gas and relaxed a little. Camile pushed a button on the dash. Music began playing. Chevalier had his usual selection of Sinatra stacked in the CD holder.

CHAPTER 43

CLAUDE CHEVALIER BEGAN WALKING. He dusted off his suit, cussing in French at his lack of street smarts. He should not have left himself vulnerable to the man flagging him down. *This is a new world*, he thought. *Perhaps things aren't always what they appear to be*. He headed in the direction the stolen Citroën had taken; figuring there'd be a town, people . . . someplace ahead.

"Claude, you should not have come here alone," he said to himself loudly. "How do you plan to return home? You have done a very stupid thing my friend." The approaching car was now a hundred meters from him. Chevalier thought quickly, decided to wave the driver down. The small car crawled to a stop. A scruffy unshaven man poked his head from the car.

"What are you doing out here walking all alone?"

"My vehicle was stolen by some hitchhikers. I was left here to fend for myself. Can you take me as far as the nearest town?"

"It is about thirty kilometers, get in."

The village was similar to many he'd seen on the outskirts of Paris. Small cars were parked along equally small streets; coffee shops in abundance. Groups of people sat outside the shops, large colorful umbrellas, and soft music from guitar strumming singers. *Just like home*, Chevalier thought. *Even the songs are the same. What is this place?*

Then he saw it, parked almost one hundred meters away, alongside a large glass building, the red Porsche.

What luck, he thought as he quickly made his way toward the car. The rear tire was flat. He looked inside the car; the keys were not in the ignition. He opened the door, found the hood latch.

"Hey mister, what are you doing to that car?"

The young man startled Chevalier, but his answer was quick and believable.

"I was asked to change the tire."

The boy smiled and gave a friendly wave. The boy said, "The car was here with the flat tire, I thought it was abandoned, but then – it is a Porsche. I expected the owner to collect it eventually. I've seen it around the village quite a lot."

"Do you know the owner?"

"No, but I've seen him in the village. His name is Trevis or Trevor, something like that."

Chevalier was not surprised. His misadventure with Travis was still fresh in his mind. The body of Laroche lying on the ground in the barn, the Porsche roaring off into the night, the futile attempts to follow the red car – all of this passed through his mind, a nightmare movie, playing over and over. He could actually touch the red car. Even sit in it.

"Can you help me with the tire?"

"Will you take me for a ride in it when you have the tire changed?"

Chevalier grinned. "Of course. A short one."

"I am Jacque," the boy said extending his hand. "Claude."

Chevalier shook hands with his new friend, *my cohort in crime*, he thought with a smile.

The spare tire was fitted. Chevalier pulled the wires from beneath the dash while the young man placed the flat under the hood, straightened the carpet covering the spare area and lowered the hood. Within seconds the engine of the red car was running.

The lid was off the Targa, and the open air felt good to Claude as he moved the Porsche through its gears.

"What is this?" Jacque asked as he ran his fingers across a bank of switches above the radio.

"I'm not sure, let's find out."

Reaching to the first switch, Chevalier flicked it to the down position.

A screen slid silently from the dash, below the glove compartment.

"It's a television." Jacque laughed.

"No, I think it's a satellite guidance system of some sort.

My friend is very knowledgeable with the latest technology."

Chevalier flicked the next switch and the screen came to life.

"It's the old farm road," the boy said pointing at the screen, "It's back a bit, outside of town."

Chevalier studied the monitor; he recognized the road as the one he arrived on when the Citroen jumped through the doorway. Below the location was a set of coordinates pinpointing the current position of the Porsche and the distance to a particular point, the nearest point being on the very same *old farm road.* Another point was located about three hundred meters from the glass building, where the Porsche was originally parked with its flat tire.

"Jacque, can you tell me exactly where you have seen this Travis person when he was in the village?"

"Sometimes he is in the tavern, other times I have seen him in the mission."

"Mission, where is that?"

"About ten kilometers from the village, it is where the monks work, where the white cloaked people live. It is where the watchers guard the perimeter."

"Watchers, what are watchers? What do they do there?"

"I heard they make things in there."

"What kind of things do they make?"

"I'm not certain but I heard they make some kind of jewelry."

Chevalier drove the Porsche for fifteen minutes. He returned to the glass building where the red car had been originally parked.

"Well my friend that is your ride. Thank you for your help. Perhaps we will meet again sometime."

The young man happily strolled off, waving back as he turned the corner. Chevalier sat in the red car staring at the screen, wondering how the guidance system operated, wondering about the monks at the mission, wondering what jewelry they produced at the mission, and wondering if *they* were the watchers.

He thought about the village. Started the Porsche up once again and drove to the village. He found a small hotel, and parked at the entrance to the lobby. He entered the lobby and checked in at the front desk. An elderly man answered the bell, squinting through thick lenses at Chevalier. He had a tussled head of white hair reminiscent of Einstein. The two men stared at each other, Chevalier wondering if the glasses, nose and moustache were attached, if they could be removed from the head like some kind of comical mask.

"Yes monsieur, can I help you?"

Yes, I'm here for dance lessons, Chevalier thought, but he said, "May I have a room for the night?"

The man opened a registry; the book was almost the size of the desk. He ran his finger down the page, readjusted his thick lens glasses and mumbled, "Let me see, let me see, let me see hmm . . . I do have one room available. It is a little more expensive. A little, little, little more expensive. It has a bathroom. Yes a bathroom, bathroom, and a shower."

Chevalier stared directly at the lenses, shook his head a little, and said, "I'll take it."

Einstein passed a key and directed the guest to his room.

It was at the far end of the building. Chevalier decided to leave the Porsche parked where he'd left it, at least a hundred meters from his room. It was damp and musty, as though no one had stayed in it for a long time. A very long time. He sat on the bed and it squeaked like an out of tune violin. He bounced a few times, tested the firmness of the mattress. Caused the squeaking to intensify.

The dusty lamp at the bedside flickered. The television opposite the bed caught Chevalier's eye. Looking around for a remote, he realized the futility of his search, stood and walked to the set. Switched it on . . . nothing happened. The clock in the room said one fifteen. He doubted the correctness of the clock. He mumbled almost whispered, "Nothing else works, why should the fuckin' clock be any different?" He checked his watch, one fifteen. *Hmm, the clock is correct.*

Smiling, he returned to the bed and sat. The squeaking kicked back in. The day had been long. Rustling in the trees outside the window played on his mind. *What if I have reason to leave in a hurry*, he thought. *The car is parked quite a distance from this room.*

The room had no rear exit. The small medieval bathroom did have a window. He sat on the bed looking in the direction of the bathroom. He stretched nervously, stood and made his way to the smaller room. The shower was old, a plastic curtain that had seen better days. He strolled back to the bed and undressed. Needed to use the toilet and shower.

He sat on the toilet, reached for the paper role. Found the role was almost empty. Pealed off the last short strip, hardly enough. When he was through, he stood and pressed the flush button, nothing happened. He stared at the mess in the bowl. Realizing the need for fresh air, he looked up at the window. Couldn't reach it. He closed the toilet lid, carefully stepped up onto it. *If I need to make a hasty escape, I can fit through this window*, he thought. *Just a bit of a lift to raise myself to the sill.*

The rustling in the trees was louder, much louder this time. He stood on the toilet seat, slowly pushed the window open. The ensuing scream startled the manager, who immediately limped from his office into the hotel's car-lot. Chevalier didn't mean to scream, but the toilet lid had dug into his leg as his foot crashed through it His foot was now immersed in the un-flushed contents of the bowl.

"OH MY GOD," he shouted aloud in agonizing pain.

His other foot found solid dry ground alongside the toilet, but as the contents of the bowl spilled over the edge it added to his difficulty, his one dry foot began slipping. He grabbed out at the shower curtain. Hanging precariously on its plastic rings, the curtain popped off. Chevalier tumbled backward onto the tiled floor. His one wedged foot placed too much pressure on the bowl. It separated from the floor, and the entire bowl tipped on its side and emptied across the bathroom floor.

It was a few minutes before Chevalier attempted to raise himself from the quagmire, to regain what could be salvaged of his composure. Not of his dignity, that was long gone. His predicament was one he would never share with his associates.

CHAPTER 44

BLAKE SPENT THE NIGHT at Camile's. The next morning she showered, and wearing a black lace negligee served breakfast fit for a king.

"Wow this looks good enough to be a man's last meal." Blake laughed.

"Please Drew; do not make a joke about it. I am so scared that you will follow the inspector and I'll never see you again. Is there some way I can change your mind? Please, it is so dangerous."

"Honey, if last night didn't change my mind, nothing will. I gotta do it. He can't stay there alone. Can't believe I let him go off without me in the first place."

"Will you try to go through the same point where he vanished?"

She paused, thought about what she'd just said.

He answered in an uncertain tone, "Yeah."

"Of course, how else can you follow him? How stupid of me. But will you return the same way?"

"I guess the vanishing point and re-entry point are one and the same. Listen Camile, I've taken greater risks in my life." He lied with a straight face as he sipped his coffee. "I'm leaving this morning. I'll take Claude's Ferrari, he won't be pleased but I feel better with its power rather than a regular sedan. First I'll need to pack a few things. You never know what I'll find when I get to wherever the hell this ride takes me."

"Drew damn it, let me come along. You mean so much to me; I do not want to lose you."

"Impossible. I'll find Claude, and this Travis character, and then we'll all return. Promise."

Camile lowered her head in a sulking gesture. The two embraced. Blake held the kiss longer than the manual recommends, but deep inside he considered this might very well be a goodbye kiss. A final farewell.

The drive back to Blake's hotel was slow. Pre-lunch

traffic was building up and the roundabouts were never a Blake favorite.

"Fuckin' French drivers!" he shouted as he zigzagged between impatient horn blowers, all going somewhere, few moving anywhere.

He opened a midsize carry-bag, packed denim jeans, sneakers, a Viking's sweatshirt, underwear, two boxes of nine millimeter cartridges, and a backup Glock. He checked the contents of his bathroom travel bag, added a few extra Advil, some Band-Aids and cotton buds. Jammed it all into the bag between the sneakers and the Glock.

The Glock was a Model 17 semi-automatic, a nine millimeter caliber. Just a tad over seven inches in length and weighing less than twenty-three ounces, it was a favorite of many government agents as well as private contractors. It had a muzzle velocity of 1180 feet per second and carried an optional magazine holding nineteen rounds. Blake's marksmanship had greatly improved since his switch from the smaller Beretta, which only carried ten cartridges.

He wrote a lengthy letter explaining his actions as best he could. He sealed the envelope, placed a stamp in the corner, and addressed it to McDowell. He attached a note to the envelope. Leaving a letter with Camile had crossed his mind, but this would only serve to distress her all the more. The note read: "To be mailed in the event I do not return by Saturday March 29." This allowed three days for him to locate Chevalier and return safely. He placed the letter on the table facing the door, easily seen by anyone entering the room.

He knew what needed to be done. Driving the Ferrari to the old farm road, he slowed and sat facing the vanishing point, the car purring like a cat about to pounce. He looked into the rearview mirror. No one. Then at the road ahead. No one. The way was clear. He aligned the Ferrari with the center of the road, gunned the motor. The Testa Rossa zoomed to top speed, Blake's head pressing firmly against the restraint.

The car shot into the vanishing point and Drew Blake saw his world spinning around him. Flashes of color. A nebula flash, and then . . . as if by magic, he was on a quiet road not unlike the one he'd just left. The car slowed to a steady speed. He looked about in awe, expecting a different world. Ahead he saw a small farmhouse. Kids were playing alongside a large haystack. *This is earth as I know it, nothing's different.*

He cruised the narrow road until another group of kids caught his eye. They were playing by the road ahead. He slowed the car, brought it to a stop, called to the nearest kid.

"Hey, can you tell me how far to the nearest town?"

The boy shook his head and shrugged.

Another of the children approached the car and, smiling at Blake said, "You asked?"

"Understand English? How far to the next town?"

He pointed along the road. "That way, about thirty kilometers."

The other kids rambled on in French, making Blake feel a little more secure, realizing at least he wasn't on a different planet. When he arrived at the hotel, his eyes were immediately drawn to the red car parked at the far end of the parking area. He slowly and quietly drove the Ferrari toward the red car. He stopped alongside, primed the Glock, walked around the Porsche. He leaned inside the open window, touched the wires dangling from the dash. He quietly locked the Ferrari, walked to the attendant's office, and pushed on the door. The door squeaked as he entered.

"Hello, anyone there?"

The Einstein man with the bulbous nose and thick lens glasses entered from the adjoining room. "We monsieur?" he said in a gravely voice.

"You speak English?"

"Of course, I am a businessman, I speak several languages. How can I be of assistance?"

"That red Porsche outside, can you tell me who owns it?"

"I know of no such car, let me look at it."

He shuffled toward the door, taking painful six inch steps. Blake let out a long breath, raising his eyes to the ceiling. As the old man made his way toward the car, Blake spun the registry book around and ran his finger down the guest list.

His finger halted, he moved closer, double checked the name.

"Christ. He's is here . . . unless there's another C. Chevalier," he said quietly to himself.

When the man re-entered the room, Blake asked politely, "You have a guest named Chevalier signed in. What room's he in?"

"In the far room, number nine. He only recently checked in."

Blake feared the worse, knowing the red car belonged to Travis. It was conceivable Travis was in the room with Chevalier, *why else would the Porsche be here*, he thought. *Christ, I'm too late to help him. Has Craven got to him already?*

Blake moved like a gazelle. Pulled the Glock as he moved, making his way toward the door numbered nine. He placed an ear to the door, listened. Nothing. There were no sounds coming from the room, no voices, no television. He stepped back from the door, raised one foot and kicked hard at the door, just above the lock.

Chevalier sprung quickly from his bed, stumbled to reach his handgun. He'd placed it on a cabinet across the room, *a mistake*. The words flashed through his mind. *A mistake. Should never leave my gun out of reach.* He fell to the floor, rolled - reached up for the pistol - had it - turned - raised it quickly in the direction of the intruder smashing through his door. But the intruder was on him.

"Jesus Christ Claude! What's that smell?"

"BLAKE!   HOW CAN YOU BE HERE? WHAT THE HELL!"

Both men lowered their weapons and embraced. The attendant reached the demolished door. He was shocked at the sight of the demolished door, even more shocked at the sight of Chevalier standing naked with Blake's arms firmly wrapped around him.

The old man grinned. He said, "*L'amour,* ah yes . . . it is so grand." He deleted the grin and said, "Which of you two will pay for the damage?"

"Ah shit, what's that fuckin' smell?" Blake said again, screwing up his face and stepping away. He looked at the naked Chevalier.

"Jesus Christ man, get some clothes on."

Chevalier pulled the sheet from the bed, wrapped it around himself, maintaining a dignified quality reminiscent of Caesar addressing the Senate.

Blake threw Chevalier a look of typical intensity. Chevalier, now blushing a bright tone of red forched the words, "I had a slight problem with the toilet, an overflowing of sorts. My closthes are still drying. I had to launder everything. They are all still wet."

"You okay Claude? That mark on your side, that's a hell of a bruise. What happened?"

Chevalier thought he may have hit his hip as he fell, but quickly realized Blake was referring to his birthmark.

"No, no, it is our family heirloom, you might say, a birthmark. My father had the same distinguishing attribute."

Blake caught a brief glimpse as Chevalier pulled the sheet tightly around his midriff.

"Kind of looks like a dolphin; you sure it's not a tattoo?"

"It is a birth mark." Chevalier replied in a snapping tone, now showing obvious embarrassment and impatience at Blake's inquisitiveness. His dignity clearly depleted.

Blake stepped toward the bathroom. The stench was unbearable. He turned away, went to the entry door now lying on its side, pushed his head into the fresh outer air, inhaled deeply and dashed back to the bathroom. He dared not breathe; he nudged the door slowly open. A blast of heat smacked his bulging cheeks. He turned away and let the breath out.

"Jesus Christ, what a fuckin' mess."

The tiled floor was slippery. Chevalier's clothing and shoes were spread about the small room. A small heater whirred away, adding to the stench that drifted from the bathroom. The acrid odor of excrement wafted into the main room. There was no respite to the occupants of number nine.

"Forget your clothes Claude. If we're gonna work

together you'll need to freshen up, dress a little more fragrantly," Blake said standing ten feet away from the destroyed door. The Einstein man scribbled on a note pad, estimating the damages. Blake peeked sideways, it was a long list.

He called aloud, "Hey Claude, I got a change of clothes in my luggage. You're about my size. Trousers might be a bit long. You'll need to roll the cuffs, okay?" He turned to Einstein and said, "Got another bathroom, he needs to clean up?"

Chevalier showered for the third time. He called to Blake from the shower, "I still have a smell."

"Splash on a little Givenchy. You'll be fine."

Chevalier sprayed himself liberally with the Givenchy. He thanked Blake for the supplies. The now overpowering overindulgence of cologne had Blake again outside of the room. He called into the room, "I'll be waiting in the car Pepe."

The French sense of humor has never been a strong attribute. Chevalier pulled a face. Blake missed the look as he walked to the front lobby, passed a bundle of notes to the Einstein man.

Once in the Testa Rosa, Chevalier filled Blake in on the events. He explained the car jacking incident and how he'd come across the Porsche, neither man fully understanding the complexities of this place they were now in. In appearance it resembled their own country, their earth. The language was the same and the people appeared to be the same. Claude had tried to place a call to his office from the hotel desk, the line was dead.

Claude filled Blake in on what he'd heard about the mission, how Travis was seen on occasions in the area, how the inhabitants of the glass building wore robes and produced jewelry. How they were guarded by watchers. Drew sat in silence, shrunk back into the seat. He absorbed each word like a child listening to a fairy tale. Every so often he'd shake his head in disbelief, followed by Chevalier's reassuring nod.

Chevalier reached into the glove compartment. His spare pack of cigarettes was still there. He lit up, took a long pleasurable draw. Then he grumbled in an unhappy tone, "You should not have brought my Ferrari."

Blake ignored him. He waved his hands about and said, "Ah jeez, d'ya have to smoke those stinking things?" He rolled his head from side to side. Chevalier stared out the window, blowing the smoke away from Blake, pretending to ignore the antics.

"Claude, have you come across a couple of Russian guys during your investigations in Paris?"

Chevalier grunted. The question caught him, but the cigarette covered for him. The grimacing facial expression could be attributed to the strong cigarette. The grunt gave him time to chew over the reply.

"We have suspected Russian involvement, what with the two bodies in the jewelry store being Russian agents."

"Have you identified the guys?"

"No."

"Two were our guys, right? From the embassy. Strange, very strange," Blake added pensively. "We still haven't made the connection. What're your thoughts?"

"I am not certain, let us see where the next few hours lead us. With any luck, the whole thing - it may become clearer."

When the white Citroën cruised by the hotel, Chevalier had his back to the road, he missed its passing. Blake watched it pass, but didn't realize who the occupants were. It passed through his mind like a slow speed movie. He thought about what Chevalier had said earlier, *a white Citroen.*

"Did you say you were originally driving a white Citroën?"

"Yes, and they were all in the car when they left me by the roadside. That son-of-a-bitch. The other one really gave him hell for letting me run off. He. . ."

As Chevalier spoke Blake started the Ferrari, whipped the car around, and headed off in the direction of the Citroen.

"HEY, HEY, HEY! What is the rush? Steady with my car. I told you not to bring my Ferrari. What are you doing, why are we heading this way in such a hurry?"

"The car that just passed, it's a white Citroën."

CHAPTER 45

THE TWO CARS HEADED in the direction of the vanishing point.

Blake could see the brake lights of the white car five hundred meters ahead. As they drew nearer, the Citroën moved across the center lines of the road, aligning itself with the doorway, increasing its speed dramatically.

Blake pushed the accelerator to the floor; the Ferrari quickly closed the gap. Travis kept the Citroën on track, momentarily glancing into his rearview mirror.

"No, it can't be," he snapped at Angelica, who squirmed with pain. She turned, propped herself up on one elbow, sneaked a glimpse of the pursuing car.

"Who is it, do you recognize them?"

"I can't believe it. The French cop from the barn. How'd he get through the doorway? How'd he find me? He was in Paris." He stopped talking and thought for a minute. "Unless he had access to a disc. THE DISC! Of course - that's it - it must be - it's the only way. Son-of-a-bitch. Fuckin' Chevalier. I should've finished him in the barn."

Angelica slowly turned to the passengers in the rear of the Citroën. She was breathing heavily, her chest wound still seeping.

"I need to get to a doctor Travis. Please we've lost enough time; I can't lose more because of them following us."

Amy was comforting Karen. Her bleeding had stopped and she continued to drift in and out of consciousness. Rick and Saffrey both stared through the rear window of the Citroën at the Ferrari now quickly closing the gap. The Citroën sped toward the doorway and vanished. The Ferrari followed on its tail. It was right there less than a hundred meters ahead, and then nothing. It was gone. Blake dropped down a gear, picked up speed, gunned the Ferrari and rocketed through the doorway.

The old farm road was deserted as the Citroën jumped

through, landing with a squealing screech. It accelerated on the asphalt surface and Craven turned it hard right. It swerved out of control; he regained the upper hand, steering through an opening and behind a row of tall hedges. He killed the engine, didn't breath, listened for the roar of the Ferrari.

Chevalier and Blake bounced hard on the asphalt as the Ferrari jumped through, bottoming out heavily on the narrow road.

"MY GOD, HIT THE BRAKES!" Chevalier cried loudly, his arms outstretched as he braced himself back from the dash.

Blake slammed the pedal down. The Ferrari swerved uncontrollably off the side of the road, hit loose gravel and began swaying. It completed a 360 degree spin, not once but three times. When it came to a stop, both men were disoriented and shaken. They staggered from the car, each falling to his knees, the dust cloud keeping them in total suspense, keeping their surroundings a surprise.

"Thank God, thank God," Chevalier gasped. "Oh Jesus, oh Jesus. We are alive, thank you Jesus." Chevalier had joined the ranks of born again Christians.

"It's okay Claude. It's okay, take it easy," Blake said gagging as he breathed the dust. He wiped his eyes free of the dirt. Chevalier coughed, smudged the tears with the backs of his hands as they ran down his dust coated face.

"Wasn't too bad huh? Come on Claude, show a little backbone for Christ's sake. It's just like Disneyland, like, like the Indiana Jones ride."

"I do not ride the fast rides at Disneyland, I dislike the uncertainty." He shuddered, glanced at Blake, said, "Where has the Citroën gone?"

"I can smell it," Blake said squinting through the settling dust. "The smell of hot rubber, a hot motor. Can't you smell it Claude?"

"I can smell something, but it is a lot worse than burning rubber," Chevalier quipped.

Blake grinned, "Don't need a visual, thanks."

The two men walked back to the entry point.

"See, here are our tire tracks, see the skid pattern, and look over here," Blake pointed to a second set of tire skids. "Here's where the Citroën landed."

The white car was nowhere to be seen. The two men strolled about the area, but the Citroën was too well hidden. The occupants were as quiet as church mice. Craven kept his weapon pointed at the passengers in the rear seat. They didn't need to be told to stay quiet. He told them anyway. Craven whispered, "Not a sound, not even a breath, or so help me, I'll leave your bodies by the roadside. I've no further use for any of you, understand?" Craven stared ahead; unaware of what had happened in the rear of the car.

Amy, Rick, and Saffrey sat frozen. They didn't hear a word he'd said. They were staring at Karen. The bleeding had stopped, in fact she was back to normal, the arm had never left her body. Karen was whole. Nothing had changed; she was as she'd been before the limousine first jumped them through the doorway.

Blake drove the Ferrari toward the city. Both men remained silent during the drive; time to rethink the whole situation.

CHAPTER 46

WHEN CERTAIN THE ROAD ahead was clear, Craven pulled the Citroën out and headed toward the city. A few kilometers passed and he slowed, swinging the car into a driveway.

"Wha – wha - what is it?" Angelica asked, the pain from her wound causing her to slur her words.

"That's the cottage. It's where the doctor lives. He took care of my leg wound."

He pulled the car along the side of the house where, well hidden from passers by.

"Out of the car, get out of the car," Craven ordered, waving the gun at the passengers, motioning them toward the house. He knocked loudly on the door. No one answered. He wasted no time. He raised one foot, splintered the jam as the lock smashed apart.

"Inside, inside, inside," he snapped lookin behind them, anticipating the Ferrari's arrival. No one came. He'd eluded his pursuers. Once in the cottage, Craven slammed the door closed, pushing a small table against it to keep it from opening.

Saffrey said, "Rick, take a look around, find a bowl, hot water, and disinfectant. Gotta clean her wound."

"When did you start giving the orders here?" Craven snapped.

Rick said, "Fuck you Craven, your lady here needs help. Ya can see there ain't no doctor here. We can use whatever stuff's around, try to make her comfortable."

Saffrey asked, "Why didn't her wound disappear like Karen's? I don't get it."

Craven grimaced, "Your girl re-entered as she left, but Angelica didn't originate in your time, therefore this is her first jump through, the way she entered is the way she is, with the wound - your luck - her bad luck."

Craven stared at Angelica, pondering their situation. He

returned his attention to Rick and said, "Okay, okay, you're right. See what medication you can find. I remember seeing a cupboard full of stuff in the room out back. But no heroics, you know I have no hesitation killing any of you."

"Rick, come with me," Saffrey said dismissing Craven's threat.

The two men began sorting through the dozens of bottles in the small surgery, placing bandages and disinfectant into a large stainless steel bowl. Rick ran hot water from the tap, ran it until it steamed. Craven helped Angelica to her feet and slowly walked her to the surgery. He removed her shirt; the congealed blood disguised the small bullet hole a few inches below her right shoulder, the surrounding skin now deep blue from the bruising.

Rick touched the blue area, said "Ouch, good thing this wasn't another couple of inches over. Would have been a chest hit, we wouldn't be doin' this."

"Pass me the forceps," Saffrey said quietly.

Rick walked to a small burner where the stainless steel bowl was bubbling, the instruments now sterile in the water.

He used a cold pair of forceps to reach into the hot water, extracted the sterilized forceps. Saffrey scrubbed up and slipped his hands into surgical gloves.

"D'ya think you can do this? Rick asked. "I mean, can you find the slug?"

"Can't leave it in there. I've done it before, could get lucky," Saffrey said as sweat beaded on his forehead.

"LUCKY? LUCKY?" Craven shouted. "You could get very fuckin' unlucky too," he growled pointing the gun at the back of Rick's head.

"If she so much as lets out a whimper, I'll ventilate the dancer here, do you understand?" Craven snorted.

Neither man acknowledged the threat; Saffrey slowly moved the forceps into the wound. As he did Angelica began groaning. Saffrey backed off, slipped a half look toward Craven. Craven, now sweating profusely, raised the gun, placed it against Saffrey's temple.

Saffrey shouted "You wanna do this? Come on you fuck! Move the gun or take over with the fuckin' forceps! Fuck you Craven, get out of my face you pretentious mother-fucker!"

Craven spun away and slammed the gun butt down hard on the table.

He shouted in rage, "IT'S TIME, GET OUT. GET OUT-SIDE. I'M GONNA SETTLE THIS RIGHT NOW, OUTSIDE - NOW!"

"What the fuck are you doin'?" Rick snapped. "Let him get on with this, she'll feel pain, and she'll make noise, but he's gotta get the slug out."

The sound of the car pulling into the driveway threw the moment into silence. They all froze, looked toward the door. Craven rushed to the window, parted the curtain enough to see the driver stepping from the car. The doctor walked to the trunk, removed two grocery bags and proceeded to the house. As he approached the door, he saw that it had been all but destroyed. He backed away dropping his groceries as Craven greeted him.

"My God what are you doing here? Why have you smashed my door?" He stared at Saffrey. "Why are you pink?" Then pointing at Rick he asked, "Are you a policeman?" Totally confused he turned to Craven, "Why are you dressed as a clown?"

"Don't recognize me huh doc? It's a long story. Thanks for the great job on my leg, never felt better. But you need to take care of my lady. She urgently needs your expertise."

He led the doctor into the room, to where Angelica was laying. He turned to Amy and said, "Push the table back against the door."

Amy slid the table over, the door looked fine; unless someone tried the handle from the outside, saw the smashed lock. The doctor administered an anesthetic shot to Angelica and proceeded to remove the bullet. The procedure was over in less than twenty minutes. The anesthetic injection spiraled Angelica into a deep sleep, while the bullet was safely removed and the wound closed.

"How did this happen, this bullet wound? Why didn't you

go to the city, go to an emergency room?"

"Our little secret doc; can I trust you to keep a secret?" Craven stared into the doctor's eyes, a cold emotionless stare on his face. He glanced around the room at the other man and women there. "I can make it well worth your while. Kind of feel like I owe you doc, what with the leg job you did for me and all this stuff with my lady here."

The doctor didn't acknowledge the compliment.

"What do you say doc? Keep a secret?"

The doctor looked at him, took a deep breath and sat down.

Saffrey looked at the doctor and quickly added, "I think you should take his advice, nothing good can come of your reporting this, and . . ," he looked at Craven and motioned with his head at the gun. "We don't want that. You might be around if we need you again . . . but only if you go along with him. Okay doctor?"

"So you expect me not to report this gunshot wound?"

"That's the most promising scenario doc," Saffrey said. "God only knows what he'll do to all of us if he eliminates you." He took a quick look at Craven. He was sitting by Angelica, gently stroking her arm.

Saffrey leaned closer to the doctor, "Let me put it more bluntly. If he kills one of us, he'll have no reason not to leave us all here. So I want YOU to do as he says, keep it a secret."

Saffrey winked at the doctor and smiled nodding. The smile was returned, although somewhat forced. It was clear the doctor had fully grasped the implication of Craven's threat and realized it was not a shallow one. Realized he'd to agree to remain silent. Craven moved away from Angelica, gave the doctor a questioning look, turned both palms up in an asking gesture.

"Agreed, you've my word that this incident didn't happen. You were never here."

"Good, now let's get something to eat, hope you have some good food in those bags doc. We can't be leaving here on empty stomachs. My mother always said breakfast is the most important meal of the day."

Rick, unable to pass up an opportunity quickly added, "You had a mom, you really had a MOM? Jesus fuckin' Christ, how about that!"

Craven sat back on a small settee, scowled at Rick, and putting his feet up on a pillow said to Saffrey, Karen and Amy. "You'll all rest for a while. We've a big day ahead of us tomorrow."

* * * * *

The early morning dew hung across the meadow like a shroud, floating just feet above the ground. Craven stepped from the cottage, wrapped his arms around his shoulders and shivered. Narrow beams of sunlight slid through the tree-tops like razor sharp sheaths, lighting up scattered spots of white dew, looking like snow flakes levitating meters above the ground.

Craven's footsteps echoed on the wooden floor of the porch as he walked to the doctor's car. He rubbed the dew from the side window, peered inside. *Doesn't look too bad*, he thought. *Much safer than taking the Citroën.*

He strolled around the car, checked the tires. Checked the doors . . . all locked. He passed a final glance over the car, nodded approval of his plan, kicked a small rock from his path, and returned to the porch.

Rick stirred and turned to Saffrey. He realized Craven wasn't in the room, he said quietly, "Saff. Saffrey can you hear me?"

"Yeah, what's up?"

"Have we got a plan?"

"Got a what?"

"A plan. A plan to get away from this fuckin' madman."

Saffrey turned to face Rick, thought for a while, stretched, rolled his head about in a stretching motion, made a few sounds as the vertebrae reset themselves, and said, "What do you want to do, escape from him or settle up the score? You know what I'm saying; he's caused some serious grief. Do you want to settle the score, or just run off when the opportunity presents itself? Not know when he's behind you, having to look over your shoulder the rest of your life."

"Nah. Not when you put it that way. Fuck him. Let's settle up the score. After all, I've got a dance date with the mother-fucker."

Craven stepped back into the room and as he passed by Amy he nudged her with his foot.

"Wake up, get some breakfast going. Hey doc, how about some coffee?"

Angelica raised her head from the pillows, groaned as Craven stroked her blonde hair: "Travis, I feel so weak, how long have I been sleeping?"

"It's morning princess. You just rest. We'll get moving after we eat. The good doctor has done well."

Craven turned to Saffrey, and then motioned to Rick with his head as he said, "You think I'm a cold blooded killer don't you? Maybe I am, but regardless of what you think, your very survival rests in my hands." He paused, and then turned to stare directly at Rick. "I've fantasized at the many ways I would cut you up, but you have an endearing quality I've found quite amusing, so maybe I'll let you live, but on the other hand, you all know too much. Hmm, can I trust you to forget our little escapade?" He moved his eyes off Rick and raised them to the ceiling, waited a few long seconds, and placed one finger over his lips. Then he spun around and pointed at Amy, spoke quickly, one word running into the next, "Perhaps I only need one of you to accompany me, a hostage, insurance of sort in case your friends get too chatty." He slid one finger across his throat, slipped his tongue from the side of his mouth, made a gurgling sound.

"You're one sick fuck," Rick steamed. "How about you and me we just step outside. Get this settled once and for all?"

Craven laughed a sick depraved taunt. He began an impromptu Irish jig, dancing slowly toward Rick: "Ouch. I'm scared of my little dance partner. Look I'm shaking." He laughed again, swiveled as he danced about, made a gun shape with his hand and fired an imaginary shot at Rick's head: "Bang. Hmm, maybe. I like the thought. Bang, you're dead."

Rick made a move to stand as Saffrey placed a hand on his shoulder, restraining him. The tension was broken when the doctor called from the kitchen: "Coffee, it is ready."

"Thank God, let me have some. Extra strong I hope," Amy said rolling her eyes. It diffused the tense atmosphere and Craven again turned his attention to Angelica who was now trying to reposition herself on the sofa.

"Hold on there princess, I'll give you a helping hand. Let me get you some breakfast. You'll feel better. Hey doc, when you're through in the kitchen, take a look at her wound, maybe change the dressing."

They ate cereal, fruit and coffee. Saffrey spent the next thirty minutes in the bathroom rubbing away at the remnants of the pink dye, his face now growing red from the incessant scrubbing. Rick took a shirt from the doctor and did his best to change his appearance from a motorcycle cop to a less conspicuous outfit. Craven, who was still sporting clown's trousers and colorful shirt turned and spoke to Amy. "Go to the bathroom and bring me a dish of warm water and some soap. I need to freshen up and get the last of this paint off my face."

"Ah shucks," Rick quipped. "I was getting to like it, especially the red fuckin' lips."

Craven flashed a look of disgust in Rick's direction. Rick puckered his lips and blew an air-kiss to Craven. Craven drew his gun from his belt, pointed it at Rick, and fired off a single shot, right between Rick's eyes. Rick appeared to stare for a second, then dropped to the floor. Very dead.

Craven Shouted, "YOU HAD TO PUSH. YOU HAD TO DO IT. YOU FACETIOUS . . ."

Amy and Karen screamed as Saffrey rushed to Rick's side shouting his name, "RICK, RICK, RICK."

Craven fired another shot, this time into the ceiling.

"YOU FUCKIN' MADMAN!" Saffrey shouted. He flung his body at Craven. Craven whipped the gun down across Saffrey's head sending him down. He lay alongside Rick, now staring lifelessly at the ceiling. The doctor stepped between Saffrey and Craven, fearing the enraged gunman was out of control, and dropped to Rick's side, felt for a pulse. Craven turned toward Karen who was in shock at the sight of her brother's execution. Craven pointed the weapon at Karen's head. His finger squeezed the trigger.

CHAPTER 47

A CAR HORN SOUNDED causing Craven to lower the weapon and rush to the window. The patrol car stopped twenty meters from the porch. Two uniformed men stepped from the car, guns drawn. One cop called, "Doctor, hey doctor, are you in there?"

"Answer him," Craven whispered. "Tell him you're fine or so help me you're all dead. Ask what they want. Quickly"

Karen cries hysterically and Amy held her hand firmly on Karen's mouth, trying to muffle her cries. The doctor paused momentarily, giving Amy time to quieten Karen. He opened the door and stepped onto the porch.

The cop called from his car, "Are you all right Paul? We heard gun shots."

"Oh it's you Geraldo. Good morning. What seems to be the problem?"

The cop hesitated, looked at his partner, thought for a few seconds then replied, "Shots, we heard gun shots."

"No shots here. Maybe it's some boys out shooting. Do not worry Geraldo, things are fine here."

The cop was silent for a few long seconds, then said, "How about my morning coffee Paul, do you have time for an old friend?"

The doctor said, "I'm sorry, I ran out of coffee and cream yesterday. I'll have to go to the store later today. Why don't you call back later, join me for a cup. We can get back to that chess game?"

The cop said, "Sure Paul, we'll see you later."

They walked back to the patrol car and slowly drove off.

"What was that all about Emile?" the driver asked his partner.

"Something is not right. He called me Geraldo. We have known each other since I was in school. He would never call me the wrong name. And just this morning we spoke at the store. He had just bought coffee and cream and invited me to stop by his house around this time. He hates chess, has always refused my offers to teach him the game. Something is very wrong."

The police car pulled to the roadside. The cop reported the situation back to his station. "Dispatch, this is car fifteen. We have a possible situation at the home of Dr. Paul Blau on the old farmhouse road, please send back up. We will wait out of sight of the house, and no sirens please."

Craven threw the dish of water onto Saffrey. He slowly raised himself from the floor. His eyes remained fixed on Rick whose eyes stared lifelessly at the ceiling. He placed a hand over the eyes, closed the eyelids. Karen continually called her brother's name, crying uncontrollably as Amy attempted to comfort her.

Angelica stared at Craven, propped herself up on one elbow. She said, "That was not necessary, we might have needed him. You are far too edgy Travis. When are we getting out of here?"

"Soon," he replied. "I gave him enough warnings. He was baiting me. Should've been smarter, he'd still be alive. Not my fault."

Craven opened the door and walked to the doctor's car. He stopped. Looking around, sensed something wasn't right; he tilted his head back, sniffed the air, and returned to the house. "Give me the car keys," he snapped at the doctor, thrusting his hand toward him. "You - Saffrey! Get up and get the bags into the car."

"Get the fuckin' things yourself. I'm done taking your orders!"

"Aw jeez," he said pointing the gun at Karen. "Maybe I'll just send this attractive kid along to join her dearly departed brother," He kept the gun pointed at Karen's head. He added, "Yeah why not, he could use company." Craven moved closer, placed the barrel of the gun on Karen's temple. She closed her eyes, didn't breathe. His finger began to tighten on the trigger as Saffrey shouted at him.

"STOP, STOP - LEAVE HER ALONE - NO MORE KILLING!"

Craven raised the gun to the ceiling and turned to Saffrey. "Get the five bags and place them into the car," he repeated, nodding his head in the direction of the doctor's car. Saffrey and the doctor immediately rushed from the house carrying the bags to the trunk of the car.

The cop hiding behind the distant bushes said, "Emile look, it's the doctor. He and another man are carrying bags from the house." The two cops crouched behind a hedge, watching the two men load the bags into the car.

Angelica walked slowly from the house, one arm around Craven's shoulder. He helped her to the vehicle, and slowly placed her in the rear seat. Amy and Karen stepped from the porch. The two girls slid into the rear seat alongside Angelica.

Craven placed the keys into his pocket and turned to Saffrey. "You get in the front; I'll be back in a few minutes."

Saffrey sat in the car and thought about hot-wiring the ignition. Reached under the dash and felt about for the wires.

Angelica leaned forward, pounding weakly on Saffrey's back. "Stop or I'll scream. If he comes you know he'll kill you."

Saffrey turned and leveled a solid blow to Angelica's chin and she promptly sank into a sleeping position, propped against Amy's shoulder.

"Shut the fuck up," Saffrey snapped as his fist struck her chin. "She'll be pain free for a while, but man, will she have some headache when she wakes."

He resumed his search for the wires. The sound of gunfire rang loudly from the house. Craven stood over the doctor lying in a pool of blood. Craven said, "Sorry doc, couldn't leave you to tell the story. After all, I did say I'd take care of you."

CHAPTER 48

INSPECTOR CLAUDE CHEVALIER SAT across from Drew Blake in his office. Neither man spoke for several minutes. Blake dialed a number, got Camile's answering machine. He listened, smiled at the sound of her voice, he said, "Hi Camile it's Drew. Just wanted to tell you I'm back. I've got Claude out safely. I've stopped for a coffee here at the station. I'll call you later today. I've missed you."

Chevalier exhaled his usual perfect smoke rings, Blake raised his arm, extending his index finger, watching as a white ring slid onto his finger then dissipated as it spread across his hand.

"Always wanted to do that, just couldn't get the knack."

"You have to pout your lips - like this." Chevalier pouted his lips forward. "Then you move your mouth like a fish, like this - making short bursts of air. You see – just like this."

"It looks very un-fuckin' cool Claude. Maybe that's why I can't seem to get it right."

"Ah yes, but it works best with the French cigarette," Claude said chuckling. He grinned and pushed the pack of Gauloise toward Blake.

"Ah, what the fuck." Blake pulled one from the pack. Chevalier leaned forward, lighting the cigarette.

Blake inhaled deeply, glared at Chevalier, and broke into a spate of uncontrollable coughing. "Jesus Christ Claude, this shit'll kill you!" He coughed a few more times and reached for his coffee, swished a mouthful as though it were mouth wash, then stubbed the cigarette into the ashtray.

"Tell me Drew, where do we go from here? I expect a call anytime on the white Citroën. It must show up soon, it cannot have just vanished again. We have got our police helicopters circling the area where we entered. Do you suppose he turned around and went back into the vanishing point?"

Blake hesitated, thinking, then answered, "I don't think

so, shot back into the hole? Nah - not likely - too much trouble getting here, not likely he'd just turn tail and head back on out. Let's drive back to the old farm road, maybe we can pick up some leads. Nothing better to do. Beats waiting around here. Let's go."

Chevalier raised himself from his seat and moved toward his office door. He reached for the handle. It exploded inward and Chevalier jumped sideways as the flustered cop burst into the room.

"Sorry inspector, downtown just reported in. Some people were killed in a fire and it sounds similar to the other burn cases."

The cop swallowed with a gulp and nodded to Blake acknowledging his presence, "Mr. McDowell from the embassy also called looking for you Mr. Blake."

Blake moved to the phone and dialed in the number.

"McDowell? Blake. What's up?"

"Drew, where the hell are you man? I've been trying to reach you for hours?"

"Long story. What the hell's going on with these burn victims?"

"Don't want to chat on the phone. Get on over to my office. How long?"

"An hour, no - make it half."

Chevalier re-entered as Blake placed the phone back on the receiver. "What news Claude?"

"An electrical firm. Three workers, all burned, there were no witnesses." Chevalier said grimly.

"I'm heading down that way now Drew, are you coming with me?"

"Just give me the address, I'll meet you there." Blake took a pen from his pocket. "I've one stop to make, give me two hours."

"I'll have one of my men drive you."

Blake arrived at the embassy and stepped onto the curb, turned to the driver and nodded gratefully. "Won't be too long; meet you back in the visitor's lot."

Adam McDowell greeted Blake with a hug and a firm handshake. Blake asked, "What's going on Adam, what's with the latest fire?"

McDowell was again sporting a seventies suit, wide lapels, narrow tie, he said, "They were electricians, and the MO is a dead match - excuse the pun - to the earlier victims. They were roasted. No damage to the immediate surroundings. Weird, too fuckin' weird."

"I've got a heap to tell you Adam, and it's gonna sound really fuckin' insane, so just hang in there with me. Give me a few days and I'll bust this thing wide open."

McDowell hesitated, he said, "Ah shit Drew, we've got two dead agents, the Russkies have two dead operatives, every fucker wants answers, so don't let me down. I'll hold off the powers that be. But rest assured, there're a ton of questions to be answered, and this poor bastard right here," and he tapped on his chest as he spoke, "is the one who's gonna be answering them."

"Leave it with me Adam. I'll tie up a few loose ends and get right back to you."

The tap on the door startled both men. They turned and stared at the frosted glass panel. McDowell said, "Yeah?"

CHAPTER 49

A TALL WELL-BUILT man in his early thirties with a surfer's crop of blond hair entered the room. He had an aura of confidence, a head held high. He had self-assurance that announced to the world he was capable of achieving anything. Extending a hand, he smiled at Blake. "Hey man, long time no see, you been on another vacation to Cinque Terre I hear?"

"Jesus Christ Dal, what're you doing here? I thought Sam had you hunkered down some place in South America."

Carson Dallas was a special agent within the American Interpol Division. Both he and Blake had resigned from The Secret Service to head up Sam Ridkin's AID team. He'd been assigned an undercover mission in South America, to do with boats picking up dope being flown from down south, then being dropped off the shores of New Orleans.

"Ah shit Drew, it's a long story, I'll tell ya 'bout it over a shake, okay?"

McDowell said, "You guys just might be heading down that way after we nail this son of a bitch Craven. Dal flew in yesterday under orders from the higher ups."

Blake was always amused by the use of the term "higher ups," the assumption being that the authorization came from some individual in high office, maybe even Washington. However, when push came to shove, finding a name to place on the dotted line was as easy as finding a pork chop in Jerusalem.

Forty-five minutes later, Blake and Dal arrived at the crime scene, an electrical company twenty minutes outside of Paris. Yellow tape surrounded the perimeter of the building. The Ferrari sat parked at the curb, patrol cars stretched along the length of the short backstreet.

"Nice wheels," Dal remarked as he passed the Ferrari. "Good money in the electrical business," he smirked as he threw a quick look at Blake.

Blake didn't elaborate on the ownership of the Testa Rossa.

Dal will discover the cars true owner in time, Blake thought, *why burst his bubble so early?* Both Dal and Blake drove Porsches, but Dal struggled each time he saw Blake driving his more highly esteemed C4 Porsche.

They arrived to find Chevalier kneeling. In front of him lay a roasted carcass resembling a human figure. There was an odor like pork on the spit – not intolerable, but then - not at all palatable.

"Smells like fuckin' pork roast in here," Dal quipped.

Blake coughed and nudged Dal in the ribcage in an effort to maintain some level of decorum.

"How's it looking Claude?" Blake asked with one hand still covering his mouth.

Chevalier slowly raised himself to his feet, brushing off his knees, "Same old scene," he replied.

The inspector took a packet from his pocket and quickly placed an Altoid onto his tongue.

"Claude I'd like you to meet Carson Dallas. He's a long time pal of mine; we've worked together since the pilgrims landed."

Chevalier gave Dallas a cursory smile, reached to shake his hand, "Mr. Dallas. My pleasure, I'm sure."

"Yeah likewise inspector, you can call me Dal."

Dal turned and unwillingly absorbed the carnage of burned bodies. He said, "Fuckin' horrific," as his hand motioned across the scene. "Same shit that Sam showed me in the video from the jeweler's store, burned bodies, but no collateral damage."

A work journal sat open on a desk. Chevalier slowly ran his finger down the entries. He said, "Look. Look right here Drew, this is the work journal of these men."

Blake studied the last few entries, steadying his finger on the final entry. "Bingo, McDonald's on Champs Elysées. Oh yeah!"

Dal shook his head. He said in an inquiring tone, "And?"

"Well . . . there was a meeting there . . . never mind, it'll make sense as we go along. Stay with me here, okay Dal?" Blake patted Dal's shoulder, a consoling gesture, an assurance that all would be explained. Blake turned to Chevalier who was still browsing the journal. "Do you see a connection, Claude?"

Chevalier scratched his forehead, squinting. "I - I don't know . . . could very well be." Chevalier waved his hands gesturing toward the bodies. "All these aromas, my stomach tells me it must be almost time to eat, shall we?" he asked, motioning to the door.

Dal kept a hand over his mouth, he leaned to Blake's ear, he whispered, "Jesus fuckin' Christ, he must have a cast iron stomach for Christ sake. I can't eat, I need to pewk."

Blake replied softly, "Give it time Dal, give it time. You'll get used to French cuisine." He killed the smile as Dal quickly made his way to fresh air.

With Dal in the lead, the three men quickly left the building. Blake and Dal stepped into a squad car. Chevalier remained on the curb. As he pushed the squad car door closed Dal asked, "Aren't you joining us inspector?"

Chevalier casually pointed toward the red car parked a few meters away; he said "I'll follow."

Dal nearly choking said "Jesus Christ, the Ferrari, it's his!"

Blake laughed aloud, "Yep, had the same initial effect on me too. Nice car, just a bit of a squeeze for a second passenger. But it goes like a bat out of fuckin' hell."

CHAPTER 50

CHEVALIER PULLED TO THE curb, placed a police notice on the dash and hurried toward McDonald's. When he entered the store he was greeted by a young girl offering to take his order.

"I wish to speak with the manager."

The manager, a middle aged man sporting a neat white moustache, moved from around the counter, carefully ushering his guests to a point as far as possible from the customers lined up at the order counter. He sensed these men were not after a Happy Meal.

"How can I assist you gentlemen?" he asked inquisitively.

Chevalier gently led the man by an elbow. He walked from the store, speaking quietly as they went. His assertive nature left no doubt as to his position of authority.

"I am Inspector Chevalier, I have questions that need answering, and you monsieur, might be able to help me."

Four uniformed cops arrived and impressively stood behind their boss. The manager seemed to struggle with his voice as he grunted. He said "Of course inspector, what is it you wish to know?"

"You had some recent electrical work carried out here by Dupont Electrical Services, correct?"

"Why yes, they did some repairs in the bathroom. Is there a problem with them?"

The manager gestured toward the bathroom and Chevalier nodded in that direction. The small procession inconspicuously made its way toward the corner of the restaurant.

"What exactly is it they were doing in this bathroom?"

"The light was not working correctly, so we had them replace it. As well as add one other."

"How did they gain access into the ceiling?"

"They raised the panels and used a ladder."

"Do you have a ladder?"

"Of course, I will get it for you."

Blake stared at the ceiling panels. He said, "You can reach this panel by standing on the toilet lid, Claude."

"Thank you very much Mr. Blake."

Blake chuckled.

Chevalier grunted, "Yes, best we wait for the ladder."

Dal sensed he'd missed something in the exchange and asked, "Care to fill me in on that one?"

"Another long story. Ask Claude to fill you in on it later. It's a doozy. He really gets a kick out of telling it."

Chevalier chuffed, saying, "Maybe it is amusing for you, but at the time . . . perhaps later, we'll see. Aha, the ladder, she has arrived."

The small ladder was placed beneath the light. It carefully straddled the toilet bowl. Chevalier stared at the bowl with hesitation in his eyes, raised the lid and gave the bowl an unnecessary flush.

"Better safe than sorry huh Drew."

"I understand Claude, I absolutely understand."

Chevalier directed one of the cops to raise a ceiling panel. The police activity attracted the attention of passersby. A large crowd now congregated outside the restaurant.

"Have your people clear the store," Chevalier said to one of the cops. "We will treat this as a crime scene until we know what we're getting ourselves into."

The vehement protesting of the manager fell on deaf ears as Chevalier glared insistently at him. The cops, together with the McDonald's staff began ushering the patrons from the shop.

Chevalier called to one of the departing men, "I want the fingerprint crew here, fast."

The flashlight shined through the maze of trusses and wiring.

"Handprints up here inspector, plenty of prints," the cop with the flashlight called out. "But all that I can see ahead are wires and building structure, no packages, nothing unusual."

Blake pushed his way between the four uniformed cops holding the ladder. He grinned slyly at Dal, looked at Chevalier, and quietly said, "How many Frenchmen does it take to hold a ladder?"

Dal passed an apologetic smirk to Chevalier who didn't seem to appreciate the sarcasm.

"Mind if I take a peek Claude?"

"Go ahead, do not touch anything."

Chevalier nodded to one of the cops and mumbled in a low tone: "Call the station and get me the home addresses and telephone numbers of the families of the deceased electricians. I want you to get right back to me as soon as you have the information."

Five minutes later the cop returned and handed a note paper to the inspector. He read through the list. Passed it to Blake.

"Take a look at these names Drew. We need to follow up on this immediately."

Blake glanced at the list and handed it to Dal. Chevalier lowered his voice to his most intimidating depth: "Keep everyone away from this area, cordon off the restroom, and leave two men here until further notice."

"But inspector," interrupted the store manager, "what of our patrons?"

"You have two choices monsieur. They can all use the ladies' restroom or you can serve women only for today."

"But, but . . ." the mumbling manager's pleas fell on deaf ears as the entourage of gendarmerie fell into line behind their inspector and the troop exited McDonald's.

Once back at the office, all three men removed their coats and fresh coffee was ordered. Chevalier made the first call.

"Are you the wife of Anders Borge?" Chevalier asked as the softly spoken woman sobbed on the phone.

"Yes I am she. Who is speaking?"

"This is Inspector Chevalier, I'm sorry to call you at such a grievous time madam; however I need to ask you some very important questions about your husband."

"Please inspector, I have answered so many questions. If there are any unanswered, I cannot imagine what they could be."

"We know your husband brought home a diamond he found."

Blake caught the quick look from Dal. Saw the question mark flashing like a neon sign above his head. There was silence. Chevalier was playing his bluff card, and it was working. He asked, "Madame Borge, are you there?"

"How did you know of the diamond? I spoke of it to no one," she replied in a quivering soft voice. "Anders found it in the ceiling at McDonald's, he did no wrong. He was going to have it made into a pendant for our anniversary."

"What of his co-workers madam? Did they also have stones?"

"Anders told me they were all well rewarded for their work at the restaurant. He said they each received a diamond."

"And you did not find this suspicious . . . oh I am sorry, ignore that question madam. Thank you Madame Borge; we will be back in touch with you."

The woman sobbed uncontrollably saying, "Inspector the funeral is in two days. Do you know who did this terrible thing? What happened? We were so happy."

"My deepest condolence madam, we are investigating the incident and I will personally contact you as soon as we have any results. Yes . . .yes . . . thank you madam, goodbye."

He placed the phone back onto its base, sighing heavily. He said, "She is most distraught, certainly not implicated."

Dal sighed and said, "So we have no leads then, right? I mean, with the electrical guys?"

"Not that I can see. Too many innocent people are dying on account of this Travis," Chevalier said. He placed his head in his hands, slowly ran his fingers through his hair.

"Take it easy, Claude, we'll get the guy," Blake said re assuredly.

CHAPTER 51

DAL STEPPED FROM THE car, stretched, and placed a cigarette between his lips. He thought for a bit and said to Blake, "No way is that guy still drivin' about in the same car. He'd have ditched it first thing. He's got hostages. I mean, how cool can this fucker be, what with choppers shootin' about the place and all. My gut tells me he's holed out someplace near where you guys last saw him. Makes perfect sense – he'd lie low, then make a move when the heat cooled down."

Blake asked, "Have there been any reports from hospitals, any emergency cases admitted?"

"No, nothing," Chevalier snapped impatiently.

Dal took a long drag on the cigarette, held the smoke for what seemed an eternity, and then quickly exhaled, saying, "Wait just a minute. Drew said the Travis guy was wounded, some type of leg injury. Maybe he needed attention. How about local doctors in the area? He didn't have to find a hospital."

Blake nodded his head, smiling at Chevalier. He said, "Sounds feasible, hell of a long shot but worth a try."

"This is Chevalier, get me the names of all doctors within a ten kilometer radius of the old farmhouse road, and get the names to me in the next few minutes."

Blake placed another call to Camile. He got the message machine again. He said, "Hey sweetie, Drew again, I'll be a little longer, we're heading out to call on a few doctors on the old farm road, guess it'll be about a couple of hours. Call me when you get in. maybe we can catch a late dinner. Miss you even more than earlier."

Dal rolled his eyes, Blake didn't comment.

The drive to the old farm road was interrupted by a call from head office. "Inspector this is Beck. We have three doctors in the area you requested. A Dr. Marcella, a Dr. Duran and a Dr. Blau," he said reading the list aloud.

"Good work Beck. We are coming up to the home of Dr. Duran as we speak." He pointed to a driveway ahead. "Pull into 322, just ahead, the red iron gate."

The driver slowly wheeled the black Renault into the driveway. A man stepped from the farmhouse carrying a large medical bag.

"Yes, how can I help you gentlemen?"

"I am Police Inspector Chevalier. We are looking for some people last seen in a white Citroën. We suspect one of them may be requiring medical attention for a wound. Have you had any such patients within the past few hours?"

"I had a local girl, she has a sprained ankle. A dog bite about an hour back, but no strangers. Perhaps you should stop in to see my friend Dr. Blau. He lives a few minutes along the road at 551."

"Thank you doctor; we will head that way now. If you hear of anything, here is my card, please call me immediately."

Chevalier turned to the two men sitting in the rear of the car.

"I have a strong feeling we are on the right track with this munch."

"With this 'munch,' what do you mean 'munch,' Claude?" Blake asked, scratching his head. Chevalier gave a quizzical grin, replying, "Munch! Munch! You know, when you have a munch about something, when you have a feeling?"

"Oh, a hunch, you have a hunch?"

"A hunch? I thought that was on the back of the bell ringer . . . the man from Notre Dame. Crazy language, this English. Yes, I have a hunch, I have a good hunch."

The Renault slowly approached the home of Dr. Paul Blau. Dal leaned forward and touched Chevalier on the shoulder, he said, "A little bird tells me we should leave the car out here and move in on foot. No harm being cautious, what do you say?"

"Good idea Dal," Blake added.

"Oh you Americans, you listen to too many little birds, too much television, always with guns firing, always shooting at each other. I do not think we need leave the car out here, it looks quiet enough to me." Chevalier motioned toward the house with a very French wave of his hand, an inference of dismissal of the possibility that any danger existed inside the doctor's house.

"Stop the car, quiet." Blake pointed toward the house as two men carrying bags stepped from the porch.

"My God it's Travis," Chevalier said.

Chevalier nearly choking as he swallowed said, "We've got him by God; we've finally got the bastard!"

"Easy Claude, you had him once before remember, let's take it easy. This guy's like a snake, he can still get the better of us."

As Dal and Blake quietly stepped from the car, Chevalier called for back up.

"I want air support; I want this place sealed up like the Louvre. No, no . . . you listen to me . . . don't tell me what you cannot do . . . just get men out here now!"

The men in the doctor's house continued placing bags into the trunk of their car. Others came from the house and began to slide into the rear seat. A few seconds passed. A loud gunshot broke the silence.

Craven stepped from the house, crossed the porch and made his way to the car. It took only minutes for the small house to be engulfed in flames. The windows shattered as the searing heat bust from the doctor's home. Saffrey stepped quickly from the car.

"GET BACK INTO THE CAR," Craven shouted, "OR I'LL DROP YOU WHERE YOU STAND."

"BUT THE FIRE, WHY?"

The noise was deafening as glass exploded and the noise of burning woodwork let off amplified crackling sounds like automatic gunfire.

"EVIDENCE, THERE'S NO EVIDENCE . . . JUST ASHES. ASHES AND UNRECOGNIZABLE BODIES."

Blake said, "We should make a move Claude. If he gets mobile he'll be harder to stop."

Chevalier wagged his head once and said, "It's you. I have you at last. This will be for Penoir, for Laroche."

They began to move toward the inferno, slowly, cautiously, crouching behind bushes, narrowing the gap.

"Steady Claude," Blake said. "We can't take the chance . . ." He didn't get the words out. The black car, a late model Audi, shot into the driveway, its tires throwing stones and dust as it sped by, almost knocking Blake into a ditch.

"WHAT THE FUCK?" Dal shouted as he rolled twice, landing in a deep puddle by a mail box, his Beretta flying from his hand and disappearing among the tall weeds.

"MOTHER OF GOD?" Blake said aloud as he firmly clutched his shoulder.

Two men jumped from the car as it skidded to a halt beside Craven. Craven was noticeably shocked. He stared at the two large suited thugs. He tried raising his weapon as one of the men placed his fist solidly into Craven's face. One of the men reached for the car door, opening it as Angelica dived to the ground in an attempt to retrieve Cravens pistol. She reached it and swiveled about. Pointed it at the large man, and fired.

He clutched at his ear, screaming in agony as blood ran down onto his shoulder. The other man got two shots off in a flash and Angelica went down.

Saffrey and the two girls huddled in the rear seat as the two men dragged Craven to his feet. One opened the trunk and quickly moved the bags into the Audi.

It was over in seconds. Chevalier was still getting to his feet when the shots rang out, one shot from Angelica, two shots into Angelica.

"Claude you okay?" Blake called as Chevalier dusted off his suit.

He called out again; his voice was totally muffled by the explosion coming from the house.

"JESUS FUCKIN' CHRIST! GOTTA BE A GAS MAIN," Dal shouted as the roof suddenly collapsed, imploding onto the flaming remains. The three men again hit the dirt as fragments of the dwelling flew around them; smoke billowing for fifty meters in all directions.

Blake groaned, "Christ, I knew I shouldn't have worn this Armani today."

Dal quickly inspected his own attire, now quite muddied by his second roll in the dirt. "Yeah well, the Men's fuckin' Fashion Warehouse will be happy to see me back too."

"Can't see the Audi, too much smoke, where's the fucker gone?" Blake called out. He stood, began running toward the flames, weapon drawn, extended in both hands. The Audi suddenly emerged from the smoke blanketing the area. The car speeding directly toward him swerved to avoid debris strewn about the driveway.

As the car swerved and slowed, Blake made eye contact with the driver. The large man slowed as he passed Blake, grinned and taunted him. He raised one middle finger as he held the grin. The other man sat in the back of the car, his gun firmly pressed into Craven's temple. The Audi passed just slow enough for Blake to get a good long look the occupants. The driver then gunned the car off of the property and onto the roadway.

The smoke from the inferno thickened. Tears streamed down Blake's face stopping him, temporarily blinding him. Dal and Chevalier dashed past him making their way toward the car where Angelica lay bleeding from two bullet holes, one above each eye, neatly positioned as though the shooter intended to place them proportionately apart. Saffrey jumped from the car pulling Amy along with him. Karen quickly followed as they all moved to a safer area below the fallen trunk of a large tree. Pieces of debris continued to smolder on the surrounding grass. Sirens could be heard in the distance. When the fire was eventually extinguished, nothing remained of the doctor's home.

"Have forensics get out here. We believe there's at least one more victim in the house," Chevalier barked at one of the cops.

Two medics treated Karen for scratches and a minor cinder burn. She was in shock and repeatedly called Rick's name, she again broke into uncontrollable sobbing.

One of the medics said, "We'll sedate her, get her straight to the hospital."

The ambulance sped off, siren blaring as Chevalier stood staring at Saffrey and Amy.

"Those were the Russian guys," Blake said. "The guys from the Au Lapin Agile. Why do you suppose they want Craven?"

The question hung there. No response. Chevalier stood in silence. They all stared at the smoldering remains of the house. After a long silence, Chevalier turned to Saffrey and Amy: "It's been a long journey, my friends. We've much to discuss. The important thing is of course . . . you are alive. The man who held you captive is a madman. Is there a fourth, another American?"

Saffrey nodded to Chevalier, saying, "He's in there. That mother-fucker shot him. That fucker's ass is mine . . . MINE . . . you understand? Who were those guys who dragged him off and shot his lady?"

Blake stepped forward wiping the smoke induced tears from his eyes and said, "I recognized the driver, the big Russian. I saw at the restaurant, smoking the black Russian cigarettes. The night I was there with a couple of friends."

"But how then did they know to come here?" Chevalier asked.

Blake stood in silence pondering the question, "Is that rhetorical Claude?"

"You have no answer Drew, is that what you are saying?"

"A question with a question, Claude . . . hmm. My guess would be they tailed me the night I was at the Au Lapin Agile, or more to the point, they followed the Ferrari. I was driving it that night."

"My French intuition tells me they might have placed a bugging device on the car," Chevalier said.

"Ah shit, Claude. You been watching American television?" Blake replied, realizing the implication, he groaned, "If they can trace the Ferrari, they'd know it went to Camile's apartment."

Blake sank into a squatting position, then onto his knees. He ran his fingers through his hair, looked up at Dal and said,

"My God, it's Camile. I left the message on her phone; she hasn't gotten back to me. She's the only one who knew what was going on. She knew we were headed here."

Saffrey and Amy accompanied the three men back to headquarters, gave a full briefing, explaining all they knew about the diamonds.

"Do you have knowledge of stones left in a McDonald's on the Champs Elysées?" Chevalier asked.

"Yeah, we stashed them there, in the ceiling," Saffrey replied. "I'll fill you in what happened."

"Are there any more of those stones spread about the place?" Blake asked.

Amy said, "Sure, we left some boxes in a safety deposit box at the Bank of Paris."

CHAPTER 52

AS THE AUDI RIPPED through the countryside, the Russian turned, grinned at the semi-conscious man and passed the near empty vodka flask of vodka to his comrade sitting in the rear seat alongside their victim. Travis Craven now subdued, sat alongside the larger of the two men, he squinted, tried to focus, saw the muzzle of the.45 Magnum inched from his nose. "What happened, who the fuck are you people?"

The driver eyed his comrade in the rear view mirror. Widened the grin. The larger Russian's hand jolted Craven's head as he delivered a heavy blow with the barrel of the .45. As Craven slumped the man slipped the revolver into a shoulder-holster, took out a cut-throat, quickly placed the razor at Craven's throat. Craven could not remember feeling like this: unable to draw breath without pain. Helpless.

The accent was heavy Russian, he said, "Let us find a quiet place where we can have a little chat." The Audi veered off the road, pulled into a heavily wooded area. It was hidden from the road and obscured from aerial observation by large heavily foliaged trees. An old barn came into view, the driver made his way toward it. The barn appeared abandoned, a large rusted tractor serving as a tombstone sentinel beside double barn doors, perhaps a reflection of better days. Its wheels embedded into the ground, rust corroding the wheel arches.

The door hinges were well rusted, and the large Russian strained as he manhandled one side of the large wooden entrance. Years of weed growth had made the door one with the earth. Vines had further consummated the arrangement. The driver cautiously moved the Audi into the barn. The door groaned back to its closed position and two large rats scurried across the damp ground, taking refuge in a damp rotting haystack. It bordered on compost.

The smaller of the two men stepped from behind the wheel, dragged Craven from the car, placed a fist firmly into

Craven's rib cage. There was a cracking sound followed by a muffled groan, and Craven slumped to the ground. Pain shot threw his body. Revenge would keep him alive. A length of rope and a roll of duct tape dropped beside him. The small man said, "These were in the trunk. They should do the job."

The two men raised Craven to his feet. Struggling to draw breath, he clearly knew the blow from the big man had broken at least one of his ribs.

"Drag him to that post and tie his wrists," the smaller man said grinning. "Here, throw one end of the rope over that beam and raise him up."

Craven now fully stretched, balanced on the tips of his shoes. The smaller Russian began to remove Craven's belt, unfastening his trousers. Craven lowered his eyes and watched in horror as the man fondled his genitals, removed his penis and stretched it out painfully from his arching body.

Craven began screaming as the pain swelled. The larger man drew back his fist readying himself to deliver another blow to the rib cage.

"No, it will kill him; we need him alive, for a little longer anyway. I need some time with him. I have waited for this." He placed the razor at the top of Craven's pubic hair and began shaving downward. Craven held his breath, *won't give this sadist the satisfaction*, he thought as he raised his eyes to the timber beams above him. He held his breath. Wanted God's help. God was predisposed.

The larger Russian grinned, enjoying the show. He moved in closer to Craven, looked down at the hair that had fallen to the ground between Craven's feet, he said "You will look just like a little boy when Vladimir is through shaving you."

Craven stared hard at the Russian, he winced a little, regained some composure and forced the words, "What is it you people want from me, I've never seen you before?"

"We understand you have knowledge of certain discs which carry information vital to the development of artificial diamond technology and time travel."

Craven looked at the rafters above and groaned. "You get

straight to the point. Why would I give you whatever it is – how do I know you'll let me live?"

"We are not going to kill you," he said woodenly. The Russian had given this some thought, what to say, wanted Craven to feel reassured, to cooperate. We have been directed to retrieve these discs at any cost, therefore you WILL talk, and you will talk now, not later. We are very impatient as you will soon discover. Do you wish to tell us of the whereabouts of the discs? Is your, uh . . . masculinity worth it?"

Craven motioned the Russian to come closer, by nudging his head in a *'come this way'* movement. When the larger Russian was inches from him, Craven spat, hitting the man in the eyes. The Russian reeled away, wiped his face and raised his hand.

"No do not beat him, not yet Dimitri," the smaller Russian said, still holding the blade, but now standing back from Craven. The smaller man placed the blade back into his coat pocket, reached for the duct tape, passed it to the big man, his face red with rage.

"Here, tape his mouth."

"Why me Dimitri?"

"Because you can reach him idiot, and you're the one whose face he spat in. Now just do it."

As the tape was roughly slapped across Craven's face, the smaller man opened one of the leather bags.

"Ah. Look what we have here, these beauties all make it worth while," he said tipping the stones slowly onto the damp ground.

Each bag was then emptied in turn. The two Russians sat cross-legged, staring at the sparkling mountain of stones, bedazzled by their brilliance.

Craven, watching helplessly, felt the fear creep through his body. The stones weren't stable. They'd already been exposed to the atmosphere for some time; at least while in the closed bags they retained a fairly safe level of inertness. But now, exposed to the open air, well - he'd no idea how long they'd remain stable. The stones were inclusive and the open air was not conducive to their fragile state. His past knowledge of timing led him to believe the stones could lay exposed for no more than ninety minutes; had to get out of this situation - within an hour. This would leave him around thirty minutes to finalize his plan. The inclusive stones were the integral part of his plan; his demise by fire would take the blood hounds off his trail forever. His carefully planned death, but not at the hands of these two Russians. *These Russians have thrown a wrench in the works, now the timing isn't right. Not what I've planned. Not even close.*

The larger man returned to the car, bringing back two fresh bottles of Smirnoff. They opened the bottles, toasted each other several times clinking the two bottles together between large gurgling swallows and loud belching.

Each man gulped down half of his bottle. No pausing for breath. The smaller man slumped forward landing face first into the diamond pile. The other roared with laughter, running his fingers through the stones. The laughter slowed to an almost girlish giggle. He held a handful above his head; he looked to the ceiling as he let the stones trickle across his face. He soon drifted into a deep, drunken sleep.

Craven struggled with the rope binding his wrists. Found looseness. Found hope. It was a slight loosening. A small glimmer of hope. *Can't maneuver my fuckin' fingers*, he thought, *need to get them into a position where I can fully loosen these knots.*

How long will these two fuckers sleep? He pondered the thought. *Are the stones going to give me an hour? I just need an hour, sixty minutes, that's all the time I need.* His mind rambled. His survival instinct peaked as he worked feverishly, sweating as he struggled to pick the knot loose.

The large man grunted. Rolled to one side opening his eyes momentarily, oblivious to all around him. Craven held still. His fingers froze, contorted in the workings of the knot.

The big man staggered to his feet, stumbled toward Craven. Standing blurry eyed and swaying, he coughed his foul breath as he stood just inches away. Craven cringed. The Russian fumbled for his zipper, relieving himself directly onto Craven. Hot urine soaked into Craven's trouser leg, running down into his shoe. He felt his foot warming, soaking.

The Russian cleared his throat. He grinned at Craven then flung a mouthful of phlegm into Craven's face. Craven held still, feeling the anger swell inside him, like lava inside a volcano.

His senses told him to kick out at the Russian. His ribs told him otherwise. He closed his eyes, hanging his head as though unconscious. The Russian laughed, spat again and returned to his makeshift bed.

The warm blood intermingled with the cooling urine, both meeting up in his shoe. His arms felt longer, stretched beyond any level of acceptable comfort. The rope cut deep into his wrists and blood ran freely down each of his arms. He strained to look down at his crotch, hardly any hair remained. Blood seeped from where the hair once grew. The dry shave had broken the skin and the pain was further aggravated by the Russians urine momentarily splashing onto the shaved area.

The stench of his surroundings was further intensified by the odor of the urine rising like steam from his lower body. Working feverishly Craven picked at the knot with his nails. It was loosening, or was this imagination playing cruel tricks? *Forty five more minutes*, he thought, *I can do this, just forty five more minutes.* He raised himself further onto the very tips of his shoes. Felt the rope slacken. His thoughts became excited, *there's slack, definitely slack, must keep working it.*

Closing his eyes he visualized the knot, could see the gap widening and began pulling at it with his index finger and thumb.

The French rodents again scattered across the dirt floor. His mind went crazy, he stared at the rats, wanted to shout, but couldn't. He thought *the little bastards are trying to wake the fuckin' Russians.* He froze as one scurried too close to the face of the larger man. The Russian grunted. He knocked over the empty vodka bottle, causing it to roll. It clinked against the gun lying in the other Russian's open hand.

The larger Russian opened his eyes, raised his head, looking about the barn. He stared at Craven momentarily, a blank look, wiped his sleeve across his grotesque mouth, and settled back down. Craven resumed his knot picking at a furious pace. It was loosening. *Yes, got it.* He freed himself, grimaced as his body refused to support his weight. Felt the ribs creaking as he slumped to the floor. He stayed frozen, stayed on all fours. Didn't move. Listened to the silence broken only by the drunken snoring of the two men. He raised his head and moved dog like to the nearest man - the shaver.

He carefully took the nine millimeter Gurza from the sleeping man's hand. A quick inspection of the gun confirmed the two men were probably Russian agents. The Magnum surprised him, *not like a Russian to have a Magnum, must be a Dirty Harry fan,* he thought. The Gurza was standard issue, adopted by the Federal Security Service, a former division of the KGB.

Craven reached into the larger man's pocket, retrieved his wallet. Felt in his jacket pocket and took out the Black Russians. Took one from the packet, sat pensively against the pole where he'd been suspended. Screwed up his nose, looked at the rotting haystack, looked at his trousers, looked at the Russians. Looked mad. He lit the cigarette, steadied his nerves, tried to gather some calm. He inhaled with great difficulty, his ribs aching as he did. His mind rambled. He examined the Gurza. It was fully loaded. He tilted his head, fondled the weapon like a child with a new toy, a crazed look in his eyes. He pointed the Gurza at each of the sleeping men, clicking his tongue to make a shooting sound, imagined firing a shot at each of his assailants. He repeated the gesture several times, savoring the moment of revenge and the satisfaction of having the upper hand. Playing God in his unsettled mind, knowing the lives of both men were now in his hands.

Reality snapped him back. Time was of the essence. *They're searching for me,* he thought, but this was not going to deprive him of the great satisfaction of revenge, slow revenge. Well . . . maybe not too slow. *These two thugs killed Angelica. They're going to suffer.*

These two were about to exit this world, a long, slow exit. He'd give them time to taste death coming, to know they were dying. Dying slow. There was nothing either man could say or do to prevent the inevitable. Neither of them deserved a quick death.

Craven remained on all fours as he finished the cigarette. He stubbed the Sobranie into the ground, exhaling the last of the smoke. Juggled the balance of the Gurza. Grinning at the gun he raised his eyes, and stared at the Russians. The grin dissipated. He crawled toward them, raised the weapon above the big man's head and brought it down. Brought it down hard. There was a crunching sound, the man lay still.

The noise woke the second man, he opened his eyes. His eyes were clouded with drunkenness. Craven whipped the gun across the Russian's face. He joined his comrade in a world of unconsciousness. Pain seared through Craven's body. The broken ribs made each breath a chore. He wheezed, felt for his boot. The large blade was missing its old friend. He slowly slipped it from its snug hiding place, placed it against the larger man's throat, paused, tilted his head to one side like an animal studying its prey before devouring it. He stared at the man's face. *This is too good a way to die,* he thought. He wasn't about to make it this easy. *Want them both awake, to see death coming. To suffer as bad as I've suffered.*

Struggling with the weight of the larger man, he dragged the Russian to the pole where he had earlier been suspended. He tied the man with short pieces of rope then dragged the smaller Russian to the post and tied him beside his comrade. Their feet were bound together, the right foot of the larger man tied to the left of the other, positioning each man in a spread eagle position.

It had taken all of his energy and some. He slumped to his knees, unable to stand. He crawled a few feet away from the two men, groaning as the pain caused tears to swell in his eyes. He took the Gurza from his belt, aiming it at the two men.

"HEY IVAN," he shouted, and the shouting hurt. He shivered a breath, regrouping, knowing he couldn't shout again. "Rise and shine you fucker." The man didn't stir.

He raised his voice slightly, repeated the call, "Ivan! Nikita! Come on boys it's play time!"

Their wallets lay on the ground, among the spilled

diamonds .He reached for them, and emptied the contents. Their driver's licenses carried the names Dimitri Zakhov and Vladimir Sobchak. The larger man carried a photograph of himself happily standing alongside an attractive woman with two children. The writing on the rear of the snapshot was in Russian.

"No surprise," Craven mumbled to himself giving the writing a cursory glance. He said, "Nice family Vlad, a shame."

"VLADAMIR!" Craven called aloud. The large man stirred at the sound of his name.

"Come on Vlad, wakey, wakey you son-of-a-bitch!"

Both men began to move, realized they were restrained. Craven coughed. Raising his voice again aggravated his busted ribs. He dropped to his knees, the on all fours, lowered his head to the ground as the pain again rose to a searing peak.

Seeing him down and weakened, the Russians struggled furiously to free themselves.

"Hey, hey, hey . . . steady boys. Take it easy. Don't want to piss Travis off any more than you have. Travis is already a very unhappy fuckin' camper."

He coughed again, breathed heavily, held his ribcage with his free hand.

The larger Russian pleaded, "Please untie us. We will help you."

"Yeah right, you'll help me bring Angelica back, right?"

"Your woman? I had no choice. She fired at us, it was just a reaction. I am very sorry for your loss. Please - you must understand."

"Bullshit. You don't care who you kill, and boys - neither does Travis. Your death is set in concrete fellas."

Craven rose to his feet, found the duct tape. Tore off four strips about eight inches long and slapped them over each man's mouth. The Russians rolled their heads, each trying to avoid the tape. Their struggle only served to raise Craven's level of excitement. He stepped back, raised the Gurza and fired a single shot at point blank range directly into the smaller man's groin. Craven said aloud, as best his ribs would allow, "Hey fucker, try pissing with that one you miserable mother-fucker." He relished the muffled screams from beneath the duct tape. The Russian's bulging eyes expressed the pain. "Come on, comrade, don't disappoint Travis. You were such a man when you pissed on me, big and brave. You won't piss on anyone again you fuck . . . but then again, why even give you the pleasure?"

Craven reached down blade in hand, sliced through the man's trousers, he snarled "You like fuckin' cock games. Enjoy this one."

He gripped the man's penis, and in one quick move separated it from his body. The Russian began making guttural sounds, rolled his head in agony as blood began pooling around his crotch. He struggled, ripping and tearing as best he could, but the bindings held fast as he lapsed into deep unconsciousness. His comrade was furiously shaking his head from side to side, tears streamed from his eyes. Craven stood over him, pointing the gun at the man's forehead. Craven said, "Now let me see. What would you prefer? Hmm . . . let me think . . . you'd prefer sheer fuckin' pain, right? Travis knows you want whatever your buddy here got, right?"

The emasculated Russian began to revive, his groaning and crying now intermixing, producing a whimpering sound.

"Yeah, yeah, yeah. Do it in high 'C' you mother-fucker. That's what it is. Where are your fuckin' balls now?" He held the severed penis inches from the man's face and said, "I know what's missing here, huh . . .what do you suppose that . . .yeah, you got it, we need a duet." He turned to the other terrified man. Moved the blade to his crotch. The man bucked and gyrated. Craven was excited. He cut through the trouser leg, reached inside the man's underwear, his left hand took a firm hold on the penis. He said, "Wow, big fucker." He flopped it out, stretched it, tilted his head, looking like a primate studying a banana. "Hey, not circumcised huh Vlad? Well fuck me dead, I can fix that."

He kneeled, placed the blade an inch back from the tip of the man's penis, squeezing the tip as he stretched it tort. He grinned ah he ran the blade the full circumference of the bleeding flesh. The Russian made silent screams, his eyes did the screaming, the duct taped killed the audio.

"So, what do you think? Neat work? Always wanted to be a surgeon. Ah what the fuck, get to cut up on people just the same. Here, how's this?" The Blade made a fast, clean cut and Craven stepped back holding the bleeding organ high. He let the blood drip onto the Russian's face, into his eyes. He moved to the first man and placed his severed organ on his forehead. Moved back to the big man, placed his penis on *his* forehead. Stood back and let out a sinister laugh saying, "Now that's appropriate don't you think, two fuckin' dick heads."

The Russian began convulsing. Craven said, "Playtime's over."

He raised the Gurza and placed a neat nine millimeter hole in the man's forehead. The Russian jerked backward. And as his skull collided with the pole behind him, Craven heard a cracking sound. He said, "Ouch, bet that fuckin' hurt. Hurt me just hearing it."

The other Russian opened his eyes wider. Struggled, his severed penis rolled from his head, leaving a blood trail on his face as it tumbled to the ground. He stared at his departed comrade. Stared at the neat hole in his forehead. Craven placed the Gurza on the ground alongside the dead man, squatting between the crying man's outstretched legs. He pointed the blade at the man's stomach, used the point of the blade to neatly remove each button of the Russian's shirt. The man's stomach heaved as it was set free of the sweat soaked shirt.

"Packing a little too much borscht in there, let's see if we can throw some light on the problem. But first, I need a break."

Craven slowly stood and unzipped his trousers. Placing one foot on either side of the Russian he stared at the quivering man. He made a blessing motion, said "Piss on you comrade."

The Russian held a dead stare, his head nodding ever so slightly. Knew he was dead. Craven grinned, stepped back and re zipped his trousers.

"Nah, that'd be too easy Nakita. I'm too fuckin' pissed off to even piss on you. Travis has something special in store. Travis can be creative. Let's get creative, what do you say huh? Let's get rid of that borscht."

Craven placed the blade against the man's navel, a

deep dark hole that offered residency for an amazing wad of lint. The Russian lowered his eyes just in time to see the blade quickly open his belly. Craven slid the razor sharp knife from his navel, up his chest to the base of his throat.

The over stretched skin parted, releasing the belly of a porker, his intestines spilling onto his lap. Craven moved the blade to the writhing man's sleeve, wiped the blood off the gleaming metal as the Russian convulsed, flailed about, blood squirting from his body. Craven stood, spat on the Russian. He gathered the stones, placed them back into the bags and walked from the barn. He stopped momentarily and turned back as the Russian groaned death sounds, his innards now spread onto the barn floor. Big rats . . . healthy fat rats, began to emerge from the damp haystack. They approached the Russian with cautious reservation, staring inquisitively at the meal before them. *Can't leave him like that*, Craven thought. He raised the Gurza and placed a carefully aimed slug into the Russian's head.

He grinned at the rats as they scurried back to the safety of the haystack, one gratefully carrying a freshly circumcised penis. "Dinner's on me." He called back to the rats. He added, "Bon appetite."

Craven placed the bags into the trunk of the Audi and slowly slid into the driver's seat. He leaned toward the glove compartment and pressed the release button. The lid fell open. Two boxes containing nine millimeter cartridges and a Couer d'Alene silencer brought a smile to Craven's face. He checked the Gurza, reloaded, attached the sound suppressor and placed the gun on the passenger's seat. The center armrest contained a collection of music discs, mostly Pavarotti with a Best of Mario Lanza for the purists. Flicking through the selection he chose a Pavarotti, *Night at the Greek Theater*.

"Fuckin' good taste for commies", he said quietly as he skipped through the tracks, selecting an old favorite, Puccini's Pagliacci. He adjusted the volume to near maximum, turned up the bass, listened to the aria. As Vesti La Giubba reverberated through the night air, Craven lit up another Black Russian, inhaled - painfully. Exhaled a neat small smoke ring and rested his head on the back of the seat as he watched the ring expand, drift off – disappear.

He raised an imaginary glass, toasted the day. "To old comrades, what a fuckin' splendid end to a day," he said, laughing loudly. He patted the dashboard, "And an Audi to boot."

For Craven, the drive into Paris was a familiar journey Tears swelled in his eyes, a mixture of pain and Pavarotti. He mimed the words of the song in perfect Italian. The sadness of this particular aria served only to increase the flow of tears. This aria held special memories. He and Angelica had often attended opera; they considered Vesti La Giubba to be *their song*. It was their song and the memories caused Craven to pound wildly on the steering wheel. A mix of rage and sadness.

It seemed to be such a perfect plan. Angelica and Travis. A perfect plan. He began slowly singing, straining to reach the high notes. The pain in his side again caused him to cringe. He cringed, paused for a few seconds and resumed his miming as the melancholy caused tears to flow freely. He pulled the Audi off the road, parked it and stared at the dark clouds above. He cried - and cried.

Ten minutes passed. Dark heavy rain clouds formed shapes as they slowly drifted overhead. When the sky began to clear, the branches hang above him caused the light to flicker through the Audi's sunroof. He laid there, his head resting on the back of the seat, Pavarotti hitting the highs in Nessun Dorma. Craven took another cigarette, lit it, and started the motor. The drive in the Audi was painful as he tried as best he could to block the Russians and the pain from his mind. He tried to bury himself in the sounds of Pavarotti. Ahead of him in the beam of the Audi's lights a shabbily dressed man stood by the roadside holding up one hand, hitching a ride. A bicycle lay on the road nearby. Craven slowed the Audi to a stop. Lowered his window as the man approached.

"What's the problem?" Craven asked softly, the pain continuing to sear through his body. Burning, restricting his every movement.

The man said, "Thank you for stopping, my bicycle has a bent wheel. I am heading to Paris. I would appreciate a ride as far as you can take me."

Craven looked the stranger up and down, waited a few seconds, thought about it, then said, "Yeah sure, not a problem, climb on in."

The man briskly rubbed his hands together and said, "Thank you, I am most grateful to you sir."

These were the last words the man would utter.

CHAPTER 53

MCDOWELL PLACED A CALL through to Blake The cell phone was on the charger by the bed. Reaching for it in the dark, Blake fumbled and cursed at the phone. Sleep hung heavily in his voice as he placed the phone to his ear. He listened to the voice saying, "Blake, you there? It's McDowell."

"Jesus Christ McDowell, what the fuck is it? It's still dark for Christ's sake."

"You need to get your ass down here pronto. We've got a break in the case."

Blake groaned, "Do me a favor, give Dal a wake up call too. Tell him I'll pick him up on my way. No reason for him to sleep while I'm working."

Blake gave it a few minutes, then called Dal. Dal groaned into the phone, "Awe Jesus, what time is it? I dreamed McDowell just called. Bad dream." The phone pressed into the soft down pillow as he spoke.

"Yeah, yeah, yeah – you know it wasn't a fuckin' dream. Get yourself dressed. I'll be there in twenty."

Blake pulled an old Volkswagen from the garage alongside his apartment. The car had been confiscated in a recent drug bust, giving Blake the opportunity to acquire the vehicle at a giveaway price. The drive to Dal's hotel passed quickly. Blake sounded the horn twice. Dal stepped from the lobby into the street, yawning as he scurried toward Blake.

"The last time we met this early we were going out fishing on the Bay before the sun was up. It was freezin'. All I caught was a fuckin' cold and that cost me two hundred bucks." He looked around the interior of the Fiat. "Hey, where'd you get this relic anyway? Looks like it could have belonged to Hitler."

"Are we in top form this morning or what?"

"If I don't kid about it I'm gonna go back to sleep," Dal said laughing.

"Yeah gotta laugh, gotta stay sane. It's a tough job," Blake chuckled.

When the two men reached McDowell's office, they found his light to be the only one on in the entire building. Blake nodded to the security guard as he approached the main entrance door.

"Morning Mr. Blake, you're expected."

McDowell nodded at the two and gestured toward the chairs opposite his desk, a large mahogany carved piece circa Bangkok 1990, but nonetheless impressive, kind of heavy and polished, like the man sitting behind it. McDowell stuffed the remainder of a large muffin into his mouth, washing it down with a swig of coffee from a Starbuck's cup.

"Breakfast guys, I've plenty more muffins in the box."

He reached across the desk, gave a white box a nudge toward them. Dal opened the box, took a muffin and passed the box to Blake.

"Okay here's the skinny," McDowell said as he swallowed the last mouthful.

"Our source at the Russian embassy tells us this guy Craven has access to a supply of diamonds. He's apparently bringing a consignment of stones into Paris with the intention of passing them on as gifts to top government dignitaries from the major powers. We believe the stones have some kind of device that can be triggered by . . ."

Blake swallowed hard. Dal coughed as though choking. He said, "You mean to say all this crap that's been goin' on is about smugglin' stones into France?"

McDowell rose from his desk and slowly paced across the room. He stood with his back to them as he pondered his reply.

"Yeah but these stones are - these stones are man-made."

"So they're counterfeit diamonds. How's this involve us and what d'ya mean *some kind of device*?" Dal asked.

"The stones contain some type of explosive device and power source. Impossible to detect even through a jeweler's loupe. Best they can see is a small inclusion, same as the majority of stones out there. Our informant tells us the Russians had a meeting scheduled to inspect some of these stones a few weeks back. We had also been contacted by an anonymous caller. That's how we happened to have two of our own people at the same shop when all the persons –"

Blake interrupted. "When all the agents were burned in the jeweler's shop, right?"

"Got it," McDowell replied, pacing back to his chair. "Yeah, that's exactly what happened."

Blake and Dal both leaned back in their chairs, each whistling out air.

Dal asked, "And this explains all the burn victims, right?"

"As best we can make out, all the cases the French cops are chasing around the city involve these man-made stones. It appears to be the most feasible explanation."

"It's a pretty shoddy story," Blake added. "Lots of holes in it."

McDowell said, "It's all we've got and we're gonna run with it."

Dal leaned forward, a very serious expression on his face. He glanced very seriously at each of them, had their total attention. Dal had one finger raised as he prepared to speak. "Can I have another fuckin' muffin?"

McDowell chuckled." Sure go ahead, knock yourself out. Blake, like another?"

"Don't mind if I do, French muffins huh, not bad, ain't too bad at all."

The three men sat eating, and no words were exchanged for several minutes. Eventually McDowell broke the silence. "The bureau suspects Craven's back in Paris and in possession of a considerably large quantity of stones. He could have some kind of backup with him. We've heard rumors of a splinter group operating in South America; they're also somehow associated with Craven. Inspector Chevalier tells me he's lost two of his best men at the hands of this lunatic, we gotta consider Craven to be very armed and very fuckin' dangerous. We believe he's indirectly to blame for all the burn victims. Chevalier's holding three Frenchmen who inadvertently distributed the first stones. Best we can figure is that these three were unaware the stones presented a problem. They thought the stones were genuine. Used them as gifts or barter of kind with a local call girl."

Blake asked, "How'd the French guys come by the stones?"

"Given them as payoff for a crime scene cleanup. Then the four Americans somehow got caught up in the whole mess. They came across some of the stones and next thing you know the four of them were kidnapped."

It's time, Blake thought, *time to fill McDowell in on my adventure through the doorway.* Explain how he'd chased Craven and lost him. McDowell listened in absolute silence. It was a long two hours. McDowell picked up the phone and placed a call. Neither Blake nor Dal knew whom he was calling. The clock showed seven o'clock. The voice at the other end answered, "Chevalier speaking, who is this?"

"Inspector, this is McDowell at the U.S. Embassy. Please accept my apologies for disturbing you at this hour. Can you be at my office in about an hour? It's extremely important."

"Yes, I suppose so, do you realize the time?"

"Yes inspector. I'm sorry but this is urgent."

"I will be there. Have the coffee ready."

When Chevalier entered the room the three men were still discussing the incidents surrounding the case. How the red Porsche had appeared and vanished, the involvement of the four Frenchmen, the related deaths, and how the stones found their way to each victim. They greeted the inspector who poured a coffee and joined the discussion.

"It is indeed a weird chain of events," Chevalier said, slowly sipping his coffee.

The four men brainstormed for almost an hour. McDowell set up a large whiteboard. He mapped out several squares, placed names in each and connected one name to another. The top square contained the name Raoul Ramirez, believed to be the original source, alongside Ramirez was written the name Eduard Heinzman. Then below those two names came the names of the four Frenchmen, the cleanup crew as they were now known. From there, connecting lines ran other squares containing the names of all the victims.

McDowell briefed the three on what they had so far: "The doctor's home that burned on the old country road, forensics tells me there were two victims in the ashes. One was a Dr Blau, the other was an American tourist, Rick Jones one of the four Americans. Of course you're familiar with his sister Karen Jones and friends, Amy Van Doren and Saffrey Bell. I've lost count of how many deaths can be directly or indirectly attributed to this madman Craven. Beginning with the Porsche incident at the restaurant, then most recently, these two bodies at the doctor's home."

Chevalier sat twirling the coffee around in his cup. He shrugged his shoulders in a typical French 'don't know' gesture. McDowell leaned forward: "Any further news on the two men who screwed up our operation at the doctor's house?"

Dal slid his eyes to Blake who said, "Russians, definitely Russians,"

More squares were added to the whiteboard. In the lowest corner McDowell added the names of Dr. Blau and Camile.

Blake stood and approached the board, tapping his knuckle on the square containing Camile's name. "This one wasn't necessary! I'll find those two and personally take care of them."

Chevalier's blood pressure shot up, his face turning red. He snapped at Blake, "None of them were necessary. Penoir and Laroche were two of my best men, my friends. They too were killed for no reason. Craven will pay for their deaths at my hands. Not the states, and not yours Blake, do not forget this."

McDowell sat back, arms folded, perhaps somewhat of a defensive gesture. He could sense the testosterone permeating around the room. "Come on now, guys. We all have to keep clear heads if we're to find this son-of-a-bitch. That of course, is if the Russians haven't killed him already."

CHAPTER 54

CHEVALIER LIT UP A cigarette. Blake walked to the window, opening it a few inches and smiled back at Claude.

The blood pressure was near normal when Chevalier said, "I suspect the Russians are after the technology more than the stones. We'll be speaking at length with the other three Americans. They spent considerable time with Craven. They have briefed me on all what they had seen. It is quite remarkable and totally unbelievable."

"Why not get a task force together?" Dal asked. "Go through the doorway and get the stuff for ourselves?"

Chevalier ran his fingers through his hair and looked across the desk at McDowell: "Shall you tell them or will I?"

McDowell replied: "What the hell. Might as well tell them now, only a matter of time before someone suggested returning through the doorway or whatever the hell the thing is. Go ahead, Claude."

Chevalier took one final deep drag on the cigarette, stubbed it into the ashtray and sat back uncomfortably in his chair: "After the most recent chase, when the red car disappeared, forensics combed the old farmhouse road and came across several tire tracks, tracks that seemed out of place. Their best guess is that two cars had dropped from a trailer and skidded along the road for several meters before rolling freely. Does that make sense? Anyhow, our team set up motion activated cameras. The cameras captured the re entry of the red Porsche."

"What are you sayin' Claude? That you've actually tried goin' through the openin'?" Dal asked.

"Yes, but nothing happened. We've driven at speed into the very spot, but nothing. We just keep speeding along the road, along the old farmhouse road."

Blake thumped his fist on the table. "I don't get it, Claude. You and I were able to travel through the opening, why can't it be done again? Why can't a task force re-enter and do the job?"

"Well, as we see it, the entry point has either moved or the doorway is closed. If we find Craven, we find the answers."

"We got us any leads on his whereabouts?" Dal asked.

"Not since he was forced into the black car and taken from the burning house by the two Russians. We have road blocks on every major route into Paris. Not even a magician can elude us. My men are door-knocking every dwelling within ten kilometers of the doctors house."

"This is like somethin' from a H. G. Wells novel, a little too much science fuckin' fiction for me," Dal said.

Blake chuckled, "Fiction huh. Not any more."

"The Russian embassy denies all knowledge of the two men who took Travis from the fire. They suggested Russian mafia ties. Absolute BS of course," McDowell scoffed.

Chevalier brushed it off saying, "It is no more mafia than I am."

The discussion was interrupted by a knock on the office door. "Excuse me sir, there is a call for the inspector."

Chevalier replied, "Thank you, can I take it here?"

McDowell nodded to the man, "Have the call passed through to this phone."

The phone on the mahogany desk buzzed once.

"Hello, this is Chevalier. Yes, yes . . . When? . . . We'll be right there." Chevalier returned the phone to its base and stared at the ceiling, he groaned, "When will it end? My God, when will it end?"

"What's up Claude?" McDowell inquired as the three men waited impatiently.

The inspector rested his head on the table, his arms folded, forming a rest. "The Russians, they do not have Craven. I swear this man is the Antichrist. The Russians have been found dead. Both brutalized. One was covered in rats that were making a buffet of his intestines. Both shot in the head. They were driving the black Audi; the car was not at the scene."

McDowell asked, "And Craven?"

"Gone of course, no doubt in the Audi."

Chevalier drove the Ferrari with Dal as passenger. Blake and McDowell followed in the embassy car, a large white Mercedes sporting an American flag on each fender. When they arrived at the old barn it was surrounded by petrol cars and media vans from several networks. As Chevalier approached the barn, a TV reporter hurried toward him.

"Inspector what can you tell us of the victims?"

He continued at a brisk pace, ignoring the woman and brushing the accompanying cameraman aside. McDowell entered the barn ahead of Dal and Blake, took one look at the disemboweled Russian, reeled about, and began uncontrollable vomiting.

"Please sir you'll contaminate the crime scene," a hardened cop quipped with a smile on his face, no doubt for the amusement of his fellow cops, all seeming unaffected by the brutality of the crime.

Adam McDowell continued dry retching.

Dal said, "You okay Adam? I got a Coke back in the car, wanna have it?"

The heaving intensified as two cops consoled McDowell, ushering him out into the fresh air.

"The rats were feeding on him when we arrived. The motorcycle cop found him, someone called it in, said they heard what sounded like shots. "

"Inspector we have IDs on the two bodies, both are Russian nationals," one of the cops said quietly.

Chevalier asked, "Nothing else?"

"Some spent cartridges inspector, nine millimeter. Also some car tracks and two empty vodka bottles, the bottles are off being dusted for prints. That is it for now sir, the ME is on his way."

Chevalier walked about the muttering to himself, "He was here, the son-of-a-bitch. He was in this very space, right here. I can feel his presence. It is the same sensation I had when he killed Laroche, again in a barn. Coincidence I am sure, but I say it is very strange."

McDowell rested outside the barn, propped against the

wheel of the rusted tractor. Blake placed a consoling hand on his shoulder and said, "Adam, are you okay?"

McDowell struggled to stand upright, his stomach muscles and rib cage screamed at him. He looked at Blake apologetically and said, "Sorry, I'm not accustomed to seeing shit like that, seeing his guts all over the place his. How could anyone do this? What kind of sick bastard is this guy?"

Blake gave McDowell comforting motherly pats on the shoulder and said, "Pretty fuckin' sick. That's the animal we're dealing with here. That's the way he gets his kicks. Can't see him changing his spots now, it's all too much fun for him. He seems to be creative in his MO, enjoys the ways he inflicts the kill. Yeah, a real creative bastard."

A cop ran toward Chevalier: "Inspector the black Audi has been found. It is parked by the river south of here, about forty kilometers."

"Go there now. Quickly," Chevalier snapped. "Place a cordon around the site. Do not close in on the car, I do not want him to run."

Chevalier and Blake arrived well ahead of the embassy car. The scene was quiet. All patrol cars were parked out of sight of the black car.

An older cop said excitedly, "This way inspector. The man is just sitting in the car, listening to music."

"Do you think he saw you?"

"I don't believe so sir. He has not shown any sign of concern."

As they drew nearer, the unique voice of Mario Lanza vibrated through the still night air. It was an aria well known to Chevalier.

The inspector said, "Hmm, he has good taste, the aria from Puccini's Madame Butterfly."

"Very good Claude," Blake grinned. "An opera buff as well as an artist. Impressive."

The opera resonated through the trees, adding an air of theatre to the scene. The man in the black Audi rested with his head against the seat, staring up at the stars flickering through the open sunroof. Tree branches swayed overhead. He appeared to be oblivious to the net now tightening around him.

Then there was a blinding flash. The flash was accompanied by intense which heat temporarily blinded all the cops within fifty meters of the Audi.

"SWEET JESUS!" Blake shouted as they all held their arms across their eyes protecting their faces from the blast.

Chevalier and Dal ran forward, weapons drawn. Blake stood back wiping his forehead as sweat ran into his eyes, the sweat temporarily blinding him.

As they drew closer, the smoldering remains of the person inside the flaming Audi bared no resemblance to a human form, nothing more than a skeleton wrapped in a blackened burned outer shell. The rear of the car emitted a strange greenish glow. A mist seeped from the trunk, forcing its way out through the edges of the lid.

"WHAT THE FUCK HAPPENED?" Blake shouted at Chevalier.

"IT APPEARS CRAVEN HAS FALLEN VICTIM TO HIS OWN DEMISE." Chevalier shouted back, struggling to be heard above the roar of the flames.

Seven cops moved warily about the scene. Fear of the unexpected adding to the caution each man placed on his every step.

"ANYTHING NOT KOSHER HERE CLAUDE?" Blake shouted, as the noise of the fiercely burning Audi grew even louder. "First impressions Claude, what do you think?"

"Nothing, I can't say, seems like the fire has ended this madman's folly. But until forensics have done a report who can say? If the prints match those we have of Craven, then our work is ended here."

Blake wiped the tears from his cheeks, the smoke still burning his eyes, "If there are prints to check. And that's highly fuckin' doubtful."

"What about the stones he was carryin', ya think their in the trunk?" Dal asked.

When the intense heat subsided to a level considered safe,

one of the cops used a wheel brace to force the trunk open. The final hisses of green mist dissipated from the trunk.

"We've got some bags in here Claude, all opened, all empty. Terrible smell too," Blake said screwing up his face and quickly backing away from the car.

The small group sat at the open air restaurant. A large bottle of champagne sat in an ice bucket on the center of the table, leaving just enough space for glasses and ashtrays.

"Well Claude," Adam McDowell said, "lives by the sword, dies by the sword."

"Yes very interesting - the whole business, our people have collected the remaining stones from the safety deposit box in Paris and are conducting very careful analysis."

Amy smiled at Saffrey saying wistfully, "I wish Rick was here, I miss him so much."

Karen lowered her head. Saffrey placed an arm around her shoulder, consoling her. She raised her eyes to meet his, smiling sadly, another tear trickled down her cheek.

Blake and Dal looked skyward as a 747 roared overhead.

"Wonder where that one's headed?" Blake said trying to elevate the atmosphere.

"If I were in it," Dal replied, "it would be headin' for Rio."

"Yeah after all that shit, it's time to live a bit. Rio would be just fine. I guess you get to continue on to that South American assignment anyway. So Rio is actually within reach for you, huh Dal?"

"Hold that thought Drew," McDowell interjected.

Blake leaned toward Dal and with his face screwed to one side said, "What's up Dal, come on man, I smell a skunk, what's up?"

Dal slipped a *help me* look at McDowell.

"Well, it's a long, long story," McDowell said in an apprehensive tone. "But the bureau asked me to ask you . . . well, how's your Colombian?"

CHAPTER 55

THE PASSENGER IN SEAT 2B stretched back, adjusting his pillow into a more comfortable position.

This voice on the PA system said, "This is Captain Andre La Torre. We are flying at twenty thousand feet and expect to arrive at Bonn on time. Weather in Bonn is fine and sunny; temperature is twenty-five degrees. We'll be turning off the seat belt sign shortly and you'll be free to move about the cabin.

The passenger in seat 2B grinned.

"Drink sir?" the flight attendant asked, batting her eyes at the handsome passenger.

He nodded toward the nearest bottle.

She passed a glass of Pinot Noir to the passenger.

The handsome man with the dark wavy black hair smiled appreciably.

The attendant handed a form to the passenger. "This is your Department of Agriculture form Mr. Cabot, would you like a pen?"

He touched his packet. "Thank you, my dear. I have a pen." The handsome passenger passed a cursory glance toward the form and grimaced occasionally, as though an annoying pain impeded his movement. He forced a smile, and began writing . . . Name: Travis Cabot. Occupation: Diamond Imports. And the Pinot Noir glimmered as the sunlight filtered through it.

CHAPTER 56

IT HUNG LIKE A death fog, the kind of haze seen in old British detective movies. Nobody knew where it came from. No one cared, they just wished it would dissipate, go back to where it had originated.

The headline read "DEATH FOG CLAIMS ANOTHER VICTIM." The victim, a young woman in her late twenties, lay hidden beneath the county morgue shroud.

Drew Blake had been back in the States for five days, his boss Sam Ridkin assigned him to a case in New Orleans. He found himself ready to view another stiff. He glanced down on his nineteenth career corpse, it was a quick look.

"What do we have on this one Doc?"

Dwayne Withers was the city medical examiner, a tall, pasty bespectacled remnant of a bygone age. He slipped the shroud back down along the body, his heavy glasses balancing on the tip of his Cyrano de Bergerac nose. The ME whispered in a gravelly forty-a-day smoker's voice.

"Don't have nothin'. She's a Jane Doe for now. She got dealt a bad hand. We're still knockin' on doors lookin' for anyone who's missin' someone. Found her in a wooded place down by the docks, in the fishin' area down near where the boats come in."

Blake turned away, stepped toward an old dilapidated church pew. He lowered his weary body and stretched out on the pew as though about to catch some badly needed sleep. But he couldn't stop dwelling on his close encounters with Travis Craven. Even though the two men never did meet face to face, their paths had crossed, he'd come close, but Craven managed to stay a step ahead. Blake had yet to hear back from Chevalier. Blake was guessing that the ash remains in the Audi were not usable. Perhaps the incinerated body was assumed to be Craven. But deep down in the darkest depths of his gut, Blake nurtured uneasiness, a suspicion that perhaps he hadn't heard the last of

Craven. Could he crawl from under some rock and strike again?

"Lookin' like the fog's liftin' Drew. Drop you some place?" Dwayne asked.

Blake raised his head from the armrest at one end of the hard wooden pew. He'd been drifting, the MO snapped him back to the present. Thoughts of Craven again faded into the past. As hard as he tried, his near encounters with Craven were indelible.

"What's that Dwayne? Ah nope, thanks. I'm okay, have my wheels down below. Do me a favor; send me a copy of the report, anything you find that might be out of the ordinary. I'll be in my office by ten tomorrow, I'm far too tired to handle any more of this shit tonight."

The tall, pasty man nodded, raising a goodbye hand as he opened the door for his guest.

"I'll see what I can turn up, but off the top of my head, it seems to be the same MO, no sign of sexual abuse."

Blake yawned and said as he stretched, "Yeah, yeah, yeah. Get it to me tomorrow Dwayne. I'm getting too old for this shit. Please get the fuckin' report to my office. Thanks."

Daybreak was painfully dawning, the coffee maker making a familiar gurgle, sending a rise and shine aroma around the room. Groaning as he stretched, Blake maneuvered his legs across the sofa and touched ground. He punched the remote, pulled up the weatherman. The weatherman postulated toward cloud masses and cross winds, clearly looking away from the blue screen yet trying to appear as though he was viewing the map appearing on the television. *Takes a special talent*, Blake thought sarcastically. He surfed the channels and showed an abundance of talented weather people, all pointing left as they stared directly ahead. *Ah, jeez, another day in the life of a special agent: coffee, news, shower, and work. I'm in a rut*, he thought.

"I'm in a fuckin' rut!" he said these were his first spoken words for the day. Then even louder, he shouted "A GODDAMN FUCKIN' RUT!"

He ran his fingers through his disheveled hair, rubbed the sandpaper growth on his chin, and realized the déjà vu of his everyday mundane existence.

"Ah, shit," he said quietly, flicking to the National Geographic Channel where a cloned Ted Baxter voice expounded the virtues of global warming and its effect on the mating ritual of the tsetse fly.

"Blah, blah, blah. Right, my mating habits too," Blake said as he sipped his first mouthful of life-giving coffee. "Mine too."

It's strange the way a hot shower can erase all of the misery of a bad day, just like wiping a chalkboard with an eraser, or punching delete to remove annoying spam.

It's a fresh start, a bright new beginning, a . . . a false security . . . Yeah, well, shoot that one down, he thought as he toweled off.

Carson Dallas teed up, staring at the expanse of water ahead of him. Contemplating the possible demise of his Titleist, he returned to his bag, sorted through the pocket, and removed a respectable looking striped practice ball.

"Okay little ball, you live to fly another day," he mumbled as he replaced the Pro V1 with its sacrificial substitute." His near perfect backswing was terminated by the cell phone blasting out The Star-Spangled Banner. His playing partners both snapped to attention, saluting in reverent jest, no consolation to Dal as he abandoned the tee, and scrambled to reach the phone prior to its sixth-ring cutoff.

"Dallas," he exhaled into the mouthpiece, trying to project a tone of composure.

Blake said, "Hey Dal. Where are you?"

"On the seventh tee. What's up?"

"Got another fog girl, I'm waiting to hear from forensics How long before you're done losin' balls?"

"I got about four left, fuckin' wise guy."

"Okay so I'll see you in about an hour then?"

"Fuckin' wise guy!"

The office door swung open and Dal wearing checked slacks, a pink sweater, and white golf shoes moved into the room.

Blake smirked, "Hmm, really styling it today, huh Dal?"

"Yeah, yeah, yeah . . . and I still have the four balls in my bag okay. So what's the rush?"

Blake asked, "Have you heard the latest on the fog victim? Another woman, around twenty-eight, attractive. Seems the local cops are being kept off the case. Still can't figure why the chief has us handling this. Can't find the angle. There's minor local involvement, but I feel that's only to satisfy the media. Keep waiting for something to break, a reason to justify our department baby-sitting a string of murders. Last time we were dragged into one of these was with that wacko psychotic, Travis Craven."

"Yeah, well . . . he's ashes, right?" Dal said with some hesitation.

"I believe, well . . . maybe . . . ah shit, yeah, he's gone."

Again, with hesitation, "You don't suppose . . ."

"Spare me," Blake interrupted. "Don't go there. Last I heard from the French cops was that Craven was passé."

Dal maintaining a serious demeanor said, "Right, and he's gone too. . . . but whoever is doin' this fog shit is definitely psychotic."

Blake deep in thought passed a sarcastic grin at Dal. He enjoyed scoring brownie points at Dal's expense. His minimal knowledge of the French language provided Blake with one of those frequent opportunities. Dal was one of the few people Blake knew with fewer French language skills than himself.

"What's goin' on Drew? I can tell when those cogs are turnin'."

"Can't put my finger on it Dal, but I know there's gotta be a connection. Why else would upstairs have us overseeing operations? The local homicide can easily handle this case."

The two men sat pensively. Blake drummed his fingers on the table. Dal removed his Nike hat and groomed his long blonde hair as though preparing for a photo shoot. His early days as a photo model had instilled an air of poise, one that Carson Dallas seemed oblivious to; yet those who didn't know Dal might misinterpret this as a somewhat feminine quality. A rather deadly mistake on their part, as the years had shown. Eight kills had established him as second only to Drew Blake, making them the most 'killingest' team in the American Interpol Division – a team that to the media and all others did not officially exist.

"Maybe they put us onto this to scare the sick bastard into slippin' up," Dal said. "You know . . . havin' the local cops . . . the bloodhounds, on his heels."

"Well, if we're the hounds you're referring to, fuckin' great hounds we are. We got no leads, no clues. We've got nothing," Blake replied in a tone of despair.

"They're not even throwin' us a bone, no pun intended," Dal smirked.

"Of course, there's just no meat on the case," Blake grinned back.

Dal replied, "No leads."

"Okay, okay. Enough with the doggy puns." Blake chuckled.

"Sure, sure," Dal replied. "The trail is stone cold, no scent leadin' anyplace."

Blake sneered, choosing to acquiesce. The cell phone played a tune, Blake said, "Answer that," as the Looney Tunes added a somewhat humorous reprise to the dying embers of their canine repertoire.

Dal flipped the cell open, and in his most official voice said, "This is Dallas."

"Hey Dal, Dwayne here pal. We think we've got an ID on Jane Doe, but we need Blake down here pronto. There's a slight problem, thought he might be able to help out. I hate this job; don't need this shit dumped on me. Gettin' too old."

"Sure thing doc. Stay cool, see you in about forty-five. Ciao."

"What's up Dal?" Blake asked.

"That was Dwayne, says there's a name for the Jane Doe. Wants you downtown, Sounds like someone's shoved a bug up his ass."

Blake chewed over this string of murders, now unofficially tagged the 'Death Fog Murders' by the press. He wondered if these events were related or perhaps just made to appear related. There had to be more to it than met the untrained eye. Considering his eye *was* trained, he felt an obligation to look below the surface, to look outside the box.

Missy Palmer exuded feminine charm with an impish undertone, yet appeared to be mature beyond her years. She had freckles, braids, and sky blue eyes that sparkled like aquamarines. She was a heartbreaker in the making, a definite work in progress. All ten years of her. The feminine steering genes were already there. She sat on a wooden bench, a twin to the pew Blake rested on the night before at Dwayne's lab. A uniformed police-woman sat alongside the young girl, one hand on the girl's, another balancing a box of tissues. The tears slowly jettisoned themselves from the blue eyes and the girl began sobbing relentlessly. Dal and Blake entered the room simultaneously. The girl raised both hands to cover her face, embarrassed by the two large men looking down at her.

"Agent Blake?" the lady cop asked softly." This is Missy Palmer." The lady cop stood and stepped toward Blake, she stretched to whisper, "She's the victim's daughter. We needed an ID on the body. We weren't able to turn up anyone else to do the ID. She's it, the next of kin."

Blake said, "Ah shit, has she been in there yet?"

"Hmm . . . actually I . . . I kind of hoped you guys would take her in to see the victim. I'm sort of new at this stuff."

Dal turned to Blake and sighed, "So the Special Agents step in, so much for the local constabulary."

Blake smiled at the kid and said, "Hi Missy. My name's Drew Blake and this is my friend, Dal."

The girl stood and reached to shake hands with both men. She forced a smile and whispered in a shaky voice, "I'm very pleased to meet you," Her southern twang was very dominant, and Blake thought, *very cute*.

The two men were set back by her maturity, each tried to maintain an air of protocol as they reached for the delicate white hand she extended to each of them.

Blake said," Well hello Missy, we're really sorry to meet you under these circumstances."

The girl slowly sank back onto the bench and resumed her sobbing. Blake felt worse. "I'm sorry, really sorry," he said sadly.

He reached toward the cop as she passed him a box of tissues. Blake sat by the girl and wiped away the deluge. His attention only seemed to increase the tears. He slowly rose to his feet and walked to the door leading to the ME's office. Stretching his head around the door he quietly called, "Dwayne, you there?" The doctor emerged from a far corner of the room, pulling nervously at surgical gloves that were refusing to leave his hands. "Hey Blake, glad you're here. The kid out there, she needs to make an ID of the stiff I got in here, wanna bring her in.? The cop out there seems squeamish."

"Dwayne, it sounds like it's probably her mom. I know what the book says, but can't we just do a photo ID? I don't want to put the kid through it; ya know what I mean, huh?"

The doctor took a long pause, screwing his face as though feeling pain. He considered the heat from his superiors if they were to hear he failed to follow procedure.

"Yeah, yeah. I saw her out there. It's a tough one I know. Maybe I'll just step out for a while, take a piss. You can bring her in, but leave before I get back. I'll make it a slow piss, savvy? Oh and by the way, we've got some good shots of the victim," he nodded toward the white filing cabinet as he left the room, still tugging furiously at the one glove strangling his right hand.

Blake nodded as he looked across at the white filing cabinet. "Thanks Dwayne, I owe you one man."

The ME passed through the waiting area and smiled at Missy, gave Dal a quick wink, closed the door softly and left the room. Blake moved toward the white filing cabinet across the room from the body, rifled through the photographs. There were several photographs of the victims, shots of faces from various angles. Blake looked for the one of the Jane Doe least likely to upset the kid. The knock on the door startled him. He turned quickly, holding the bunch of shots behind his back. Dal edged into the room as though he might be disturbing Blake's conversation with the deceased.

"Hey Drew, this kid's really startin' to get on my nerves. I can only handle so much, I'm gonna be cryin' with her myself soon."

"Jesus you came in here to tell me that?" Blake said tongue in cheek.

Dal whined, "The cop had to leave man, some kind of emergency at home, asked me to take care of the fuckin' kid."

Blake slowly raised his eyes and spoke at the ceiling. "And you said?"

"Well I thought - seeing how's we, hmm . . ."

"Oh great, thanks Dal. Thanks a bunch man. I guess you're volunteering *your* services to baby-sit, huh?"

Dal lowered his eyes, leaving Blake feeling very alone. He'd drawn the short straw. Not that he felt uncomfortable around kids. Blake loved kids, preferably when they were on loan.

"Uh Drew, I've been chattin' with her out there between the tears."

"Her tears or yours Dal?"

"That's tough Drew; the kid kinda gets to ya."

"To you Dal…she gets to *you*. I've plans for the next few hours so why don't *you* run the kid home?"

Dal stared at Blake. He clearly was lost for words, a rarity, and a moment Blake savored. With the photographs in hand, he pushed by Dal and moved from the room. He slowed his aggressive pace and sat by the girl. She raised her eyes; they were now blurred with a red hue covering the blue.

Blake held the pictures face down in the hand furthest from the girl. He tapped the stack against the pew as he spoke. "Missy, I got a few photos here of different ladies to show you honey. They're all hmm . . . kind of sleepin'. I'd like you to take a look and tell me which one of these people you know - okay?"

She nodded, a cute smile feigned confidence, an air of style the kid carried well. She held Blake's smile, the kind of exchange he didn't expect from one so young.

"They're dead people aren't they? They're all dead."

Her response took him by surprise. He hesitated as he tried to find the gentlest words, but she was quick to follow on. Blake stared as she replied, "I know my mom is in there. Please don't treat me like a kid."

The tears began flowing again as Blake reached for the tissue box. It was now almost empty.

"Okay Missy, I'll treat you like a grown-up. Yeah, we think it's your mom in there, you know that's why you're here, right, to tell us if it's her?"

"So why don't I just go in and see her? That's what they do on TV. They go in and say, 'yeah, that's her.' Right Mr. Drew?"

Blake wasn't ready for this bravado. He stared at the kid, swallowed hard, and let out a long slow breath. He shuffled the photos between his fingers and hung his head hang between his shoulders. The beads of sweat ran down from his armpits. He thought about the last woman who had this effect on him, quite a different situation, but same effect nonetheless.

He wanted to say, '*Ah shit kid, no need to play tough guy with me. I've seen tough guys before, so knock off the fuckin' bravado,*' but instead he said, "Okay Missy, let's do it." He rose from the pew and moved toward the room.

She stood by the shrouded body, her back straight, like a military cadet at attention, her head held high, and her nose uncontrollably running as Blake passed her yet another tissue. More tears slipped from her eyes. Blake couldn't help notice her biting on her bottom lip as though preparing for a painful injection. He reached out and held the top edge of the shroud and hesitated, Missy's small hand increased its grip on his. He paused and looked down at the kid. She turned her head to him and quietly asked, "Mr. Drew can we just look at the photos?"

He felt a wave of relief. Releasing his hold on the shroud, he kneeled beside the girl.

Blake said softly, "Let's get out of here and take a ride. We can talk later."

The first few miles passed in silence. Blake thought of a million ways to start a conversation, none seemed appropriate. He pulled the car into a burger joint. He said, "I'm hungry kiddo, how about you? Like a burger?"

Blake was really proud of himself. He'd struck a cord, a means to break the ice, a common denominator, almost escapism, a way to get far, far away from the horrible reality of the moment. He pulled the car up to the drive-through window. A bell hung suspended on a heavy rope, the type used for securing a buoy or tying a large boat to a dock. The sign by the bell read "Ring once for directions. Ring twice to order."

"Guess you get a few lost tourists these parts, huh Missy?"

"Oh sure, they're always stopping by asking for this or that. Some are real city slickers, big cars, some even wearing ties. You can tell them as soon as they pull in. Black windows, always two or more people, dark glasses too, even when it's cloudy and gray." Missy jiggled about in the seat, as though preparing herself for the ensuing treat. Blake reached for the rope, gave it two tugs. He ordered shakes and fries, pulled the car to a quiet spot under a towering elm, tuned the radio to a soft rock station and the two sat in silence and ate. As they got near to finishing their food the kid said, "Mr. Drew you can show me the photos now. I'm really okay, really." Her voice was monotone.

He was relieved and wanted to get this behind him. He reached into his coat pocket and he took the photos out, spreading all five between them on the car seat. Missy leaned toward them, and her small shaking index finger with a spluttering of ketchup still covering the nail, moved toward the middle picture. Her voice quivered, her lower lip trembled, and tears began to once again slowly make their way down her pink cheeks.

"That's my mom."

Blake called through to the local station and asked for Officer O'Brien, the cop who'd brought Missy to the county morgue. Fate worked in strange ways. The woman cop, O'Brien - had signed off for the night. This he thought, is why he and Dal were on the case and not the local keystone cops.

Blake flipped his cell shut, looked at the girl who was searching for the longest fry in the bag.

"Missy can you direct me to your house?"

She dipped the long fry into her strawberry shake, twirled it around, scooped up some cream, and passed it to Blake. He swallowed hard, a dry gulp. He thought, *oh God, please make the phone ring, anything, a gunshot, even a carjacking, just give me something easy to handle, something I'm comfortable with.*

His plead to God fell on deaf ears. God was off duty for the night.

"Do you have any brothers or sisters? What about your dad?"

"My dad went away when I was a kid; my sister went with him so I suppose I really don't have any siblings. No family at all now. She was my twin you know. Her name was Simone."

"Listen Missy, you're gonna have to stay with someone, I just need to figure out who. I could call Protective Services, but I'd rather place you with someone I know, I've a feeling we'll be needing to see you again soon, after you've rested up."

"Mr. Drew, if you can take me to my house I can get some of my things. It's not too far from here. It's down by the water. I haven't been home for three days; I was staying at a friend from school's place for the holiday weekend. Mom was home. She was going to bake my favorite pecan pie while I was away. She makes the best pecan . . ."

The kid didn't finish. Her head fell into her hands and the tears again began to flow. Blake rubbed his lips together, they were dry and tight. He wanted to ask where the kid's father had gone, wanted more information about her twin sister. He thought about it, passed the kid another tissue said, "Okay then, Take it easy, how about an aunt or uncle?"

Missy sniffled, wiped her face and blew hard into the tissue. After doing this, she wiped the back of her hand across her nose, and sat silently staring ahead at car tail lights as they passed by, vanishing into the distance.

She answered, "No, no aunts or uncles."

Blake kept trying to remind himself that *he* was the adult, *she* was the child. But her resounding emphasis on her never being childish left no room for conjecture, and Blake was darned sure he was not about to contradict anything she'd said, not now, not alone with her in the car, different if Dal or a another cop was with him.

They drove for over twenty minutes. The night air became

heavy as the marine layer moved in. There was a fog-like pall precariously balanced on the tops of the street lights that hung from lamp posts. The fog formed a white ceiling, hiding the stars and moon from earthly eyes.

The girl said, "This is it, turn here. Be careful of the potholes, there are quite a few."

Blake didn't speak, turning the car in the direction the kid was pointing. She lowered her hand and dipped another fry into the bottom of her shake. She stretched across to him, placing the cold soggy fry on his lower lip, catching Blake by surprise. His immediate reaction made him jerk away, causing her to laugh in a coy, girlish manner.

"Oh Mr. Drew, my mom used to me let me feed her my dipped fries. Come on just one."

"Thanks Missy, but I'll pass this time. Okay kiddo?"

God must have clocked back on, the cell phone broke the silence.

Blake saw the name of the caller on the screen. "Dal great to hear from you, where the fu.." He paused, glanced sideways at Missy. He said, "Where are you? I'm here with Missy, just driving to her house, yeah, she's fine, me too, thanks for asking. No, no, I'm not being sarcastic. Say Dal, can you hook up with us? You can? Great, I'd really appreciate it. I'm at the old wharf down by Lamb Cove. And Dal . . . make it snappy. Yeah, yeah, thirty minutes out of the city. At Lamb Cove, okay?"

Saved by the bell, good old Dal. Good old God, Blake thought as he gave Dal clear directions and hoped he would arrive soon, very soon.

"Is Mr. Dal joining us? How nice."

"Yeah, yeah. Dal's going to be here soon kiddo, real soon."

Blake recognized the feeling inner fear. He didn't want to be alone with Missy, not right now. *Maybe it's me,* he thought. But the situation felt like a scary movie scene where he was the prey, the idiot who was about to get the shaft. Blake hit the CD button and a soft blues melody changed the mood offering him a brief respite. Time dragged by, Missy continued to eat her fries, concentrating on each dip she made into her shake. Blake checked the dash clock; twenty five minutes had passed since he spoke to Dal. The sudden blast of a car horn caused them both to jump. Missy squeezed Blake's arm in a death grip. The midnight black paintwork was hard to spot and Dal, with his warped sense of humor, added to its invisibility by slowly rolling toward them with the lights off. Dal peered from the window of the Porsche. "Hey pal what's up? You sounded a bit loopy on the phone, anythin' wrong?"

"Jesus Christ Dal, you scared the shit out of us, oops - sorry Missy. Here, take a look at the curtains, there are shadows in there. Missy says the place should be empty. What do ya think?"

Blake looked at Missy who sat innocently smiling up at Dal.

"Hello Mr. Dal, so glad you could join us."

"Me too, I'm sure," Dal replied.

Dal looked across at Blake; it was a look searching for an explanation, one that Blake couldn't give. He shrugged his shoulders, slowly shaking his head in an *I don't know* gesture.

Missy, Blake and Dal moved slowly toward the house, about sixty feet away. Missy walked between the two men, holding both Blake's and Dal's hands. They were now just feet from the wooden house. They stepped onto the porch, their arrival announced by the wooden flooring creaking. A shadow continued its dance against the curtains.

Dal whispered, "My mouth's pretty dry Drew. Pretty, pretty, dry. How about you?"

Blake glanced across at Dal whose apprehension clearly showed on his face . . . a face now clearly more pale than usual, his blonde hair adding to the lack of color.

Dal began quietly singing his '*I don't feel too brave*' melody: "Whenever I feel afraid, I hold my head erect, and whistle a happy tune, so no one will suspect, I'm afraid . . ." His singing did nothing to eliminate the tension the three were feeling.

Blake reached inside his jacket, fingering the nine millimeter Glock. He hoped it would stay in the holster. Dal followed suit, reaching for the shoulder holster, releasing the safety strap.

"Want me to go round back?" Dal whispered.

"Yeah good move, I'll wait here and count to thirty then try the front door. You do the same, take the back okay?"

"Missy I want you to stay back in the car until we check out the house."

She smiled at Blake, the same smile he first saw back at the ME's rooms. Her eyes held his, and for a split second nothing around him existed; he was totally linked in some way to this kid's magical charm. They could have been anywhere, any safe place . . . for those few seconds the night held no fear, had no uncertainties. Blake cocked his head to one side, blinked a few times, and his hand went to his forehead as he ran his fingers slowly through his hair.

"Okay, okay, sure you can come along. Everything is gonna to be fine. Hey Dal, come on back. We'll go in the front. Things are fine."

When Blake was a kid, he had had a fascination for a scrawny kid with pigtails and freckles. She always had a wide brim straw hat stuck to her head, and she incessantly chewed gum. Blake guessed he sort of fell into that pattern until the time she was having her sixteenth birthday bash. The party was talked about for years after. It seemed her old man pulled in a favor from a friend who was a bigwig hypnotist back up Boston way. Anyhow this guy turned up at the party and broke into his act. He pulled a few of the kids from the group and proceeded to hypnotize them. He told the party girl she was a goat. The straw hat wasn't on her head, but there was a young kid there about eight who just so happened to be wearing a wide rimmed straw hat. So the kid who thought girl who thought she was a goat strolled over and began chewing off chunks of this kid's hat. The kids all went nuts, rolling about hysterically, not a dry eye in the house. Best laugh the town had in years.

The weird thing is the guy seemed to mess up on the 'snap out of it' part of his routine. For months after that, each time anyone wearing a straw hat got close to that kid, she snapped the hat from their head and proceeded to rip at it with her teeth. The weirdest thing, completely normal one minute, a ravenous beast the next. Blake had a feeling of déjà vu watching Missy; she had been calm and rather cute for most of their drive to the house.

Blake stood to one side of the door, Dal on the other. Dal nodded to Blake, waiting for him to knock. Blake stood staring back at the kid.

"Drew you're miles away man. Are we goin' in or what?"

"Yeah, yeah. Got a theory going through my head here. I just need to think it out. I'll get back to it later. Let's check and see who's inside."

CHAPTER 57

BLAKE RAPPED ON THE door not knowing who or what to expect. Dal stood to one side, his nine millimeter held outstretched in both hands, ready to move into the room. Blake turned the handle, the door wasn't locked. He nudged Missy back out of sight of the opening door, which creaked as he slowly moved it with his foot.

"Anyone in there?" Blake called hesitantly. There was no reply. "This is the police. Come out with your hands held above your head."

He nodded to Dal, who was slowly lowering onto one knee and extending his arms into a firing position, his nine millimeter raised ready for any movement. Blake moved slowly into the house. He saw the flickering light was caused by an electric fan blowing the curtain. The curtain's movement cast shadow effects on the window.

"Drew, over there by the sofa." Dal pointed to a man's sneakers protruding from behind an old Chesterfield.

"Missy stay out on the porch. I'll come get you in a tick, okay?"

Missy gave an uncomfortable smile, biting her bottom lip, looking more nervous than he had seen her earlier.

"Yes sir but I'm scared," she said with a quiver in her voice.

Dal reached behind the sofa, placed a finger on the man's neck, he turned back to Blake and said, "He's very dead, fuckin' stone dead. Cold as marble." He pointed at the floor, "dark stain over here by the table, he's got a head wound. Looks like a .22 caliber."

Blake squatted, looked at the darkened area, took a tissue from his pocket, went to the kitchen sink, wet the tissue, returned to the dark stain, dabbed it with the tissue and watched as the paper turned red. "Yep, no doubt, it's blood, probably his. Or might be whoever took this guy out, could've been a struggle.

You know the drill Dal. Call in and get forensics out here. We need this whole area combed. See if you can find some ID; take a look if he's got a wallet. I need to show the kid a photo ID, see if she can put a name to this guy."

Dal carefully slid a wallet from the man's back pocket. "Looky here, he's got an out of state driver's license."

Sliding his thumb under the license Dal hesitated, looking up toward Blake, his head cocked to the side, puzzled.

"Drew, take a look at this, this guy has three licenses in his wallet. Same photo on each, but each with a different name. One's from Missouri, one's Louisiana, and this third one's from Georgia."

Blake browsed though the contents of the wallet. Sirens were getting closer and it was only minutes before the flashing lights created an atmosphere around the old wooden house like that of a Hollywood movie set.

"Christ Dal, this guy was a private dick. Look here, his credentials were tucked away behind this flap. Reese Branson, heard of him?"

"Sounds kind of familiar, but I might've heard it in a movie. Sounds a bit too good, know what I mean, Reese Branson?"

Blake had often been accused of creating his own name, he was often told '*Drew Blake huh? Great name, sounds too good to be true*', he looked at Dal and said, "No I don't."

Dal sulked for a second and said, "That was – hmm - what do you say . . . rhetorical?"

Blake played him along. "His name . . . rhetorical?"

"Not his name . . . the fuckin' question."

Blake moved out to the porch. Missy was sitting on the top step picking pebbles from a small shell and flicking them toward the patrol car now blocking the walkway. Two cops were stretching yellow tape around the perimeter. The ME was busily gathering his tools of trade from the rear of a van prior to making his entrance.

"Evenin' Drew, see you still have the kid," he said nodding toward Missy. "Can't shake her huh?"

"Yeah, yeah, yeah Dwayne. Gotta find some place for her to stay, any ideas?"

"Yeah I noticed when I drove through town that the Hilton

has its vacancy sign flashing. Maybe they have a junior rate."

Blake gave him a half-grin and squinted in his direction, his eyes partly blinded by the beam from the patrol car now lighting the scene.

Blake's half-grin vanished as he held out a hand to shade his eyes from the glare, "Hey, can you guys kill the lights? I'm going blind here."

The larger of the two cops made one more wrap with the yellow crime scene tape around a skinny sapling by the edge of the house, tied it off, snapped off the tape and quickly moved to the car.

Dal was still in the house. The forensics had arrived and Dal hung back to watch *'real cops'* as he called them, at work. Blake called to Dal, "Hey Sherlock, come on out here."

Dal reluctantly stepped from the house and sat on the other side of Missy.

"Missy I'd like you to take a look at this photo and tell me if you recognize this person." Blake said.

Blake passed the Georgia license to Missy and studied her reaction.

"Do you know this man?"

"He's one of the men from the black boats. He's been to the house a bit. He was a friend of my mom's."

Blake passed the wallet back to Dal, and nodded to the forensic guys. "Ah shit, this is getting more confusing by the minute. Let's leave the rest to them. I don't think we can do much more here tonight. Let's head back into town and let the boys finish up. We'll touch base with Dwayne in the morning and try to piece together this fuckin' puzzle."

The woman cop was a welcome sight, and was quick to comfort Missy. Blake smiled a wide smile.

"Glad to see you O'Brian. Real glad," Dal said.

The cop chatted with Missy for a few minutes, and reassured Blake and Dal, "She'll be fine inspector," she said to Blake. *Hmm inspector, I like the sound of that.* Dal smirked and Blake threw a defensive glance at Dal who didn't have time to make he's usual smart crack.

O'Brian said, "I'll take her back to my place, if that's

all right with you, and you can reach me at the station in the morning."

Blake smiled appreciably. "You're a real Florence Nightingale! Sorry you had to rush off earlier tonight. I tried to reach you at the station but was told you had some kind of family emergency. I hope everything turned out okay."

"Thanks for asking. It was my dog actually. The pound picked her up. It's a three strike situation, so I had to get her out fast. If you've got a dog, you'll know what I mean."

Dal said, "Three strikes huh? Can't say I've heard of that for dogs, must be a Louisiana thing, gotta watch them Cajuns. Gotta be a French thing goin' on." they'll cook anythin'."

Dal leaned into Blake and murmured with no lip movement, "Fuckin' French."

She smiled a broad smile and continued to comfort Missy. Dal tried to make amends to the woman cop, fearing his last comment may have offended her. "So then, your name's O'Brien, is that from an Irish dad?"

She glanced down at the name badge on her chest, buffing it with the cuff of her coat. "Yes my dad was Irish, my mom is French. Perhaps you'll join us for dinner some night, since you've got such a gourmet appreciation for our cooking."

Blake swallowed hard, a dry sandy grating swallow. "You gotta excuse Dal here; his culinary appreciation is somewhat impaired."

Dal smiled at him, whispering, "Touché."

O'Brien tilted her head toward Dal. "And that one word is probably the extent of your French language skills, right?"

Blake turned to face Dal, rubbing the side of his nose with his middle finger.

Blake leaned to Dal's ear, he whispered, "Oh yeah, a real fuckin' low blow to the boy from Minnesota. Ten points to Officer O'Brian."

Smiling she nodded to Dal, gave him a quick wink, she carefully walked Missy from the room and left Blake and Dal standing like two school boys caught with their hands down their pants. Dal said, "I think I'm in love, did ya see the way she looked at me?"

They weren't expecting a prolonged stay, and their Hotel really was pushing its four star rating.

Dal looked about the small room. "Hey Drew, I think they penciled the fourth star onto this room directory."

Blake pushed down on the mattress. "Betcha right, we'll check out a few other places tomorrow, depending on where this case looks like it's heading."

Blake sat on the side of the bed, which appeared to be a squeaky, heavily sprung remnant of the fifties. It sagged a foot under the weight of his two-hundred-plus pounds. Placing a pillow across his legs, he shored up a makeshift desk and fired up his laptop. The name on the Georgia license came up as legitimate. It gave an Atlanta address, near a golf course Dal and Blake once golfed, by Lake Lanier. The other two licenses were fake, no match with addresses, and no past history.

Dal called from the bathroom, "Find somethin'?"

"Yeah, Reese Branson from Georgia, a good ol' Southern boy, thirty-eight years old, no priors, no outstanding warrants. Nothing. He's cleaner than a baby's ass. Has to be something somewhere, I had HQ run his prints, and guess what? Eureka! The guy was using all three licenses and none were legit. The son-of-a-bitch had a history on file back in Detroit - extortion, grand theft, assault with intent. Got himself a hot shot attorney and had all cases kicked out of court. He ain't this Branson person, his name is Jake Fortessi. Mixed in real bad circles, his sheet reads like a who's who of East Coast *don't fuck with us* mothers, ya know - Mafioso, Colombian cartels – this boy had no scruples."

Dal called out, "Sounds like he was just missin' a good Catholic upbringin'."

Blake made a loud farting sound with his lips.

The next day kicked off early, the windows of the hotel rattled like a spoon being run down a washboard in a Zydeco band.

The six o'clock morning freight train rumbled through. It made a noise like a shaker registering eight on the Richter scale. Blake reached across and turned the knob on the old radio. Too sleepy to surf the dial, he accepted the fact that whatever the thing was tuned to would it.

A desperately lonesome sounding voice sang in French, singing of lost love and heaps of heartbreak, a fiddle adding plaintive harmonic drones with an accordion accompaniment, all staccato providing bounce and substance. Beneath this conglomerate of instruments, accordion, fiddle, a six-string guitar, and an oversized iron triangle which jangled out a crude ring-a-ding sound, the result was the unmistakable sound of the south Louisiana bayou, Cajun music.

Dal rolled over and squinted broadly, straining to focus. "Jesus fuckin' Christ . . . what are you tryin' to do to me?"

It started Blake's day off on a good note. Anytime he could cause Dal to start his day with anything resembling a smile, well - any reaction resembling a thought process - that was a good day.

The red light on the old dial-up phone by the bed blinked intermittently. Blake reached across, holding the hand piece between his index finger and thumb for fear of contracting God-knows-what diseases. He was right. It'd been quite some time since any antibacterial cleaner had graced the phone in this room.

A sleepy voice came though from the desk phone. "Ah good morning sir, this is the desk. You have an urgent message to call this number." Blake wrote down the number. It seemed vaguely familiar, he thought about it, and realized any conversation on his part would be far more intelligent following a coffee or two.

"Hey Dal," Blake called. "Wake up, let's rock and roll. A new day's a dawnin' man."

Dal raised himself from the lumpy mattress, feeling the cold air in the musty room. The heater wasn't doing much at all. In fact on closer inspection it was clear the pilot light was extinguished. The view below onto the small courtyard was pleasant enough and actually offered some respite from the ten-inch television screen from which Blake was unable to get any kind of a picture. It seemed to be playing a looped version of *Poltergeist*.

They made their way to a small breakfast room. The

elderly waitress resembled an actress Blake had once seen in the front row of a guillotine scene of a movie set during the French Revolution era. *In fact she might have existed during the French Revolution,* he thought. *That makes her a few hundred years old, and that's being kind.*

"Bonjour, bonjour," she sang as though auditioning for a Parisian musical. "Coffee?"

Dal nodded, covering his mouth with one hand in an attempt to restrain his mirth.

"Se vous ples," Blake replied, which was utterly more than Dal could handle. He burst into a coughing fit of laughter which just encouraged the waitress to quickly begin beating on his back. While the scene played out Blake sat back and began on his first cup for the day.

"Well at least the coffee's good."

The coffee and biscuits went down well, fresh and tasty. The check for twenty-five dollars was something else.

"I'll get that," Dal said using his power charged in control voice. The last time Dal had picked up a tab, it had been for coffee and a cookie, a four dollar and fifty cent check in a small diner in south Los Angeles. Blake slid the check across to Dal. Blake stayed as serious as he could, anticipated Dal's reaction. Dal looked at the amount on the check and proceeded to choke on his last piece of biscuit. He fumbled his cup, spilling it as he attempted to wash down the biscuit with the remains of the coffee.

While this was taking place, Blake made his way toward the rest room, leaving behind the plaintiff cries of Dal groaning, "Jesus Christ! Jesus Christ!"

The two men sat in the Porsche, *befitting* Blake thought, while Dal still bemoaned the cost of the biscuit and coffee.

Blake chuckled "Yeah, yeah, yeah. But you pay for the atmosphere not the fuckin' coffee," Dal didn't buy it.

"What?" Blake laughed sideways at Dal.

"C'mon Drew. This is criminal, and they get away with it."

"Yeah, so next time we'll go to fuckin' Starbuck's and vacation on the savings."

"Yeah right," Dal replied nodding, yet in a somewhat subdued dejected way.

Blake reached into his wallet and pulled out the card with the scribbled phone number. "I know this number but can't put my finger on where I know it from."

Dal leaned across the gear shifter and squinted at the card.

"That's the chief's home number."

"Yeah, yeah, yeah right, sure it is," Blake said making a dubious face at Dal.

"Really it is, I remember it 'cause it has the year I was born in the last four digits, 1973."

"Hmm. Why would Sam be calling me after hours? Must have come in after we hit the sack."

Blake dialed in the number and waited as the phone reached its fourth ring. A voice answered: "Ridkin."

The voice was gruff, authoritative and intimidating. It was all there. All present in that one word, Ridkin.

"Hey Sam, how are things going back there?"

Blake used his best easy going *everything's fine here* voice.

"What the fuck are you two clowns doing over there? The bureau sent you on a simple investigation and all hell breaks loose. I've got media crawling out of my ass here. So now you've got another body. Of course you couldn't sit on it a bit, keep it discreet, oh no. You had to have fuckin' license checks run. What the fuck Blake? I give you brownie points for brains! It'd be different if that shit-for-brains fuckin' sidekick Dallas had made the license check move, but for Christ's sake man. I've had you there explicitly because *you* are able to think on the fuckin' run!"

Blake was able to stay calm in most situations He bit his tongue until it felt like it was drawing blood. Dal had his ear pressed closely toward the cell phone, almost choking Blake with his overindulgence of cheap cologne. He flicked the cell onto speaker mode and placed it on the dash, leaned back away from Dal, and listened to Sam's continuing barrage. The voice on the phone continued for several minutes, blurting out expletives, highlighted by numerous exclamation marks.

At last Blake had heard enough. Dal was going through a chameleon stage, his face now reaching a deep red hue.

"ENOUGH!" Blake shouted into the cell. Dal pulled away and made a face.

"Sam we've been here now for four days, we've been baby-sitters to a kid for some of it. We've slept in some miserable fuckin' flophouse hotel, for which we both express our heartiest appreciation to the Department, and to boot we've been given no indication as to why the hell we've been assigned this case. It seems the local cops could have taken this one. It's their jurisdiction. But that's no big deal. Nah let Blake and his trusty side-kick hang on it."

Blake stopped to draw breath.

"Hold it there mister!" Sam Ridkin was pissed. He didn't dillydally with words and Blake knew he'd overstepped the line. Then he surprised Blake: "I'm sorry, Drew, it's been difficult for me not to fill you in with the gist of this one, but 'til now it's been classified."

"Classified? What the fuck Sam? Who are you talkin' to here? It's me, Drew. Since when do I need clearance for a case?"

"Comes from up above Drew."

"Up above? You mean God? You mean fuckin' God is running this show Sam? Jesus Christ that's rich. That's really fuckin' rich."

Dal grinned.

There was a few long seconds pause, and then Sam replied, "God? Nah but you're close. Try the president, or more to the point, the CIA."

"Central Intelligence? Why are they on top of these murders in New Orleans?"

Drew I'm sending a special operative to work with you guys, a top CIA operative now transferred to our department. Now I recognize that look you're getting on your face, but stay with me on this. She's a great gal and –"

"Whoa, hold the phone, hold the fuckin' phone!" Blake snapped back at him. "SHE . . . SHE? . . . It's a fuckin' FEMALE agent?"

Sam was silent for a few moments, then added, "Oh yeah, and I'll fly in myself. I'll see all three of you real soon."

The two men sat patiently in the Coffee and Beignet Shop in the west lobby of the New Orleans International Airport. The Aero Mexico arrival was now two hours late. This was the third round of beignets.

"Fuck me Drew," Dal said nodding toward his last beignet. "I'll need to take out an equity loan to pay for this stuff."

"Yeah, yeah," Blake replied. "At least it tastes good and this one's on Uncle Sam so enjoy."

CHAPTER 58

THE GIRL WALKING TOWARD them moved like a tigress, a predatory attitude. She was everything every man could fantasize over as the perfect looking woman. It was obvious the two men were both staring. Dal nudged Blake with his elbow.

"Close your mouth, you're drooling," he said below his breath.

"Oh . . . my . . . God," Blake said very quietly. She was still twenty yards off and moving in slowly, but definitely sauntering toward them. She had it all in the looks department. She had even more in the walks department.

Angelina Jolie lips, Marilyn Monroe hips, and a knock-me-down-and-fuck-me attitude that would cause the pope to have wet dreams.

"Hello boys. I have your files. You're far better looking in real life Blake. Your file photo doesn't do you justice." She reached out and took Blake's hand. It wasn't really a shake, more of a soft lingering squeeze. Blake felt his knees weaken, swallowing becoming a conscious task.

"My pleasure I know," Blake said. Not being one lost for words, he made a mental note of this exception.

"I'm Carson Dallas but you can call me Dal." Dal reached across trying to hide his enthusiasm, and Blake felt he could have kicked Dal for interrupting his own prolonged hand shake.

"Dal, pleased to make your acquaintance, I'm sure."

Dal turned toward Blake and whispered, "The chief is full of surprises. God bless the old bastard."

"Yeah bless him for me too, and if you're not master of your domain in the morning I'll understand."

"I'm Patrice Bellinger, Bell for short. I understand you boys have been a bit out of the loop on this one. I know your department is, how can I put this, hmm . . . elite . . . yeah, elite. What is it you're unofficially called, the AID boys? That's

American Interpol Department - or is it Division? Always thought that was pretty cute," she said, smiling at each in turn.

Blake raised his eyes unapologetically and answered, "No shit, that's us - elite, I like that." Blake interlocked his fingers, showing an ounce of impatience, stretched his palms toward Bellinger and cracked his knuckles. "So now that we all know who's who, tell us what the hell has been going on here? Tell me it's more than straight out homicides. Things were going routinely until we sent off a few fake licenses for checking, then wham. The entire wrath of the White House seems to be bearing down on us."

She grinned. "I can see why this has your nuts in a knot."

Dal coughed. "Um, if you'll excuse me for a minute, I need to use the head." Dal raised himself, slowly placing his mouth by Blake's ear as he whispered, "Yeah - but can she cook?"

She nodded his way and watched as Dal stumbled over her luggage, trying clumsily to regain a semblance of composure for the remainder of his short journey to the restroom.

They made their way back to the table where Dal and Blake had earlier spent hours indulging in coffee and beignets.

"Would you like a coffee?" she asked.

"Nah not really, perhaps Dal, when he joins us," Blake replied smiling. "He's big on the coffee and beignets. So how was your flight?" he asked, feeling like a schoolboy, lost for meaningful conversation. He tried to regain composure, to adopt a voice more in keeping with his rank and reputation.

"Tell me, um, you flew in on Aero Mexico. Where'd you come in from?"

She reached for the coffee, stirred it slowly, and sipped. There was a lingering silence, as she raised her eyes in the direction of the rest rooms. Blake instinctively followed her gaze, turning his head in the same direction. Dal was making his way back toward the table. The question remained unanswered. Dal pulled his chair and eyed the fresh pot of decaf.

"Ah coffee, how refreshing, a nice change," he said

scowling at Blake who slipped him a knowing wink.

The CIA gal was now all business. "I think we can now dispose with the frivolities guys. You'll both check out of your hotel and check into the Hyatt. There's a suite reserved for you in the name of Bollinger, Beauregard and Oliver Bollinger. In this envelope you'll find licenses and credit cards to validate your ID. Any questions so far?"

Dal was quick in asking, "So who's Oliver?"

"You are. Blake is Beauregard."

"Oh, shit," Dal whined. "I don't want to be fuckin' Oliver, why can't I be a Brad or a Brent, okay even Beau, can't we manage that?"

"Sorry. It's all done, Ollie. I'll see you at the Hyatt. I have a few errands to take care of. I'll meet you both in the Mint Julep Lounge at eight o'clock. I'll have some guests who are just dying to meet you both." She sauntered off as gracefully as she'd appeared.

The two men sat in silence as the minutes passed. Finally, Blake stood and brushed off his trousers, and Dal stretched out as though yawning, both men falling back on old nervous habits. Blake didn't need to brush his trousers, and Dal certainly wasn't tired. They looked at each other. Dal scratched nervously at the side of his nose. Blake tightened his lips, a nervous habit he'd acquired as a child, yet one he believed added a touch of intellect to his pose, as though his thought process was in top gear.

"So, what's the scoop?" Dal asked.

"No fuckin' idea," Blake replied. "If I tried to make something out of all this I'd be either guessing or straight out lying. Let's get our stuff from the flophouse and move into something more befitting our status. No point sitting around here playin' with our weenies."

Dal snapped to attention. "Yeah, the Hyatt suite - I got dibs on the remote, okay?"

They loaded the luggage into the Porsche, *probably the first real set of wheels to grace the car lot since the place was built back in the horse and carriage era,* Blake thought.

The drive to the Hyatt was a short one, just one mile from

the French Quarter, Bourbon Street, and Jackson Square. Their suite faced the Louisiana Superdome, with the New Orleans Arena also in view.

"Looks a lot better than the Katrina days huh. Definitely the place to be now, great view," Dal snapped in a happy tone. He dropped heavily on the bed opposite the large TV which was ceremoniously placed above a huge bar area, more than amply stocked with Johnnie Walker.

Blake reached for the wine list, glanced at the offerings. Veuve Clicquot, Perrier-Jouet Fleur Champagne, Cuvee William Deutz, Bollinger, Piper-Heidsieck by Gaultier, and last, but not least the ever popular Dom Perignon. No prices, but then Blake figured if you want this stuff, what the fuck, you don't need sticker shock in advance, and after you've drunk it you don't give a fuck anyway. He slid the list under the bed not wanting Dal to go comatose when he saw the check-out bill, *if we ever check out*, Blake thought.

"Man just feel these beds. Heaven man, heaven. I'm starting to hope this case really drags out," said Dal.

Blake peeled his coat off and gently stretched out, both hands clasped behind his head. "Yep, I was feeling like that way back at the airport," Blake replied. "Way, way back." He smiled, and Dal got his drift. Blake said, "Have a Pepsi, it's in the bar." Then said very slowly, very clearly: "But just a fuckin' Pepsi, okay?"

CHAPTER 59

T HE HYATT AMBIENCE WAS a stark contrast to their previous eatery. Hotel guests were attired far more elegantly than the gaggle of backpackers who had sat across from them at the flophouse. It seemed amusing how their former accommodation progressively deteriorated with each improvement to their current situation, their daily lifestyle was now more one to which Blake was accustomed. The only stable standard seemed to be their mode of transportation. The Porsche was Dal's baby. It sported a turbo wide body, sitting on ten-inch rims. It looked as though it were speeding when it sat at the curb. But to a Porsche purist, this 911 was a hybrid to say the least. A mongrel breed.

Three years earlier Dal had stepped on the peddle once too often and painfully ceased the motor. Dal was on a trip from New Orleans to Saratoga, New York. On the return trip he noticed a clacking and checked the oil. The dipstick in the Porsche just barely registered any oil in the motor. He pulled into a gas station and added another two quarts. *Better safe than sorry*, he thought. It seemed the extra oil was just a tad too much. The subsequent smoke cloud billowing skyward in his wake caused oncoming vehicles to flash their lights, thinking he was on fire. The following week the German engine went into retirement.

The transplant was a good ol' 454 Chevy Big Block, this monster being way too much weight for the finely tuned and balanced body of the Porsche. Dal put in considerable track time being reeducated in how to gun the 911 without the rear end spinning and facing the direction he was driving. Ah yes, Dal loved that car, but alas, the course of true love never runs smooth.

The Mint Julep Lounge was quiet. Four couples sat chatting, waiting for tables in the restaurant. A voice announced, "Walton, party of two." Dal grinned in Blake's direction saying, "Seinfeld party of four." Dal was the shows number one fan and was quite skilled in quoting lines from the series verbatim. He had all of the episodes and replayed them on a regular basis. He truly believed Seinfeld together with Frazier might one day both become a quiz show topic, giving him his big break on the entertainment scene.

"Drew - look to your right." Dal gestured with a nod of his head. "Tell me I'm seein' things."

Blake looked around and squinted to sharpen his vision. Patrice Bellinger was approaching them accompanied by a young girl, well dressed, almost a stranger until she came closer.

"Hold the phone," Dal snapped loudly.

"MISSY?" Blake said loudly. "IS THAT YOU?"

The man at her side spoke for her. "This is Missy's sister Simone. I'm her dad, Dick Palmer."

Bell pulled back a chair and nodded to her two acquaintances to have a seat.

"Dal, Drew this is Missy's dad and twin sister. I know you were told they disappeared in a boating accident, but this was necessary because of events which will make sense to you in the next hour or so. It's a long story, but I'll try to keep it brief and as simple as possible. If I lose you at any time, please stop me and ask any questions okay?"

The two men sat and nodded, neither of them wanting to say anything that might delay Bell's explanation from getting underway. "When Simone and Missy were five years old, their dad Richard was a special operative with the department. He was a top CIA operative working undercover as a distributor for 'Boleros."

"Boleros, what's that?" Blake asked.

"Boleros are a South American organization dealing in the development of satellite technology."

Blake interrupted her, rubbing his chin quizzically as he asked, "South American based, but where does the backing originate?"

"Drug cartels we believe. Back in the late nineties we Dick Palmer right there, in the heart of Boleros."

Blake turned his eyes toward the man sitting opposite

him. "This Dick Palmer?" Blake said flicking a thumb in his direction.

"In person," the man replied.

"Things went badly, and Dick's cover was blown. We needed to get him out of there pronto. This kind of backfired. At the same time a dissident within the Boleros organization chose that very week to abscond with an assortment of discs containing their most valuable research from the past six months. Boleros had come up with a means to perfect tele-transportation with the use of satellite programming. It's a precursor to the Star Trek phenomena, the old 'beam me up, Scotty' travel trick. My discussions with Sam Ridkin – well. I'm aware of your travels with Chevalier."

"Okay," Blake said, now dropping the surprised act. "So now they can move something from one place to another by beaming up? Like the Eldridge, but got it right. I'm experienced with the technology; my time with Chevalier and Craven was an experience to say the least."

"Yep, now it's making some sense, the tourists, the Navy SEAL Reese Branson, Chevalier and Co, huh?"

"I've been briefed on that whole incident with Travis Craven," Bellinger said softly. "The same way Craven was able to transport through the wormholes, to jump from one location to another, so too can Boleros transport objects, but not just a Porsche or Limousine. These guys can teleport a nuclear weapon, gold bullion, a president. In fact, if they can see it, they can take it. They've evolved way beyond the pre set coordinates Craven was using; now they can virtually beam the object to any pre-set destination."

"Oh shit – sorry kiddo," Dal said smiling apologetically, momentarily forgetting that ten year old Simone was at the table, her nose in a comic book yet obviously not at all in tune with the conversation.

"Yeah if they want to get their hands on your Porsche Dal, you have it one second, then you blink and it's gone. Try explaining that one to your insurance broker." Bell smiled. The thought had really struck a nerve with Dal; his visualization skills clearly forced a squeamish expression on his face.

Dal thought for a minute, and then smiling said, "But if it's out of sight, say in a garage - they can't see it. In that case it's safe, right? Like, they can snap up the president when he's walkin' his dog on the White House lawn, but can't touch the man once he's back in the Oval Office, right?"

"You're getting warm Dal, the early system developed by Boleros operated exactly that way. But - and here's the cruncher guys - the latest technology actually only requires coordinates and mass. The weight of the object, to within ten percent accuracy we believe. Once this information is fed through, they can transport any object from any location to any destination without so much as ruffling the hair on little Barney's back."

"Oh shit," Blake said running his fingers through his hair again. "Okay then, so where's the connection between all that shit and our episode with Missy?"

"Let's not get ahead of ourselves. The bureau immediately pulled Richard –"

Dal being one to not pass up on a quick shot interrupted, "You pulled Dick? Ah, sorry kid, really sorry," he said nodding.

He turned to Blake and lowered his head, "Jeez, Drew, can't we have this discussion without the ankle biter sitting across from us? She's giving me the willies."

"As I was saying, we got Dick out of there and lost two agents in the operation. The Boleros organization sent their best bloodhounds after our boy. We were tipped off they were planning a hit during a day's fishing excursion on the lake. Unfortunately Simone was in the boat with her dad. Her sister Missy was out of town with her mother. We had the two Boleros guys under observation during the entire time they were staking out the lake area. The twist is this; one of the Boleros boys was on our payroll. As planed he disposed of his sidekick, we staged a boating accident, and there you have it. Objective accomplished. Our Boleros agent returned to his bosses, reporting a partially successful mission. That discs, of course, remained un recovered."

Blake interrupted. "Again my question . . . how does that tie in with the reason we're in New Orleans?"

"There's believed to be some advanced information on discs, if so these newer discs need to be found, period. The discs are said to contain information about an even more advanced diamond operation, a stage that's evolved beyond what Craven had. If he hadn't been terminated, this new stuff would probably be in his hands right now, we know one of the discs was deactivated in Paris. These discs probably contain the technology on the development of time travel and invisibility. It's no longer considered as science fiction. The disc that was eventually deactivated had found its way to Paris with the guy called Ramirez. Boleros sent one of their favorite contractors after Ramirez to recover the disc, he of course being Travis Craven. So things got messy when the American tourists who you met up with, got a hold of this one disc and had it deciphered through as far as a preset lock-down stage would allow. It seems each of the remaining discs is also programmed to lock-down if incorrectly viewed. The code must be entered correctly before being downloaded, otherwise – a white monitor."

"So how did Missy's mom end up in the morgue? Who played out that killing? We found a dead guy at the house, the one we ran the license checks on, was he from this, what is it again...?" Blake asked.

"Boleros. Once we realized the Paris disc was a lost cause, we placed an undercover agent at the Palmer house in New Orleans, figuring that sooner or later Boleros would be sniffing around to recover the remaining discs. The agent was close, real close . . . then turned up dead. You guys actually found the body and then proceeded to blow the whole cover wide open by doing a trace on his driver's licenses. He was our guy."

"Aw shit!" Dal cried in a frustrated groan. "What a snafu, what a fu . . ." he whined, rubbing his closed fists into his eye sockets, again sending an apologetic smile across the table to Simone.

All Blake could muster was a long exhale. Every drop of breath just wheezing out, he sounded like a balloon deflating. "Oh boy, the old assumption screw up," he said. "Assumption, the mother of all fuck-ups." He quickly shot his eyes toward the kid. "Ah jeez, sorry Simone."

Bellinger raised her voice an octave, possibly in an attempt to regain the podium and revert to a "G" rated conversation: "He operated as Reese Branson, a name you're both now familiar with, in fact one that the entire New Orleans traffic division is familiar with, thank you both very much. When you boys blow a cover, you really do it to the max."

This Bellinger chick is a cool operator, Blake thought. She knew exactly how to slowly feed out the story, painfully, in small doses, each fragmented segment sequentially leading to an even better follow up, smacking them each over the head with the license check fuck up. Blake sat wondering just when the whole story would reach a crescendo. He sat with both elbows propped on his knees, his fingers once again slowly running back through his hair, his head now hanging way down between his shoulders. "Bell, I'd love to say let's cut to the chase, but somehow I'd just hate to rush your delivery," he said with a half forced smile.

"We're nearly there Drew, patience please."

He looked at her with his head cocked to the side, wondering if this gal did everything as slow as this. Again the smile returned. It was his best Michael Madsen smile, but for a whole different reason.

Dick Palmer, shaking his head slowly from side to side, stood and looked about, "If you don't mind, I think I'll take Simone for a soda. Besides, you guys can clear the air a whole lot better without trying to censor the lingo for a ten-year-old."

"Good idea," Dal snapped, pointing in the direction of the nearest empty table.

"Subtle, Dal, real subtle," Blake said giving Simone a small departing wave.

When they were beyond earshot Blake turned to Bell, regaining his composure and some of his deflated self-confidence.

"Okay blue eyes, cut the shit and tell us why the fuck we weren't in the loop from the very start?"

The tough guy bravado noticeably set Bell back. She sat more upright - as though regrouping, cleared her throat, moved her head uncomfortably from side to side, and replaced the smile that had slipped away during Blake's uncensored outburst.

"We placed Branson in town as a fisherman. His assignment was to stay close to the Palmer house, keep an eye on Missy and her mom. We assured Dick Palmer we'd look out for his family 'til we got things on track some of our guys had hits on their homes; Palmer was concerned about his family."

They were interrupted by the public address system. "Bollinger, Beauregard and Oliver Bollinger, a call for Mr. Bollinger."

The desk call went over both of their heads. Dal looked around curiously, watching to see who moved toward the desk, to see what characters belonged to such extravagant names.

Bell said grinning, "Hmm . . . I believe that call is for you guys."

The two men stood as one, realizing their alias of Bollinger had slipped completely from their minds. As they stood Bellinger crossed her legs, very slowly. She had a way to manipulate a man's gaze; the two men predictably dropped their eyes to watch the legs crossing. She lowered her eyes slowly, as though inspecting the hemline on her now raised skirt. Then as if rehearsed, she raised her eyes, catching both Dal and Blake as they stared at her exposed thighs. She flicked a slight smile at Blake, and a similar smile at Dal. Each man fidgeted about, looking like school boys caught in the act.

"Beauregard Bollinger, you have a call at the desk."

The voice on the phone was gruff. Sam said, "So I suppose you guys are all over Bellinger. Just keep off and get the job done."

Blake's voice had a smile in it. "Hey Sam, thanks for the upgrade."

"Glad the room suits you."

"The room? I'm talking about the agent."

Dal leaned toward the phone and added, "Yeah boss, I'm thinkin' they're real. Spectacular too."

Ridkin was an old-school cop who'd worked his way up the ladder, starting off beating pavement in Jersey. He was well respected and it was common knowledge he never took a dime from anyone, albeit known he had had some pretty heavy cash thrown his way by one mob boss. The boss denied at the time that the money came from him, only to have it dumped in his cell the first day he landed in the federal pen. They all joked at how he panicked when twenty other cell mates caused a near riot, scrambling to lay claim to as many bills as they could get their hands on. What made it even more memorable was that Sam Ridkin had arranged a closed circuit camera to be positioned to record the whole incident, catching the boss screaming, "Get the fuck away, it's mine. It's all mine."

Sam could easily have kept that money. He didn't. The guys in the department respected him for that, many of them admitted that they would've stuffed it away. The whole half mill.

"Patrice is extra special Blake. Don't underestimate her professionalism. She topped her CIA class, so far ahead of the rest she made them look like rejects. I was kind of thinking she might be a bit too aggressive for you and Dal."

"You're kiddin' me, right?" Blake said grinning into the handset.

"What's he sayin'? What's goin' on?" Dal asked, straining to pick up on the conversation. Blake placed a hand lightly over the mouthpiece. "He says rumor has it you're a fag and to tell you to try to act macho around this Patrice Bellinger chick."

"Fuck you Blake, fuck you."

Blake laughed. Sam got a kick out of it at the other end. They got good kicks at Dal's expense, but they knew when to get down to the business at hand.

"Drew let me fill you in on some of the events leading up to the incident at the Palmer house. Firstly the father, Dick Palmer, worked for the CIA. He was planted undercover at the Boleros stronghold. His job was to get his hands on the information which, I believe Bell has explained to you by now - the tele-transportation r shit. Okay so far?"

"Yeah, yeah, yeah. Go on, we've been told most of that," Blake said impatiently.

"The stiff you found in the house was an operative named Fortessi. He carried a few covers, his most recent being Reese

Branson. Fortessi was one of the best undercover guys the agency had. It's a huge loss and the bureau is chafing at the bit to get their hands on the one who whacked him. His record was exemplary."

Blake blinked a few times, shaking his head as though not comprehending Sam's explanation. He thought about it as Sam spoke.

"So the fog murder victims were coincidental?" Blake asked.

"Yeah, when Savannah Palmer turned up dead we thought we'd leak it out to the press as being under investigation as another fog murder. We needed breathing space, time to get you guys into place, time to move Bellinger in there to help you guys get all your ducks in a row. It brought us that time, making Palmer another serial killing victim. You can see now why the local cops have been spoon-fed this whole thing. You know - on a need to know basis."

Blake said very slowly. "Yeah I'm with you Sam, keep going."

"After the attempt on Dick Palmer, we moved him and his daughter Simone to a safe house. We needed to stash them away safely until we were able to get our hands on the discs, the ones that –"

Blake interrupted impatiently…

"Yeah, yeah, Sam, come on, cut to the chase for Christ's sake."

"Okay so we put Fortessi in place as Reese Branson, he goes in as a fisherman, in a black boat. I'll explain the relevance of that later. Fortessi actually uses his warmth and charisma to become very close to the Palmers. We assume the mother was hit by someone from Boleros after the location of the discs, they could only assume that Dick's wife shared their location with her husband."

"That's a shit load of assuming Sam." Blake said. "And you know what Benny Hill said about assuming."

Sam didn't bother answering; he was well accustomed to the '*makes an ass out of you and me*' line.

Trying to keep up with the whole scope of the events left quite a few empty spaces, but Blake could feel some of them slowly filling, like a jig-saw puzzle nearing completion. He thought out aloud. "So the killer turns up at the lake house, takes out the mom, can't find Missy, and somehow knocks off Branson, uh, Fortessi a few days later right?"

There were a few seconds of silence. Blake waited.

"Sam, you there?"

"You got it Drew, sounds about right. But you might want to jot it down with a few circles and arrows so you don't lose track of the sequence of events. I have one more piece to add."

"Jot it down? Jesus Sam, It's a goddamn movie script. I think I'll do a manuscript and sell it to one of the fuckin' studios on the West Coast. We can have Jack Nicholson play Fortessi. Tell me though, where was Fortessi when Savannah Palmer was hit? If he was supposed to be planted to protect her, where did he screw up? It was days between her death and Fortessi's. Something's missing Sam, what am I missing here? Am I missing something, Sam? Hello - Sam?"

Blake listened for breathing; *surely he can't hold a breath this long.*

"You know what Drew? We've been asking ourselves that very same question. And that's right at the top of our list of questions we've yet to answer, where was Fortessi the night the killer hit Savannah Palmer? And even more importantly, who carried out the hit? We know it's supposedly been orchestrated by Boleros, or someone acting on behalf of Boleros. We believed we had all of their operatives covered. The powers that be over here are hinting this was done by a contractor, not by Boleros. If that's the case, we aren't as smart as we're paid to be. The contractor we suspect is an old associate of yours, any clue where I'm going with this Drew?"

"Sam I'll call you at ten sharp tomorrow. It's been a hell of a day, my brain is scrambled, and I need time to sort things out. Guess I'll get a whiteboard and draw a few circles and arrows, that kind of shit, you know the stuff."

"Now there's an idea. I would never have thought of that,

but there's no need to call me, I'm already booked on the first flight tomorrow, so I'll see you at the Hotel first thing. Best I give you the last bit of your puzzle face to face. Want to see your reaction first hand."

"I can hardly wait. Catch you early domani, ciao."

Dal and Blake said their goodnights to Patrice Bellinger, Dick and Simone Palmer. As they walked off, Blake turned and gestured to Palmer.

"Ah say Dick, one question. When will you be getting back together with Missy?"

He gazed at Blake, his mouth open, but no sound coming from it. Bellinger interjected on his behalf. *What a surprise,* Blake thought. *Taking the reins again. How predictable of her.*

"We haven't quite got our ducks in a row on that one Drew. I'll cover that with you tomorrow. But for now, Missy believes she's an orphan, and the bureau believes this is the most acceptable scenario all around, while things are, hmm - let's say, as they are."

"Are as they are?" Blake quipped. Then raising his voice to anger level, Blake snapped. "As they goddamn are! And how the hell are they Patrice?" This was the first time Blake had called her by her first name and it felt good, as though they knew each other better, as though they could share the intricacies of the case a little more than they had to this point. As though now, at last, he was no longer below her. He could set her back well, just a nudge at least.

"I'll bring you up to date on the bureau's rationale in the morning."

"Darn right you will," Blake snapped with an air of authority, at the same time turning to Dal who, scratching the top of his head, resembled Stan Laurel.

Blake looked at him, smiled and said, "Let's go Ollie."

CHAPTER 60

THE NEXT MORNING BEGAN earlier than it should have. The room phone buzzed impatiently and Blake played possum, leaving Dal to pick up the call.

"Hello? . . . Yeah . . . Yeah. . . . Yeah. . . . Aha. . . . Aha. . . . Aha, right. . . . Right, sure. . . . Okay, we'll be there."

Blake rolled over to face Dal, "That's your intelligent start to the day, huh bozo?"

"It's the boss. He's here. He's been on the phone with our lady Patrice. She's gonna open up the rest of the doors; *put us in the loop* was actually the way Sam put it."

"Thank you God," Blake groaned. He propped himself on one elbow, and grimaced as he caught the rear end of Dal disappearing into the bathroom.

"What else did Sam say?" Blake asked.

Dal called from the shower, raising his voice above the noise of the water. "He says either he or Bellinger will call us before nine to set up breakfast and a briefin'."

Blake rolled onto his back, felt for the remote and flicked through the channels. "Hey Ollie, don't use all of the hot water okay?"

"Fuck you, and I ain't too comfortable with that chick, don't like her one bit."

Following breakfast, the three agents quietly sat over coffee, conversation was at a minimum. Sam joined the table at twenty minutes after ten. He placed a large green folder on the white tablecloth beside him. He cleared his throat and nodded in turn to Blake, Dal, and Bellinger. "Good morning, trust you all slept well. Yes I had a pleasant flight thank you very much. Today is going to go down in your memory as one of disbelief. But doubt me not, what you're about to hear is true, and it's happening as we speak. Save all questions until I'm through. I don't want to lose my train of thought or the sequence of events."

Blake coughed and in a deprecating grunt said, "Good

morning to you too."

"Make those the last few words you say Drew until I'm done," Sam grumbled.

Dal, not so much as raising his eyes, nudged Blake under the table. Patrice Bellinger sat like a storefront mannequin, not moving, but looking intimidated.

"You have a basic knowledge of what's been happening here in New Orleans. But that's the extent of your knowledge, very basic. The reason you guys have been assigned this case is simple. The guys up top were hoping they'd penetrate the problem area and that would be the end of it. But, as they say, shit happens. If things had gone well, you and Dal would have returned home after a routine crime investigation, one which no longer required our intervention. And make no mistake; we had several believable reasons which initially justified your both being assigned to the case, serial killings not being amongst them."

Blake exhaled. Sam paused and gave him the eye, the *don't even think about it star*e. Blake raised both palms, face up, and shrugged his shoulders.

"This case involves far more than satellite research. It's a direct attack on the United States, an offensive that Washington is aware of. But they seem to lack cohesion, to be unable to muster a defensive force to squash the movement. Make no mistake, the DEA is working with a number of other federal law enforcement entities – the FBI, the U.S. Attorneys' offices, the Criminal Division at the Department of Justice, the U.S. Customs Service, the Border Patrol – as well as several state and local law enforcement organizations, to respond to the serious problems caused by organized crime groups from South America and Mexico. In order to effectively face the significant challenges that arise from sophisticated drug trafficking organizations . . . and make no mistake Drew, don't underestimate the Mexicans; they don't all come to the States to cut grass, blow leaves and wash cars – it's necessary for us to attack the command mechanisms of the organizations. As communications technology changes, we need to maintain the highest level of defense . . . a cohesive attack.

"If you're familiar with Operation Reciprocity and Operation Limelight, these two operations clearly demonstrated the importance of the DEA's ability to successfully target the leadership of international criminal organizations. In both of these operations the DEA, with the cooperation of other federal and state law enforcement agencies, targeted cocaine distribution cells commanded by the Boleros organization. The investigation resulted in the arrest of one hundred and twenty individuals in thirteen U.S. cities. Those Boleros cells subsequently demolished in these two operations show that the traffickers from Puerto Rico and Mexico are expanding their reach across the United States, and as far as the Canadian border.

"These Boleros syndicates whose leadership is primarily situated in Puerto Rico have dumped tons of cocaine on New York City, and they are moving closer to eclipsing the Colombians and controlling the U.S. drug market.

"The DEA started Operation Reciprocity a few years ago by identifying the command elements of the Boleros organization dealing drugs in New York and Los Angeles. Working through a multi-agency investigative approach, the DEA identified how the traffickers transported cocaine across the country in tractor trailer loads and returned the illicit profits in the form of bulk cash, using drivers hired largely from the Grand Rapids, Michigan area."

Sam paused and poured a glass of water from a pitcher on the table. He took a short drink and continued on. "Operation Limelight began in '96 in Imperial County, California, focused on the transportation and distribution cell of the Boleros organization. By targeting the command and control communications systems of this group, the DEA identified how they smuggled drugs across the country by tractor trailer truck through California, Texas, Pennsylvania, Illinois, and New York.

"These traffickers are able to pass orders on movements, places, and times of delivery and mode of transportation of thousands of tons of cocaine and methamphetamine with a more than reasonable certainty that U.S. law enforcement will not be able to intercept their communications. The DEA faces a number of difficulties, which may threaten our ability to combat these organizations and undermine the ability of all law enforcement agencies to deal effectively with the problem. These problems are tactical, strategic, and interagency."

Sam gulped down the remainder of the water and topped up. "The first problem is tactical, and potentially threatens the lives of every U.S. citizen. These international criminals have shown they are extremely violent and willing to use violence when and where it suits them to carry out their lethal trade. Violence along the southwest border has escalated. The media tends to play it up as illegal immigration, tunnels going under the fence, Mexicans being rounded up by border patrol vehicles. Unfortunately, the violence that is attendant to the drug trade in Mexico is spilling over the border into U.S. towns like San Diego and Eagle Pass. The recent armed civilian border reinforcement group is a direct undercover movement to send a message to the drug cartel, although the media has played it up as an illegal immigrant deterrent."

Blake said, "So how'd this effect Dick Palmer?"

"If these criminal drug gangs have unfettered access to our cities, then they'll be able to do more than issue orders for transporting drugs. They'll be able to issue with impunity 'death warrants' for U.S. law enforcement officers, for witnesses, or for innocent civilians. This is exactly the case with Dick Palmer. They'll be able to continue their reign of drug terror in the United States, a very immediate bloody threat to the national security, in addition to the threat from the drugs they sell."

"So where's their main entry point?" Dal asked.

"Recently large shipments have been traced to New Orleans entry points, the chosen means of transport being black boats. It seems their stealth design helps them slip under radar more easily. It's utilizing stealth technology. They also strictly use cell phone communication which also eludes our radar. Are you getting the connection yet? Don't answer, it's rhetorical."

Sam paused, took a long gulp of water, sighed heavily, and opened the green folder.

"The funds from the drug trade are funding an even bigger

threat, global dominance, the satellite program. Our sources are following a strong source who has uncovered a multi national conspiracy with a single philosophy, world dominance through the moral destruction of the United States. The initial attack comes in the form of a free flow supply of drugs into the States. And to further exacerbate the problem, there is also a free flowing market of counterfeit prescription drugs believed to initially be originating from China and India; these are also endangering the American public. We've got tens of thousands if not millions of people who believe they are taking medically prescribed drugs to cure cancer, cholesterol, blood pressure as well as every other ailment you can name, when in fact they're taking capsules and pills consisting of plaster dust and coloring, much of which is toxic in itself. The Chinese are thumbing their noses at the world.

"But let me tell you guys, one word: decoy. The whole drug rousts certainly nets big bucks for the South American cartels as well as the Chinese, and they love it. But they're the footmen, the advance legions. Mark my words, once this country's groveling about like mindless idiots, the resistance level will be so low that Tasmania will be able to march into the Pentagon and plant its flag and not lose a single man. Final blow, satellite tele transportation of any item up for grabs, the booty being fairly distributed between those nations putting up the largest initial investment, devoting the most sweat equity into the campaign.

"There you have it, the rise and fall of the United States Empire. Sound familiar? So Dal, can you see your Porsche sitting in a garage in Colombia next week? Sounds nuts, I know, but it's getting close to reality, except for one thing, and that's where we come in. They need the discs to complete the encryption. Without them the satellite program has ground to a standstill. The most they can do without the additional discs is the fixed co ordinate transportation, which is the episode you experienced in France with Craven, not total tele transportation of chosen objects and people."

"Oh good," Dal snapped in, smiling. "Guess I'll enjoy my Porsche a little longer."

"Can I speak, Sam?" Blake said raising his hand school boy style.

"Sure Drew, go ahead."

"As I see it, we were sent here under the pretense of a murder investigation, which actually turns out to be an international drug cartel, but in reality is an effort to attack the United States with satellite warfare. Is that just a bit close to what you've been saying Sam?"

Dal sat staring at Blake with a bewildered expression, and then, as if the light had been switched on, began nodding his head and grinning. "I get it," he said. "I get the whole ploy . . . I think."

"So why can't the CIA handle this shit on their own?" Blake asked.

Sam rubbed his chin, replying, "The FBI has been haunted by a very real problem due to the discovery that veteran agent Robert Hanssen had been a Russian spy for over twenty years. The FBI was scrutinized because they didn't possess a serious attitude regarding internal security issues. The lack of a cohesive management structure indicated respective FBI departments weren't aware of each other's activities. In response to the Hanssen scandal, Congress approved the creation of a new position within the Justice Department to oversee the activities of the FBI. Some believed this action assisted in the spawning of our Department....the AID. This enabled the bureau to move more unilaterally without 'Big Brother's' perusal. The AID was unofficially called in to slip under their radar, so to speak. We have access to all bureau files, without the Justice Department and Congress interfering or, more politically correct, overseeing. So we do have an almost open slather, the CIA however has more carte blanche, more leverage."

Blake followed Sam's delivery, but he still felt wanting on the situation, on where they were heading at their end. He needed time to digest, to draw out a plan – a plan with plenty of circles and arrows. Dal looked at Blake. Sam was once again sipping his now cold coffee. Bellinger raised a hand and a young man in a Hyatt uniform quickly appeared, refilled the water pitcher and refreshed the four coffee cups.

"Ah cream here buddy, I'm all out," Dal said to the neatly uniformed young man.

"Certainly sir, I'll be right back."

He shuffled off without a care in the world. A senior employee stopped his passage, pointing to the young man's shoes. The young man appeared to apologize. *Not shiny enough*, Blake thought. He watched as the young man moved toward the service area. Now clearly concerned with the apprehension, he reached below the counter and removed a polish cloth. He then buffed the toe cap on one shoe, inspected it, and smiled to himself.

Blake thought, *If only you knew what devious plans are going down in the outside world. How insignificant your fuckin' shoe is. How meaningless you are in the scheme of things. Like an ant, amounting to nothing – you step on it and move on; you're worth exactly that, nothing.*

"We have two objectives," Sam said quietly.

"One, we need to infiltrate this Boleros organization. And two, if we can we need to secure the discs and bring that information home."

"Okay, so all it amounts to is that we need to find the discs?" Blake said.

"It goes deeper than that," Sam answered. "We've been told the person responsible for the development of the transportation program is dissatisfied with the regime. He's a possible candidate for defection. His name is Galatea. We need to assess the situation. If Galatea's conducive, and we don't know if he will be, we bring him out alive. If not – we eliminate him and destroy the facility. We're also expected to retrieve appropriate files on their personnel, these files reveal the names and locations of Boleros operatives who, the Bureau suspects, are double agents and have access to our facilities.

"Gardner Hunter is a bureau plant who's been working for Boleros for the past six months. A very scary assignment, there have been two previous agents uncovered in South America; their bodies are still hanging from a tree for the crows to snack on. Hunter will be a major plus in helping you toward a successful mission. He'll be your main contact in Colombia. Don't underestimate his demeanor. He's quite the 007 prototype, lethal and stealthy. Interesting character I hear. Actually saved the Boleros chief from an assassination hit. That's how he won favor with the organization. Sad thing is, the bureau set up the hit, one of their more disposable agents. Hunter had been tipped off by the bureau as to the attempt and given instruction to eliminate the intending assassin. He staged it to perfection, jumping the killer from behind and struggling with him just long enough for the Boleros security to arrive in the scene and watch as Hunter sliced the man's throat. Very convincing, especially when you consider that the man he just killed was one of his fellow associates, a golfing buddy from Connecticut. Hunter's a scratch golfer, maybe a bad loser too."

Dal appreciated the golf comment.

"Remind me not to play with this dude anytime soon. I hate poor losers," he said, tongue in cheek.

Sam reflected for a moment. "Well gentlemen – and young lady, that's the gist of it, almost in a nutshell. We have to cut off or infiltrate the black stealth boats from bringing the stuff into New Orleans, and we need to stifle the Boleros organization. But primarily we don't want to fall into the trap of focusing on just those two, because people," he paused for a breath, "listen when I say, they are *decoys*. In the course of events, if we can bring Andreas Galatea back to the States, that will be a huge bonus. Once we have him, we have, in effect, stifled the entire cartel operation. He has names, formulas, missions. The man is a walking computer. He is the sum of all the discs, all the manuals. The man has a photographic memory unparalleled. We must get him out of South America, and we can't do it under any departmental bullshit. You will be there strictly as mercenaries. No knowledge of your operation will be on record or ever acknowledged. With that said I'll add this, I'll do my best to muster mercenary back up, but we can't count on it….I'll be trying my best."

He slowly gazed at each person in the room, made noticeable eye contact with each. "But, make no mistake," Sam added with a serious tilt on his head, nodding as he spoke. "If we can't get this Andreas character out of South America alive, we leave him there, very, very fuckin' dead. Comprende?"

"Ah Christ, the old Mission Impossible shit. Don't ya just love it?" Dal quipped.

They looked at each other. Bellinger sat filing her nails. *So cool* Blake thought. *Would be different if she was going.*

Sam leaned across the table and forced a smile. "Bellinger will head up the mission. Her Columbian dialect is impeccable. She speaks it like a native, because . . . well she is, I guess, right Patrice?"

Blake's jaw dropped. Dal sunk into his leather chair. The two men again looked at each other, replying in unison . . . "Ah, shit!"

CHAPTER 61

T HE NEXT TIME THE group met, it was for a recon briefing. Sam and Bellinger sat across from Blake and Dal at a conference table in a Hyatt business suite.

"In front of each of you is a file. Open them now and we'll go through this together," Sam said in his most solemn tone.

Blake opened the green file and was greeted by a photograph of a handsome, fair-haired man dressed in a Hawaiian shirt, beads, and a large diamond ear ring. His smile was broad, showing two rows of perfectly crowned teeth.

"The first photo is of Gardner Hunter. He's to be respected in a militaristic sense, trusted in a cautionary sense, and observed at all times in a self-survival sense. Don't, under any circumstances, dismiss this guy lightly. He can go from mellow to ballistic in three seconds flat. That's why he's where he is, and remember this . . . he slit the throat of a friend just to convince Boleros he was on their team. Hunter has no qualms about killing. He kills first, and he's a CIA man second. He does his job. Trouble is I believe he enjoys it."

They each moved the photo to one side, looking at the next, a picture of a Latin guy, in his late thirties, holding a large fish between his outstretched arms.

"This guy looks like a sporty type, good catch too," Dal said.

Sam picked up his copy and smiled. "He's okay. This is your target. This is Andreas Galatea, the brains behind Boleros. He answers only to the Consort. We believe Galatea has traveled to the Consort's world, with your old adversary Travis Craven."

There was silence as all three studied the man, his eyes, his smile, and his appearance which projected him as a fun person. Bellinger grinned and said, "He seems to be a normal enough guy, loves his work. He owns Boleros, it's his baby. I've spent many fun hours deep sea fishing with Andreas. In fact it was I who took this snap of his catch about four months back. Hunter was standing alongside me when the shot was taken He's quite the hunter too. I watched him dive into a swamp and ride the back of an alligator just to win a ten dollar bet. When he walked out of that swamp he took the ten dollars and gave it to some kids who had been cheering him on. That's the way the guy is. You love to hate him, but God help you if you make the mistake of loving him."

Blake looked at Sam, who was anticipating a reaction from either Dal or from Blake. He received none. Blake said, "So if we have trouble with this Hunter character, the odds are in his favor, right Sam?"

"He's your backup for Christ's sake, Drew, not your adversary." Sam didn't appreciate the inference. "Trouble? Why would you even feel that way? Do you suspect a potential testosterone clash? I'm kind of hoping I can one day sway him from the CIA to join the AID. Tell me there won't be any macho bullshit going on. Perhaps Patrice can keep you tethered sufficiently enough that you can all get on with the task at hand."

Bellinger grinned, saying, "You'll all do just fine. Let me do the talking, Hunter do the slaying, and you and Dal can tidy up the mess and escort Andreas home to mama."

Dal stood up, more than pissed off at her remark.

"Steady boy." Sam snapped.

"It's okay, it's okay," Dal said calmly. "I'm just needin' to relieve myself, ya see, I'm really pissed." Dal stormed off in the direction of the rest room.

"Sam," Blake said. "Why do I get the feeling this operation won't be any cake walk?"

Sam placed his folder on the table, slowly raising his eyes to meet Blake's. Blake once again ran his fingers slowly and deeply through his hair, a dead give away that stress was setting in. He felt the hair was decidedly thinner than it was yesterday.

"Oh, and before we wrap things up," Sam said. "I thought I'd save the one-two punch 'til last. Take a look at the final photo in the stack; it's one you'll recognize. In fact, he may very well be your boy. I suspect he's the contract hit man."

Blake flipped through the many Latino faces. He stopped at the bottom picture. "No fuckin' way. He's dead. . . . I saw the fire."

CHAPTER 62

THE FLIGHT TO SOUTH America started off routinely. The plane was an old Douglas DC something or other, no jets, two props. *Strange*, Blake thought, *but there must be a reason.*

There were two characters on the flight deck. Neither man appeared to have shaven for days, and neither wore a uniform. Body odor was the cologne of the day. The more senior of the two appeared to be the pilot. He wore a holstered revolver. The other man puffed furiously on a large cigar, holding it firmly between his tobacco-stained teeth.

Patrice Bellinger wore army fatigues, and both Dal and Blake had been issued with similar garb, the style you associate with guerilla jungle warfare.

Blake struck up a conversation with Bellinger, who hadn't said so much as a word since they had left the ground.

"Seemed to me we had a pretty clean exit. No customs, no security checks, no body scans,: Blake said. "What's the deal, Bell?"

She stretched out, her knees cracking as she pushed them as far from her hips as possible . . . and that was quite a stretch. "Oh boy, oh boy, oh boy. For two supposedly slick agents, you boys have been slow on the uptake. You guys trained in Minneapolis, right? Hmm, I guess that qualifies you as city cops?"

This aggravated Blake, and Dal was quick to jump in, leaving little time to simmer. "Who the fuck do you think you are, for Christ's sake? You've been stickin' it to us from the offset. And missy, don't misinterpret any hesitation on our part as inadequacy. We're too fuckin' polite, or have been, to this point, and you know what? I'm done with it! So fuck you, and fuck your attitude, and you can shove your batterin' blue eyes . . ."

Before Dal could bury himself deeper, Blake jumped right in. "Bell, come on missy, give us a break here. We've been treated like understudies from day one on this. I still haven't quite figured out the shit with the kid, Missy. That was some pretty weird stuff. Then you bring in her twin, Simone, and her supposedly dead father . . . Jesus Christ, what a spin this is. What's your take on all that shit that went down at her place on the lake?"

Blake really didn't expect an answer and was set back when Bellinger replied, "Listen Drew, we could go back three years and still not have you understanding the depth of this case. And as far as your insecure sidekick here, if he ever . . . " she stressed the r's in *ever*, "if he everrrr again launches a verbal attack on me like that, I'll take great pleasure in personally repositioning his balls somewhere between his tonsils and heaven."

She sat staring directly at Dal, holding her breath. Dal returned her stare, and that, barring the breath holding, was how things stayed for quite some time.

Oh boy, Blake thought, *flying the fuckin' friendly skies*. Blake was a chopper pilot and possessed a strong desire to avoid planes. Somehow choppers never worried him, but planes . . . well, when it came to planes he'd rather walk.

The sun was getting low on the horizon and they could see tree tops below. "Where are we landing?" Blake asked. He didn't direct the question to anyone, just kind of threw it out there.

"We're not," Bellinger answered.

"Not?" Dal said with a questioning overtone, his head cocked to one side. "What the fuck does that mean, 'not'?"

"My boy," she said, twisting the knife a little more into Dal's ribs. "My boy, we're jumping. Do you think we're dressed like this to impress the locals? We flew out incognito. We never left the States, and we'll never land either. No welcome committee, no existence."

The two men stared at her. Neither of them had reason to comment. Neither of them had saliva enough to produce a response.

"I assume you boys have made a few jumps?"

The silence lasted a few seconds, while they each pondered which of them would deliver the most convincing lie.

"Sure we have!" Blake quickly proclaimed, nudging Dal

with his foot as he spoke.

"But we're probably a little rusty. You know, some chutes are different from others. Beside, we don't know who folded ours. Where do we land? How high will we be for the jump?"

Bell grinned, looking through Blake. She raised her hand, gave him a thumbs up. In unison, Dal and Blake returned the gesture. And there they sat, all three with thumbs in the air.

Blake thought about the stupidity of his comment, and pressed his lips tightly together, realizing he had screwed his face into the stress position. Dal sat slumped forward, his face now buried deep into his hands, and whimpered. "Toto old son, you're not in Kansas any more. Ah shit, another fine mess Drew. Another fine fuckin' mess."

CHAPTER 63

TRAVIS CRAVEN HAD LIVED a secluded existence since his encounter with Blake and Dal in France. His bank account was tucked away, also secluded, in a far-off Swiss bank. His nationality was generic, one month American, another British. A chameleon, Craven had long since learned the survival art of "blending." His only extravagance was his 911 Porsche, gleaming red, fitted with jet black glass and all wrapped up inside a factory wide body, considered by connoisseurs to be the ultimate Porsche. For the rare occasion when Travis felt safe enough, it sported a removable Targa top, which would let the sunshine in but restrict the constant gaze of admirers.

"Jesus Christ, what the fuck have you done to this motor? It strains at a hundred and fifty."

The mechanic grinned at Craven.

"Did you see the switch below the fuel knob?"

Craven leaned toward the left side of the small, tight steering wheel and touched the small, hidden black switch.

"It's nitrous. You flick that switch and it's 'see ya!' You become a blur! Nothing, and I mean fuckin' nothin', will catch you. It'll top out at two twenty, and that's in fourth, you still got fifth. Man, I mean you still got fifth. Unless he's been to see me, of course, then he ain't gonna catch ya." The mechanic laughed a satisfying chuckle. He knew his product well.

"So, who else out there do I need to worry about?"

The mechanic scratched at his three-day beard growth with the tips of his grease filled nails.

"Not many, there's this rich fuck, who brought me a 'vette. It's fast, but no way it's this fast. Man you better be ready for fuckin' whiplash."

Travis Craven was a killer, the very best kind. He was a five-star assassin. His price per hit was the highest. Those who needed to contract him were aware of his six-figure fee. He had a perfect hit record. He had a very private cell phone and a very elite list of clients. He had a clear escape record, but Craven had come close to failing just one time.

His encounter with Claude Chevalier, had caught Craven off guard, and it had cost him dearly. His lifestyle had changed because of Chevalier. He had vowed to settle the score. Inspector Chevalier was blessed, some might say lucky. When Craven had the opportunity to dispose of him back in the old barn, his clip was empty.

Craven spent hours reliving his close encounters with Chevalier as well as his near brushes with Blake. He still had recurring nightmares of Chevalier, Blake, and Dallas, the three who almost had him, the three who had almost ended the infamous Travis Craven's run.

"Fuck 'em, fuck 'em!" Craven shouted as he relived the encounters.

He dropped the Porsche into fourth and pulled alongside an ominous looking Corvette. He lowered his window, smiled at the attitude sitting behind the 'vette's wheel, and then Craven flicked the switch!

"Jesus Christ!" he shouted, as the Porsche swung its tail around the lane. Fighting to regain control, Craven burst into uncontrollable laughter.

"I love it!" he shouted.

"I fuckin' love it!"

He glanced into the rear view mirror and found the Corvette, laboring some three hundred yards back, with what seemed like a hundred yards per second separating the two cars. Craven could feel his head pushing into the restraint and his cheeks stretching back as the car entered warp speed. He passed the Modesto sign at a speed which made the name appear no more than a blur.

Sacramento was a quiet city compared to most. Travis Craven was able to maintain a secluded lifestyle, yet still have reasonable access to the snowfields of Tahoe, the golfing of the Bay area, and Seventeen Mile Drive encompassing his favorite domain of Pebble Beach. And with his connections, he could even manage an occasional tee time at Cypress Point, an envious treat Dan Quail himself was unable to achieve as Vice President. It was Cypress Point where Craven was headed now.

Craven had fond memories of his youth; days spent playing the courses around the Monterey-Karen area. His first kill occurred after a confrontation with a member at Cypress Point. It was a foggy morning. Travis had just celebrated his sixteenth birthday and had a brand spanking new set of clubs. This particular morning, he decided to sneak onto the fifteenth hole at Cypress, a secluded par three with easy access from the road. Neglecting the "Private Property" signs as he always had in the past, young Travis hit a few balls across the small water inlet, over the heads of the barking seals.

On the final ball, a perfectly struck eight iron, Travis Craven posed in a perfect finish and watched as the ball found the bottom of the cup. He looked around, wanting someone to have seen it, anyone. *Please, God*, he thought. Then a voice called from behind. "Hey kid!"

Travis turned and smiled. "Did you see that?" he shouted in absolute joy.

The stranger quickly pounced on the boy and began dragging him toward the boundary fence.

"Seen you here before, you smart young fuck. Get the hell off the course! This is a private club! Now get off and stay off!"

In the excitement, Travis had left his bag on the ground where he had teed the shot.

"Hey mister, my clubs! Can I get my clubs?"

The member walked to the bag, picked it up, and in one fast motion flung the new set of clubs into the Pacific. Three weeks later the man was found floating in the same inlet. Word on the street was that he'd slipped in while trying to retrieve a ball, and that was how it stayed. The bruise on his head no doubt caused by his landing on the rocks below. Only the seals would know the truth. The seals and young Travis Craven, who always did swing a good club.

Playing at Cypress Point years later bore great irony. Craven wasn't sure if his favor was on account of his somewhat fearful reputation or his outstanding playing ability. On the one hand, who would dare tell Travis Craven he couldn't have a tee time? But then, on the other hand, maybe they enjoyed playing with a scratch golfer.

Craven sat pondering the sunset and listening as the piper played Amazing Grace, a tradition at the course this time of day. As the final notes dwindled from the bagpipes, the cell phone came to life.

"Ah shit, spoiled a perfect moment," he mumbled softly.

"Craven," he answered quietly.

"This is Andreas Galatea. We're anxiously awaiting your arrival. When can you join us?"

"Give me forty-eight hours, will that work?"

"Yes, don't delay. You know where to find me, okay?" Galatea asked rhetorically.

"Sure. You know my fee, agree?"

"Si, si. I'll transfer the usual amount to your account immediately. Just get here."

That was the conversation, a typical contractual call. Succinct, to the point, a done deal. Someone, somewhere, was in deep, deep trouble. Someone, some poor bastard . . . was about to leave the building.

CHAPTER 64

BELLINGER CHATTED QUIETLY WITH the
co pilot. Blake sat opposite Dal, each of them with
that pre-root-canal look, the *nothing's going to get better today*
expression hanging on them like a soggy Halloween mask at the
end of a long wet night of trick-or-treating.

"Jesus Drew I've never jumped. What if we get hung up
in tree tops? I've seen that in movies, you know. The guy crashes
through the tree top, cracks a few ribs, snaps his leg . . . then just
fuckin' hangs there 'til someone discovers his skeleton danglin'
from the tree a few years later."

Blake slowly raised his face from his hands, his fingers
pulling his cheeks down as his hands slid down toward his
neck. "Well shit. Happy fuckin' trails to you too fella."

"Aw come on. This is a nasty situation."

"Nah could be worse. The plane could be going down."

Bellinger turned away from the co-pilot and moved the
few yards to join them.

"Slight change of plans." Bell raised her arm and quickly
extended . . . a nine-millimeter pointed directly at Dal.

'"This boys, is where we part company, and I don't mean
with chutes attached."

"What the fuck? What's this all about Bell?" Blake
asked.

"Well Drew, let's just say Uncle Sam's old pension fund
isn't quite what I need to keep me living in the style to which I've
grown accustomed."

"Fuckin' CIA. It's in your blood. You've been bought,
right?" Dal asked unintelligently.

"Oh, ya think, huh blondie?" she said sarcastically,
wobbling her head from side to side. "No Dal, I'd rather think of
it as being rewarded. Rewarded for years of service, for risking
everything for Uncle fuckin' Sam."

Blake saw his life flashing before his eyes, the sound of

the plane, its propellers vibrating through the cabin, Dal sitting white faced opposite him. He drifted back to a safer time, a more secure time, a country bar in St. Paul. The singer telling about the loss of another love, tornado took the house, dog got scabies, the daughter's pregnant. *Yeah*, Blake thought, *just another typical country pick-me-up.* Then he got to thinking, *is there a single happy, upbeat country fan? Not on this fuckin' planet! Morbid, morose bunch of losers.*

The plane jerked violently, shaking him back to reality. The sudden drop in elevation threw Bellinger off balance and in that split second the nine millimeter discharged, the bullet passing into the cabin. Dal pounced, forcing Bellinger to the floor.

"GRAB THE GUN, GRAB THE FUCKIN' GUN!" Blake shouted.

Bellinger's head connected with the edge of the seat as she went down, the co pilot rushing by her as he scrambled from the cockpit.

"You've shot the pilot," he shouted as he ran from the cabin brandishing a small side arm.

As he passed Dal, he raised the weapon, waving it menacingly toward Dal. Dal reeled about with Bellinger's nine millimeter and fired off one quick round. The shot passed through the rushing man's throat, shattering the front glass. Blake swallowed hard as the drop in cabin pressure caused papers and debris to swirl furiously about the plane.

Bellinger slowly raised herself onto one knee, one hand resting on the copilot who lay eyes open looking for God . . . but God was not on this flight.

"DREW, IT'S GOIN' DOWN!" Dal shouted over the roar of the wind and engine noise.

"Get the chutes on. I'll get one onto Bellinger."

Blake pulled Bellinger to her feet and strapped the chute under her bust, pulled the straps, and fastened his own, as Dal followed suit.

The pilot struggled frantically with the stick, an obvious losing situation.

The trees seemed to be getting closer, much too close to make a jump.

"THROW BELLINGER OUT!" Dal shouted.

"ARE YOU SERIOUS, I CAN SEE THE GROUND? WE'RE TOO LOW, I MEAN - I CAN REALLY SEE THE GROUND!"

He shouted into the pilot's ear, "JESUS CHRIST, CAN YOU LAND THIS THING?"

But the pilot said nothing. Blood trickled down his temple; his eye's glazed, staring into the tree-lined horizon. The pilot now had his very own wings.

"HEY, HEY YOU!" Dal shouted louder, grabbing the pilot's shoulder. The man slumped to one side, leaning on the stick as his chest pushed forward.

The sudden dive threw Dal against the controls.

Tree tops self-destructed about the plane's interior, its tail pulling away. Blake watched as it disappeared into the smoky haze bellowing in its wake. Bellinger slid uncontrollably toward the rear opening where the tail end was once attached, her chute snagging against the bracket of a dislodged seat. She began flapping about, like a rag doll in the wind, her head bleeding profusely from a gash to the forehead. Blake could see Dal, now stripped to the waist as the force of the wind shredded his shirt, leaving him bleeding from cuts to the upper body.

Impact was sudden, like anesthetic. Wham! . . . Nothing but blackness.

CHAPTER 65

RAINDROPS TAPPED ON BLAKE'S forehead, small fingers beckoning him to wake.

A soft painful whisper said "Drew . . . Drew . . . Drew."

It was his eighth birthday. He sat by his father, lines dangling in the creek below the jetty. He always believed there were fish to be caught, but his father would reiterate to him that the pleasure was the anticipation of the catch. They never did pull any fish from that creek, but the memory of the hours spent in anticipation of the catch far outweighed the disappointment. These were priceless memories, and as he lay on the damp ground, those times flashed through Blake's mind.

The anticipation of the catch, words he used many times later in life . . . "the catch." Would he ever play the game again? Or had fate finally delivered Drew Blake's death knell, in this damp, green hell?

The odor of fuel permeated about him, blending distastefully with the smell of burning rubber. Blake's body began to move, dragging across the thick, damp ground cover.

Opening one eye, he could make out a silhouette, but one which was indistinguishable, just a shape.

His effort to speak was stifled, his mouth moving, but no sound came out.

"Hey man, this one's still kickin'. . . . No wallet, nothin'."

"Cut his fuckin' throat and get it over with. Not worth wastin' a slug on him."

"Fuck no; the critters gotta have fun . . . let 'em do the job. Come on vamoose."

But the hands dug deeper. Blake could feel the hands rummaging through what remained of his jacket, then the hands rolled him over and began digging into his rear pockets.

"Nah nothin'. Throw me your blade."

His head was wrenched backward as the cold steel touched a few inches below his chin.

"I said leave him be, better he's found without your added touch. Don't want that fuckin' signature; they'll tie it all together."

The deafening sound that followed splattered blood across Blake's face. Contorting it sideways, the hand released its grip on his hair. His body jerked as his assailant became airborne, landing some yards away.

A barrage of shots continued for several agonizing minutes, the deafening scream of bullets insatiably searching for targets as though on some insane guidance system. Blake's mind was zooming back into another universe, swirling around and around as though on the end of a long rope, spinning, spinning. Blackness encompassing him, he retreated at a million miles per second, retracting from the insanity around him. His mind seemed to pause for an instant, hovering like an observer above the melee, an observer safely suspended in another world, a safer Drew Blake, immune to the dangers below.

Was this death? The thought swirled, sharing itself with a million similar screaming thoughts, each consuming a nanosecond of his brain time. Seconds, or maybe minutes, passed. Silence . . . or was it death?

Blake raised himself, propping up on one elbow, trying to focus, his head throbbing, pain so intense he wished for sleep, or whatever . . . but not conscious agony.

As he squinted, movement from nearby bushes created the only sound.

"I'd kill for a fuckin' Starbuck's. You okay Drew?"

"Dal? Jesus . . . is that you?"

Dal waved the bush aside, an M16 still smoking in his right hand.

The answer came as a long protracted groan.

"My fuckin' head, man. Don't move. I'll get over there, just a slight problem." Dal began his slow crawl, a piece of fuselage protruding from his thigh.

"Ah shit man, I hate flying," Blake groaned. "Who the hell were those bastards? Thank Christ you had that M16."

It was a rhetorical question, one Blake knew Carson

Dallas wouldn't answer, yet he seemed to hold out in anticipation of a reply. It was just a need, the need to rejoin life, to once again converse, an acknowledgement of survival.

"We're alive man, we're fuckin' alive. Can you believe this?" Dal grimaced, forcing a half grin and propping himself against Blake, the two men taking great comfort in their solace. No bullets, no screaming, just life. Life again, beautiful, beautiful life as though death had granted each man a reprieve. But with a massive dose of pain. Enough pain to serve each of them a reminder, a brutal appreciation of the precious value of life.

The two men stretched out as best they could, each lying face up, the sunlight filtering down through the thick rain forest canopy, the destruction around them now a part of their existence, no longer carrying shock value. Each knowing, *this is now, this is real, this has to be dealt with.* A new day, perhaps a new beginning, in far more ways than either Blake or Dal were prepared to accept. But there was something mysterious, something treacherous, requiring sharp presence of mind, a quality neither man fully possessed at the time. Yet each was instinctively, internally assessing the situation. The silence became protracted, and sleep won the day.

Day became night, mist became rain, and the wetness washed the blood from the faces of both men. Blake groaned as his eye sockets pooled with the small dams of water. He blinked and tilted to one side, allowing the pools to escape, trickling across his cheeks. As he coughed, Dal shuffled his body toward Blake's, his arm dropping across Blake's waist.

"Dal, Dal. Wake up, you okay?"

"Ah shit, are we still here? *Alive* I mean. I feel like I jumped and the chute didn't open."

"Well it didn't, Dal you didn't jump, remember?"

"Yeah, yeah. Fuckin' plane. Where *is* that bitch, did she make it?"

"Don't know, last I saw of her she was ready to fly out the back of the thing. I'd say she's wasted."

"Fuckin' shame, good pussy getting' wasted like that,"

Dal snapped back.

Blake grinned, his blue eyes regaining some of their former sparkle.

"You sound like you're feeling a bit better." Blake nudged Dal and both men chuckled for the first time in their new lives.

The small strip of metal was clean. Blake tore a strip from the tail of his shirt and carefully wrapped it around Dal's hip. Dal grimaced, but tried not to make his pain obvious.

"Florence Nightingale would be proud of you, Dr. Blake. Good job. Not too deep huh?"

"Deep enough. Just try to lean off this side for a bit okay. Otherwise we might have to open it up, clean you out, and throw in a few dozen stitches. My embroidery was always a weak point, so you don't want that."

"Yeah, yeah. Thanks." Dal relaxed, folded his arms behind his head, fingers clasped and stared into the overhead branches. "Funny how you think over the past, when you're up the creek with no paddle," Dal said wistfully. "Been thinkin' about those guys who got themselves fried in Paris with those diamonds. Never did hear more about that Craven son-of-a-bitch. I sure liked his Porsche though."

"Yep," Blake answered.

"Guess he's layin' back on some beach in Rio."

"Yep."

"Too clever for us huh?"

"Yep."

"What the fuck? Who are you, Gary fuckin' Cooper?"

Blake grinned, knowing only too well how to push Dal's buttons.

"Chevalier got close. He got closer than *we* ever did. Cost him some good men. I remember those two Russians the prick cut up in the barn. Jesus, they had some guts." Dal laughed.

"Yeah lots of guts," Blake said quietly. "Lots of guts."

"Ah shit, any idea where we are? I mean - I know it's the fuckin' jungle, but you know, I'm lost without a guide. Can't find my way to the supermarket without a guide, and I've lived on the same street for three years."

Blake realigned his aching body, tried to move into a less painful position. He groaned and replied, "You're rambling Dal, got a fever?"

"Fuck the fever, when I get back to the States I'm gonna find Sam Ridkin and . . ."

"Shhh," Blake interrupted. "Listen."

Both men turned their heads to the left. They could here voices in the distance.

"Quick! Under those bushes," Blake said as each man crawled on all fours into nearby cover. They lay dead silent, not daring to breath, Dal clutching the M16.

"How much ammo in that thing?" Blake whispered.

Dal looked down at the weapon, slowly shaking his head from side to side. "Not a single shot, zilch. Just thought I'd hold onto it for sentimental value."

"Okay. Good thought, could come in handy," Blake said in a reaffirming way, yet grimacing as he spoke.

The faint cry seemed to come from a small heavily grassed area fifty or so yards nearer the wrecked fuselage.

"Hear that?" Dal asked quietly.

Blake raised a finger to his lips, indicating silence. Both men turned facing the same direction, waiting, listening. Again, someone calling, "Help me, hello. Help me."

The call was now louder, clearly a female.

"Shit do you think . . . ?"

"Yeah sounds like our Mata Hari," Blake whispered, still showing pain as he grimaced, spitting a distasteful wad of dried blood away from Dal.

"Fuckin' mouth feels like someone practiced a tongue transplant," Blake groaned. "Shit it hurts."

"Yeah, I'll swap you for my leg, now *that* fuckin' hurts."

"Stop whining," Blake winced spitting more blood.

They crawled on all fours, moved painfully in the direction of the cries as they grew louder, becoming more frequent.

Blake stopped, pointing his right index finger off to the right of a clump of small shrubs, indicating to Dal that he circle in that direction.

Blake moved to his left so that he and Dal were opposite each other, the cries coming from the bushes between them.

"Someone there?" the voice whispered in an almost inaudible plea.

"Please - help me."

Dal parted the green cover, slowly pushing the branches to one side, pausing momentarily as the bushes opposite him moved. Blake stared back across at Dal from ten feet. Then as each man lowered his eyes, the bloodied body of an almost naked Patrice Bellinger lay staring up at them.

"Jesus! The bitch is alive - is she alive?" Dal asked.

Her eyes moved toward Blake and her lips quivered, "Please help me, my legs, my legs!"

Her recovery was slow, yet by the time the sun filtered through the dense canopy, Bellinger was able to sit upright, and slowly return to minimal body movement.

"So what's the deal, why the fuck up?" Blake asked.

"What's the use? You won't believe what really was meant to happen."

"Try me."

CHAPTER 66

"IT WENT WRONG, HORRIBLY wrong," Bellinger whimpered. "The whole plan got screwed up."

"You got that right," Dal chirped in.

"The pilots, the two guys in the plane, they were with Boleros. We knew this and I was decoyed to join them, take you guys in as my ticket for membership. It was our way to win over their trust. Once you were inside, we had backup plans for a full recon. Sam told you he'd try to get mercenary support, that's actually the plan, off the record. We needed you guys inside the prison complex. Hunter has it all set up; the escape plan was meant to originate from inside the prison compound. I was going to take you both in, then we'd all leave with the information and the man."

She paused, caught her breath.

"Go on." Blake said inquisitively.

"The plane going down was not part of the plan."

"Oh that's really fuckin' rich," Dal snapped in.

"I know it looks bad," Bellinger pleaded. "But it went wrong, it went terribly wrong." Her tears could no longer be held back.

Both men sat and let her cry, neither comforted her, neither showed sympathy, neither wanted to believe her story. They each raised their eyes from the whimpering blonde, catching each other's stare; both men timed heavy swallows as though synchronized. Each took a deep breath and shakily exhaled. Blake's nervous habit kicked in. He ran his fingers through his matted hair.

"What now?" Dal asked.

"What now? Well first thing that comes to mind is how I'm going to enjoy watching you ram whatever it is you had in mind, right up Sam Ridkin's ass. In fact I'm next in line when you're done."

Bellinger coughed, holding up one hand. "No please,

Sam's not to blame for this, it screwed up, but the plan was sound, sometimes you know . . . Murphy's Law."

Blake snapped in, "Fuck Murphy and fuck his Law - that Irish prick nearly got us killed."

Bellinger burst into tears.

"Jesus, Mr. Diplomacy. That sure went well didn't it?" Dal chortled sarcastically.

"Yeah well," Blake grunted, "good move on the department's part. Keep it secret, keep it tight."

Bellinger turned off the tears, tried to smile, an acquiescing gesture, conceding their disapproval. She said, "I'm sorry you weren't in the loop. We do aim to please."

"Yeah well, if that's aiming to please, you need some serious fuckin' target practice," Dal replied turning away in disgust..

CHAPTER 67

GARDNER HUNTER EXPECTED THE plane, it was now well overdue and he now was looking worried. *What could have gone wrong? Why no news, no landing in alternate clearings?* The search was now into its eighth hour. The density of the jungle along the flight path made aerial reconnaissance impossible. A land search could take weeks. Unless you were good at finding the needle, this haystack would eat you up and pass you from its bowel movement so fast you wouldn't feel its mouth closing around you.

"Hey man, pass me the Marlboro," Galatea said reaching toward Hunter.

"Where the hell do you think the plane went down?"

"Got me, but it's down, that's for fuckin' sure. Toss me that lighter."

Both men lit cigarettes.

"Andreas if Bellinger's alive, she'll find a way to get through to us. She's a tough lady."

"What about these two agents, what of them? Are they dead, they alive, what the fuck? I do not like uncertainty."

"Jesus Christ, do I look like I've got fuckin' crystal balls? Stop grinding my nuts man. I'm here with you in this hell-hole. Nothing either of us can do but wait."

"For what, wait for what?" Andreas Galatea was not a patient man; his intolerance of inefficiency was reputed. His punishment for those performing at a level slightly less than less than divine was swift and non negotiable.

"I'm expecting an old friend today. My boys are meeting him at the airstrip. You'll find him most interesting. Travis Craven, heard of him?"

Hunter was very familiar with the reputation of this surprise visitor, yet played his cards close to the chest.

"Craven - I've heard a few stories about the guy," Hunter said.

"What's his main claim to fame?"

"Let's just say he solves problems, gets jobs done."

"And what job might you have in mind for him in? Are you holding back on me?" Hunter asked, his eyes lowered.

"Hmm, feeling threatened Hunter? Your curiosity belies your reputation. You'll find out when Craven gets here."

"Craven, Travis Craven?" Hunter said, with a question in his voice.

Last Hunter had heard, Craven was a pile of ash in an Audi outside of Paris. *How could this be? The man was dead. The department had his file. He was absolutely dead, both Chevalier and Blake had signed off on Craven's incineration. Could they have messed up? If so, it would be a first*, Hunter thought. This arrival needed thought, it was not a part of the grand scheme of things. The department had no contingency in their plans for the deceased Travis Craven being resurrected and scripted into the possible scenario. Hunter realized quickly he would need to play this very carefully. Should he feign ignorance of Craven's involvement with the French incident? Should he admit any knowledge of the man's history? Wouldn't be the smartest way to handle the arrival of Craven. *Quickly!* He thought. *Get it together. How much does Craven know about me? Am I supposed to know anything about Craven? Is my cover destroyed?*

"Señor Travis Craven, the infamous killer himself."

Andreas tilted his head back, sucked in deeply through the nose, made a guttural noise as he sucked from the rear of his nasal cavity, then ejected a golf ball sized spit, just missing Hunter's right ear.

Hunter quickly jerked toward the left. "You fucker, ever do that again and so help me God, I'll slit you from your dick to your Adam's apple you fuck! You might run Boleros, you son-of-a-bitch but you don't run me."

Hunter was intentionally over reacting, using this opportunity to quickly change the subject and leave the small compound. He needed to gain sufficient time to call back into the agency, to try to resolve this latest turn of events.

"Andreas is scared, think I'm peeing in my pants." He laughed quickly removing his Glock. In a flash he raised the weapon and pushed it firmly into Hunter's chest. Abruptly ending he laugh.

"What the fuck?" Hunter froze. "Come on Andreas, lighten up. This is getting crazy."

"You fuckin' better listen and listen good. You work for me understand. I own you, and right now I'm considering your worth. Hmm, not too much worth, maybe I should reduce my overhead. What is it they say in your homeland - hand you a pink slip?"

The muzzle of the Glock pressed uncomfortably into Hunter's chest. Andreas began squeezing the trigger. Hunter held his stare, each man holding the other's glare. The hammer dropped and the click of the empty clip caused Andreas to erupt into a raucous laughter.

"Oh God! Oh God!" He laughed aloud as he slapped the empty Glock onto the table, sending the half-full bottle of Corona hurtling across the room.

"Your face, you should see your face! You look like a fuckin' ghost!" The laughter was growing uncontrollable.

"You crazy fuck, I owe you for that and I've never backed off on a debt." Hunter stood quickly, his chair falling sideways. He stormed from the room, remembering the amount of planning the department had gone to placing him into the Boleros "family," how he had eliminated a good friend to prove his worthiness. The price was high, and Hunter realized his pride was a small price. His chance would come, and when it arrived he'd even the score with Andreas.

Andreas strode down the wooden stairs leading from the shack toward the Chevy speeding through the large guarded entrance, the Chevy's wheels spinning in the muddy driveway. The vehicle came to a stop and the men greeted each other and took seats at a table.

"Travis, how was the flight?"

"Uneventful. What's the deal here Andreas?"

"I hear you caused some havoc with those diamonds in Paris. They were not meant to be removed from their containers. You knew the consequence of that mistake, right?"

"Accidents happen." Craven replied.

"I pay for accidents not to fuckin' happen."

"Don't imply a threat, Andreas. I don't handle that too well." Craven kept his eyes low.

Andreas moved away slightly, feeling the inference and developing a self-defensive posture.

"I'm sorry, what I mean to say is, well, you know, the stones are the doorway coordinates. They're only of value if all are in their individual containers and placed strategically at the proposed entry and exit points. After all my dear Craven, how could we ever get that grand Porsche of yours through safely if someone so much as removed one coordinate? Do you realize the implication of such a fuck up?"

It may have been a question not requiring an answer, but curiosity was strong, and Craven had to ask.

"No Andreas. What's the implication?"

He played on the word *implication*, giving it the same South American accent Andreas had used.

"Well putting it simply it would be what our scientists have termed, 'The Philadelphia effect.'"

Craven coughed, took a tissue from a box on the table and leaned toward Andreas. "Go on," he said impatiently.

"If the coordinates are fucked up or not aligned as they should be, whatever attempts to go through the doorway, mightn't come though cleanly. He'll probably encase."

"Encase?" Craven asked.

"Hmm, how can I put this clearly? On the Eldridge, when the ship re-appeared, many of the crew men were partly encased in the ship's structure. They didn't materialize cleanly. This is what I mean by 'encase.' This is why the diamonds must all remain in their individual sealed boxes. They're safe that way. Their power's utilized for their original intent, not as curiosity pieces for some thief to give as a gift to an unsuspecting recipient."

"Well put, Andreas, at time your English amazes me," Craven said smiling.

"Thank you, Travis, I do try. Are you sure you fully understand the use of the sealed containers?"

"Fully. Ramirez and Brown obviously didn't."

Andreas shook his head sadly from side to side.

"Obviously not. Bad, bad mistake. Anyway, let's move on. I hear you got your ass kicked by some cop, a Frenchman?"

"Don't believe all that shit. You hear what you want to hear. And that's probably a lot more information than you need, so drop the French cop bullshit, okay?"

"Hey, whoa! Touchy subject huh amigo? Aw poor Craven."

"I have a score to settle but that's down the track. Chevalier's day will come. Retribution will be swift."

"Ah yes Chevalier. And a certain agent named Blake wasn't it? Drew Blake?"

"Yeah Blake. You got it, Blake. Never did actually meet the guy but we came close, too close. But I have the upper hand with those boys Andreas. You see last I heard they think I'm dead. So I'll just pay them a quick ghostly visit, say, hmm, about summer? I hear the French summers are something special in the South of France, a nice fast Porsche 911. Yeah Chevalier and I have a little dance number we need to finish."

"A tango in Paris?" Andreas laughed.

"Could say that. Yeah, last tango in Paris."

"And the discs, what of the discs?"

Craven ignored the question, his eyes remained lowered.

Andreas asked, "The discs were *never* recovered. Correct?" He placed a serious lean on the word "*never*."

"One was deciphered by some computer nut. A group in Paris fucked up the works. The disc shut down. Not one of my better laid plans, you might say. Cost a few souls, they went directly to hell, didn't pass go, didn't collect two hundred dollars."

Andreas stared coldly at Craven, an icy stare. Andreas returned a blank stare, oblivious to the board game reference.

"Ramirez and his accomplice Brown, they tried a double cross, wanted to retire early, long story."

"A long story? I've got time Craven. Tell me the long story. There are answers I need to hear." The tone of Andreas's voice showed curious concern. He definitely wanted the whole story from Craven. He wanted to hear why the French incident went so badly. Craven's body language made it clear he was not prepared to discuss the issue further. Sensing this Andreas raised a hand, motioning to one of his henchmen. The large brown man moved toward the table. Andreas faintly nodded his head toward Craven. The large man placed a hand on Craven's shoulder, a huge brown lobster claw of a hand. Craven raised his eyes slowly and stared directly at Andreas.

"Hey we're on the same fuckin' side here. I'm counting to ten. If his hand's still here," he dropped his eyes toward the hand on his shoulder, "I'll kill the fucker."

The two men held each other's stare. Andreas ran the tip of his tongue across his bottom lip. The large brown man stood his ground. The claw increased its grip on Craven's shoulder.

Craven grunted the words, his eyes staying lowered. "You're either the dumbest mother-fucker or you have a death wish. Either way, not good for you."

There's fast and there's warp speed. The large brown man didn't see it coming. In an instant Craven turned, reached down to his boot, flashed the large blade, and plunged it directly into, and up the large man's stomach.

The large man let out a gurgling belch, his hands grabbing uselessly at a surge of intestines now hanging loosely over his belt. The man sank to his knees. Andreas in shock, jumped back from the table gasping, his hands covering his mouth. Craven wiped the blade clean on the large man's shoulder, slowly leaned to one side and slid the blade back into the side of his boot.

Straightening the chair he regained his composure He sat again and reached for the beer. He passed a disinterested glance at the large brown man who stared in disbelief at his employer, his hands now hopelessly supporting his intestines.

"Happy fuckin' trails amigo," Craven said quietly sipping the Corona.

Andreas stood frozen, his hands now either side of his face, forcing his cheeks forward, his mouth distorted in a fish like pout, his eyes stared trans-like at the bloody mess kneeling on the floor ahead of him.

Craven took another long swig of beer, reached nonchalantly into his jacket, removed a nine millimeter handgun and instinctively without turning to aim, pointed it at the man's head and fired off one shot. The large brown man was gone.

"OH SHIT, OH SHIT!" Andreas shouted over and over, louder each time.

Craven raised a hand, palm facing the shouting man as if requesting silence. Then he raised the second hand, spreading his fingers and wriggling his ten fingers at Andreas.

Andreas continued shouting.

"Oh shit, shit, man, you're fuckin' crazy."

"Count them, I got ten, and that's what I give, ten. Ten seconds, Andreas. I shit you not, ten seconds. Next time I say I'm counting to ten, you'll take notice."

The car door slammed and the approaching man leaped up the steps three at a time. The door flew open as Hunter stormed into the room, gun in hand.

Craven spun around, caught unprepared. The two men had finally met, gun to gun, face to face.

Andreas shouted, "STOP – ENOUGH, ENOUGH," as the sound of running men shouting grew nearer. Several more brown men entered the room, crowding around the body. One unable to hold his food headed for an open window and, hanging over the sill, heaved uncontrollably into the moist jungle air.

A fine rain began falling. The crowd dispersed and the dead man was dragged by his feet from the room. An entourage of similarly colored compatriots walked behind, trying to avoid slipping on the gruesome entrails attached to the dragging body.

"CLEAN THIS MESS!" Andreas shouted.

"What a day! What a fuckin' day!" he said, waving his arms frantically in the air as he dropped into an old leather sofa adjacent to the table.

"What do you know about the black boats in New Orleans?" Hunter asked Craven.

The quick call to the department had resolved his quandary, Sam clearly advising Hunter to play along, to show he had in fact heard of Craven. It was decidedly a better plan, Sam believed, preferable to handling Craven as an unknown entity. It was a plan devised on the run. No time to mull it over.

"I've heard a few stories about you. Mostly sound like they've been embellished along the way. Mostly bullshit, right?"

The question was meant to jolt a reaction. Craven was unfazed. "Yeah, mostly bullshit. I'm really a nice fuckin' guy. Only kill the bad. People misinterpret my intentions. Big mistake . . . misinterpreting my intentions. Don't ever misinterpret my intentions, it has a history of being a last mistake. Last one, no question about it. Just leaves a nasty mess for someone to clean up." He gestured toward the red pool, its insidious trail leading to the door.

Hunter raised his fingers to his chin, slowly massaging his two-day stubble. He exhaled slowly, bit on his lower lip, considered how his demeanor was being perceived, how best to play his hand, how to maintain his image, or rather how not to appear intimidated by this killing machine, how to deliver the most appropriate first impression.

CHAPTER 68

IT WAS SLOW PROGRESS, both men helping Bellinger as struggled with her legs.

"Think she'll be okay Drew?" Dal asked quietly.

Blake grinned, "Sure she will. She ain't one of the good; she's too fuckin' evil to die young."

Dal nodded disagreement and said "I'm still here. Kinda shoots that theory down," he replied smiling.

"Jesus my body's aching." Dal nodded. Blake rolled his head about, stretching his neck. "Yeah, yeah. Yours too, huh?"

Dal grinned nodding. "Let's take a break, rest here by the tree." Blake grimaced. The two men had figured they were heading north. The sun had risen to their right, so it had to be north, they surmised. The three collapsed to the ground for some much needed rest.

"You were a boy scout, right?" asked Dal seriously.

"Yeah, yeah, whatever," Blake replied.

"You know, Blake, just lying here thinking back on things, I kind of feel that fate has something planned for us. You know that feeling, like, what the heck, everything happens for a reason, right? This is taking us somewhere. I have a strong gut feeling we're meant to be here."

Blake hadn't heard a word. He was in another world. Sleep had caught up.

"Drew. Hey, Drew. Ah jeez, it was one of my more deep conversations too. Ah, well. Sweet dreams, buddy."

A few minutes passed, and all three slept soundly.

The following morning a light drizzle bathed the three with a welcome shower. Blake sat up slowly and tried to stretch but realized his body still hadn't regained its flexibility.

"Dal, rise and shine," he called.

"Yeah, got it. Cream 'n one sugar."

"Sure, dream on. Would you settle for that strawberry shake?"

"Please man, don't fuckin' tease me like that." Dal rolled to his side, the expression somewhere between a smile and a grimace.

"I had the weirdest dream last night. It was about the kid back in New Orleans, Missy Palmer. I remember the song she was singing in the car when we stopped in for fast food. It was that 'Alouette,' says her mom sang it to her. I woke during the night, Dal, or at least I think I did, and I swear I heard that same tune being whistled out there."

"Out where?" Dal asked.

Blake raised one hand and pointed into the thick brush.

"Out there, someone was whistling, and it was the same tune."

"Nah, you were dreaming," Dal said.

"Maybe," Blake replied, still staring curiously in the direction he'd indicated. "Maybe, strangest thing, really fuckin' strange."

"Amigo's," the voice called. The large brown man pointed an Armalite AR 30 at the three as he stepped through the bushes and approached. They were totally unprepared, the M16 lying on the ground too far away for Dal to reach.

"Welcome, gentlemen, we've been expecting you. Glad to see you are all alive and well. Señor Galatea will be very pleased. Is the woman badly injured?"

Blake and Dal each turned toward Bellinger.

"Are you badly injured, Patrice?" Blake asked sarcastically.

She forced a grin and said very quietly without moving her lips, "Listen to me; remember what I told you about the plan. You are my prisoners. Play along with me and we'll all get out of this alive, with our people from the compound."

She turned to face the man with the weapon. She said, "Sure, I'm okay, a bit sore, but I can move along slowly, with some help. How far is the compound from here?"

He reached out and helped Bellinger to her feet. Gave a quick cold stare to Dal and Blake. "You two stand and help the woman. Walk that way."

He pointed the gun toward a track leading down by a small stream. They followed the stream for some five hundred yards, though it seemed like much further. The three needed to stop twice to rest, and the journey finally ended when they arrived at two large gates, tire tracks and a rough road clearly indicating motor vehicles had been entering the gates on a regular basis. The brown man raised the Armalite, using the butt to beat on the gate. It clanged loudly and within seconds, began creaking as it opened.

Three more brown men wearing dirty white clothing, each carrying automatic weapons, moved toward the three, helping them move through the gates. They directed them to a large shack. The stairs seemed to be stained with blood, diluted by the morning drizzle, yet still clearly blood.

"Well, well, well. At last, our elusive jet-setters have arrived, none the worse for wear, I hope. I am Andreas Galatea. You may have heard of me. Of course I know you have heard of me my dear. He smiled at Bellinger, arms outstretched.

Bellinger who stood behind the others smiled at Galatea.

"Andreas, it's good to see you again. We made it." She limped toward him, and the two gently embraced.

"I appreciate your best efforts to bring me these two my dear, but I'm sure your little plan didn't include the rough landing." He gave her a slightly skeptical glance.

Bellinger stopped to think. She was not sure which way to go with this. If she clearly lied, she would ruin the entire plan. If she bluffed, could she do it well enough to convince Galatea? Not an easy call. She stayed silent.

Dal dived across, landing a blow on Bellinger's face. "You bitch, selling us out. Fuckin' bitch."

Bellinger pulled away in shock. Blake picked up on the ploy and joined in the retaliatory action. Both men struggled toward Bellinger. The three white garbed men pulled Dal and Blake off of Bellinger, who played along nicely with the attack.

"Good girl, you did well," Andreas said smiling.

"Take her to her quarters and give her clean clothing and shower goods. I'll have Maria help you with your wounds. The doctor will be here soon to take care of you, but 'til then, we'll do our best to make you comfortable."

Bellinger limped from the shack, looking at the two men lying on the floor, weapons pointed at their heads, concerned but not allowing it to show.

"You two, huh. Stupid, very stupid. Take them to the far shack and chain them. The doctor will tend to them both after he's taken care of the woman."

Hours passed.

Blake said to Dal, "Pretty smart of you back there, fast thinking. I'm impressed."

"Had to do somethin'. A plan's a fuckin' plan, gotta get it back on track. Hope Bellinger can pull it together. Smart lady."

"Me too," Blake replied. "Because I gotta tell ya Dal . . . I've no idea where it goes from here, none whatsoever."

"Me too," Dal added. "Me too."

Two days passed, the chains stayed on. The doctor called each morning, changed their dressings, cleaned the deep gash on Dal's hip. A trust developed, he took the chains off and had one of the large brown men escort Dal and Blake to a makeshift shower room. They showered and shaved. The food was good, better than prisoner standard. Three square meals each day, and coffee. A clean set of clothing, and disposable shavers now made the two men indistinguishable from the rest of the men in the compound.

"Try to pull the waist in a bit," Dal quipped as Blake attempted to tailor fit the baggy white shirt.

"Ah shit, can you believe this?" Blake said in frustration, pulling at the oversize garb.

Dal sat quietly watching Blake's unsuccessful attempt to turn his outfit into anything remotely resembling an Armani creation.

"Hey Drew, come on man. Can't put a shine on shit, give it up," and they laughed for the first time in days.

Andreas Galatea strolled into the shack, looked at the two more presentable men and smiled.

"Do you mind if I join you?" he asked.

"Be our guest," Dal replied.

"Yeah sure, pull up a box, kick back. Excuse our decorator,

he's aesthetically impaired," Blake said smiling.

"He's what?" Andreas queried with a screwed up face.

"What's the deal here, why've we been treated like this? Not that we don't appreciate the medical attention, three squares and the exquisite couture," Blake added.

Andreas paused, exhaled with lips pouted, and raised his eyes to meet Blake's.

"Gentlemen, Miss Bellinger was kind enough to spoil your little supposed surprise visit. So Andreas has to ask himself, what if these two fuckers had of slipped into my world, what would they have planned for me? So gentlemen, Andreas asks you both, what did you have planned for me? I'm aware of the international escapades of the American Interpol."

Blake's eyes moved toward Dal as he tried to absorb the depth of the question. The American Interpol Division was not endorsed or recognized by any law enforcement body.

"We need to think about this. Can you give us an hour? It's been confusing for us as well," Blake said softly.

"Interesting Mr. Blake, does this look like a fuckin' country club? Did Mr. Dal here bring his clubs along?"

Dal coughed, smiling.

"I'll give you ten minutes, gentlemen. You'll do one of two things, let's just call them plan A and plan B. Which would you like to hear first?"

Blake held up his right index finger.

"Give us plan A first," he said.

"Plan A Mr. Blake: You discuss your reason for coming here then maybe you live."

"That sounds workable," Blake said.

Dal sat up showing gathered interest, aiming both hands in the shape of pistols at Andreas and asked, "And plan B?"

"Plan B is very much like plan A. You meet a very special surprise guest, you lie like mother-fuckers and my special guest gets to have his way with each of you. And I know from personal experience this guest would especially enjoy spending time with you Mr. Blake."

"Well I'm just fuckin' flattered," Blake said grinning.

"So please, my curiosity is definitely needing satisfying here, who is this hmm, *'special guest'*?"

"Does the name Travis Craven satisfy your curiosity?"

Both men quickly stood, a reaction Andreas was not prepared for.

"Steady, steady. Whoa there boys. Well aren't we touchy?"

"Craven? Here?" Blake snapped in stunned disbelief.

"Mother-fucker!" Dal grunted.

"Ah yes, the Paris farce. Seems your French friend Chevalier will be getting a surprise visit from Craven in the not too distant future. I believe he referred to it as a hmm, what was it? Oh yes a *'last tango in Paris.'* Mr. Craven did a very clean job for me in New Orleans, the operative known as Branson or Fortessi. We sent two other members of our team in to take care of Dick Palmer and his family, then we lost one man, but the other was in and out before the authorities knew what hit them. The media tagged them all, ah yes, the 'Fog Murders.' Travis Craven set a dummy trail with a few killings before he took out the mother Savannah Palmer, just to mess with the boys in the local Louisiana department."

Andreas chuckled as he placed a cigar on the table, trimming its end. He lit the cigar and, after exhaling a burst of white smoke, he said, "They're still looking for a serial killer."

CHAPTER 69

IT WAS OBVIOUS TO Dal that Blake was tactfully digesting the information passed onto them by Galatea, digesting than reacting to it.

"You see, when there's a problem needing to be solved, I have Craven. He's not cheap, but he never fails, never. You don't want him after you, not ever. I'll have you join us for lunch. Meanwhile, you can think about your introduction speech, what you're going to say to Mr. Craven. Oh, and also to Mr. Hunter, I believe he used to be on your team, but saw the error of his ways. Interesting, don't you think? Hunter, Bellinger, no longer members of the Uncle Sam's Club. Oh, and the box of cigars, please be my guest, go ahead, help yourselves."

He laughed at his pun on words as he left the room.

"Uncle Sam's Club, very good, very good Andreas," he said as he departed.

Blake moved across the room toward Dal, both men watching Andreas through the wooden louvers of the window. In the far corner of the compound were two shacks. Light flickered from a lamp indicating lack of electricity in that corner of the yard.

"Look at the wires in here. They're old but still carrying power. The light switch works."

Dal flicked the switch and the small bulb came to life.

"Okay so what's your point?" he asked Blake.

"Somewhere in this compound there has to be Internet or telephone connections. We need to get word out to McDowell or to Sam, or even through to Chevalier. We need all of the backup we can get, and the French have an ongoing interest in this, maybe more than we're aware. That shack over there with the flickering light, it's possibly a gas burner, so I'll bet it doesn't have power. I don't see wires leading to it like that shack alongside of it. It's got the wires. That's our best bet for outside communication . . . we might only get one shot . . . first chance we get."

CHAPTER 70

IT WAS A STEAMY day in Paris when the phone rang on Claude Chevalier's desk.

"Chevalier," he snapped with authority.

"Hello Claude, McDowell here. How's it goin' over there?"

"Oh my God, this is a surprise. To what do I owe the pleasure my friend?"

"Business. Our deceased friend Craven, seems he's back in action."

There was a minute of silence.

"You are, as you would say, shitting me, right?"

"As we would say Claude, I shit you not."

"We sent Blake and Dal to South America on a lead we had on more of the discs. Meanwhile we had an undercover agent in place, he got a call through to us this morning. We knew a few days back that the plane our guys were flying in on went down. Our satellite guys picked up the wreckage, so our recon team has already turned up wreckage, tracks leading into the jungle. We've a rescue and recovery squad ready to swing into action. A group of SEALs."

"And you're calling me to tell me what exactly?"

"Claude it's a messy story. We need to glue some of the bits together. It seems the South American syndicate Boleros is in cahoots with the Consort with developing the disc technology, the tele transportation, the doorways that Craven did his comings and goings through. It was a covert operation, disguised as common drug running. In fact, the DEA boys in New Orleans were onto the operation, with aerial drops from South America being picked up at sea by what've become known as 'black boats.' But the drug arm was just a money-raising front, the true operation was the placement of the technology, the diamonds. The Russians were after them as well as a few other high rolling contenders. You saw what Craven did with the Russians."

"I'm having trouble keeping up with this, where's it

going?" Chevalier asked.

"Craven is ready to make a move back to Europe. He's the contact man for the sales, the broker as such for Boleros and the Consort."

"Blake and Dal, are they on top of this?"

"Well we'd like to think so. We've a plan in action, or a plan of sorts."

"How is my department able to help you?"

McDowell drew a deep breath. Partly confused himself, he continued on. "We're going to allow Craven to escape our net in South America. We believe he'll proceed directly to Paris, he's main stomping ground, he's most at home there. Want your guys to be ready for him getting there. Want you to let him go untouched, no intervention. He's a small fish; we want the big guys, the buyers. We need to find out how much of this technology they already have in place and more importantly, how much more advanced technology Boleros is offering to the players. We believe once Craven's in France, he'll set himself up to deal with the buyers."

"Why don't they just transport the goods, same way the Porsche went and returned at will, are they are able to do that?" Chevalier asked.

"From what we understand, the portal needs a recipient, not an open-ended arrival point. It can't just shoot through like the Porsche did. Craven can't drive it through as there isn't an established departure door for him at the South American coordinates. We think it's a loose end they haven't yet tidied up. We have to think there on the verge of getting it sorted out. Once they can dispatch from any given spot, the world is in big trouble. When Craven arrives back to familiar territory, to Paris, he'll probably set up a recipient point. This's the reason I'm calling you Claude. Like it or not, it looks like the ball's back in your court."

Hunter had done well. He'd established contact with his stateside man. Thanks to Hunter, the recon move was in place. They were prepared for what was ahead.

Bellinger tapped on the shutter of the shack. Blake, surprised, quickly nudged Dal, and both men quickly had their ears to the shutters.

"Listen quickly. Hunter's gotten the word back to headquarters and a SEALs force is about to storm the compound."

"Jesus –" Dal was stopped before he could add to his sentence.

"Shut up and just listen. It's absolutely imperative Craven is untouched. We need him to make a clean getaway, our guys back home to track him. He's the rat and we're about to spring the trap."

"So what can we do, just hang back like a couple of observers?" Blake asked.

"Well not really . . . We'd like you to make a run with Craven. To make sure he gets away safely, to nursemaid him out of here."

"You're fuckin' shitting me right?" Blake asked.

"I shit you not. Craven knows you're a chopper pilot, Blake. He needs to get out of here, and we know he can't transport out because the coordinates in South America haven't been fine tuned. We're having our guys come through in two choppers. They'll take out the Boleros guys, no problem there. So the chopper will be sitting in the middle of the compound, and Craven will know that a chopper is his quickest way out, and you're his only way to get the chopper out of there."

"And Dal? What about Dal?"

"I'm kind of fond of Dal. He'll be fine here helping clean up at this end, and he'll return with the recon crew. We'll collect all the data and people we need from this end, and complete the assignment, but this thing with Craven, well…it's a last minute directive from the boss, so…what can I say, good luck Blake, he's *your* boy, take him home."

Dal looked at Blake and nodded. "Sounds like a plan. I'm cool with it, how about you?"

"Up, up and away, let's do it. No one I'd rather fly the friendly skies with than Craven." Blake turned his head and spat his disapproval.

The timing was as though it were scripted. Andreas arrived at the door, two of his large brown men accompanying him, M16 weapons in hand. "Well, gentleman, the hour is at hand. Be good boys now and be polite to Mr. Craven. He anxiously awaits your company."

The two agents walked between the two large brown men. Suddenly the whup, whup. whup of chopper blades brought the group to a stop, all staring skyward. Men poured out of the larger shack, they were all carrying weapons and began frantically firing shots skyward, in no particular direction. Shouting and general disarray added to the panic.

Craven, Hunter and Bellinger ran to the center of the courtyard. Hunter dropped his gun to his side and waved toward Andreas, "Andreas quickly, this way!"

Andreas seeing this as an escape opportunity ran toward Hunter. "HUNTER, CAN WE TAKE THE CHOPPER?" he called out aloud, panic in his voice.

Hunter shouted, "SURE WE CAN, GET OVER THIS WAY QUICKLY."

Andreas ran toward the chopper. When they arrived at the chopper Hunter raised the nine millimeter and placed a hand on Andreas's shoulder.

He shouted, "HEY SPIT-MAN, YOU FUCKER." Andreas turned as if in slow motion. Hunter held his Smith & Wesson Sigma 9mm an inch from Andreas's forehead, smiled and placed a slug between Andreas's eyes. Andreas's head kicked back, then rebounded toward Hunter as he dropped to the ground. Hunter quickly ejected the clip and replaced it with a spent clip, tossing the empty weapon to Bellinger; she caught it, still standing open-mouthed at what she'd just seen.

Craven spun around, losing his balance as his shirt snagged on the side of the shack. The buttons ripped open and the rusty iron sheeting cut into his chest. The choppers were now twenty feet above the ground, ropes dangling like so many spider legs, supporting the dragon flies hovering above. Uniformed men slid down the ropes, automatic weapons firing from beneath each of their arms as they annihilated the Boleros crew on the ground.

Men scurried in all directions. The charging SEALs broke through the dust storm now enveloping the choppers sitting predator-like in the middle of the compound. The noise was deafening, the confusion disorienting.

Bellinger shouted into Craven's ear, "THE CHOPPER, GET TO THE CHOPPER. TAKE MY GUN, GRAB BLAKE. HE CAN FLY A CHOPPER."

Craven smiled quickly at Blake who stood just a few paces from the chopper, its blades only now beginning to whup, whup, whup to a stop. The rescue crew played their roles as though it were a scripted movie. Eight large brown men lay dead, completely outmatched by the Navy SEALs onslaught. It was like putting a High School football team against a NFL side – no match at all.

Dal, Bellinger and Hunter stood looking down at Andreas Galatea. He was laid out face up, eyes hidden beneath blood.

"Nice shot man, but a bit close I'd say, not really sporty," Bellinger called to Hunter. "A bit off to the left too, don't you think Dal?"

Dal said, "Fuck sporty! What with all the dust flying, I'd say it was a pretty good shot. Bit of a hook perhaps."

Hunter snarled, "The guy was a swine. I told him we'd have our time to square off."

"Yep," Dal said aloud. He kept his head low as dust continued blowing about the compound. "You squared off nicely. Remind me not to fuck with you on the course. I hear you play a good game. Let's get together for a round sometime."

The chopper bobbed and weaved its way through the valleys, staying just above the treetops. Blake really didn't need to babysit this son-of-a-bitch, but that was the plan, that was what Adam McDowell and Sam Ridkin wanted.

Craven placed the nine millimeter into his belt.

"You're bleeding," Blake said I an unemotional tone.

"It's a scratch, I'll be okay." "But thanks for your concern."

"It ain't concern Craven. I'm just surprised to see you bleed. Thought you had ice in those veins. Kind of a relief, shows me you're vulnerable."

"I'm not fuckin' vulnerable to you Blake. You're not up to it, you never were. Like that Frenchman, his days are numbered too."

"Listen you fuck, I'm flying this beater. If I go down you follow right? So shut the fuck up and let me get us out of here."

Craven stared, a cold, long, lost-for-words stare.

"Good we're cool then" Blake said.

"Yeah, cool," Craven replied in an unconvincing voice. "Just fly the fuckin' thing. Fly it west toward the sun."

The flight lasted almost two hours. Craven directed the chopper toward a hangar. Blake put the copter down, a Lear jet stood ready nearby.

"Craven," the voice called, "we're expecting you. Come on, get on board. We're outa here."

Jesus, Blake thought, *so organized. The department really wants this guy to perform.*

Craven hesitated. He stood back suspiciously then asked, "Who the hell sent you guys here? How'd you know?"

"Boleros tipped us off to your escape. We tracked the chopper, knew you'd come here. Only place you'd be able to link up with one of our planes. After all, those drops to the black boats, they all started here. You knew that."

"Really?" Craven asked. He quickly raised his weapon, pointing it at the man. He said, "Why are you using past tense? Why are you saying the drops 'started' here and not 'start' here?"

"Hold it, hold it, hold it!" the man snapped defensively. "It's just a figure of speech. Jeez you're fuckin' touchy man."

Craven stared the man down, as all three moved into the jet. The turbine whirred and within minutes the Lear cruised at twenty-five thousand feet.

"Pretty good how you picked up on the past tense shit," Blake said smiling. "I missed it but you're right, he was talking about it as though it's all over. Maybe you've got nothing to go back to?"

Craven paused and considered the implication of Blake's comment. He said, "You took it too literally. I've got a plan and it'll work just fine.

Blake felt a chill travel up his spine, a feeling almost

foreign to him. He needed to settle this lunatic down. The pilot came forward asking, "Everything out here okay?"

"Sure," Blake replied, "just a bit of premature ejaculation – ouch – celebration."

The Lear touched down several hours later on a dark, warm night.

"Where are we?" Blake asked the pilot.

"South of Paris, private strip."

"Shit really?" Blake said surprised.

The pilot turned to see where Craven was at, then quickly turned to Blake and gave a quick, reassuring wink. He whispered to Blake, "Chevalier is by the old barn road. Everything is set, understand?"

Blake coughed, hoping to drown out any chance of the words leaking to Craven. The cough was accompanied by an agreeing nod.

"Over here!" Craven snapped. He moved quickly toward a covered shape in the far corner of the hangar, kicking aside a pile of cardboard boxes. He reached for one corner of the canvas cover and pulled it carefully from the car. There it sat, the red Porsche in all its glory.

"Hello baby, daddy missed you." He ran his fingers along the front guard.

"Tell me Blake, ever had a pet name for a favorite car? Like Christine, Genevieve or Betsy. Have you?"

"Yeah sure. I had a '67 Chevy rag-top. She was white, called her Marilyn. You know, blonde and all."

"Yeah good name. I'd like you to meet my Marilyn. Name's Fang."

He pointed to the Porsche, waving the gun in a matter-of-factish way toward the passenger's door.

"Slide into Fang, she's about to take us on one wild, wild ride."

CHAPTER 71

THE RED CAR COUGHED twice, shot out a puff of white smoke, and roared from the hangar.

Blake turned and nodded toward the pilot who gave him the thumbs up as the 911 roared by, thumbs up being the internationally recognized sign of "Glad it's you and not me."

Craven drove a few kilometers and, before too long, was cruising down the old barn road. Blake recognized the scenery. He pulled the car to the roadside, stepped out and pulled the hood. He reached into the storage area and returned to the car with two small clear boxes.

"Oh shit!" Craven said loudly, looking at the containers under the light of the dash panel.

"What's up? Problem?" Blake inquired.

"Yeah more than you'll understand. These numbers on top are supposed to match, but these don't."

Blake looked at the numbers. One container was marked TC 34, the other carried the numbers TC 41.

Blake asked quietly, "So?" He paused, and then continued. "What's the problem with the numbers not matching?"

"They need to be the same so the fuckin' coordinates are balanced, imbalanced coordinates can lead to transcription error."

"Okay." He paused again. "What exactly does that mean? Transcription errors? Do I need to be worried about that?"

"Well," Craven answered turning to face Blake.

"Are you familiar with the Eldridge? Way back in the '40s, it was known as the 'Philadelphia Experiment'?"

"Yeah I know a bit about it," Blake replied.

"You heard how some of the crew were impaled into the hull and deck of the ship? Well, even though they had neither the technology nor the terminology down, that malfunction was the direct result of a transcription error. When the exit or reentry coordinates are not balanced, you risk becoming a part of the vehicle or vessel on which you are being transported."

"Oh shit, that's a real fuckin' gem. So I guess I do need to worry?" Blake asked sarcastically.

"Got that right, big time worry. But we'll give it a try. Here, hold these," he said to Blake as he slowly rolled the Porsche further along the roadside. He counted the white posts at the edge of the hard top.

"Twenty-two, twenty-three . . . yeah, right here." He pulled the car to the edge, took the two boxes from Blake, and placed one on either side of the roadway, about twenty feet apart. The sun was rising, and Craven swung the Porsche around and headed back a few hundred meters.

"Okay hold onto your toupee, here we go!" Craven gunned the Porsche, and as it neared the two boxes, Chevalier drove the Citroen out from its hiding place behind a stand of tall roadside bushes, drove the patrol car directly across the path of the speeding Porsche.

Craven swerved, clipped the front of the Citroen, spun it sideways and sent it careening toward a large tree. He spun the Porsche around the Citroën, slowed to a crawl, and made a U-turn. Cruised by the smoking Citroen saw the man falling to the ground. Blake seized the moment and jumped from the car. Craven laughed and called back at Blake, "Dead weight anyway, you'd just slow me down! I'll be seeing you around."

He nodded to Blake, held up one hand, *a friendly gesture* Blake thought. *If I didn't know his background I might like the guy.*

The Porsche sped toward the doorway, but the motor was tired. It had been standing too long perhaps, not an endearing habit for a Porsche. The car spluttered, sliding sideways toward the doorway. Three patrol cars closed in on the Porsche.

The Porsche crossed over one of the boxes, shattering the casing, sending sparkling gems scattering across the roadway. The front half of the car appeared to vanish into the doorway, Craven's lower body vanishing along with it, just his torso remained, looking like an appendage jutting from the dashboard.

Blake ran toward the wreck and could see that Craven's

upper body seemed to be fused into the dash. Craven was shaking, trembling, his shirt hanging by threads.

Embedded nose first into the trunk of the large tree, the Citroen groaned, spewing steam from under its hood. Chevalier lay on the ground beside the smoldering wreck as three gendarmes sprinted toward him, panic on their faces. Chevalier struggled to hold up a hand, slowing the approaching cops. The ultimate victory belonged to him, he alone would claim the prize. He alone would take out Travis Craven. Any of his men could have taken Craven, but this madman was Chevalier's prize. The long, painful search was at an end and he alone was destined to bring it to fruition. He rolled to one side, reached for the glock. Raised it, groaned, took aim.

Fired.

Blake shouted, "CLAUDE STOP! HE'S DONE - HE'S FINISHED!"

Chevalier lowered the weapon, and his head slumped to the ground. He rested it momentarily, unable to hold it upright.

Craven gasped in agony. Blake quickly ran to the Porsche, standing over Craven. His shirt was hanging open, and Blake stared down at the large dolphin shaped birthmark on Craven's lower left side. *The same mark*, Blake thought. *Chevalier's fuckin' birth mark.*

Craven raised the nine-millimeter, waved it in a *'help me, what the fuck happened'* gesture.

Blake stood back, momentarily stunned by the gaze in the pastel hue of Craven's eyes, saddened by this final gesture; he smiled at Craven sympathetically and said quietly, "The gun is empty. Take it easy Travis."

Chevalier saw the gun raised toward Blake. He fired off two rounds, hitting Craven in the shoulder with the first, his forehead with the next.

Blake reeled about shouting angrily at Chevalier, "No! No! It's empty, his fuckin' gun is . . ." The cry echoed and hung there, suspended in midair. It reverberated in Blake's head for what seemed an eternity.

A victory smile spread across Chevalier's face. In pain he

limped toward the dead man, making his way toward this man he'd searched after for so many years. The son he would never meet. Blake could see Chevalier getting nearer, he looked down at the dolphin shaped birthmark on Craven's lower rib cage, reached down, pulled the shirt across, covered the birthmark.

Chevalier let out a cry, the words it reflected his hurt. His voice wavered, "AT LAST I HAVE YOU. YOU SON-OF-A-BITCH!"

Blake rushed between the inspector and the wreck. "Yeah you found him Claude. He's gone, move away. Don't come any closer." He steered Chevalier away from the carnage, away from what remained of the Porsche as it erupted in flames. The two men turned, squinted at the destruction taking place, each raising an arm to shield his eyes from the tremendous heat.

For Chevalier the search had ended. And as he limped away, he placed an arm around Blake's shoulder. His mood was melancholy.

"My friend, I'm finished with this police work, this has ended it for me Drew. With more time on my hands I've a long lost party I need to find, I've put it off long enough. Perhaps you can help me a little with it. His name is Trudeau, he must be around thirty six years of age now, I have never really told anyone but . . . I have a son . . . I have a son." His manor became melancholy. Again he dropped to one knee. "Did I ever tell you about Trudeau? I would like to tell you about my boy." He stumbled, Blake righted him, took a few long seconds to steady him. Chevalier went quiet, said: "Maybe tomorrow Drew? Yes, tomorrow. My boy, my Trudeau. I will tell you tomorrow."

Blake swallowed hard, choked a little, felt a tear swell, and replied softly, "Yeah Claude. Tomorrow sounds good. A son huh?" He placed an arm around Chevalier's shoulder, steered him away from the smell of roasting pork. "A son you say, huh. We'll talk about it tomorrow."

Chevalier swallowed hard, forced his voice. "Just like his mother. I was told his eyes are the color of the moon in a daylight sky."

JASON DENARO'S

a

PASSAGE

to BURMA

THE ANTONOV WEAVED AND veered sideways. Then Harry put it into a steep ascent. He struggled with the controls; the Antonov was heavy when asked to perform steep turns and quick maneuvers. The chopper stayed close by, it was now less than three a thousand feet off of the plane's tail. It sent another burst of gunfire into the Antonov's fuselage. Harry and Slade instinctively lowered their heads as they felt the impact of the hits. Blake shouted from the rear of the plane, trying to attract the attention of either man in the cockpit, but the intercom headsets between the Harry and Slade blocked out Blake's shouts. A further burst of gunfire raked the fuselage behind him. The engine noise in the Antonov was loud up front; the plane's exhaust was positioned just two feet from Slade's right foot. Normal conversation between pilot and co-pilot was impossible. Blake shouted again but the two men up front could only hear each other's voices through their headsets. Blake stepped into the cockpit and removed Harry's headset, he shouted directly into Harry Ching's ear, "COME ON HARRY, FOR CHRIST'S SAKE DO SOMETHING DIFFERENT. THINK OUTSIDE THE BOX MAN." Harry ignored Blake's shouting; he continued pushing the Antonov to a height of thirty eight hundred meters. "WE'RE OVER TWELVE THOUSAND FEET AND THAT CHOPPER CAN'T GO MUCH HIGHER," Harry shouted back at Blake, his message barely discernable above the noise of the engine. The single prop motor had taken a hit and smoke began billowing along the length of the fuselage.

Harry shouted, "I'M GONNA TRY PUSHING HER A BIT HIGHER." Harry had a look of uncertainty. His voice lowered and he spoke at the gauges. "Feels like we've lost some of our horses. This little girl has a thousand horses; right now she feels more like eight hundred. If we can maintain this ceiling, that chopper can't stay with us. If I'm right his ceiling is around thirteen thousand feet, that's just over four thousand meters." Harry looked about, strained to see the chopper, flipped a thumb in its direction. "He can make one ninety miles an hour. Were just gonna have to go higher, get above the clouds. If we can get to fourteen thousand feet, enough to stay above him, we can give him the slip." Harry waved a hand at the clouds and added, "If the cloud layer doesn't break."

Hunter debated on going into the cockpit; felt he needed to be where the controlling was happening. But the chopper held his gaze, like a flame to a moth, he wished it wasn't there, saw the muzzle flashes from the automatic as it sprayed the tail section of the Antonov. He could see the pilot and co-pilot inside the chopper, the co-pilot was making a take it down gesture with his hand, Hunter rescinded with one finger in a going up gesture. This angered the co-pilot, he shouted to the man at the control of the chopper. Hunter realized he shouldn't be able to see the men inside the chopper. Something wasn't right. It took a while for him to realize the occupants were being illuminated by an ever brightening glow. Then in a flash the chopper ignited in an orange ball of flame.

The two men in the cockpit of the Antonov shielded their eyes from the blast. "Jesus Harry, what just happened?"

"They've blown off the tip from our starboard wing." Harry pointed as he spoke. Slade looked in the direction Harry pointed and saw a meter long section missing from the wingtip. "I saw it rip off, it flew back into their rotor. Lucky we were above them or it would have missed."

"Can you still control the plane?" Slade asked.

"Yeah, but it doesn't feel good. The motor's been hit and were losin' oil pressure fast. Our air speed's dropped to a hundred and forty kilometers, if we drop to ninety we'll stall." Harry tapped on the gauge. It was showing one twenty-five. It was still dropping.

"How much further before we reach the border town?"

"I'd say we've got to be there in thirty minutes."

Blake came into the cockpit, leaned into Harry and raised his headset. "So . . . will we make it Harry?"

There was no reply as Harry stared at the gauges. "Look at this." Harry tapped on the fuel gauge, he was shouting over the engine's roar. "This should be showing three quarters full. It's dropped below half in a few minutes. Go aft, see if you smell gas."

Blake moved from the cockpit, and as he stepped into the cabin area Dal shouted, "WHAT THE HELL'S THAT GAS SMELL BACK HERE?"

Blake moved to the rear of the plane. Hunter and Slade both moved aft to join Blake, the three men peered from the windows at the gasoline spray clearly visible in the Antonov's wake. The plane rolled to the left then began a vertical descent. It was an uncomfortable feeling with only the stars to show which way was up. The plane refused to respond to Harry's efforts at regaining control. Harry tried several procedures to get the aircraft back on track, none worked. He decided it was time to tell all on board to strap on their chutes.

"Go back, have the guys hand the chutes out."

Blake was mortified. The last time he had to jump was on a mission over South America, both he and Dal were mentally ready to go, but the ground had other ideas and rose to meet the plane. Blake had a sudden feeling of deja vu. He quickly moved into the cabin and made eye contact with Dal. Sung waved at Blake and made finger jabbing motions at the tail. He placed his hands around his mouth to form a megaphone and yelled, "THE TAIL, IT'S BEEN HIT."

The hits to the tail section and engine cowling were too much for the old warhorse. The plane continued losing altitude as Blake shouted to Dal and pointed to the parachutes.

"ARE YOU SURE HARRY'S CORRECTLY ASSESSED THE SITUATION?" Dal shouted to Blake, not wanting to jump out of a solid aircraft. Blake nodded yes. He was a good liar. He'd always been good. He moved closer to Dal and placed a reassuring hand on his shoulder and shouted, "WHERE'S THAT CALM DEMEANOR YOU SHOW IN STRESSFUL SITUATIONS?"

"SCREW YOU. I DON'T SEE YOU IN ANY RUSH TO GET OUT," Dal shouted back at Blake.

Harry considered his options, of which there were two, fly the aircraft to a safe area and parachute out. The other option, attempt to land the disabled Antonov. Slade looked at Harry and shrugged his shoulders in a *what are we gonna do* gesture. Harry shouted even though he had the intercom connected, "I CAN DO ONE OF TWO THINGS, TRY TO LAND A PLANE THAT'S BROKEN, OR JUMP. . . AND I AIN'T GOT A NATURAL INSTINCT TO DO THE LATTER."

Blake heard the shout, he re-entered the cockpit, his parachute strapped on and gave Harry a *what's happening* shrug. He dropped into the seat alongside Harry and slipped the headset on. Harry glanced sideways. "I guess it's my call about whether to jump or attempt to land this baby."

Before anyone could throw their two-cents worth into the mix, Harry made sure Blake was comfortable that the decision to land or jump was Harry's and Harry's alone. The plane dropped another hundred meters and the gas gauge now showed a quarter of a tank. The decision was clear. Harry now had no doubt in his mind that he was not going to attempt to land that airplane while the light was so bad.

"If we could stay up here 'till first light, I could put it down safely." Harry dropped the starboard wing and looked toward the ground. "Look down there. Pitch black. It'd be guesswork in this darkness. I can't risk it."

The passengers sat in silence, feeling every vibration, smelling the gasoline. Billy and Sung chatted in Mandarin as Bellinger reached across the aisle and tightly grasped Hunter's hand. Blake moved into the cockpit and took over Slade's position, he placed the headset on and faced Harry who was now a lather of perspiration.

"Shit man, can't remember being this wet flying since I landed a Cessna in the Hoover Dam. That was wet man. That was wet."

"Harry, give it to me straight. What do you think our best chances are? It's going to be your call man. No one's going to hold you to blame for the outcome. Wha d'ya say?"

"Well, there's plan 'A'. I could stay up here long enough to see what's below. My money says I can put her down. Then there's plan 'B'. If we run out of gas, and it's still dark, we jump."

"I guess that's it then, plan 'B'. We keep flying 'till she splutters. Can you glide her?"

"Yeah sure, she'll glide like a rock," Harry said without taking his eyes from the nose of the plane, "Yeah. She'll glide alright, straight down."

Blake, wet and white, returned to the rest of the group and discussed what he and Harry had figured to be their best chance.

"So, we wait 'till the gas goes and jump?" Dal asked.

"Yeah, that's about it. Harry will keep her as high as possible. When the gas runs dry he'll see if the horizon's visible, if he can see the ground he'll assess our chances for a safe landing. If not . . . we jump. So, with that in mind let's all be clear on the jump procedure."

Slade offered to go through the jump procedure and Bellinger began to sob.

"Hey Bell, come on, take it like a man," Dal said and gave her a thumbs up.

"Yeah sweetie, I'll take care of ya," Hunter said reaching over his seat and squeezing her shoulder. Ten minutes passed and the Antonov was still airborne.

"GET READY TO GO," Harry shouted trying to be heard above the engine scream, "WE'RE LOSING ALTITUDE FAST," in the next breath, very loud and clear Harry shouted, "GO, GO, GO!"

Slade opened the door and the wind screamed into the Antonov. Magazines and Styrofoam cups shot about the cabin as Slade gave an extra tug to the buckle securing his backpack containing the Tara. He gave the thumbs-up to the others, hesitated, stared down into the blackness . . . stepped from the plane. Bellinger gave Hunter a final hug and a quick wave to those standing behind her and followed Slade. Hunter shouted to Blake and Dal, "JUST LIKE THE FLYIN' FUCKIN' ELVIS'S." He pointed at Dal, they both laughed and Hunter disappeared from sight. Billie came around and half-stood, half-kneeled by Sung and gave him a thumbs-up sign. Sung and Billie both pointed down toward terra firma and within seconds of each other they were on their way down. Blake and Dal hung back.

"HARRY, GET YOUR ASS OUT HERE," Blake shouted into the cockpit.

"I'LL BE OUT IN A TIC, YOU GUYS GO ON AHEAD."

Blake had a bad feeling about Harry, thought he might have a *go down with the ship mentality*, knowing how much this aviator loved his baby.

"IF YOU TWO DON'T GO IN THE NEXT TEN SECONDS YOUR GUTS WILL BE HANGIN' OFF OF BRANCHES."

"HARRY, GET OUT HERE!" Dal shouted. Both Blake and Dal tugged at Harry's shoulder but he waved them off.

"LISTEN . . ." Harry shouted still squinting ahead, "I

THINK I CAN LAND HER, JUST NEED TO HOLD HER AT TWELVE HUNDRED FEET 'TILL I SEE THE LIGHT ON THE HORIZON, ANY MINUTE NOW."

"WE'LL STAY WITH YOU," Blake shouted.

"OKAY, OKAY. LET ME GET OUTA THIS SEAT." Harry made his way into the cabin and got into his 'chute, he stood alongside Dal and Blake and nodded. He pointed down and shouted, "GETTING TOO LOW, GO, GO, GO."

Dal and Blake leaped from the plane. The moment they'd jumped, Harry pulled back from the opening, slammed the door shut and scrambled to the controls.

*****

JASON DENARO'S VATICAN FILESS

Drew Blake glanced at his watch, his concern over Dobbs' dive time was showing. Paul Dobbs had been submerged for almost an hour. Allowing for around three minutes of descent, five minutes securing the line to the bottom, plus time to do a brief observation He had an hour of ascent time with the appropriate decompression stops, he was expected to break surface at any time. One hour and thirteen minutes after entering the water Dobbs walked from the lake, removed his face mask and headlight, and gave his team the thumbs up. "All systems go Wolf. Almost zero viz, but the line's secure. I didn't see much. You might need to use the cyalume sticks."

The two SEALs swung into action with an instinct born of countless hours of training. With an air of confidence, Brandt and Gerbler moved quickly from the truck nearest the waterline, down the embankment and into the lake. They each moved with the aura of men totally skilled in what they were doing. The two men quickly prepared for the deep descent down Dobbs' yellow polypropylene anchor line. Even with his illuminated compass strapped to his wrist, and his headlight switched on at twenty feet, Brandt's vision was limited to a few feet in the inky black Lake Como water. But, as a tap on his shoulder reminded him, he was not descending down the line alone. Franz was down there with him. They each shared the danger as they made their way toward the debris field but for the two SEALs it was just another day at the office.

Drew Blake gave his watch a quick glance then slipped Dal a look of dubious intensity. As the moon projected spots of light spasmodically atop Lake Como the two Navy SEALs paused at the water's edge, turned, gave a half-wave and within seconds both men had melted into the black water. Three minutes later the two divers touched down on the lake bottom. Brandt's depth gauge showed two hundred and twenty four feet. He could sense Mussolini's gold had to be within meters of where he had bottomed. But a man's mental capability is reduced to that equivalent to a child's level when subjected to the nerve wrenching pressure of the lake at this depth. The trimix that Brandt and Gerbler were breathing would certainly assist the two SEALs in staying as clear headed as possible. Brandt pointed into the black that surrounded them. He pointed his light, but its penetrating power was greatly reduced by the silt now rising from the movement of the diver's fins, reducing visibility to just a few inches. Although the boxes were scattered at a depth between two hundred and twenty and two hundred and fifty feet, they couldn't be seen. The first few minutes were spent getting a feel for the site. The two divers sat . . . waited. They allowed the silt sufficient time to settle, neither diver moving his fins. After a few minutes had passed, Brandt and Gerbler slowly moved off in a northerly direction, feeling sharp edges, seeing debris shapes that could be ammunition boxes. When they ran out of shapes, they turned and slowly swam off in a southerly direction, retracing their path, making mental notes of the debris field. It seemed there was around seventy feet of lake-bed on which several ammunition boxes had been jettisoned. Then to his amazement Gerbler was trapped in what felt like a wooden room.

He stopped unexpectedly and Brandt edged into Gerbler's fins. Both men reached out and felt the edges of what seemed wrapped around them. It quickly became clear to the divers that this was some type of large wooden barge. Perhaps explaining how the boxes were brought so far out from the shore. Mussolini's men somehow loaded the gold onto this craft and, once in deep water, scuttled it. They felt the shapes of boxes laying about the barge. It became a visualization exercise. They'd been down for eighteen minutes, their bottom time was done. They moved back to the anchored line and began their ascent. Once they reached forty feet, they stopped for a five minute decompression, then at thirty feet for another ten minutes and finally at twenty feet the two divers stopped for fifteen minutes.

They walked from the lake and slipped out of their gear. As Brandt sat and chatted with Gerbler one thing was clear, the two men were in agreement. There was a boat on the lake-bed, probably some type of barge. They had located four dominant boxes that appeared to have settled without breaking open, one appeared to be sitting on top of another. The lower box felt as though it was badly disintegrated. Consensus was that this box had suffered the landing rather poorly and could have fragmented as the barge hit bottom. To identify each of the four in tact boxes, and to give reference points to the field, Gerbler chose to name the boxes Matthew, Mark, Luke and John. Brandt would have labeled the boxes A, B, C and D but Gerbler was first to make the identification move. He pulled the tag-pad from his belt and scribbled each of the names, affixed one to each of the boxes, a touch of irony considering the likely Nazi origin of the contents, Brandt thought. Might have been better had it ended up in the Vatican Bank with the rest of the Nazi hoard. Fuckin' Mussolini.

One box had strewn its content into the silted lake-bed. Several gold bars now covered in black slime laid scattered about the lake bottom and Brandt had attached a fifty pound lift-bag to one bar. The temptation was more than he could handle. He slipped a loop onto the bag and released it so that it made an ascent along the yellow 'anchor' line. Brandt had also brought two larger lift bags and a harness net to the lake-bed. To prevent an out-of-control lift, Brandt tried to match the lift capacity of the bag to the weight of the unopened box, and the two bags were the result of a pre-dive best guess estimate. He ran his hands around the edges. His senses told him each of the ammunition boxes were thirty-six inches long, twenty-four inches high and twenty-four inches wide. Brandt could only hope the contents were gold bars. Gerbler moved to the opposite side of the Matthew box as Brandt set about attaching a five hundred pound lift bag either side of the only box on which he had sufficient clearance under which the two men could feed the harness. Brandt vented the excess air from the bag, never generating more than five hundred pounds of lift. With these large bags, Brandt could also vent excess air from the bag as it rose to the surface. Both men were familiar with lift-bag salvage and knew too well that they must never get above or below the load and should not exceed the recommended safe ascent rate, stopping to decompress at forty feet, thirty feet, twenty feet and ten feet for the correct times. However the box failed to rise. The lift-bags failed. Pontoons would float the heavy box, but the nearest pontoons were at Ramstein and even if they were flown in, the size of pontoons would definitely attract unwanted attention to the dive.

The box defied the lift-bags and remained stubbornly on the lake-bed. Brandt knew better than to struggle any longer with the box. This would only result in a quicker depleting air supply. He pointed at the box and Gerbler made hand signs that suggested they return with a crow-bar and pry the box open. This would allow the contents to be raised by lift-bags a few pieces at a time. It would be a slower process, but far easier than raising the sealed box.

Brandt looked toward the surface, his eyes straining through the unclear face of his dive mask, he tried tracking the anchor line, but the yellow polypropylene line secured from the box to the tree trunk faded from sight in the weak glow of his light. The beams struggled to pierce the blackness of the water. Air bubbles from the tanks disappeared from view just a few feet from each man's mask. Aside from the few feet of anchor line visible, each diver's peripheral awareness of the bubbles was his only indication of which way was up.

Each diver tried not to move too quickly along the bottom, their dive fins acted like large fans, one gentle kick stirring up an opaque wall of black silt. Even the minimal amount of movement made around the debris stirred up silt, creating black clouds that forbad any penetration by the beams from the flash lights; visibility was now only three feet in the black cold murky water of Lake Como. Brandt knew that just a matter of a few feet away the bottom of the lake slid into a deep trench, bottoming out at over one thousand four hundred feet at its deepest point. Gerbler signaled to Brandt, pointed to the surface then tapped on his air gage. It was showing near empty, they had exceeded their bottom time and both men immediately moved toward the backup tanks that they had sat on the box fifty feet north of their present position. Gerbler lit up the face of his compass, pointed in the direction of the tanks and both men calmly moved through the grave-like blackness. Their survival depended on finding the tanks and making the changeover. They swam for what seemed an eternity; Brandt trailed closely behind Gerbler, following his dim light.

Silt formed a greasy film on each of their face masks. They paused a few long seconds, wiped the black sludge away, and then resumed their move toward the tanks. They began swimming a little faster, panic in each man's mind, but a feeling that would never be discussed . . . if they made it to the surface. They'd been here before; each man knew too well that the key to survival was careful pre-planning and the ability to remain calm in all situations. When they reached the box, Brandt ran his hands across the surface. Gerbler stared into Brandt's cold blue eyes. He shined his beam onto the top of the box. It was bare, black silt showed that no tanks had been placed on this box. There were no tanks! The careful pre-planning had gone array. Okay gotta stay calm, Brandt thought. He tapped on his watch. Gerbler shrugged and pointed to his right. Brandt nodded and followed Gerbler as they ignored the reality of disorientation.

They each entertained the thoughts of dying on the bottom of Lake Como, and they each avoided the even worse thought of the painful alternative . . . rocketing toward the surface and dying from certain narcosis. The trimix in their tanks kept them thinking clearly. More clearly than had they used regular scuba air, both men realized that had they dived using regular scuba mix, they might very well be dead instead of having the ability to strategize, to search for their lost stage tanks, to maintain a more peripheral awareness of their surroundings. The trimix kept each man clear headed enough to calculate the correct decompression times on their ascent . . . but only if they could locate the back up tanks. Making a bolt for the surface was not an option.

Clouds of silt were illuminated by the lights from each diver. Wolf Brandt could hear his heartbeat pounding in his chest, the sound of distant drums, and the drum beats were growing louder with each minute he was spending on the bottom. His breathing rate increased. This shouldn't be happenin' he thought. I'm usin' too much air.

Franz Gerbler could feel the difficulty as he tried to take breaths from his tank. To further compound his misery, his head-mounted light piece died, and he fumbled for his backup hand-held light. *Oh Christ*, Gerbler thought, *this is not going well. This is not going well . . . not going well . . . not going well.*

Gerbler was mentally repeating himself, a sign of early narcosis, then his backup light slipped from his grip. It began drifting, drifting . . . drifting slowly away from him. He found himself staring at the light, mesmerized by its beauty, his mind telling him to reach for it, but his body didn't respond, *"Franz, reach out . . . reach out . . . Franz reach out . . . Franz reach out . . . reach for the light Franz."* But his muscles refused to obey. His mind made the move to reach for the light, but his body was far too entertained by the fading beam, he just wanted to enjoy its drift.

For a few brief moments the narcosis further tightened its deadly grasp, and Franz Gerbler listened as the light called to him '*Franz . . . Franz . . . follow me . . . Franz . . . follow me.*' The martini delight of narcosis had tightened its grip. Gerbler had tasted death many times. But he had always avoided swallowing.

Gerbler understood full well what his years of experience had instilled into him, but he looked at the glow like a moth mesmerized by a flame. Wolf Brandt turned as the drifting flashlight moved by the beam of his headlight. He moved a few feet and grasped at it. As he approached Gerbler he made a *'what's wrong'* gesture. Gerbler shook his head, and pounded on his dead head-light, he tilted his head, pounded on his temple like a swimmer trying to clear his ears. Gerbler gave the *okay* sign to Brandt, and the two men continued in the direction where Brandt recalled leaving the backup tanks. The air supply for each man was now indicating empty.

Lieutenants Franz Gerbler, Karl Grosser and Wolf Brandt each had many hours of wreck diving experience. They had all dove the Andrea Doria in the bitter cold Atlantic. Each man was familiar with the pain of hypothermia. They'd made their acquaintance with the demon narcosis. They were there in the pre trimix days, and they had each pioneered the new rebreather technology. They were great admirers of legendary divers Bill Nagle, John Chatterton and Richie Kohler, and each man was a student of their achievements and contributions to deep sea diving. Nagle, Chatterton and Kohler are the epitome of the professions most esteemed divers. They set the standard. Chatterton and Kohler are now pioneering rebreathers, finally moving the rebreather technology into the area far more trusted than a few years earlier. None the less, Brandt and Gerbler chose to stay with trimix. The rebreather involved the recycling of exhaled gases. Bubbles that would normally be exhaled and find their way to the surface stayed within the unit and are filtered through a closed-loop system. When the diver inhales and exhales…there are no bubbles, great for remaining invisible to surface observers.

Franz Gerbler, in a moment of bravado threw in the idea of using rebreathers, but two things stopped the crew from choosing them. One, they were night diving, so the bubbles weren't an issue, and two, several divers had died using rebreathers. Gerbler believed, as did many others, that the deaths were more the result of inexperience. The challenge was learning the new technology before placing ones life two hundred feet below the surface, and experimenting. Brandt shared Gerbler's point of view and all of the team was somewhat relieved to go with trimix without the rebreathers. And as each man had said many time *'we don't trust the plumbing.'*

Brandt reached back toward Gerbler and waited until they were side by side. He again tapped on the glass of his dive computer. The dive profile was beyond the danger level. The decompression stops would require all that the backup tanks could provide. There was no time to keep searching. Brandt drew hard on his air supply, but nothing came through, his tank was empty, a few seconds passed and he felt the demons of narcosis beginning their stampede into his brain. The narcosis spiraled deeper with each passing second. Brandt remained calm. He reached to the rear of his weight belt, trying to feel the cyalume stick each man carried as a last light source resort. As he fumbled Gerbler grabbed the stick from the rear of Brandt's belt and ignited the flare. The chemical light stick illuminated a radius of twenty feet. Gerbler spotted the white outline of the back up tanks some ten feet away and darted toward them. Brandt hung motionless in space, his arms and legs extended like a mannequin floating, weightless . . . lifeless.

Gerbler retrieved the tanks and dashed back to Brandt who managed to raise one hand. Brandt drew strongly on the regulator as life returned to his limp frame. Gerbler placed a hand in front of Brandt and gave him the okay signal. Brandt nodded and pointed back in the direction of the yellow line which was now clearly visible in the glow of the cyalume. Gerbler stared up toward the surface still over two hundred feet away, hoping the strong glow of the light did not find its way to the top of the lake. He speared the light stick into the sand, partly wedging it beneath one of the boxes. It could not be extinguished and would continue to burn for several hours.

It was time to begin the ascent along the line earlier attached to the tree by Dobbs and Apollo. The two men would have preferred to just float to the surface but this could not happen. Gerbler checked his dry suit for neutral buoyancy, Brandt did the same. Gerbler observed Brandt, feeling he needed to be sure his friend was thinking clearly. At fifty feet both divers paused for the first decompression stop. It was a slow and very long weightless suspension. Brandt occasionally shook his head from side to side giving Gerbler grounds for concern. Gerbler repeatedly tapped Brandt on his face mask and gave him a questioning okay hand signal. The ascent would take the two men ninety minutes. As their decompression continued, Gerbler continually focused on Brandt whose breathing seemed far more shallow than normal. At twenty feet Brandt and Gerbler again paused. When the two men broke the surface they were greeted by five excited members of the team. Blake, wading waist deep shouted for more help from three of the SEALs who were caught unaware by the delayed surfacing of Brandt and Gerbler. Dal and Apollo each took a hold of Brandt and quickly pulled him from the water. The two divers were literally dragged to the bank and each man lay motionless.

Blake was almost in Brandt's face. "What the hell happened? You guys are way over time. Did you decompress?"

Brandt rolled to his side and threw up a pint of water. Neither man answered Blake's question.

Blake shouted louder, this time directly into Gerbler's face, "DID YOU DO YOUR FUCKIN' DECO?

*****

Visit the author's website at www.denarobooks.com or email jasdenaro@yahoo.com for information regarding upcoming Drew Blake novels.

Printed in the United States
108779LV00009B/13-21/P